GUY'S GIRL

GUY'S GIRL

EMMA NOYES

Berkley
New York

BERKLEY
An imprint of Penguin Random House LLC
penguinrandomhouse.com

Library of Congress Cataloging-in-Publication Data

Names: Noyes, Emma (Emma Virginia Rideout), author.
Title: Guy's girl / Emma Noyes.
Description: First edition. | New York: Berkley, 2023.
Identifiers: LCCN 2022057951 (print) | LCCN 2022057952 (ebook) |
ISBN 9780593639009 (trade paperback) | ISBN 9780593639016 (ebook)
Subjects: LCGFT: Romance fiction. | Novels.
Classification: LCC PS3614.O976 G89 2023 (print) |
LCC PS3614.O976 (ebook) | DDC 813/.6—dc23/eng/20230201
LC record available at https://lccn.loc.gov/2022057951
LC ebook record available at https://lccn.loc.gov/2022057952

First Edition: October 2023

Printed in the United States of America
1st Printing

For Lauren

Dear Reader,

I had to hit rock bottom before I could bring Guy's Girl *into the world. I was twenty-five, fresh off a breakup, and hopelessly lost in a disease that I hadn't even admitted to having yet. That is the power of an eating disorder: it burrows into your thoughts, your routines, your comforts, your* life, *seducing you with promises to soothe the chronic anxiety that plagues so many of us.*

I struggled with anorexia for seven long years. Shortly after the pandemic began, it morphed into bulimia—but not the kind you see in movies. Not the dramatic overeating, followed by a sprint to the bathroom and a finger down the throat. It was far subtler, driven by forces that felt totally out of my control. And it's because my disease didn't "look like bulimia" that I was able to stay in denial for so long.

Shortly after I (finally) got into recovery, I started to write. It felt like a different kind of purging, the exorcising of thoughts and secrets and emotions rather than the food in my stomach. Gradually, those words became a character, and Ginny Murphy was born.

The reason I care so deeply about Guy's Girl *and have fought so hard for its publication is that it is the book I so desperately needed in my early twenties. All eating disorders are isolating, but bulimia is doubly so; the self-loathing you feel when bingeing and purging is so intense that revealing it to anyone feels like admitting to murder. When I wrote this book, I essentially took the thing I hated most about myself and plastered it across the sky, because I knew that my courage could help others heal.*

I am very active on TikTok and Instagram and have recently begun posting videos about my recovery experience. I wasn't expecting much of a response to them, but I have now received dozens of messages—especially from teenage girls—saying that they've never seen anyone talk about bulimia on social media before and that it has made them feel so much less alone.

That is why I wrote this book. That is why I sincerely hope that you read it and love it, too—because everyone deserves to feel seen.

All my best,
Emma

GUY'S GIRL

Ginny isn't sure which came first—the bad habit or the boy. They showed up at almost exactly the same time, like two trains pulling into one station from opposite directions. And when they left, it took much longer for one to go than the other.

On the surface, the two seem completely disconnected—one a human being, the other a human defect—but at their core, they're both powered by the same thing: false versions of love. One, the wrong way to love another; the other, the wrong way to love yourself.

She didn't mean to become bulimic. Does anyone? Does anyone go out looking for mental illness? Well, she didn't, in any case. It just kind of happened. Just the way things did with Finch—piece by piece, she fell into something intoxicating, something dangerous; and by the time she realized what was happening, it was already too late.

Adrian remembers the exact moment he decided not to fall in love.

He was eleven. His mother hadn't stopped crying in a week. He didn't quite understand what had happened with her and Scott. In fact, it would be years before he grasped the full breadth of his stepfather's betrayal.

He climbed the rickety stairs of their new home in Indianapolis, one half of a duplex they shared with a cloudy-eyed couple who had strange pockmarks all over their faces. A bowl of porridge balanced in one hand, a mug of coffee in the other. His mother wouldn't eat, but he still had to try.

He nudged open her bedroom door. Inside, she was curled up with her head on the pillow. Even half conscious, she looked miserable. Wrinkled forehead. Puffy eyelids. Lips moving silently, as if in prayer.

He set the bowl and mug down on the bedside table.

I don't want it, he thought. *I don't want it, and I never will.*

PART I

Ginny Murphy is wasting away again.

She can feel it as she drags her suitcase up the fifth and final staircase of her friends' walk-up in SoHo. The tremble in her limbs. The pop of stars at the edge of her vision. It's 6 p.m. and she hasn't eaten a thing all day.

If Heather were here, she wouldn't let Ginny get away with starving herself. She would pull out her phone and find a list of every muscle, every neuron, every organ that needs energy to survive. Then she would force-feed Ginny a donut.

When she reaches apartment 5E, Ginny pauses to straighten her skirt and blink away the lights clogging her vision. She hesitates. Alone in Minnesota, where she lives, hiding her habits is easy. But here, visiting a group of boys who have known her since their freshman year of college?

Not so easy.

She raises one fist and knocks twice.

"*There she is!*" comes a voice from inside. She hears footsteps, then the door swings inward, revealing a bushel of red hair and a grin so wide it seems to take up the whole doorway. "Ginny fucking Murphy," says her best friend, Clay. Then she's swept up in a frenzy of freckled arms and spun around the hallway. Ginny laughs. She can't remember the last time she heard that sound come out of her mouth.

Clay sets her down and grabs her suitcase. "Welcome to Manhattan."

Adrian Silvas is on his 6 p.m. break. Fifteen minutes to leave Goldman and pick up a coffee from the Gregory's on East 52nd: cold brew, no sugar, a splash of almond milk. A pick-me-up for what's sure to be another long night. It doesn't matter that it's Friday. It doesn't matter that the managing directors left already. Analysts are to stay at their desks until their eyeballs bleed.

Adrian went into investment banking because that's what everyone said he should do. Just like he applied for the scholarship to Harvard because that's what everyone said he should do. Just like he became the vice president of his final club because that's what everyone said he should do.

When he signed with Goldman Sachs, he had no idea what he was in for. How long his hours would be. How mind-numbing the work was. How truly and utterly it would suck the soul out of his body. Now he's a man with more money than he knows what to do with and no time to spend it.

"*Eső után köpönyeg*," his grandfather would say. *After the rain comes the raincoat.*

Clay leads Ginny down the short hallway toward the living room. They don't make it more than three feet before she's accosted by a flurry of curly light brown hair and grey cotton.

"Gin-a-vieve!" yells the flurry, crashing into Ginny and squeezing her tight. "You made it!"

"Tristan," Ginny says into her friend's shoulder. "How many times do I have to tell you? My real name is—"

"'*West Virginia*,'" Tristan sings, releasing Ginny's shoulders and throwing one hand into the air. Clay leans up against his roommate, and together they sing: "'*Mountain mama, take me hooo-me, country roads.*'"

When they're done, Clay grins down at Ginny. "Bet you missed us."

"I saw you came in on a seven fifty-seven," Tristan says, suddenly serious. "Was it wide-bodied? God, I would give my left arm to be on a sweet, sweet wide-body right now. Did you know it's been over a month since I've been on an airplane? I think I'm going through withdrawal. But I downloaded this app, look at this, and—"

And he was off.

When they met freshman year, Ginny didn't think she would like Tristan; he talks enough to fill three conversations at once, and his favorite topics are finance, finance, and finance. He is obsessed with shorting stocks and would love nothing more than to ruin a small country's economy.

However, he will also say yes to anything, laugh at anyone's jokes, and try any food you put in front of him. He is insatiably curious—and strangely childlike in his obsession with airplanes.

She adores him.

Ginny loves boys. Not in a sexual way; frankly, she hasn't felt attracted to anyone in years. No—what she loves about boys is their company. Male friendships aren't like female friendships, she thinks. They're easier. Free from the drama.

She loves male bodies, too. Their sloppy haircuts and predictable clothing. The strange shape of their calves—thin at the ankle and round in the middle, like telephone poles swollen with last night's rain. The stupid, honest way they make themselves laugh.

But she loves *her* boys most of all.

Now Tristan chatters eagerly about the flight-tracking app on his phone as he leads Ginny and Clay into the living room.

The boys' SoHo apartment is the quintessential postgrad shithole: creaky floor planks, white wall paint, and a shower that looks like it was built before the fall of the Berlin Wall. Every boy living in this apartment is over six feet tall; Ginny isn't sure how they fold their legs up tight enough to shit on the pint-sized toilet.

"Tristan," says a low, raspy voice from inside the living room, "if I have to hear one more fact about domestic flight patterns, I'm going to throw myself off the fire escape."

Ginny inhales. He's here.

Finch.

She steps into the dim light of the living room, and there he is: Alex Finch, the fourth and final corner of their friend group. Sitting in a low armchair, aux cord plugged into his phone, guitar balanced on his lap. Finch is studying to become an orthopedic surgeon at NYU. He has close-cropped blond hair and a crooked smile. He's completely brilliant and also stupid, in the way that all brilliant men are also stupid.

When Ginny thinks about freshman year, she thinks about Finch. About his hands on her waist, on the hem of her shirt. The feel of the fabric as it peeled over her head. His eyes as he took her in for the first time. She thinks about kissing until her cheeks are red with the burn of his stubble.

Stop, she thinks. *Turn it off.*

She forces a smile onto her face and steps forward. "Finch. Hi."

"Gin." He sets aside the guitar and stands. In two long strides he's before her. "It's great to see you." He wraps both arms around her and pulls her in for a hug.

Ginny tries not to inhale for fear that his scent will be too familiar.

After untangling herself from Finch's hug—which lasts just a second longer than is appropriate—Ginny walks over to the worn grey couch and sits. Now that all four of them are standing in the small living room, there isn't much space to breathe.

"So." Clay sets her suitcase on the floor beside the television and crosses the two steps that take him into their tiny kitchenette. "Tonight, we're thinking poker and pregame until Adrian gets back, then hit the bars."

Clay is their ringleader. He may not talk the most—that award rests firmly with Tristan—but he holds the most power. He makes plans and leads the charge. Right now, he works for a government consulting firm, but will probably one day be president of the United States. The man could make friends with a houseplant.

"I bet I can get us a table at Tao," Tristan says. "The owner is a personal friend of my father's. Just last year, we visited his house in the Hamptons, and—"

"Shut up, Tristan," say Ginny and Clay in unison. It rolls off the tongue—their old mantra, words they spoke whenever their friend started going on about his father's connections or late-stage capitalism. They flash surprised grins at each other. Clay's teeth are brilliant white beneath his red hair, and the sight is so familiar it nearly cracks Ginny in half.

"So." Clay winks and turns around, opening the small refrigerator in the corner. "How's work, Gin?"

"Oh, you know," she says, shifting on the couch. "It's work."

"But you work for a *beer* company," Clay says over his shoulder as he rummages around, looking for cold alcohol. "That's epic."

"Right," Ginny says. "But I live in Minnesota."

During the fall of her senior year, Ginny signed with Sofra-Moreno, a global beer conglomerate. When SM started recruiting her, she was a senior in college studying history and literature—proof that your degree means absolutely nothing and you can do whatever the fuck you want after college, provided you're a good enough liar. What? She was going to get paid almost six figures a year to study the history of beer? Absolutely not. She has to at least *pretend* to contribute to the company's bottom line.

When she signed her contract with Sofra, Ginny was ready for an exciting global career. She imagined visiting breweries around the world. Rubbing elbows with executives. Climbing the ladder. Maybe even getting her Cicerone Certification, becoming a sommelier of beer.

Right up until they placed her in Minnesota.

She was going to say no. She was going to look for another job. But then her classes picked up in earnest, and all Ginny's free time disappeared, and she just sort of fell numbly into her future. Into the path assigned.

"The Twin Cities!" Tristan claps. "You're lucky to live there. Did you know you can fly to a hundred and sixty-three different cities out of MSP? It's one of Delta's primary hubs, and Delta is the best airline in—"

"*Tristan.*" Finch cuts him off before he can really get going.

Tristan and Finch don't get along. It's not that they don't like each other; it's more that they are two sides of the same coin. Both are stocky, both have lopsided grins and curly hair—Finch's short and blond, Tristan's long and light brown—both come from money and attended East Coast private schools where they rowed stroke on the varsity crew team. During freshman year at Harvard, they were often mistaken for brothers. As college wore on, however, the two split, as if in direct reaction to this unwanted comparison. They leaned as far into their differences as they could. It's the same logic behind why neighboring countries are always at war with each other: we despise those who are too similar to us.

For his part, Tristan became the quintessential finance kid: majored in economics, joined Harvard's consulting club, interned at a bank, dressed in button-downs and Sperry's. Kept a close shave and an even closer eye on his portfolio.

Finch, on the other hand, shed as much of his upbringing as he could. He grew out his hair, traded slacks for joggers, and spent all his free time either with his guitar on his lap or in the physics lab with a bag of weed in his backpack.

Ginny looks away from Finch, forcing her mind in a different direction. To the final occupant of Sullivan Street. The absent party: Adrian.

Of all the boys living in apartment 5E, Ginny knows Adrian the least. He was a last-minute addition to the boys' apartment. An outlier. Back in college, in the limited interactions Ginny had with him, he was roughly as friendly as a potted cactus. But if she wants a place to sleep during her visit to New York, she has to put up with him.

Finishing his search in the fridge, Clay pulls out the ingredients for mixed drinks—exactly what Ginny feared he would do. *One shot of tequila is 100 calories; 8 ounces of lemonade is 100 more . . .*

She stands, crossing the tiny room to crack open a window. Cool air filters into the room. She inhales deeply before walking back to the couch and sitting down.

Clay pours four cups of tequila and lemonade. Finch lights a cigarette and fiddles with the Bluetooth speaker, setting up a play-list of songs for their pregame. Tristan tries unsuccessfully to steal the aux cord from Finch. All the while, they chatter—about work, about sports, about the girls they're seeing. Every time Tristan mentions wide-bodied airplanes, Ginny and Finch throw napkins at him.

Their voices wash over her, and she finds that, for just a brief moment, her anxiety dissipates. It feels good not to be *the girl* any-more. To just be one of the group. One of the guys.

She inhales, filling her body with cool air and secondhand smoke.

Adrian pushes open the door of 200 West Street, which houses the headquarters of Goldman Sachs, and heads out into the long-since-black night. He can't remember the last time he left while the sun still shone.

By some miracle, he made it out of the office before midnight. This will be his first chance to go out with his roommates in a long time. His roommates and the girl. Ginny.

Adrian didn't know Ginny well in college. He saw her around campus—rollerblading down Plympton Street or dancing on a table with Clay in the Delphic—but he didn't *know* her. From what Clay tells him, after graduation, she signed with that big beer company and moved to Minnesota. Normally, he couldn't fathom why anyone would want to live there, but right now he hates his life in New York so deeply that living alone in the Midwest sounds like a dream.

He would never move there, of course. If he were to go anywhere, it would be back to Budapest, where he was born.

His phone buzzes in his pocket. He pulls it out. It's his mom, checking in about his week. *"Milyen volt a heted?"*

"Kiváló," he responds. *Excellent.*

His weekly lie.

He tucks his phone away and heads for Sullivan Street.

Adrian's favorite part of the commute is the three blocks he walks down Prince Street. Artists line the block, paintings, jewelry, and woven blankets laid out before them. Tables spill out of restaurants and onto the sidewalk. Diners play footsie under white tablecloths. The scene reminds him of Váci Street. Of Budapest.

His years in Hungary were the happiest he can remember. Though his mother had her own apartment—in which Adrian lived with his older sister, Beatrix—she worked constantly, which meant he mostly lived with his grandparents outside Budapest in a house his grandfather built by hand. There were cherry trees in the backyard and cabbage wraps on the stove. They lived near a slew of Adrian's great-aunts and -uncles, who regularly gathered to celebrate the holiday of some obscure saint. Someone was always too drunk. Someone was always fighting with someone else.

Years later, Adrian would long for those fights.

When Adrian turned eight, his mom put him into English classes. Once a week, he biked to the home of an ancient Hungarian woman and listened to her jabber at him in a language he neither understood nor wanted to understand. He never participated. Never even opened his mouth. Why would he? Everyone in his life spoke Hungarian.

When he turned nine, his mom announced they were moving to America. She told him in the kitchen of her downtown Pest apartment. Adrian never liked that place. He preferred the colorful homes and cobblestoned streets of Szentendre.

That afternoon, his mother sat him down at the wooden table in her kitchen and said, "*Távozunk.*" *We are leaving.*

"*Hová megyünk?*" *Where are we going?*

"America."

His mother was remarrying, she said. A man whose name Adrian had never even heard. A man who lived far away, in the foreign land of *Indiana*. He didn't know how she met this man, though he would later overhear Beatrix whispering on her cell phone about some sort of online matching service.

Adrian stared as she bustled about the kitchen, unwrapping

groceries and tucking away spices. She moved casually, as if she hadn't just told her son that his entire life was unraveling. He was so angry he could have thrown a fit—if he were the type to do so.

But he wasn't. So, instead, he bottled it up, all that anger, all that sadness, all that grief for the only home he had ever known.

"*Pakold össze a cuccaidat,*" she said. "*Egy hét múlva indulunk.*" *Pack your things. We leave in a week.*

When he reaches the front door of his apartment building, his phone buzzes. He checks it, expecting another email from an MD.

Instead, it's his future landlord.

He found the studio on StreetEasy. He hasn't yet told Clay and the others that he's moving out, that he won't be re-signing their lease. Living with them has been fun, but Adrian is ready to try out proper adulthood. To have a place where he can lie down and turn everything off, every switch and lever of his personality.

On their front stoop, a plastic bag filled with cardboard boxes waves in the breeze. Delivery from Mamoun's. Clay must not have heard the delivery man buzz. Typical. He was probably regaling Ginny with some story.

When Adrian agreed to move into this apartment after graduation, Clay was the only one of his roommates he really knew. They met in the Delphic, of which Clay was the president and Adrian the vice president. It was a natural pairing: Clay, with his easy charisma, was the face of the club, while Adrian did organization and behind-the-scenes strategy. He didn't mind the arrangement; he's never been one for the spotlight.

As he climbs the four flights of stairs, plastic bag dangling from his hand, Adrian imagines what living in a studio will be like: his own space, a bed and a little kitchen, a TV to watch movies, and a bookcase filled with novels. Stacks and stacks of them.

In his rare moments of free time, Adrian reads. Fiction, mostly. He likes stories that drag him into the narrator's psyche, that force him to feel. Because he *does*. He does feel. He feels in a way that seems impossible in real life. Characters die, and he is sad. Characters fall in love, and he is happy. He might not cry or laugh out loud, but there is a stir in his chest, a pit in his stomach, a flutter of excitement that reaches his very toes.

Perhaps it is the safety of the unreal. The knowledge that he can close the book or turn off the television, and the emotion will shut off with it. Like guardrails around the heart.

Right as Tristan flips over the card that completes Ginny's full house, the apartment door swings open, and in walks Adrian Silvas. His face is cast in shadow from the tight hallway. He's dressed in the typical investment banker uniform: a jacket and button-down, pressed pants, and leather shoes.

Ginny sighs inwardly. *There goes my good mood.*

"The zombie returns," says Finch, setting down his phone. "And so early."

"MD has a weekend in the Hamptons." Adrian shuts the door and walks out into the living room. From his hand dangles a plastic bag and the telltale odor of fried chickpeas and shaved lamb.

Ginny zeroes in on the food and takes a few deep, steadying breaths. She can do this. This is what she prepared for, why she didn't put any food into her body all day. To create a cavern within herself. She can eat, and the food will fall deep into the cavern— far, far from her hips, her thighs, the ring around her belly.

It's just one night.

In her pocket, Ginny's phone starts to buzz. She pulls it out and checks the screen. It's a FaceTime from her sister, Heather. As she so often does, Ginny hits IGNORE.

"Hi, Ginny."

She looks up. Adrian stands above her, setting the food down on the coffee table and unbuttoning his jacket. He smiles. It's a small smile, a flash of white teeth and crinkled eyes amid dark hair and five o'clock shadow. His jawline is long and crisp, eyes so dark brown they could almost be black. He looks tired, so tired, but genuinely happy to see her.

That small smile—it does something strange to her. Like a rumble deep within a long-dormant volcano. The feeling shocks Ginny. She looks down at the floor, cheeks heating. When she looks back up, Adrian is watching her curiously.

Remembering her manners, she jumps up, causing her phone to slip from her hand and her head to spin. "Adrian, hi!" Her voice is too high. She blinks through the stars speckling the edges of her vision. "It's been so long! How are you? How was work?"

"Work was soul draining, as usual," he says.

She blinks, and her vision steadies. "You don't like investment banking?"

"No one likes investment banking."

"Oh." Ginny tilts her head, studying him. He's handsome. Far more handsome than she remembered. "You look surprisingly good for someone who hates his job."

She regrets the words as soon as they leave her mouth. *Shit. Was that an insult or a compliment?* It's been so long since she's socialized; she seems to have forgotten how.

For a moment, Adrian just looks at her, lips parted, eyebrows pulled together. She opens her mouth to apologize, to say she was kidding—but then, without warning, Adrian's face splits into a grin. The smile transforms him, cracking every hard, tired line of his face, erasing the standoffish boy she remembers from college. It shocks Ginny so much that she almost stumbles backward.

"Thanks," he says. "I think."

"We're about to start Texas Hold'em," Clay says. "You want in, man?"

"I need to shower and change." Adrian turns away, waving over his shoulder as he heads into his room. "Nice to see you, Ginny."

His door closes. Ginny stares at its chipped white wood.

Huh.

Adrian pulls off his jacket and throws it onto his bed. His walls are bare, his desk undecorated. He spends almost no time here. He doesn't have the energy to care.

The zombie returns.

There aren't many people that Adrian actively dislikes. If his emotions were a graph, they would hit only subtle peaks and valleys—never exponential dips or highs. He cannot feel love, but he cannot feel hate, either; toward most, he feels entirely neutral.

But Adrian doesn't like Alex Finch. He cannot even explain why, really. It's a feeling he gets. One that stuck to the pit of his stomach the first moment he shook Finch's hand, at once slippery and sticky, a leech that slides right through your fingers every time you try to pull it away.

It's not that Finch is rude or unpleasant. On the contrary—whenever Adrian speaks, Finch goes out of his way to lean forward, squint his eyes, prop his chin onto his hand. Anything to make it clear that he's listening, *really* listening.

But it's something behind his eyes. Something Adrian cannot read and does not like.

Now he shakes away the feeling and pulls off the rest of his clothes. As he wraps a towel around his waist, he thinks of Ginny's smile. Her cheeks flushed from tequila. She's cute. Far cuter than he remembered.

The game begins. The boys dig into their fried entrées while Ginny picks at a hummus and tabbouleh plate.

"I'm all in," Tristan says into a mouthful of fries, light brown hair bouncing as he chews. He pushes all his chips into the center.

"Dude, what?" Finch asks. "It's the first hand."

Tristan shrugs.

Finch throws his cards onto the table. "I fold."

"Always the conservative." Tristan licks his fingers and rakes in a small stack of chips.

"Says the man whose father is the literal embodiment of the Republican party," Finch grumbles.

In the next round, Clay flips over the river—eight of clubs, six of clubs, nine of clubs. "Who's got that straight flush?" he asks before tossing a dollar's worth of chips into the center.

Tristan whistles. "Big dick energy over here."

Finch shakes his blond hair. "This asshole doesn't have shit."

Clay grins and presses his fingertips together.

"I call," says Ginny, parsing out a dollar from her chips.

Tristan smiles even wider. "That's our girl. As my father says, *No money was ever made without spending money first.*"

"Shut up, Tristan," say Ginny and Clay together.

They play for a half hour. Clay mixes more drinks. Tristan loses all his chips on a bad call and immediately buys back in. Finch slowly leaks money, dripping chips onto the table like a bad faucet. Eventually, he gives up entirely, picking up his guitar to pluck a rendition of "Slow Dancing in a Burning Room." Ginny does her best to ignore what it does to her stomach.

When Ginny thinks of freshman year, she thinks of Finch's voice. The first time she heard him sing—across the beer pong table, a crowd of Four Lokos between them—her stomach bent and flexed. His voice was lush and smooth, like taffy between his teeth. She watched his lips form the words to a song she could only half hear. She wanted to cup her hands around those lips. To capture the melody between them and bring it back to her dorm to listen to whenever she wanted.

When she thinks of freshman year, she thinks of his eyes, how they followed her wherever she went. She thinks of standing in Tasty Burger in jean shorts and bare feet, splitting a bagful of French fries, Harvard Square spinning around them. She thinks of him inside her. Of his whisper—*I like you so much.*

Here's the thing about being a straight woman in a friend group of all straight men: there will inevitably be a complication. Either you'll fall for one of them, or one of them will fall for you. Sometimes it's mutual. In most cases, it isn't. And in the worst situation of all, one of them will chase you. He'll chase you hard, despite your repeated insistence that it's a terrible idea. He'll chase until you give in. Until you fall for him.

Then he'll break your heart as hard as he possibly can.

Ginny checks her cards for the sixth time, studiously keeping her eyes from drifting over to Finch's armchair.

Clay sticks out his falafel and fries and shakes them under her nose. "Want?"

Ginny eyes the grease. Once upon a time, she would have. Once upon a time, dinner was guerrilla warfare, Ginny versus her three brothers, everyone stealing food from everyone else's plates, Heather rolling her eyes in the corner. Once upon a time, Ginny fought for her share of macaroni and onion strings and French fries and every other delicious calorie bomb she could get her hands on.

Not anymore.

Ginny reaches out and plucks exactly one fry from the stack, popping it into her mouth. "Yum."

Clay's eyes narrow. Ginny tenses, anticipating a comment, a question, even an interrogation. She mumbles something about refilling her drink and pushes off the couch, heading to the kitchenette.

On the way there, she passes the bookshelf. She pauses to scan the authors: Zadie Smith, Sally Rooney, Kurt Vonnegut, Chang-rae Lee. "Whose books are these?" she asks.

"Mine."

Ginny turns around to find Adrian leaning against the wall. He smiles, pulling at his collar.

"Really?" she asks.

"Really."

Her gaze lingers on the sharp length of Adrian's jaw. His white T-shirt is cut with a low vee, thin curls of chest hair peeking out. Dark hair still wet from the shower.

For years, Ginny has had no interest in men. None. Finch was the last person she ever remembers actively wanting. She tried, in college: pick the cutest boy at the party, touch his arm, go back to his dorm. Once in his bed, she would do her best to rev herself up, to tell herself she was enjoying it. But when he finally pushed inside her, she was dry as sandpaper.

Every time, a dull, muted sadness unfurled in Ginny's chest. She didn't understand what was happening. She thought she wanted this boy, but now that she had him, she didn't any longer. She didn't want anything. She faked an orgasm. She draped herself over his torso and wore his body heat like a sweater until a dreamless sleep pulled her under.

Eventually, she stopped trying altogether.

Ginny is broken. She knows it, but she can't *do* anything about it. Her brokenness isn't like a grammatical error or a bad subject line, which she can fix by writing and rewriting. Her brokenness is anxiety without cause, a weight on her chest as heavy as first snow.

But when Ginny's eyes travel over Adrian's chest, over the dimples pressed into his cheeks, her heart flips suddenly, unexpectedly, in a way she hasn't felt in a long time.

She clears her throat. "You have some of my favorite authors."

"And, one day, you'll be up there with them, Gin," says Clay, raising his plastic cup.

Tristan and Finch yell, "Hear, hear!"

"You're a writer?"

Adrian's question drifts over the merriment. When Ginny looks back at him, something has changed in his expression. It's no longer detached, elsewhere. He looks genuinely interested in her answer.

Ginny pulls at the hem of her skirt. "Not really. I've never published anything."

"Hey, now." Clay leans over the back of the couch and pokes her in the side. "I read what you sent me right after you moved to Minnesota. Stuff was legit."

And she's *still* writing. Every single day. See, the thing about working a nine-to-five right out of college is that after work Ginny has five whole hours to fill before it's acceptable to go to sleep. *How am I supposed to live?* she asked herself over and over during her first weeks in Minnesota. *How am I supposed to fill my hours? What makes a proper adult?*

She could've joined a club. Could've taken piano lessons. Could've gone out to a bar and tried to make friends. But, during the day, she eats so little and works so hard that, by sunset, she's exhausted. She doesn't have the energy to join a club, take piano lessons, or make friends. She's sad and hungry and alone.

So, one evening, she opened her laptop and started to write.

She wrote without purpose. Whatever came to her—a fisherman in an Alaskan bay, a mother who goes for long walks beside old train tracks, a boy growing up near the Boundary Waters. She wrote about being sad and hungry and alone.

She hasn't stopped writing since.

She sent her first story to Clay, but not the rest. The rest are just for her.

What she likes about writing is that it captures her attention and fills the empty hours. It captures her emotions and fills her empty body. It takes her somewhere else. It lets her live, for just a moment, outside a self she does not particularly like.

"What about Sofra-Moreno?" Adrian asks. "Don't you work in communications?"

Ginny shrugs. "That's for now. Not forever."

Though Adrian doesn't ask any more questions, she feels the heat of his gaze linger. It makes her squirm. She drops back to the couch and checks her cards for the seventh time.

Ginny doesn't think of herself as cute. She doesn't think of herself as quirky or bubbly or creative or any of the other words people often use to describe her. In fact, she thinks of herself as little as possible—and only ever in terms of whether her waistline is expanding or not. To be frank, she would prefer that she not exist at all.

She only sees herself as desirable when her weight is below a certain number. Any higher, she believes, and her chin will double, her face inflate, and with it will go any sexual appeal she might hold.

Yet Ginny doesn't even *want* to have sex. With anyone. She hasn't for years.

Right?

Her eyes flick to Adrian, then quickly back down to her cards. For the second time that night, she feels a clench low in her belly. The same place that used to squeeze whenever she looked at Finch.

From his place in the straight-backed wooden chair beside the TV, Adrian watches the strange girl in his apartment. She hands him a drink. She deals the next round. She laughs. Adrian likes her laugh—it's loud, startling. A sound that could scatter pigeons.

"So, Finch," Ginny says, not looking up from her cards. "How's Hannah?"

Hannah. Finch's girlfriend and high school sweetheart. Adrian has never met her, but his roommate talks about her so much that he feels like he has. They met playing the leads in their school's production of *West Side Story*. She's a year younger than Finch, currently attending school at Ohio State University. As far as Adrian knows, they've made it almost six years without breaking up.

Finch sets down his guitar, eyes shining. "She's great, yeah. Loving senior year. I'll see her at Thanksgiving when we're both home in Cleveland."

Ginny smiles at Finch. It doesn't touch her eyes. "That's great."

Her focus returns to her cards, but Adrian continues to watch her. What was that in her tone? That tightness, that sharpened edge? The Ginny he knows is all laughter and warmth, quick with a joke, Clay's partner in crime. Not angry. Not restrained.

What is she hiding?

Before Adrian can think too long on it, Tristan throws his cards on the table and yells, "Ha! Royal flush!" He leaps up from the couch, spins around, and starts shaking his butt at his friends. "Eat that, ladies and gentlemen."

"No, thanks." Clay places both hands on Tristan's rear and gives him a good shove. Tristan falls headfirst onto the couch.

"Wow," says Ginny. "That's a good hand." Her lips pursed in mock confusion, she sets her cards on the table and asks, "Does a straight flush beat that?"

All eyes turn to her.

Clay and Finch burst into applause.

Tristan, upside down on the couch, lets out a long wail.

Clay claps Ginny on the shoulder. "*That*'s my girl."

She winks and rakes in every chip on the table. "Can we go to the bar now? I'm ready to dance."

"Easy, tiger." Clay holds up a hand. "I need another drink or three before we head out."

"Right." Ginny nods grimly, hands resting on the chips before her. "You all do. God forbid we subject the good people of Manhattan to the sight of Tristan dancing sober."

"Hey!" Tristan sits up on the couch and elbows her in the side. Ginny giggles and elbows back.

Adrian watches on and wonders if this is what it looks like to be totally comfortable in one's own skin.

Ginny and the boys spill out into the balmy October night. Clay reaches out one hand to hail a cab. Tristan says something about his father only ever being driven around in black Escalades. Finch pushes Tristan into a recycling bin.

Ginny bounces in the toes of her white platform shoes—a new purchase, her attempt to blend into the fashionable New York crowd. Goose bumps rise on her arms. Cold as always.

"You okay?" comes a voice from just behind her.

Ginny turns to find Adrian peering down at her. A light breeze feathers the black locks peeking up at the top of his head. Instinctively, she drops her hands, which were rubbing her arms. "Yes," she says quickly.

"Cold?"

"No," she lies.

Adrian tilts his head but says nothing, so Ginny looks away, studying the street around them.

New York is everything Minnesota isn't. Gone are the chubby, bearded Norwegian men. Here—leggy women the size of mountains. Bodies shaped like telephone wires. Eyes thick with dreamy desire. Ginny wants to drown in it all.

And it isn't just the models. It's everyone. Gangly teenagers. A man whose face appears to have gone through a trash compactor. A big-breasted woman with eyes like steel, dressed in a suit Ginny has only ever seen on James Bond.

The *style*. They reek of it. Chic, tailored women in black tights and heeled boots. A waif-thin photographer crouched low on the corner, jeans dangerously close to falling from her body. Hasidic men with curls swinging beneath boxy black hats. A dog with three legs. A thick-browed man in enormous black headphones, pushing through the crush and belting out the words to a song no one else can hear.

Heather would fit in here, Ginny thought.

"Cabs ah he-ah," says Clay, using the Jersey Shore accent.

"*Cabs ah he-ah!*" Finch and Tristan yell back.

They all cram into the tiny yellow sedan. Somehow, Ginny ends up on Adrian's lap. Neither acknowledges the other. The car speeds off, whisking them toward the bar.

Niagara steams with bodies. Bodies by the front bar. Bodies by the back. Bodies by the photo booth. Bodies by the arcade. Bodies on the dance floor.

The boys lead her through the crowd. They scream over the music and the voices. Clay heads up the group, holding his hands over his red hair. Ginny keeps close to the flagpole that is Adrian's figure. Finch elbows Tristan into a group of girls ordering vodka sodas.

Once they make it to the back, all the boys melt onto the dance floor, bouncing up and down and flailing their necks side to side. All the boys except Adrian. He leans down to Ginny and asks, "Should we get drinks?"

Ginny nods, so they elbow over to the small bar shoved into the back corner.

"Coronas?" Adrian asks.

"Sure."

Adrian turns to the bartender. "Five Coronas, please." He pulls out his wallet and hands over his credit card.

"Thank you," Ginny says. Adrian shrugs. When the bartender presents them with five open bottles, each with a slice of lime pointed from the rim, Adrian hands two to Ginny.

She hesitates. *One Corona is 150 calories, plus the tequila lemonades earlier, and . . .*

You know what? *Fuck it.*

Ginny squeezes the lime wedge into her bottle and takes a swig.

She must drink three Coronas. They must dance for hours. The DJ plays songs from the early 2000s, and Ginny sings as loud as she can. She dances with her boys. Clay picks her up and spins her around the dance floor as if she weighs nothing.

She can't remember the last time she had this much fun.

Ginny wanted to make life in Minnesota work. She did. She wanted to strike off on her own and prove to herself that she didn't need anyone else to live happily.

She was sorely mistaken.

Her whole life, Ginny had a brood of siblings around her. Siblings and friends and friends of siblings. They filled her life. Distracted her from the inside of her head, which, more often than not, was an extremely unpleasant place to live. Made her laugh, even when she didn't think she could. Until now, Ginny hadn't realized how essential other people were to her own happiness.

I want to move to New York.

The thought hits her like a shovel to the head.

I want to feel like this all the time. I want to move to New York.

At some point, through the haze of realization, Ginny becomes aware of Adrian talking to a girl in the corner. She's petite, draped with mousy brown hair and a snow-white romper. She stands on her tiptoes to yell into his ear.

Well, Ginny thinks, *that won't do at all.*

Adrian has never known what to do with his good looks. To him, they're a gift he never asked for. One that he doesn't mind but has ultimately brought him more confusion and unwanted attention than anything.

Take now, for example. All he's trying to do is have a night out with the boys, but girls whose names he cannot remember keep coming up to him and practically screaming into his ear.

It's not that they're ugly. The girls who hit on him at bars—who offer to buy him drinks, lean in too close to his collar, or place their hands on his shoulder—almost never are. They're confident, beautiful, obvious in their interest. If he wanted, he could have any of them.

It's just that he never wants them.

He's never had a serious girlfriend. Never actively pursued a woman for much longer than a few weeks. Never wanted to. He's not gay. Or, at least, he assumes he isn't, because he's never wanted any men, either.

It's as simple as this—every time Adrian tries to let himself fall in love, he fails.

While White Romper vies for his attention, Adrian notices something out of the corner of his eye. It's Ginny. She's swaying her hips around the rim of the dance floor, moving toward him. Adrian breathes a sigh of relief. She's coming to rescue him.

As the music changes to an Outkast song, Ginny enters Adrian's orbit. She doesn't touch him or even look at him. Just dances nearby.

Ginny is different from most girls he knows. Loud. Unfiltered.

Lives in Minnesota. Works for a beer company. Likes to roller-blade. Beat them all at poker. If he's being honest, she's sort of weird.

He thinks he likes it.

Which is why, without any of his normal hesitation, Adrian pats White Romper twice on the shoulder, then turns to Ginny and holds out a hand.

Adrian doesn't normally ask girls to dance. He's more of a *stand on the side and watch the action* kind of man. But something about this girl makes him want to grab her hands and spin her around. To sing along with her. To mirror her smile.

Ginny dances without inhibition. She spins and sways and laughs so hard he can hear it over the pounding music. She watches him with these enormous green eyes that flash in the lights moving over the crowd. A slight smile seems to invite him closer, telling him to pull them chest to chest and dip her backward.

He can't remember the last time he had this much fun.

Adrian pulls Ginny back to vertical, and she stares up at him. They're so close now that he can feel the heat echoing off her body. Can watch as an unreadable set of emotions flickers across her face. She looks like a puzzle he desperately wants to piece together.

He can feel his heart beating in his stomach. Is that normal?

Maybe it's her strangeness. Maybe it's her smile. Most likely, it's because she lives in Minnesota, which means this can never turn into anything real. It's low stakes. It's safe.

Whatever the reason, right there in the middle of a hundred flailing bodies, Adrian takes Ginny's face and presses his mouth to hers.

In the cab on the way home, Adrian cradles Ginny's hand like a child in a swaddle.

G inny collapses onto the boys' sofa, tequila and Corona swirling the corners of the apartment into a vivid dream.

"Should I get out the blow-up mattress?" asks Clay.

"Why don't you sleep with Finch?" Tristan says. "Reprise of
freshman year."

Ginny's cheeks turn pink. Tristan *loves* making uncomfortable
jokes about her and Finch. Just as she opens her mouth to tell him
to shut up, Adrian appears in the living room, dressed in nothing
but boxers and a button-down.

"You can sleep with me if you want."

He says it so simply, so matter-of-fact. There is no implication
in it, no innuendo. He might as well be offering her a sandwich.

Before Ginny can think too hard about it, she says, "Sure.
Thanks."

As she follows Adrian into his room, she glances once over her
shoulder. Clay and Tristan's eyebrows are so high that they look
like they might fall off their foreheads. She widens her eyes at
them, and then she's inside Adrian's bedroom, and the door is
closing, and she's alone with a man for the first time in a year.

Sweat pricks her neck. What if he tries to have sex with her?
What if, as they make out, he starts to push her head downward,
the way so many men have before? Ginny knows that, if he does,
she'll go along with it—whether she wants to or not. She won't
want to make him angry. She won't want him not to like her.

Before she talks herself out of it, Ginny hops onto the bed. The
mattress bounces beneath her as she takes in the space: bare walls,

an empty desk, a closet filled with running shorts and collared shirts.

"Not into decorating?" she asks.

"Haven't had the time, really." Adrian unbuttons his shirt, then shrugs it off. Ginny tugs his sheets up around her.

Adrian is tall and concave, his chest and stomach scooped with patterns of muscle. His left rib, she notes, juts out of his torso like a broken piano key. She takes in his slim, muscular thighs. Runner's thighs. Despite spending most of his life at a desk, Adrian is effortlessly skinny.

Ginny hates how envious she is.

He flicks off the lights and crawls into bed beside her. Moonlight filters in the lone window that looks out on the building next door. It illuminates the pale stretch of his body. Long and ethereal, like the ghost of a spider. Ginny waits for him to pull her on top of him, to stick his tongue down her throat.

Instead, he wraps his arms around her and lays his head on the other pillow. "What's it like in Minnesota?" he asks.

Ginny hesitates. *He wants to talk?*

She thinks for a second. "Miserable," she says at last. "What's Goldman Sachs like?"

"Miserable," he says, and they both laugh.

"Where did you grow up?" she asks.

"Indianapolis. But I lived in Budapest until I was nine."

"Really?"

"Yeah. Then my mom married an American and moved my sister, Beatrix, and me to the Midwest."

Ginny notices that he doesn't mention his dad. "Do you miss it?"

"Sometimes." Adrian runs a hand down the length of her arm. "Mostly I miss my grandparents."

"Are they in Budapest?"

"Just outside, in a town called Szentendre."

"Do you visit?"

"Every year."

She's waiting for him to push. To lean in and slide his tongue into her mouth. To pick up her hand and drag it down to his boxers.

But he doesn't. He just holds her.

They talk for a half hour. Ginny jabbers at him about Minnesota, about Sofra-Moreno, about her life back at Harvard. She's halfway through a story about Finch convincing Tristan that Martha Stewart is the leader of the Illuminati when Adrian interrupts her.

"Ginny?"

"Yes?" She adjusts her body inside his arms. For being such a skinny boy, he's surprisingly warm and soft. "What is it?"

In response, Adrian lifts a hand and moves it tentatively toward her face. He brushes her cheek with his fingertips. At his touch, Ginny goes very still. Breath drags unsteadily in and out of her lungs. Adrian settles his palm on her cheek. Then he leans forward and presses his lips to hers.

The kiss is sweet. Tender. He doesn't try to push further. He doesn't move his hand down her back, grind into her, or inch his fingers up her shirt. He just kisses her.

Even warm and still on his mattress, Ginny feels as if she's falling.

It might have been Adrian's beauty that caught her eye. But what hooks her—what makes her heart beat way down in her stomach—is that he never touches her below the waist. That he refuses to acknowledge she has a body below the torso he holds so gently. That he refuses to acknowledge she has a body at all.

And that—that, more than anything—is all Ginny has ever wanted.

PART II

Six Months Later

Spring awakens in New York with a fervor Adrian has never seen before. In Boston, winter dragged her feet as long as she could, leaving grey-brown piles of slush dripping on the sides of the road well into May. Not in New York. In New York, the seasons work as efficiently as the city itself. They have distinct beginnings and ends, and no one is allowed to overstay its welcome.

April. A year out of college, and he still has another to go before he's fulfilled the standard two needed to prove to other companies that you're dedicated to your job. But Adrian isn't dedicated to his job. His job makes him want to pour lighter fluid all over 200 West Street and burn the building to the ground.

Is this adulthood? Is that why people tell you not to grow up?

In moments like these, Adrian thinks of Budapest. He thinks of biking along the Danube, legs flying as he tries to break his record for getting from his mom's apartment to his grandparents' house. He thinks of the crumbling bars, the castle on the hill.

An email *dings* into his inbox, the third in five minutes. The higher-ups are chattering about their newest deal: a bid to buy a craft beer company. Every email they send means more work for Adrian. More juggling numbers in Excel. More edits to the deck. More mind-numbing clicks of *F2, F2, F2.*

All for a stupid beer company they probably won't even buy.

Beer. Beer makes him think of Ginny. Clay said she's moving to New York this week. When Adrian first heard she was moving here, his heart sank. He likes her, but . . . doubtless, she's going to expect that they start dating, and Adrian simply doesn't have the time.

He sighs, opening Outlook to see exactly how fucked the rest of his week will be.

The door to Sofra-Moreno Companies, LLC, is made of all glass, half of which is plastered with hundreds of beer brand labels. Ginny recognizes them all—some from her year with the company, some from drinking warm cans in sweaty fraternity basements.

It took six months. Six months of gently nudging her manager, then not so gently nudging her manager, then emailing HR, then interviewing on Zoom for a dozen different roles. But her hard work paid off. Today, Ginny begins her life as the youngest member of the global communications team.

She lives in Manhattan.

She lives in Manhattan.

Ginny grew up far from New York City on the Upper Peninsula of Michigan in a thimble-size town called Sault Ste. Marie. Locals just call it "the Soo," an Americanized version of its French name. Every house has a stack of firewood out back. The airport has one gate. The outskirts are nothing but chipped red barns and bales of hay. The biggest attraction is the bridge that carries tourists out of the city and into Canada.

Before she could even spell her own name, Ginny knew she was going to leave.

Ginny's best friends were her brothers. Two above, one below: Tom, Willie, and Crash. One serious, one funny, one who likes to blow things up. They spent nearly all their free time playing video games, driving to Wendy's, organizing the neighborhood into giant games of ghost in the graveyard, and finding things for Crash to light on fire.

And, of course, there was Heather.

As kids, Ginny and her older sister didn't get along. Not even close. It's kind of sad when she thinks about it. After six years as the only female in the family, Heather was probably excited when she found out her mom was pregnant with a girl. Probably she wanted a doll, a two-foot-tall, porcelain-necked American Girl with plaid skirts and a symmetrical face. Whose hair she could cut however she wanted. Who she could cover in lipstick, make pretty.

Instead, she got Ginny.

From the start, Ginny wasn't what her sister wanted. She didn't like dolls. She liked dinosaurs and digging holes. She played dress-up, but only to turn herself into a Viking, vampire, or backwoods explorer—never a princess.

Heather, on the other hand, isn't just feminine; she's *aggressively* feminine. She wields womanhood as a weapon against all who would harm her. Handbags heavier than rifles, heels sharp enough to draw blood. She's unreasonably beautiful, like staring straight into the sun.

As a kid, when Ginny watched her sister move through a crowd—purse swinging, miniskirt stretched tight, giant sunglasses balanced on the bridge of her nose—she felt that she knew a secret no one else did: *this tiny blonde could fucking kill you.*

Inside, a security guard sits behind a sleek black desk. To the left, turnstiles flash from red to green as employees trickle inside.

"Hi," says the guard, a bald man whose name tag says GARY. "Visiting?"

"No." Ginny smiles. "It's my first day."

She's excited about her job in internal communications. In Minnesota, she was left off every announcement, every all-hands, hardly a part of Sofra-Moreno at all. She knew firsthand how it felt to be forgotten by your company. She would fix that. She would be the bridge that connects everyone.

On the side, she imagines learning the ropes of external media from her boss—how to liaise with journalists, pitch a story, navigate a crisis.

New York. She can hardly believe her luck.

For the longest time, Ginny thought she could make things work in Minnesota. She made it to Harvard, didn't she? How difficult could it be to last a few years in the Twin Cities?

What she didn't account for was the loneliness. The grief. How badly she would miss her brothers. How badly she would miss her friends. How she needed them around. A year of starving herself and crying herself to sleep and convincing herself, each and every day, that she was okay, even though she wasn't. A year, then she was gone.

And when the boys' lease came up for renewal last month and Adrian Silvas announced he was moving to a studio, she thought she might perish from happiness. Two days ago, she moved into his old bedroom, hanging her posters on his bare walls and setting photo frames on his bare desk. When she inhaled, she thought she could smell the secrets he left behind.

Now Ginny spends every minute of free time in the living room. Now she sleeps with her door open, just to hear the sounds of her friends' existence.

She's starting over. Anything is possible.

If Heather were in her place, she wouldn't be nervous. She runs her own business, for Christ's sake. Nothing scares her sister.

Clay, Finch, and Tristan helped her move in. They carried her boxes—only six in total since she left half her life in a dumpster in Minneapolis—up four flights of stairs and deposited them in Adrian's old room. Tristan made continuous jokes about Ginny moving into Adrian's old room, dubbing it "the last place she touched a penis." Finch told Tristan to stop obsessing over other men's genitalia. Clay told them both to never mention *Ginny* and *other men's genitalia* in the same conversation again or he'd have to throw up.

Little do they know, Ginny thought as she watched them argue.

Adrian Silvas. Ginny spent the last six months thinking about him. Not constantly but consistently. He followed her to sleep, appeared in her dreams, popped into her mind as she dozed off in meetings. To be honest, it was somewhat unsettling; for years, her brain only had space for food, exercise, and work. Food, exercise, work. Food, exercise, work. But when Ginny woke up the morning after her first night in New York, it was as if a new pocket had opened in her brain. And into that pocket slid Adrian Silvas.

She didn't try to repress the fantasies. Part of the fun of Adrian Silvas was that he lived a thousand miles away, which meant their relationship could never come to anything. There's safety in that.

But then her company finally assigned her to a new role, this time in their corporate strategy office in New York. And suddenly, Adrian Silvas went from fantasy to reality.

Not that she's seen him yet. But she will. She knows she will.

And when she does, she can't wait to see what will happen.

Her first day is a blur. Back in Minnesota, Ginny would get to work at nine, greet her coworkers, chat by the coffee machine, then sit down for a leisurely day of work. The New York office is something else entirely. Bright lights. Open-concept seating. Glass conference rooms. Cold brew on tap and a fridge full of free beer. Coworkers weave throughout the space, holding laptops and plastic containers of salad. Someone is always getting up to take a call. Someone else always has to jump onto a *very* important meeting, *right* this very second, I'll be *right* back with you.

It's madness. It's a buzzy hive of productivity.

Ginny loves it.

She's a good worker. There's no other way to say it: just as she threw herself into her college studies with a kind of manic obsession, so too does she attack the tasks assigned by her new boss, Kam. She pulls her desk up to a standing position. Opens Slack and Outlook. Delves into her first assignment and doesn't come up until lunch.

As a global manager of communications, Ginny's first task is to create the newsletter that will be sent out each week to the entire company. She has total creative control over the newsletter's design. It's a test. She knows it is. How well can she establish communication within such a disconnected organization? How deep is she willing to dig? How the hell will she figure out what is happening inside a division with more than two thousand employees and offices on five different continents?

Ginny isn't worried. She got perfect grades in high school. Earned *magna cum laude* with her college thesis. Lost twenty pounds while living in a state whose primary foods are tater tots and cheese curds. Never touched a slice of bread. Ran every morning.

She can do anything.

After work, Ginny meets the boys for drinks in Washington Square Park. Technically, drinking outdoors is illegal, but, as Clay said, "Anything is legal when it's wrapped in a paper bag."

"To our girl in the Big City," he says now, raising his paper bag over their blanket.

"To our girl!" echo Finch and Tristan, clinking their beers together. Ginny grins, stupid big, and takes a long pull from her bottle.

It's almost eight o'clock. The April sun has only just set, casting their group in long shadows that play over the matted grass. No one has eaten dinner.

"Do we want Thai or shawarma?" Tristan asks, scrolling through his phone.

"Are you seriously going to Seamless food to the park?" asks Finch.

Tristan waves a hand. "It's on the hedge fund's dime."

"Let's do Thai," says Clay. "I'm craving pad see ew."

Finch wipes an invisible tear. "Our little picky eater, all grown up."

It's true. When they were freshmen at Harvard, Clay wouldn't touch anything that didn't resemble a cheeseburger. Now he eats sushi twice a week.

"Gin, what do you want?" Tristan types into his phone.

"Chicken cashew nut," she says automatically. "With lots of veggies."

Clay makes a face.

It takes Ginny a second to be embarrassed. Here she is again, ordering protein and vegetables. Didn't she tell herself things would be different in New York? Didn't she swear she was turning over a new leaf?

"Listen to this." Finch picks up his guitar and starts plucking a string of unrecognizable notes. "Today in class, I get this text from Hannah, right? Telling me how she's at some frat party—on a Wednesday, mind you, God I miss being a senior—and just did a beer bong with the son of the CEO of *Beck Pharmaceuticals*. I swear to God. Apparently they got in some big argument over patent laws."

"Of course they did." Clay laughs. "Hannah could argue with a rock over health care."

"Beck Pharma?" Tristan says. "That's nothing. If you look at their stock price compared to Pfizer, they're not even in the same *ballpark* as—"

"Shut up, Tristan," Clay and Ginny say without even looking at him.

Forty minutes later, the food arrives, slung over the wrist of a harried-looking man on a bicycle. Tristan distributes containers. Across the blanket, Clay's phone lights up with a text. He picks it up. After scrolling, he says, "Silvas is getting fucking crushed at work."

Ginny nearly chokes on a bell pepper.

"Silvas, eh?" A strange grin twists Finch's mouth. "Have you seen him yet, Gin?"

She pounds her chest. "I moved in two days ago."

"But you *will* see him, right?"

Ginny hates when Finch does this. Gets overly pushy about her dating other men, as if forcing her to find happiness will somehow erase what he did.

"Maybe," she says.

"*Maybe*." Finch rolls his eyes. "She'll be in his bed by next Friday. I'd put money on it."

Ginny resists the urge to hit him.

Of course—not that she would ever tell them—she secretly hopes he is right.

The next day, Ginny stands at her desk, trying to pay attention to the task of putting together the newsletter. She came in at 8 a.m.— a half hour before Kam, as planned—and spent the first hour at the office trolling through Slack, trying to figure out who works for which brand. She spent the second stalking Sofra-Moreno employees on LinkedIn, jotting down any big wins they posted about recently and pulling their photos to add to the newsletter. *Everything is content*, she tells herself.

It doesn't take long to hit a wall. She ran three miles this morning and didn't eat any breakfast. By 10 a.m., her attention has already started to wander. Her mind grows fuzzy, the world hazy at the edges. She can't stop glancing from her laptop to her iPhone, which lies facedown on her standing desk—Ginny never works sitting down; she prefers to multitask, to type and burn calories at the same time—irritatingly silent. It's only her third day in the city, but for some reason she desperately wants to text Adrian.

Stop, she tells herself. *You don't even like texting.*

Of course, there was a time when she *did* like texting. Before college. Before food took over every last inch of her mental space. She had boyfriends in high school—the longest being Andy. She loved the way they would text flirt, an ongoing conversation about nothing. Sporadic reminders that someone was thinking about her. That she was worth something. That she was desired.

Of course, the last person with whom she texted like that was Finch, and look how *that* turned out.

She glances at her phone. Back to her laptop.

Stop.

She reaches out and flips her phone over. Its screen is blank. She types in her passcode, clicks MESSAGES, and puts in Adrian's name.

GINNY: Hi! What r u do

She stops typing. Is she really doing this? When Ginny gave her phone number to Adrian last October, she thought she'd hear from him at least a few times. But his name never once appeared. Does that mean all his kindness—his gentle touches, the kiss that lingered on her lips for weeks afterward—was just for show?

Her thumb hovers over the blue arrow. It's 10 a.m. He's probably at work already.

When you have anxiety, every text you send feels like jumping out of an airplane with no parachute.

GINNY: Hi! What r u doing Friday night?

She presses SEND.

The bubble leaks up into the conversation, turning the deep blue that tells her that yes, you sent that, there's no taking it back. She flips her phone facedown and puts it as far away from her laptop as she can.

The one and only benefit of working at an investment bank—besides the money, of course—is that Adrian rarely shows up to work before ten. No one does. Everyone was up until four the night before.

Whenever he can, Adrian gets up early to run. Physical exercise has always been the easiest way to keep him sane. Out in the fresh air, limbs moving, mind focused. In Budapest, he rode his bike along the Danube; in college, he rowed the Charles; now he runs the Hudson.

Last night was particularly gruesome. This morning, he wakes to a text from his VP telling him not to worry about coming in before noon, so he laces up his running shoes and takes off toward the river. Just as he turns onto the bike path, his phone vibrates. Expecting another text from his VP—likely telling him *never mind, come in ASAP*—he pulls it from his pocket.

GINNY: Hi! What r u doing Friday night?

Ginny. Interesting. Adrian tucks his phone away. He'll respond, just not now.

He keeps running. In all likelihood, he won't be able to go out on Friday. He hasn't left the office before nine in months. But if his associate doesn't crush him with anything new—

Maybe it would be nice to see her, even if just for an hour.

This thought surprises him. Normally, he craves solitude. But after a month in his studio, it's become clear that too much alone time is bad for him. His mind—it races. Jumps from one thought to the next like a moth flitting from flame to flame.

As he jogs along the Hudson, Adrian is surprised to find those thoughts wandering to Ginny. To her smile, sideways on his pillow. To the sound of her laugh. To the way she tasted—limes from the Corona, mint from her toothpaste.

Adrian shakes his head. He's barely thought of Ginny at all since that night.

Better not to start now.

t takes twelve hours, but he responds. Another two and they make a date: drinks at Dante in the West Village.

Ginny floats through the rest of the week. Every morning, she eats breakfast. A small breakfast, but breakfast nonetheless. At lunch, she goes out with her coworkers for tacos at Tacombi. At dinner, she allows herself a fistful of starch. One afternoon, she even goes out for ice cream with Clay.

Adrian's long response times are intentional. To him, this thing with Ginny is nothing serious. It's cotton candy: sweet and whimsical, inherently transient. Meant to dissolve as quickly as it hits the tongue.

Of course, what he can't know is that the more he neglects her, the worse Ginny wants him.

On Friday, Adrian is the first to arrive. Unbuttoning his jacket, he settles into one of the rickety wooden chairs out on Dante's patio and orders an Aperol spritz. He made a nine o'clock reservation, and it's now 9:05, but Ginny strikes him as the kind of girl who shows up ten minutes late to anything.

Adrian isn't even sure why he agreed to come on this date. He has no time for nor interest in a serious relationship right now. By all accounts, it would have been more chivalrous of him to say no.

And yet—

And yet there's something enchanting about Ginny Murphy. Maybe it's her choppy, shoulder-length hair. Maybe it's the delicate, creamy waif of her wrists. Or maybe it's that here she comes now, speeding down MacDougal Street on a pair of fucking *Rollerblades*, hair tucked into a stickered helmet.

She really is weird.

Adrian has never allowed himself the privilege of being weird. How could he, when he moved to America at the age of nine, speaking not one lick of English? He spent his pre-pubescence— one of the tenderest parts of life, when kids are unabashedly cruel and selective—trying to understand the new culture into which he had been unwillingly thrown. To Adrian, success hinged on assimilation. On learning the language, making friends, and fitting in.

Ginny quite literally rolls up to their table. "Hey!"

"Uh. Hi."

"Sorry about this." She plops down into the chair opposite his and starts unsnapping the blades. "This is my ride."

"You skated here from SoHo?"

"From work, actually." She yanks off the first Rollerblade, wiggling her socked foot around before tucking it into the shoe she pulls out of her backpack. "I stayed late tonight. First week sending out our newsletter."

"From work? Wait—don't you work up in Flatiron?"

"Yep." She yanks off the second.

"But that's—"

"Twenty-three blocks. I know." She grins. "Fun, right?"

Adrian shakes his head, amused.

"Anyway. What are we drinking?"

He holds out the flimsy paper menu and says, "I ordered an Aperol spritz."

Ginny crinkles her nose. "How very European of you."

"Technically, I *am* European."

"Don't I know it."

There's a long pause.

"I think I'll have a beer," she says.

When the waiter returns, Adrian orders a burger, Ginny a beer and kale salad.

"That's all?" Adrian asks, handing the menu to the waiter.

"Yeah. I'm not that hungry."

Adrian thinks she looks like she's been hungry for years.

"So," Ginny says, propping her chin onto one hand. "Tell me about Hungary."

This pulls Adrian up short. He'd expected her to ask about work or what he did last weekend. The things people their age normally talk about. In all four years at Harvard, he could count on one hand the number of people who asked him about growing up in Hungary.

"Like . . . about the country?" he asks.

She shrugs. "Whatever you want to tell me."

"Well." Adrian leans back in his chair. The waiter arrives with their drinks, setting them down on the wooden table. "For one, it's corrupt as hell. The prime minister, Victor Orbán, has been in power for, like, twenty years, even though he overtly funnels money to his supporters while letting the country's infrastructure crumble away. Plenty of people call him a dictator."

Though Ginny doesn't respond, he can tell she's listening.

"None of that was really part of my world growing up, though. I lived out in a small artist's village with my grandparents. We were pretty disconnected from the politics of the city."

Adrian doesn't know why he feels the need to add this. He doesn't talk much about his past, but something in Ginny's eyes makes him feel as if she wants to know. As if she's waited all her life to hear about this.

"You didn't live with your parents?" she asks.

Adrian takes a sip of Aperol. It's cool and bitter. "On occasion, I stayed with my mom, but she was always working. And my dad . . . he died a long time ago."

Grief crosses Ginny's eyes. Adrian braces himself for it—for the pity and apologies that always accompany this information. A familiar desire to leave pulls at him. To put a stop to this before it begins. He doesn't understand how they arrived at this conversation, just ten minutes into their first date.

But Ginny doesn't apologize. Instead, she asks, "How did he die?"

"Car accident." When Ginny doesn't react, he continues: "It was winter, and . . . well, there was ice on the bridge." It's a story rarely spoken aloud in his family, but one that Adrian has told himself a thousand times. Every time, he looks for ways it could have been different: if his father had taken a different route, if it hadn't been dark outside . . . "It happened a week before I was born."

Ginny blinks. "Are you serious?"

"I am."

"That's . . . one of the most tragic stories I've ever heard."

Adrian looks down into his glass. Here it comes. *I'm so sorry, I can't even imagine . . .*

"What was he like?"

He looks up. "Who? My dad?"

She nods.

Adrian almost laughs. "Did you not hear what I just said? I never met him."

"No, no. I mean—what do you know about him?"

God, this girl loves to ask questions. Adrian doesn't think he's ever met someone more willing to stick her nose into places it doesn't belong. He waits for annoyance. For the familiar recoil that comes when people pry into his past. But when he looks into her wide green eyes, so open, so curious, genuine, and without judgment, he finds that he *wants* to tell her. About his dad. About Hungary. About *everything*.

What the hell is happening?

He says, "He was a professor."

"A professor of what?"

"Mathematics."

He thinks of the limited times he's asked his *anya*—his mother— about his father. Of the way her eyes shut down. The way she physically folds inward. Her clipped answers, no more than a word or two, as if to speak any more would physically injure her.

They were deeply in love. That much Adrian knows.

And then she lost him.

Adrian thinks about his father every day. Mostly in passing, like a road sign between thoughts, because to linger any longer opens the door to the guilt. Sticky black guilt, thick as tar. It leaks into his chest, coating his bones and blood vessels. And every time he scrapes the guilt straight off the hard bones of his chest, wiping it away until only a faint residue is left behind.

His mother keeps exactly one photograph of his father, but as far as Adrian knows, she never looks at it. Adrian discovered the photo as a child when he was looking under the sink for the spray that would clean his orange juice out of the carpet before Scott saw. Beneath a box of Swiffer wipes, hidden among all the plastic bags and cans of Shout, was a Bible.

This made no sense. His mother is a devout Catholic; to this day, she attends mass every afternoon and keeps a rainbow stack of Bibles out in the living room, where everyone can see them. To find one hidden away was strange.

Even stranger: when he cracked it open, the inside was hollowed out, pages knifed away until all that remained was an empty stomach.

His mother defaced a Bible?

There, inside that stomach: his father.

Adrian knew right away that it was him. He had never seen his father before, but he knew. It was the stack of books under his right elbow, the long fingers that rested on the door of a pale-yellow car, the unkempt dark hair and the brown eyes, so dark they could almost be called black. It was exactly the way he always imagined his father would look. When he flipped the photo over, in the bottom left-hand corner, his mother's tight, all-caps handwriting read: *ADRI, 1992.*

Adrian stuffed the picture into the pocket of his shorts and slammed the cabinet shut. He raced up the steps to his room. He would return the photo later that week, but for now he wanted to keep his father all to himself.

"He must have been brilliant," Ginny says.

"He was. And well respected." Adrian smiles, thinking of his grandmother's stories. Unlike his mother, *Nagyanya* glows with pride every time her son comes up. "Practically the entire city showed up to his funeral." He points at her glass. "You haven't even touched your beer."

"Yes, I have." She lifts it to her face and takes a long gulp. When she lowers it back to the table, froth lines her upper lip. "See?"

Adrian laughs. He feels an urge to lean across the table and kiss the froth from her mouth. Instead, he picks up his napkin from his lap and offers it. "You have a little—"

"I *do*?" Ginny gasps, covering her mouth. "How humiliating."

This makes Adrian laugh even more.

Ginny grins, wiping the froth from her lip with her own napkin. "So." She drops it back into her lap. "What was school in Hungary like?"

"School?"

"That's what I said, isn't it?"

"Hmm." Adrian sips his Aperol, considering. "Pretty similar to school in America."

"Really?"

"Well." For the first time in years, he thinks back to his old schoolhouse on the outskirts of Budapest. He remembers desks and blackboards. Lockers and hallways. A stern teacher. The starched cotton of his uniform.

But he remembers other things, too. He remembers stark Soviet architecture. Boxy beige meals. Ceilings that threatened to fall on your head. Marching.

"We used to march," he says, surprising himself. "In gym class."

"You would . . . what?"

"We would march. For, like, thirty minutes. That was our exercise."

For a long moment, Ginny just stares at him, eyes wide. He thinks he might have frightened her, but then she tips her head back and laughs so loudly it fills the entire restaurant.

"What?" Adrian asks, bewildered.

"That is . . ." Ginny wipes at her eyes. Their green seems to glow even brighter. "That is the most former–Soviet Union thing I've ever heard."

A smile sneaks onto Adrian's face. "I suppose it is."

"Has no one ever asked you about this stuff before?"

"Not really."

She shakes her head. "And then you moved to the US when you were nine. What was that like?"

"Hard," he says. "I had no idea what anyone was saying."

"You must have missed Budapest so much."

"I did."

"I can't believe no one asks you about this stuff. You have the most fascinating life of anyone I know."

Adrian laughs. "If that's true, you really need to get out more."

Ginny doesn't smile. Instead, she takes another sip of her beer. Studies him.

"No," she says finally. "No, I don't think I do."

When they finish dinner, Adrian isn't ready for the date to be over—a fact that surprises no one more than himself.

"Well," she says as they turn down MacDougal Street. "This was really—"

"Would you like to come back to mine for a drink?"

Ginny stops walking. "Okay."

"Let me carry those." Adrian reaches out for the Rollerblades.

"Are you sure?"

"Of course."

In Chelsea, Adrian unlocks the front door of his studio walk-up and leads Ginny up the stairs. He's never brought a girl back to his apartment just to hang out before. It's not that he hasn't had the opportunity; girls practically throw themselves at him when he's out at the bars. But if they come home with him, it's for one thing and one thing alone, and it doesn't require much conversation.

Adrian's apartment is the only unit above a small restaurant. It's one room, spacious, with a bed pressed up to the white molding beneath wide bay windows. A nonfunctioning fireplace sits in one corner. A long couch in the other. But his favorite part of the apartment, the place that keeps him sane during long weekends spent working alone, is the patio, the doors to which sit just beside the couch.

"Wow," Ginny says, setting her purse down on the floor. "This place puts my shithole to shame."

"Hey, I used to live in that shithole."

She smiles. "So you did."

"What do you want to drink?" Adrian walks over to the kitchenette. "I have tequila, whiskey . . ." When he opens the cabinet above his refrigerator, he pauses, noticing the two-liter Coca-Cola bottle jammed into the corner. "Actually . . ." He reaches over and pulls it out.

"What's that?" Ginny appears by his shoulder.

"Homemade sour cherry wine. My grandma sent it to me."

Her eyes widen. "She *made* that? In Hungary?"

Adrian pauses. When the bottle arrived in the mail, he hadn't intended to share it with anyone. He thought he would drink it after long days of work, one tumbler at a time, savoring it for as long as possible. But something tells him Ginny will appreciate it. "She did."

After pouring two glasses of wine, Adrian leads Ginny out onto the patio. She inhales, taking in the high brick walls, the dangling lights, the cushioned outdoor sofa.

"I can't believe you live here," she says.

"I can't, either." And he can't. The apartment had been a steal, a well-kept secret passed from analyst to analyst at Goldman.

They settle onto the sofa. Ginny crosses her legs, setting the glass on her knee. "So," she says. "If I remember correctly, you hate your job."

Adrian thinks of working until 4 a.m., of incessant emails from associates and MDs, of work so rote and mind-numbing he sometimes thinks his brain will ooze right out of his ears. Sometimes, he wishes it would. "I do."

"Why not quit, then?"

"I consider it every morning."

"You do?"

"Yeah." He stares through the double doors at the bed where he has spent far too little time since college graduation. "I don't want to work in banking forever."

Ginny shifts closer on the couch. "What *do* you want to do?"

A memory passes through his mind: a woven rug on the wood floor of his grandparents' house. A bottle of orange Bambi. The old Zepter television set, on which Adrian watched Hungarian cartoons and dubbed Disney movies every Saturday morning. A treat. Something his *nagyanya* only let him do for an hour or two before she sent Adrian out on his bicycle.

And after he came to America: another floor, another television set. This time lit by the hazy Indiana sunshine. Animated characters jabbering in blocky, unpolished syllables—entirely unrecognizable from his home tongue. At first, trying to watch American television was just as frustrating as the long days at school, when his classmates moved their lips, voices raised, as if volume would somehow make him understand. But as time went on, TV and movies became a refuge. A place he could practice English without fear of messing up. A place he could hide.

"Movies," Adrian says.

"What?"

"I've always wanted to work in movies and TV."

"Seriously?" At this news, Ginny visibly brightens.

"Yeah. When I moved from Budapest to Indiana, TV kind of saved my life. I couldn't understand a word the kids at school were saying, and I was scared to even try to talk to them. But TV—that was a safe way to learn."

"That's fascinating," Ginny says.

Adrian smiles. They stare at each other for a long moment, saying nothing, and Adrian is surprised by how much he wants to kiss her. He's done it before, right? *Take face in hands, lean down, press lips to hers.* It's simple. Why can't he do it now? Why do the six inches between them feel like so many more?

"So." Ginny clears her throat, looking down. "Have you ever had a serious girlfriend?"

Adrian almost chokes on his wine. "You really don't beat around the bush, do you?"

She shrugs. "You're terrible at texting. In my experience, that usually means someone has never had someone to consistently text."

"No," he says. "I'm terrible at texting because I hate it. Even if I did have a serious girlfriend, that wouldn't change." He glances at Ginny. "I won't alter who I am to suit someone else."

Ginny's eyelids flutter.

Kiss her. The words drift to him from some hidden pocket of his mind.

I can't, he thinks. *Not right now. Just one more drink. One more is all I need. Then I'll be brave.*

Ginny asks, "Have you ever been in love?"

Adrian almost laughs. Not only has he never been in love, he's never let anyone get close enough to even approach the *idea* of love. Whenever relationships surpass a date or three, he cuts things off. He's never liked anyone enough to let it go further. And if he isn't 100 percent certain he's in love, he would rather be alone.

He'll probably do the same with Ginny.

But, for now, he enjoys their conversation. He enjoys the way she looks up at the night sky, as if each time she sees it is the very first. Her presence carries some sort of tonic. A restorative for the life Goldman drains away. Around Ginny, Adrian doesn't feel quite so empty. Around Ginny, he feels oddly at home.

Ginny doesn't understand what's happening. By now, it's past midnight. She's spent almost five hours with Adrian. They've each had three glasses of sour cherry wine, and he hasn't even tried to hold her hand.

It's sad, Ginny decides. That she's even still here. He's so clearly uninterested. No man has ever passed up the opportunity to kiss a girl who has been sitting on his couch for three hours. Not unless he isn't actually attracted to her.

And yet—how could he not feel what she does? The faint buzzing between them, the air thick as smog, clogging her throat, making her dizzy. Every time she looks at him, her chest tightens painfully. She longs to reach out to him. To rest her hand on the hard planes of his chest. To press her lips to his.

If she did, she'd only make a fool of herself.

She brushes off her pants as she stands. Earlier that night, she put on those pants with the expectation that later on someone else would be taking them off. What an idiot.

"Well," she says. "Guess I should probably head out."

"What?" Adrian asks. He's visibly surprised. "You're leaving?"

Ask me to stay. "Yes."

Adrian looks into his glass of wine. "Okay."

"Okay," Ginny repeats.

He hesitates. Then he stands and says he'll walk her downstairs. When they reach the landing, Ginny lingers, waiting to see if he'll lean down and kiss her. He doesn't. Instead, he wraps her in a hug. His grip is limp. It contains nothing—no hidden messages, no lingering meaning. Ginny thinks fleetingly that it's the kind of hug you could shrivel up and die in.

"Bye," she says.

"Bye," he says.

She pulls away from him and steps out the building's door. She doesn't look over her shoulder.

Outside, Chelsea is uncharacteristically quiet. The bars, normally boisterous and bustling, sit silent on their street corners. Ginny cuts across Seventh and starts walking south. Inside her chest, a hole, patched over by years in the safety of solitude, re-opens.

Rejection. She could choke on the word. She can't believe she's spent six months thinking about someone who doesn't even want to kiss her good night.

"Fuck this," she says aloud.

"Yeah, fuck this!" echoes a man across the street, pumping a fist.

Ginny cries. Warm tears stream down her cheeks. They stream into her open mouth, which gasps softly in and out, spreading a familiar saltiness across her tongue. She cries until her head aches and her cheeks are stained. She cries until she finally accepts the truth: that Adrian is simply, obviously, painfully uninterested.

She wants to hit herself. The crying was supposed to end with her move away from Minnesota. New York was supposed to fix her.

"Fuck this," she says again, a whisper this time, the words intended only for her.

Why didn't I go for the kiss?

Adrian stares at the back of his building's door. At the cold metal that, seconds before, framed Ginny's warm smile.

B ack at Sullivan Street, Ginny pushes open the door to 5E. She kicks off her shoes and wraps her arms around herself as if they can somehow protect her from her own anxiety.

It's just past eleven on the West Coast, where Heather lives her perfect life with her perfect husband. Ginny could Face-Time her now; she'd probably pick up. But she doesn't. She never calls her family when she's sad or anxious. She doesn't want them to know.

In her bedroom, Ginny strips naked and stands before the mirror. There they are: growing hills at her breasts, gentle protrusions at her hips, and—worst of all—a soft layer of fat around her stomach.

For Ginny, it's been five. Five years of keeping her weight *just* low enough for her body to be permanently uncomfortable, but not so low that it would raise any eyebrows. She's never been Ginny Murphy, Scary Stick of a Woman. But she shaved away her butt, her boobs, her stomach, her thighs. Just enough to satisfy that deep craving for emptiness.

When Ginny came home after sophomore year, her mother opened the door with a big smile, ready to receive her daughter. It slipped from her face when she took her in.

"You've lost weight," she said.

"And?" Ginny said, shouldering past her with a duffel bag in tow.

"And I thought you were supposed to *gain* weight in college."

"Old wives' tale."

The bag disappeared from her hand as her mother scooped it up. "Sweetheart." Ginny stiffened. Her mother hadn't used that word in years. "You didn't have any weight to lose in the first place."

At school, she could avoid her mother's worry—out of sight, out of mind; her mom *did* have two kids still living at home, after all—but whenever she came home, the issue resurfaced.

It all came to a head a few weeks ago, when she spent some time at home in Michigan between her move from Minnesota to New York. Ginny's mom tried to force carbohydrate after carbohydrate upon her, bringing home all the treats she'd loved as a child: glazed twists from The Queen's Tarts, cupcakes from Thyne's, boxed brownie mix that burbled thick chocolate when it came out of the oven. Ginny did whatever she had to do to avoid eating them. Sometimes she made excuses and feigned a stomachache. Other times she put them into her mouth, chewed and smiled for her mom's benefit, then spit them out into the sink when no one was looking. Ginny became an expert liar. A world-class cheat.

At the end of the two weeks, Ginny's mom gazed at her, tearful, as she packed her bags for New York. "I don't understand," she said, voice cracking. "I fed you so much."

Heather was home that week. She drove Ginny to the airport. When she dropped her little sister off, she looked Ginny dead in the eyes and said, "Get your fucking shit together and gain some weight, or I will fly to New York and beat your ass. Got it?"

She got it.

On the plane back to New York, afloat in that in-betweenness of air travel, a state in which anything seems possible, Ginny made a vow—*No more.* That period of her life is over. She will throw down her walls. She will eat bread and rice and candy and all the other foods she hasn't allowed herself to touch in years.

The room swims before her. How did she let this happen? She

knew the risk of eating carbohydrates. She knew that things like burgers and bagels and beers would cause her body to grow.

And yet—she grew lazy. She allowed herself to indulge in the newness of New York City, in its many delicacies and delights, and she did not exercise. She did not run, bike, lift weights, or do any of the other activities that kept her body an obsessively tight, muscled board back in Minnesota. All she had done was roller-blade, hardly enough exercise to keep herself skinny. Of course her body grew. She did this to herself. It is her fault. All her own.

Ginny is dizzy. So dizzy. The angular body bends and swims before her. And all the alcohol in her stomach—it begins to inch back up her throat. *Shit*. She knows what will happen next. She's seen it countless times, performed by countless drunken college kids, all of whom drank so much they hurled the contents of their stomach over Mt. Auburn Street.

So she does the same. She runs into the bathroom, places a hand on either side of the toilet, and vomits.

In the morning, the first thing Ginny does is return to the mirror. She's in nothing but a baggy cotton T-shirt and lace underwear. She lifts the hem of the shirt, turning sideways to inspect her belly.

To her great relief, she sees none of the pouch from the night before. Her 2 a.m. vomit must have reversed the damage.

Hmm, she thinks. *That's a neat trick.*

"You were together five hours last night, and he didn't even *kiss* you?"

It's Saturday morning. Ginny picked up bagels from Blackseed for the boys. Now they're gathered around the coffee table, spreading cream cheese and picking apart Ginny's night. In the corner,

Tristan and Finch fight wordlessly for control of the aux—a daily ritual, for them. Finch always wants to play indie bands they've never heard of. Tristan always wants to play Doja Cat.

Ginny digs out a mournful glob of chive spread with her knife. "No."

"But you guys have already slept in the same bed," Tristan says over his shoulder as he tries and fails to grab the aux out of Finch's hand.

"I know."

"And he had no problem kissing you then."

"I *know.*"

"Oh, come on." Clay takes a bite out of his sesame bagel. "This is Silvas we're talking about. No one knows why he does anything."

Ginny drags the knife through the cream cheese, carving a long valley. She doesn't want to eat her bagel. She doesn't want to eat anything. "Maybe he just doesn't like me."

Clay waves a hand. "No guy spends five hours with a girl he doesn't like."

Ginny disagrees. It may have been years since she last desired to be desired, but she remembers how the game works. She remembers from Andy, and from Finch. She remembers how physical actions—kissing, touching, sex—are evidence of a man's attraction. If Adrian didn't kiss her, what else is she supposed to assume?

Growing up, Ginny never worried about her physical appearance. About her desirability. Between her streaky blond hair, symmetrical face, clear skin, generous hips, and thin waist, she knew boys lusted after her. Even after Andy broke up with her, his continuing desire to sleep with her told her that she was, at the very least, still wanted. Still worthy.

During freshman year of college, she began to doubt. Began to suspect that maybe there was something wrong with her. It was just a quiet thought, a seed, but it dropped into the soft soil of her mind and started to sprout.

Of course, once she bought into the internal dictatorship that is anorexia, men fell out of her thoughts. There was no space; her mind was utterly consumed by food. Ginny threw mud atop the seed and pretended it wasn't there. It worked.

Until now.

"Don't stress, Gin." It's the first thing Finch has said all conversation. Ginny looks over at him. He doesn't meet her gaze, instead scrolling through music on his phone. "Silvas is a great guy, but when it comes to dating, he never takes initiative. Ever." He clicks on a song, causing twangy guitar music to filter out of the speaker, and looks up at her. "You need to be with someone who will fight for you."

Ginny stares back at him. *You mean, like you never did?*

On the table, her phone buzzes. Everyone looks down.

It's Adrian.

Ginny hiccups.

"Well, would you look at that?" says Clay, leaning back into the couch and cupping his hands behind his red hair. "Things are only just warming up."

She's watching Netflix in bed when the bagel starts inching up her throat. It's the strangest sensation—a lump right at the center of her esophagus that seems to knock at a door just below her chin. *Hello!* the food says. *Us again.*

She presses two fingers to her larynx. What's happening? Why isn't the food going down? Is it the cream cheese? She knows dairy is harsh on the stomach. Of course, it could also be all the puking yesterday. Maybe her esophagus is stuck in reverse.

She glances helplessly about her room. An empty Nalgene sits on her desk. Able to think of nothing else, she unscrews the lid. Presses its lip to hers. Then she pushes slightly with the muscles of her throat, and—

A quiet *splish-splish-splish* as chunks of barely digested food drop to the bottom of the Nalgene. She peers inside. The food is thick and viscous, a corpse just beginning to deteriorate. It isn't long before she feels more knocking at the door.

It takes six pushes. Six pushes, six splashes, a snake of stomach acid slithering headfirst out of her mouth. Her food reborn. Pooling at the bottom of her water bottle. It's so easy. Too easy. *There's something wrong with me*, she realizes. *Acid reflux?*

When her stomach feels empty, she holds out the Nalgene and stares at the yellow-brown mush caking its insides. She supposes she'll have to wash it out later.

Before anyone can see it, she stuffs the bottle into her backpack and zips it all the way shut.

There is no lull between anorexia and bulimia for Ginny, no respite. She transitions from one to the other as seamlessly as the passing of a baton. Life as a relay race run by many flavors of mental illness.

t's Monday again. Adrian is editing his fifth spreadsheet of the afternoon when his phone buzzes. He flips it over, expecting a text from Ginny. Instead, it's an email. Not to his corporate account—to his personal.

SUBJ: [DELPHIC] Analysts wanted—come work at Disney!

Adrian's heart starts thudding in his ears. He glances over his shoulder to see if his associate is nearby. She isn't. He swallows a glob of spit and clicks OPEN.

Hi all,

Writing to let you know about an opportunity to come work for Disney in international strategy. Full job description below. I've worked here since graduation, and I can't think of a better . . .

"Texting your girlfriend?" comes a voice over Adrian's shoulder.

Adrian jumps, fumbling with his phone. It slips from his fingers and tumbles onto the carpet. "Shit." He dives under the desk. When he pops back up, he finds Chad, the analyst who sits one desk over, lingering behind his chair, Chopt salad in hand.

Chad cocks an eyebrow. "It's okay, dude. We all watch porn at work."

Adrian's cheeks color. "I wasn't—"

"Yeah, whatever. I won't tell if you won't." He winks and whacks Adrian's shoulder.

Adrian sighs, slumping back into his chair. He doesn't bother reading the rest of the email. Too risky. It'll have to wait until he gets back to his studio. He lays the phone facedown on his desk and tries to sink back into Excel.

When Ginny returns to her apartment after work that day, exhausted and drained, she walks in the front door and finds Finch lounging on the forest green sofa.

"Oh." She sets her backpack on the floor. "Hi."

He waves one hand. "Hi."

"Back from class already?"

"Lecture rarely goes past four o'clock." He points at the open textbook on the coffee table. "Clay and Tristan work until all hours of the night. So."

"I see."

"So it's just you and me."

Ginny knew when she agreed to move in with the boys that she would spend plenty of time with Finch. She just hadn't counted on that time being spent alone, with neither of their other friends as a buffer.

"You hungry?" she asks. "I'm making stir-fry for dinner."

"Sure."

She lines up a row of onions beside a pot of boiling water. Reviews the steps.

First: peel.

Second: halve.

Third: chop.

She digs her fingernails under the onion skin and starts to pull.

If she's being honest, Ginny is out of practice. Though she cooked extravagant meals for her friends every week in college, when she moved to Minnesota, all she did was scramble eggs and roast vegetables. She saw no point in deboning a chicken for one.

In Minnesota, Ginny spent the empty hours after work writing. It was her link to sanity, the only way to make it to bedtime. She had an endless stream of ideas. Dialogue popped into her head as she stared out the office window at the snow falling in thick drifts. It played on a loop, like the words to a song. She wrote them down: on a Word document, in her phone, on the back of a draft for an instruction manual. One story spread across a half-dozen documents, with her journal open, too, to record the thoughts she had about her own life. Thoughts from the journal often made it into the imagined story—blurred lines, reality bleeding into fiction.

Onions peeled, Ginny picks up the chef's knife and slices the first onion in half.

Growing up, Ginny often cooked for her family. It's not that her mother didn't like to cook; it's just that Ginny liked it more. She loved to see the look on her brothers' faces when she pulled out a tray of freshly baked cookies, homemade pizza puffs, or pretzel bites with a cheesy dipping sauce. The boys would spill into the kitchen, falling over one another to get a bite while it was still hot.

Heather, of course, would roll her eyes and say she didn't like cookies, pizza puffs, or whatever Ginny was serving. But when Ginny woke up the next day, a cookie was always missing.

At Harvard, cooking steadied her. Took her mind off the pressure of midterms, finals, social life, romance—or lack thereof. She loved the heft of a big knife in her hand. Loved the concentration it takes to properly mince garlic or chop cilantro. Loved the gratitude in her roommates' eyes when she presented them with a heaping bowl of guacamole.

This is all I want to do, she would think as she watched the boys dig in, as they shouted *thank you* through full mouths. *This is all I will ever want to do.*

So, after freshman year, when most of her peers were interning at banks and start-ups and consulting firms, Ginny went to culinary school.

Onions halved, she lines their flat bottoms up on the chopping block, presses the point of her knife into the chopping block, and starts cutting rapidly down the onion, watching the little crescent moons spill over onto the wood.

The first rule she learned in culinary school: always keep your knife sharp. It's the key to cooking well. The sharper your knife, the easier flesh and bone give way. When Chef set up for demonstration each day, he took out an enormous black briefcase—heavy, oblong, protected by a tiny silver padlock—and splayed it open on the counter before them. Its pockets rolled open, extending to twice the briefcase's length, a magazine's centerfold.

Then he started to sharpen.

Now Ginny uses the back of the knife to scrape the onions into a frying pan.

Culinary school is where she lost most of her weight. It's a paradox, she knows—when she came back to campus, every girl who saw her exclaimed, "Damn, girl. You're the only person I know who could go to cooking school and *lose* weight."

In truth, losing weight wasn't difficult. Ginny walked two miles to the local cooking school in Sault Ste. Marie every day that summer, then stood on her feet in the practice kitchen for almost six hours. They weren't allowed to eat anything they made; when they tried, Chef shouted, "This isn't a restaurant."

Lunch was a half hour. Hardly enough time to eat the salads she packed. Ginny wasn't a coffee drinker before, but at CIA, she started pounding espresso shots like water. It was the only thing getting her through the day.

By the end of week one, she understood why so many chefs do cocaine.

Ginny barely noticed the slimming of her body. When she did, it was only to admire. She liked to think that, as she sharpened her knife skills, she sharpened her body, too.

Inside the frying pan now: onions, baby corn, snow peas, garlic.

When Ginny arrived back on campus, she felt invincible. For the first time in her life, after existing firmly in the middle of a sea of children, firmly in the middle of the sea of popularity, firmly in the middle of the sea of academics at Harvard, Ginny had an identity. She was the Food Girl. And who doesn't want to be the one who makes the best food? Who doesn't want to spend all afternoon cooking for her best friends, making them three-course gourmet meals served on paper plates in a dorm room with no coffee table, insisting that they eat it all, every course, never taking a bite herself?

Ginny reminds herself of the vow she made on the plane ride here: *throw down your walls. Eat bread and rice and candy and all the other foods you haven't allowed yourself to touch in years.* She can do that. Tonight, she'll even have rice with her stir-fry.

She'll just throw it up afterward.

When she finishes cooking, there's enough food to feed a family of seven.

"Whoa," Finch says, setting down his guitar. "Are we expecting company?"

"No. I just made too much dinner."

He cranes his neck to peer into the kitchenette. "No kidding."

"Anyway." Ginny ladles a few scoops of stir-fry into a bowl, then turns around to take it into her bedroom. "Enjoy."

"Hold up." Finch stands from the armchair. "Aren't you going to eat with me?"

"Um." She moves the prongs of her fork around her bowl. "Sure?"

"Cool."

Ginny settles onto the couch, maintaining one full foot of distance from Finch.

He picks up the remote. "Want to watch something?"

"Sure."

"You like *New Girl*, right?"

"I do."

"Cool." He presses the center button on the remote, queueing up an episode from season three. For the first ten minutes, they eat quietly, laughing at all the appropriate moments. Then, during a scene in which the roommates are searching for Winston's cat, Finch turns to Ginny and asks, "So, how's the boss?"

"Fucking robot."

He laughs. "Really?"

"Swear to God. I mean, don't get me wrong—she's absolutely amazing at what she does. She lives and breathes communications, and she runs our team like a well-oiled machine. But the woman wouldn't know creativity if it hit her with a semi."

"Damn." Finch leans back in his armchair. "That must be really frustrating for someone like you."

Ginny sets her empty bowl onto the coffee table. "How do you mean?"

"I mean—you're creative, Gin. You always have been. It's one of the things I like most about you."

She waves a hand, dismissing the compliment. "It's no big deal. If anything, her lack of creativity gives me space to shine."

"Of course it does." He grins. "I'm serious, though. The story you wrote in Minnesota—"

"Wait." She arches an eyebrow at him. "Clay showed that to you?"

"Of course he did. Me *and* Tristan."

Ginny rubs her forehead. "I'm going to kill him."

"Why? It was good. Like, really good. You shouldn't be wasting your time at a corporate job. You should be chasing your dream."

"I don't have a dream."

"No?"

"Not really."

"I don't believe you."

"You can believe whatever you want. Right now, I'm focused on my career. I'm trying to learn as much about communications as I can, impress my boss, climb the ladder. You know." She nudges his leg with her toe, the first contact they've had since their stilted hug when she first moved in. "Boss-girl shit."

Finch holds up both hands. "Fair enough."

She changes the subject, asking about med school. The longer they talk, the more they slide back into the easy rapport they had five years ago, when they used to sit on his rickety dorm bed and laugh about all the outrageous people they met at Harvard. It feels, to Ginny's surprise, as if no time has passed at all.

The episode ends. A new episode begins. Ginny pays no attention. She is focused entirely on Finch, on his description of being in the OR for the first time.

Eventually, their conversation peters out. Ginny looks at the TV screen, but she can feel Finch's eyes on her.

"I miss you, Gin."

Her heart skitters. She doesn't look back at him. "That's absurd. We live together."

"You know what I mean."

She does. She remembers their walks by the Charles. She remembers listening as he sang for her, usually Eric Clapton or John Mayer. She remembers talking for hours, never running out of things to say.

He was her best friend those first few months at school. Not Clay. Not Tristan. Finch.

Finally, she meets his gaze. "What are you saying, exactly?"

"I want to try again." Finch scoots closer to her on the couch. "I want to be friends. *Real* friends, like the way we used to be."

Ginny looks down at the empty bowl on the coffee table. She considers the soy sauce staining its sides, the bit of red pepper clinging to the rim. At last, she looks back up. "Okay." She smiles. "I want that, too."

But even as she agrees, even as she thrills at the image of Finch smiling goofily at her, a voice switches on at the back of her mind, a whisper that asks: *Were we ever really friends?*

Freshman Week, Harvard. Ginny moves in below three boys who quickly adopt her as their fourth roommate. She spends almost every night on their futon, drinking Keystone Light, playing Mario Kart, and ordering Domino's at 2 a.m.

She does not miss her brothers. She has found three more.

Freshman Week, Harvard. Adrian doesn't cry when his mother drops him off at his dorm. He tries to picture his dad standing beside her, the way he often does, but the image wobbles and quickly vanishes, shaken by the guilt that bubbles up within him whenever he thinks too long about the man he never met. He wishes his grandparents were there.

As soon as he's moved in, he sets up his computer and calls his *nagyanya* on Skype.

During their weekly Skype calls, Adrian and his grandparents always cover the same three subjects: the weather (cloudy), their relatives (fine), and Hungarian politics (corrupt). After a decade of having the same conversation, Adrian could easily beg off these calls. Say he's too busy, that he'll try again next week.

But then he would miss the sunlight streaming through the kitchen window. The jars of pickled vegetables lined up along the sill. The wrinkles around his grandmother's nose, the squeeze of his grandfather's hand on her shoulder, knuckles calloused from building the house in which they live. The proof that love does exist. The glimpse of a life he could have led.

Freshman fall. Finch starts to pursue Ginny. She avoids collision for as long as possible, going home early, skipping nights out, begging off with excuses of homework or exhaustion. She doesn't want to screw up the dynamic of their friend group. She doesn't want to lose the first best friends she's ever had.

But Finch is persistent. He works for her.

And there's just one other problem: she likes him, too.

Freshman fall. Girls like Adrian. They like him a lot. They fall all over him at parties. Twice in the span of a month, a girl cries because he doesn't want to have sex with her.

His new friends look at him sideways. Why doesn't he take what he could so easily have? They don't understand. They don't know what it's like to live inside his body, a vine on a river, following the current of life, rarely driven by desire.

Freshman fall. Finch and Ginny have sex. He is her second, the first she's let inside her since Andy.

Afterward, they lie twined together on his twin dorm bed. Finch sings her to sleep.

Freshman fall. Adrian sleeps with three different women, all of whom he tells he doesn't want anything serious.

At his age, most people have already been in love—or, at the very least, *thought* they were in love. Adrian knows he hasn't. He's only just beginning to suspect what will later feel obvious: that he's incapable. That love is a coarse handful of sand that will slip right through his fingers, no matter how hard he tries to keep hold.

Freshman fall. Everyone goes home for Thanksgiving break.
Finch gets back together with his ex.

He tells Ginny on their first night back on campus, seated cross-legged on the bed on which they had sex a week before. As he speaks, a roaring fills Ginny's ears, like the sound of a summer storm rolling across Lake Superior.

Ginny tells Finch that it's fine. That they're fine. She tucks it away, all the pain and hurt. Stuffs it into a pocket somewhere. She does it for the sake of their friend group, for the sake of not losing her boys.

The next day, she eats one hard-boiled egg for breakfast and nothing else until dinner.

The first time they meet, it's for lunch at the Shake Shack in Madison Square Park. NYU Med School is in Gramercy, Ginny's office in Flatiron. They opt to meet in the middle.

Madison Square Park teems with activity. Men walk dogs. Nannies push strollers. Trainers lead sweaty groups of women in kickboxing. A man who can't be younger than seventy pushes himself around and around the curving paths on a skateboard. Ginny winds through it all, making her way toward the crowd right at the center.

Finch comes into view just as Shake Shack does. He sits at one of the green tables just beneath a string of dangling lights, waving. Ginny waves back.

"Hungry?" he asks, standing.

"Starving."

Finch orders a fried chicken sandwich, a Shackburger, French fries, and a milkshake. It takes all Ginny's effort not to order her burger wrapped in lettuce instead of a bun. They carry their trays over to one of the green tables and sit facing each other.

"So," Finch says, picking up the fried chicken sandwich with one hand. "Friendship Trial, Day One."

Ginny smiles and sips from her plastic water cup. "I suppose you could call it that."

"What should the first test be? Should we talk shit about people we know and see if our opinions align?"

"Oh, come on. That's cheating. You already know they do."

"That's true." Finch nods, taking a bite out of his sandwich. "I think that's how we bonded so quickly freshman year. Do you remember when we used to stand in the corner during Wiggles-worth dorm parties and psychoanalyze all the people in the room?"

Ginny laughs. "How could I forget? Tristan almost beat you up when he heard you call him the 'quintessential Oedipal head-case.'"

Finch holds up both hands. "Hey, now. It's not *my* fault that the guy reeks of repressed desire to murder his own father."

"I think it's more the bit about sleeping with his mother that bothered him, Alex."

Finch sits back. "Alex," he says. "No one calls me Alex any-more."

"Not Hannah?"

Finch picks up a fry, then puts it back in the cardboard carton. "She's the only one." His eyes flick up to Ginny's face. "And you now, I guess."

"If you'd like."

"I would, actually."

"Okay, then."

They sit in silence. Ginny looks over at the family seated at the table to their left. A mother and father drink plastic bottles of cranberry juice, two kids eat peanut butter sandwiches, another simply runs in circles around them all.

"Have you heard from Adrian?" Finch asks.

She shakes her head. "I might text him and see if he wants to go out this weekend."

"Might you?" Finch leans back in his chair, holding a hand to his heart. "My, my, Virginia Murphy, how very *modern* of you."

The mother has run out of cranberry juice. Her husband leans over and pours a measure out of his own bottle into hers.

"Right," she says. "Because acting like a desperate, lovesick puppy is *so* modern."

"You're not acting desperate. You're inviting him out. It's not that big of a deal."

"Okay, but it *feels* like that big of a deal."

"That's just because you're in love with the guy."

"I am not in love with anyone, thank you very much."

Finch lifts the milkshake to his mouth and sips lengthily. "Ah, now *that's* a true shame."

On Thursday, during his 6 p.m. coffee break, Adrian digs his phone out of his pocket, hoping the buzz he feels will be a response to the application he submitted to Disney a few days before. He knows it's early, but—

It's a message from Ginny.

GINNY: Hey, brunch this weekend?

He pauses. He has a choice. He can let Ginny down easy, the way he would with most girls. It would be so simple. Three words, tapped out with the rough pads of his thumbs: *Sorry, I'm busy.* He's done it so many times.

But then he thinks of Ginny's laugh. Her enormous green eyes focused only on him, as if trying to peel back his skin and study what's underneath. He thinks of the thickness that fills the air whenever she's around. The fist at his center. The *want.*

ADRIAN: How's noon?

The next weekend, Ginny has bottomless brunch in the East Village with Adrian. She drinks too many mimosas, and Adrian laughs as she skips through Tompkins Square Park.

They pick up coffees from a street cart and sit on a park bench.

"So," Ginny asks. "When did you lose your virginity?"

Adrian chokes on his coffee. "Seriously?"

"Seriously."

He thinks for a moment. "I was eighteen."

"Who was she?"

"A girl from back home."

"Girlfriend?"

He shakes his head. "What about you?"

"Seventeen. My boyfriend."

"That sounds nice."

"It wasn't."

Ginny was supposed to lose her virginity on her birthday. That was what she and Andy agreed to. He would've preferred it happen sooner, of course, but to his credit, he never pushed. Never even asked. *She* was the one to set the due date. *She* was the one to tell him: seventeen years old is good. Seventeen years old is enough.

At the back of her mind, Ginny had doubts. Sometimes, when they were kissing on his bed, she would become suddenly, terrifyingly certain that she needed to break up with him. Right then, right that moment. *He isn't the one*, her brain would whisper.

But I like him, she would whisper back.

But do you? Do you really?

It was anxiety. She knew it was. Anxiety is a surgeon skilled at carving things open that were never meant to be touched in the first place. She will examine your life from every angle. Look for cracks, abrasions, weak spots, doubts. And when she finds one, she will pick it apart, bone by bone, worry by worry, until you can no longer tell truth from fiction.

And so it was with sex.

Back then, Ginny was still recovering from the guilt uploaded into her body by a decade and a half of Catholicism. She liked the *idea* of sex—liked the way it felt when a certain part of her pelvis rubbed up against a certain part of Andy's thigh—but she knew it was bad, too. Naughty. And every book read, every movie watched, every article in *Seventeen* magazine—they made it seem like losing your virginity was some sort of threshold: once you crossed, there was no turning back. You are no longer the same. You never will be.

The closer her seventeenth birthday drew, the more Ginny started to panic.

She started to think. Hard. Made a list of pros and cons: *To do it now, or to wait?* She drafted messages to Andy. Deleted them. Drafted more. Deleted them again. The surgeon was hard at work. By the end, Ginny couldn't remember why she wanted to have sex in the first place.

Here's the thing about Anxiety: once she grabs hold of an issue, you cannot think or reason your way out of her. It's the mental equivalent of chasing cars down the highway.

On the night of her birthday, as Andy's hand crawled down her stomach, she panicked. Started to sweat. "Actually . . ." she said. "Can we just . . . ?"

His face darkened.

In the six weeks that followed, the two fought more than they had in all the previous year combined. She went around and around on what to do, decided to go through with it, took it back, and then, one rainy afternoon beside the soccer field, they broke up.

"Were you in love?" Adrian asks.

Were they in love? For a long time, Ginny thought so. That first year—she remembers long walks by Lake Michigan, making out in the spiny grass of the dunes; long summer days in the pool in his backyard, sneaking beers from his dad's fridge; long summer nights atop his shoulders at Lollapalooza, body caked with glitter, fake ID tucked into the pocket of her cutoffs.

"You're not like other girls, Ginny," he used to tell her. "You're magic."

When Andy dumped her, Ginny spent an entire weekend in bed. She told her brothers she was sick. She told her guy friends she needed time. Then she set her phone on the bedside table and stared at it for forty-eight hours straight, waiting to see Andy's name appear.

It never did.

With every hour that passed, Ginny's depression deepened. She felt like a hole was slowly widening in her chest. Like a hole was slowly widening in her life.

I love him, she realized. *I always loved him.*

Sunday night, she picked up her phone and sent him a message.

GINNY: We need to talk

ANDY: When?

GINNY: Now

Ginny stole her parents' Volvo and drove to his house. She snuck into his basement through the door in the garage. Ginny motioned him over to the closet, afraid his parents would walk down.

Inside, a single light bulb hung from a string on the ceiling. Whiskey and cigars lined the shelves.

"Well?" Andy asked.

Ginny inhaled. "I want to have sex with you."

"What?"

"I want to have sex," she repeated. "With you."

So they did. She let him have clunky, unpolished sex with her in the broom closet where his dad kept the whiskey and cigars.

She thinks back to that night. The way her spine scraped up against the shelves. The way it drew blood, leaving long red streaks that eventually turned to scars. Ginny never told him she was in pain. She never even *noticed*. Because there was another pain, stronger, more acute, more alien, happening between her legs.

It went on like this for months. Ginny would sneak over to his house, they would have sex, and then she would leave. Whenever she brought up the idea of them getting back together, he said he wasn't ready.

It was strange, stealing like a thief into a home in which she had, for so long, entered as a welcome guest. On the way there, knowing that she would soon be in his arms, the hole in her chest would fill in with a porous, temporary putty. On the way home, it all spilled back out. She cried. She hated herself. But she couldn't stop. She loved him. And because she loved him, she needed to be around him, and sex was the only way she could.

"No," she says finally, answering Adrian's question. "No, that wasn't love. I thought it was, at the time, but now . . ."

Adrian lets her trail off. Lets the silence fill in the rest.

They spend two hours on that bench. Ginny peppers Adrian with question after question, knee jiggling up and down as she listens to his responses. The coffee has her blood rushing at double its normal pace. Or maybe it's simply how near Adrian is to her. Barely an inch separates their legs, and that inch feels pregnant with buzzing electricity, begging her to close it entirely.

Eventually, Adrian turns the spotlight onto Ginny. "What were the summers like in Michigan?" he asks. "Similar to Indiana?"

Ginny smiles. There's nothing quite like Michigan in the summertime. The drone of cicadas. The flash of fireflies. The air, obese with humidity, having sucked the Great Lakes up like soda through a straw. During the summers, Ginny and her brothers loaded the whole neighborhood into the back of their Dodge Ram and trucked out to one of Lake Huron's sandy beaches. On the rare occasion that Heather joined them, she always took shotgun, forcing Ginny, Willie, and Crash to squeeze into the Ram's back seat. They brought footballs and bags of Franzia rosé. Everyone got drunk; everyone played in the waves. Ginny wore purple bikinis. Most boys knew that she was off-limits; those who didn't learned their lesson quickly. Despite being both the youngest and smallest of the group, Crash was rather good with his fists.

Ginny does her best to explain all this to Adrian. He listens intently, eyes screwed up into little slits. When she finishes, he says, "Tell me more about your brothers."

From a young age, it was clear where her brothers would end up. Tom would be a lawyer in Detroit. Willie would go to the Second City in Chicago. And Crash—well, they just hoped he'd make it to eighteen in one piece. By all accounts, there would be nothing left for Ginny in the Soo.

So, she studied.

School came naturally to Ginny. She sat in the last row of all her classes, where she could both play crude hangman on crumpled sheets of paper with her guy friends and lean over to help them through the hardest questions. She never went out on weeknights. She put homework before everything else. The boys all called her *Harvard*.

But she could also chug a can of Busch Light as fast as any of them. She never wore makeup. She liked George Strait and Bob

Dylan and giving her friends wedgies in the middle of the hall-way. Roundly, she was known as the fourth Murphy brother.

Which isn't to say that she wasn't compared to her sister. Of course she was. Heather Murphy was the most beautiful student to ever grace the hallways of Soo High. She made all her own clothes and starred in every school musical. She was the Upper Peninsula's Gigi Hadid. She got into fashion school in Los Angeles and now lives a glamorous life out West, with the sunshine and the supermodels and a business account on Instagram with more than two hundred thousand followers.

They say that sometimes we define ourselves not by the ways in which we are like others but the ways in which we differ. And so it was with Ginny and Heather. Ginny wanted to leave the Soo, just as her sister did—but on her own terms, using her own skill set.

She thought: liberal arts degree. She thought: University of Michigan or Indiana, or Northwestern, if she was lucky. She applied to Harvard as a joke, a spoof on the nickname she'd worn her whole life. She never expected to get in, let alone to land a scholarship.

Ginny tells all this to Adrian. She scoots closer, brushes her knee against his, rests a hand on his shoulder. Anything to demonstrate her interest. By now, she's quivering with anticipation. Every time he smiles—fleeting, infrequent moments that light up every tired line of his face—shivers run up her arms. His body has a strange power over her. When his emotions shift, she feels it. Surely he must feel it, too.

But as the sun moves across the sky and the mimosas start to wear off, disappointment sets in. He hasn't reached for her hand. He hasn't brushed her cheek. He's not going to kiss her. He doesn't even *like* her. Ginny doesn't know what this is, but it certainly isn't a date. She stands and says she should head back to her apartment.

To her surprise, Adrian leaps to his feet. "I'll walk you."

When they reach Ginny's front door in SoHo, she waits again. Makes small talk and taps her heels on the stone stoop. Adrian still makes no move to kiss her. She says goodbye and sticks her keys into the door. Already she feels the hole in her chest starting to widen.

"Wait," says Adrian, reaching for her wrist.

Ginny turns.

Before she makes it all the way around, his lips are on hers. Startled, she steps back, bumping into the door. Adrian catches her and pulls her in close. She is liquid against him; she has no solid body left.

Too soon, Adrian pulls back. "Bye," he whispers, then turns down Sullivan Street and disappears into SoHo. Ginny presses her fingers to her mouth. She feels as if she might float away.

The minute Ginny walks through the door, Clay and Tristan mob her. In their hands are two glasses of white wine. Over their shoulders, through the hallway, she spies an open bottle of chardonnay on the beat-up coffee table.

"Well?" asks Tristan.

"How'd it go?" asks Clay.

"Did he kiss you?"

"You were gone for a *long* time."

"Did he pay for brunch?"

"A *very* long time."

"Did he make you split the bill?"

"More than enough time to—"

"*Guys.*" Ginny laughs, shooing them away. "At least let me get through the door."

She follows the short hallway, Clay and Tristan on her heels, still pestering her with questions. She shoves Tristan when he asks what kind of credit card Adrian has. When she reaches the living room, she's looking over her shoulder, laughing. Then her gaze turns forward, and she halts. Clay bumps into her, wine splashing over the rim of his glass.

Finch sits in his usual armchair, plucking at the guitar. He looks up coolly, as if just realizing Ginny is back. "Hey."

She hesitates. "Hi."

His gaze falls back to the guitar. "How was the date?"

Adrian's kiss still tingles on her lips. She raises her fingers, wanting to feel it, to remember his warmth, but the cold air drifting off Finch is slowly wiping it away. "Good."

Finch nods without looking up.

Clay and Tristan, unaware of the tension, usher Ginny over to the couch and pour her a glass of wine. They sit to either side of her, bouncing up and down. "Well?" asks Clay.

Ginny looks into her glass of cheap chardonnay. In her peripheral vision, she sees Finch glance over. "Well, what?" she asks.

"Well, how did it go?" Clay asks. "Better than last time?"

She watches as pale-yellow liquid swirls about the inside of her glass. Finch's stare is a hot light burning into her cheek. What is that? Anger? Jealousy? Neither? She is certain of one thing: what she says next is important. It means something to him.

She just doesn't know what.

At last, she looks up from her glass into Clay's warm blue eyes. As always, they're crinkled at the edges, a result of the near-constant grin on his face. Seeing those eyes makes her instantly warm, wiping away the chill that seeped into her the longer Finch stared.

Ginny smiles. "It was perfect."

t's Saturday, and Adrian is working. Again. An IRR, urgent, that his associate says he needs first thing tomorrow *or else.*

His phone pings with a text from Ginny. He lifts it and sees that she's asking if he wants to get coffee at the ELK on Charles Street. He does. Lord knows, he would rather get coffee than sit scrunched up at his laptop at the tiny desk in his tiny studio. But he has no other choice.

Ginny will be disappointed. He knows she will. She wears her emotions like brightly patterned scarves; they're the first thing you notice and the last thing you see as you walk away. Their colors fill the entire room.

They've been on two dates now. Adrian is approaching his limit. The place at which he normally cuts things off with girls. He should probably do the same with Ginny. Should give the monologue he's recited hundreds of times now.

And yet—

And yet, none of those girls were *her.* None of them laughed the way that she does. None of them rollerbladed through Manhattan or spent their free time writing novels. None of them asked him so many questions about Hungary that he ran out of stories to tell. None of them made him forget the need to pretend.

Ginny is the first girl who's made him want to stay.

But he can't. Not right now. If all the dates he's had to cancel are any indication, Adrian is physically incapable of maintaining a serious relationship in his current job.

Why is he still with Goldman? It's not like he wants to climb the ladder. Become an associate, then a VP, then an SVP, then an

MD. Buy a house in Fairfield and have kids he never gets to see. He told Ginny he wants to work in movies, but sometimes, he's not even sure that's true. Sometimes, he's not sure of anything.

When his mom uprooted their family and shipped them across the ocean, Adrian had neither warning nor say in the matter. All he could do was board the plane and accept his new life. After that day, he understood that this is the natural way of things. That we do not have control over our own lives. That we are leaves adrift in the wind, following whichever breeze is the strongest, the most logical.

Maybe that's why he's never been in love. Maybe love is a choice. One he'll never be able to make.

Ginny is proud of this week's newsletter. She went above and beyond her usual three sections—articles, HR resources, Win of the Week—by interviewing two coworkers and including snippets from the conversations as internal spotlights. She didn't even ask Kam for help. She did it all on her own.

Words have always been Ginny's specialty. As a child, she carried a notebook all over the Soo. She filled it with descriptions of her brothers and the bridge and the fudge store on Interstate 75. She wrote everything down, a hoarder of details and memory. She dreamed of one day writing books, *real, full-length.*

In college, she traded her journal for a spiral notebook. There were essays to write, textbooks to underline. She found a new, more immediate dream: to stay afloat. She let her old dream fall into the Charles and drift far, far away.

Now, in New York, Ginny does the same. She sets aside the short stories that filled her time in Minnesota in favor of emails and newsletters and hour-long meetings with their PR contractors. She stays late at the office. She wants to do well. She wants to impress Kam.

Between meetings, she finds ways to puke discreetly.

It's much easier to hide vomit than you'd think. In the movies, puking is always this big event: it's sprinting to the bathroom, tearing open the door, falling to the floor, and maneuvering your face over the toilet *juuuust* in time to let loose a waterfall of red-green stomach acid, most of which will splatter the clean porcelain anyway. But that's not the truth. At least, not for Ginny it isn't.

The trick is to not make a big deal out of it. Speed-walking to the restaurant bathroom and retching like a barn animal? Yeah, no. That's amateur hour. Ginny can vomit an entire bowl of popcorn into a coffee mug while snuggled up next to her roommates on the sofa. Seriously. All she has to do is quietly open her esophagus and let the puke leak back up into her mouth. Then she lifts the mug to her mouth and pretends to sip something inside while really spitting out the half-digested buttery popcorn, letting it dribble down the ceramic and pool at the bottom. Then she does it again. And again, and again, repeating the action over and over until her stomach is wonderfully, blissfully, fabulously empty.

That's all. That's it.

For work, she buys an opaque Nalgene and keeps it at her desk, the way Kam does. But instead of filling it with coffee or water, she fills it with breakfast or lunch, leaking it slowly back out until she is clean again.

Every evening, she scrubs the bottle out with dish soap, but the tangy stink of vomit never fully washes away.

Adrian can't stay away. He tries. Lord knows, he tries. All that next week, he plunges himself into work, anything to distract him from thoughts of *her*. But Ginny is black ink in the clear water of his mind; all it took was one drop.

The following weekend, his schedule is clear. No requests for decks or reports in Excel. After sleeping in far too late, he buys two iced lattes and meets Ginny on the West Side Highway.

The Hudson is still that day. Ferries and tugboats carve smooth lines onto its surface. On the walkway, joggers—Adrian often among them—speed past. Out on Pier 45, couples sprawl on blankets with plastic cups and bottles of rosé.

"What do you think it's like to be in love?" Ginny asks.

Adrian looks out at the water. He cycles through his past relationships—all years before, none longer than a few weeks. "I haven't the slightest clue."

"I've read that it's like being a drug addict," she says. "You get this feeling of euphoria around them—giddiness, increased energy, a rush of dopamine—and then, when they leave, you crash. You want them back right away."

"That doesn't sound very stable."

Ginny shrugs.

"I thought love was supposed to be about comfort and certainty." Adrian tucks his hands into his pockets. "That, one day, you'll be with someone, and you'll just *know*. You'll be a hundred percent certain that this is the person with whom you want to spend the rest of your life."

"Maybe. Maybe both are true."

Out at the end of the pier, a man offers one sweaty palm to his girlfriend, tugging her to stand by the railing.

"Well, in any case," says Adrian, "you would know better than me."

"Why is that?"

"You once thought you were in love. With your high school boyfriend. Right?"

Ginny looks down. "I did."

"What did that feel like?"

She's quiet for a long time. She watches her feet, lining them carefully up with the cracks in the sidewalk. A minute passes, and Adrian thinks she won't answer, but then she says, "It hurt."

He inhales. On one side, his hand clenches into a fist.

Ginny continues, "I let him hurt me, over and over, because I thought I loved him, and I wanted so desperately for him to love me back."

Adrian doesn't respond. He wants to, but something strange has happened to his throat. It has become blocked by a brick of anger, of violence. By the desire to find whoever hurt Ginny and sink his knuckles into that man's face.

This impulse startles Adrian. He is not the violent type.

Out on the pier, the sweating man fumbles around in his pocket.

Adrian clears his throat. "So where did you read all that? About love and dopamine?"

"Where else? The Internet."

"A highly reliable source."

Ginny laughs. "I quiz people, too," she says. "People who have been in love. My mom, my brothers, my sister, Clay, Finch . . . They all say the same thing: that they just knew." She sighs. "So unhelpful."

Out on the pier, the sweating man's hand closes over a little velvet box.

"You're really invested in this subject, huh?" asks Adrian.

Ginny kicks a pebble out of their way. "I just get scared, you know? That I won't recognize love when it's right in front of my face."

Adrian looks out across the pier. He sees a flock of seagulls, a gathering storm cloud, a man and woman leaning against the railing, the man's hand jammed into his pocket.

Adrian decides he isn't scared about not recognizing love. Why would he, when he already knows he's incapable of feeling it at all?

By the time they return from their walk, it's four o'clock—that strange in-between hour, too late for lunch, too early for dinner. Outside, clouds hide the sun. Inside, the walls of a studio hide Ginny and Adrian.

They're at his place. They're always at his place. They say it's because of the privacy, because the boys clog up the Sullivan Street apartment, and, in a way, it is. It is because of the privacy. What they don't acknowledge is what that privacy affords them: invisibility. The promise that, if this relationship implodes, they can pretend no one knows. They can pretend it never happened in the first place.

When Ginny steps into the studio that afternoon, she feels that the entire space is cloaked in that four o'clock in-betweenness. That hazy break in reality. It clings to every surface like a thin layer of dust.

She knows, then, that they're going to have sex.

It's been a long time for Ginny. In college, the more she restricted her diet, the less she thought about boys. While sober, she thought only of food, of what to have for her next meal, of what she shouldn't have eaten at the meal before. But, when drunk, her mind wandered. She noticed the cute boys at the final clubs. She made eye contact with men across the rooftop of Felipe's. But when she kissed them, she felt nothing. No butterflies. No arousal.

Sometimes, they would even go back to her dorm room. The minute Ginny found herself in bed with a man, however, she panicked. She would start fast-forwarding in her head to when he would take her pants off and try to have sex with her, and her throat would close up. Her back would start to sweat. She wanted to run away. Only she didn't know how to run away without being rude, and Ginny *hates* being rude.

So she went through with it. Went through the motions of sex—the sighs, the heavy breathing—even though no part of her wanted to. Even though she was dry as a bone, nipples soft, insides cold and rigid. Even though the idea of having something, *anything*, inside her body made her almost retch with disgust.

Until now.

Ginny sits on the end of Adrian's bed.

"Want some water?" he asks, pulling two glasses out of the cabinet.

"Mmm."

He carries the glasses over and sets them on the bedside table. As always, he sits next to her but keeps a hand's width between them. He opens his mouth, probably to say something about the weather seeping in through the open window, but before he can get even three words out, Ginny takes his collar and pulls his lips down to meet hers.

Adrian's mouth is warm and familiar. He has full lips that always feel as if he's just applied ChapStick, though Ginny has never seen him use a tube. His lips taste like coffee. He never touches her with his hands, not at first. Never runs them through her hair or cups them beneath her breasts. In fact, he stays so still that Ginny sometimes wonders if he's still breathing.

Ginny is all touch. She wants to feel every part of his body. To push back his hair and unbutton his shirt and cradle the hard line of his jaw. Adrian gives her no direction. She crawls up onto the bed and throws one leg over his lap, straddling him. She grabs the bottom of his shirt and pulls it over his head. Even though it was over seventy outside, there isn't one bead of sweat on his body. There never is. Ginny wonders where all the sweat goes.

That simple act—stripping one layer from Adrian's body and tossing it aside—does something to him. Causes him to loosen. He wraps his hands around her sides. Pulls her gently toward his pelvis. His eyes are dark, hooded, even closer to black than usual.

Ginny places a hand on Adrian's chest and nudges him backward until he's lying flat on his back. He doesn't speak. Just watches as she pulls her own shirt over her head. She isn't wearing a bra. She never is, with breasts as small as hers. Her stomach rolls over once, right at the bottom. Ginny hopes he doesn't notice.

Adrian reaches up one hand and runs it slowly down the length of her torso, from collarbone to pelvis. Ginny closes her eyes, leaning into his touch. The brush of his fingers feels completely foreign, as if they're the first thing to ever touch her bare skin.

"Do that again," she whispers without opening her eyes.

"Okay."

But when his fingers find her skin again, it isn't at her collarbone. It's at the sensitive area atop her breast, where they trace slow circles. Her nipples harden. She lets out a low moan.

Normally, now would be the time that Ginny panics. That she questions whether she even wants to sleep with this person, or if she's doing it simply because it's what's expected. Normally, Ginny would be so far up in her head that she would leave her body entirely.

She opens her eyes. "Take off your pants."

Adrian does, unbuckling his belt and kicking off his dark jeans, causing Ginny to raise up slightly from his lap. Underneath, he wears tight black briefs. Again, she's struck by how thin he is. How his stomach is like a crater, how she can see every rib. She wants to fill all that open space. To press her chest to his concave center, the illusion of two bodies fusing together.

She lays one palm on his chest and starts to rock her hips back and forth. Her skirt billows over his hips. He slides his hands up

her legs, under the folds of her skirt. As she moves, pressure starts
to build at the base of her pelvis. Heat, familiar yet long forgotten.
She pushes it into the hard length inside his briefs. It isn't enough,
not even close.

She feels no anxiety about what's happening between them. No
doubt. No guilt. Adrian's lips part. She wants to hear him speak.
To hear her name. She realizes, then, that she can't remember him
ever saying it aloud.

"Do you have a condom?" she whispers.

Adrian pauses, hands still warm on her legs. "Are you sure?"

"Yes."

And she is. For the first time in her life, she is.

Adrian can't get the wrapper off the condom. He's naked, and so is Ginny, and he can't get the goddamn wrapper off the goddamn condom.

"Let me." Ginny appears at his side. She kisses his shoulder, then takes the condom from his hands and tears it open with her teeth.

Adrian isn't motivated by sex. Not the way some men are. He enjoys it, obviously, but he doesn't spend weeks pursuing women for the sole purpose of sleeping with them. He wasn't even planning to sleep with Ginny today. But now that it's happening, it feels inevitable, a wave finally reaching shore.

Almost every one of the women with whom Adrian has slept have been one-night stands. Flings he met at a bar or the Delphic. He felt no emotional attachment to those women. Just basic, alcohol-fueled desire.

With Ginny, it's different.

She positions herself above him, holding him with gentle fingers. He finds as he watches her that what he feels isn't basic desire. He isn't thinking about her breasts or her hips or the soft curve of her lips. He's wondering if she's cold, if he has the air-conditioning too high. He's wondering if she's comfortable, if she likes to have sex this way. He's thinking about all the moments they've shared in the past month. The questions she's asked. The secrets she's told him. The way she listens when he talks. The way she makes him feel like he's finally allowed to be comfortable in his own skin.

Then she lowers onto him, and he sinks into her, forgetting all that entirely.

Ginny's head dips back, shoulder-length hair floating down her shoulders. She uses the muscled length of her thighs to raise and lower her body. Adrian can hardly think straight, but he knows he doesn't like the idea that she has to do all the work, so he pushes himself up into a seated position and wraps his arms around her back, holding her tight to his chest. Ginny loops her arms around his neck and lowers her forehead onto his shoulder. Waves of pleasure roll from his pelvis up through his stomach, his chest, in every place that Ginny's hand touches. Together, they move her body up and down, up and down until they're both panting, sweat running down their bodies in long rivulets.

"Adrian," she whispers.

The sound of his name coming from Ginny's mouth does something to Adrian. His muscles tighten, drawing her closer. A strange tension is building within him—different from the typical one, the escalation before release. It feels warm and dense, like the soft roots of a plant taking hold in the soil. He can't identify the feeling, and something about it scares him.

He flips Ginny over, maneuvering so that her head lands softly on his pillow. He lays his chest atop hers. The heat from her skin seems to seep all the way through to his stomach. This doesn't feel like normal sex to Adrian. There are no tricks, no theatrical moans. It's just him and Ginny and the soft music of their breathing.

The waves of pleasure build and become almost overwhelming. He tries to time things right, to not come before she does, but she feels so good that he isn't able to hold back for long. When he finishes, it doesn't feel like the tension within him releases into the air, into nothing. It feels like it seeps from his body into Ginny's, like she now holds a piece of him.

He rolls off her and onto the tangle of bedsheets. He holds out an arm, and Ginny crawls under it. She lays her head on his chest.

Her toes slide down his calf, one leg fitting itself between his thighs.

"That was nice," Ginny whispers.

"Yeah." He smiles, tracing circles around her shoulder. "It was."

They're quiet after that, bodies adrift on a gentle sea. Adrian shuts his eyes. He's tired. He's always tired. But he finds that of all the ways in which he's fallen asleep since moving to New York—in his bed, on the couch, under his desk, on the subway ride home— he likes this one the most.

After they have sex, Ginny does her best to keep things casual. She doesn't bring up *what they are*, or speak of the bleak sadness that normally seeps into her body after sleeping with someone. She gives him the light version of Ginny, the same one she gives everyone else.

But she's fighting a losing battle. She knows it. You see, Ginny gives love too freely. Doles it out like flyers on the side of the road. She will accept anyone, befriend anything. By the time she finishes distributing every ounce of love within her, she has none left for herself.

They see each other more and more, after that weekend.

Adrian's favorite Hungarian photographer has an exhibition at a gallery in SoHo; Ginny stares so hard at each photograph that he's surprised they don't light on fire.

They speed down the paths of Central Park, Adrian on a bicycle, Ginny on her Rollerblades. They weave through bridal parties and moms with strollers. Ginny grabs onto the back of Adrian's bike seat and he pulls her up the steepest hills.

They go to a coffee shop in Brooklyn where board games and cards are spread out on low-rise tables and refurbished trunks. They drink three cups of coffee each and, by the end, Ginny's leg fidgets faster than a woodpecker. When she wins at Yahtzee, she yells, "Fuck yeah, motherfucker," so loudly that half the shop turns around.

Each time Ginny asks him to meet, he almost says no, then changes his mind.

Adrian refuses to think of them as being in a relationship. He went to Harvard because it was the logical decision. He ran for vice president of his final club because it was the logical decision. He took the job at Goldman because it was the logical decision.

He will not fall into a relationship because it is the logical decision. He will wait for love, no matter how long it takes, even if he's ultimately incapable, even if he's alone forever.

n the morning, Ginny arrives to work pumped full of zero breakfast and a headful of endorphins left over from an hour spent forcibly wringing sleep from her body on the treadmill in their building's basement. She heads over to her standing desk, nods at her coworkers, opens her laptop. She answers an email or three and scrolls through her list of tasks for the day.

At eleven o'clock on the dot, her phone dings with a message from Finch. *Shake Shack?*

This has become their ritual. Every week at noon, they meet in Madison Square Park, where, after quickly scarfing down two burgers and French fries, they pick up their Diet Cokes and do laps around the maze of pavement.

And talk.

And talk.

They do not shy away from the painful, the uncomfortable. They discuss every relationship, every heartbreak, every moment they wish they could take back. They know the names of all each other's exes by heart.

"Was Cara the one who tried to punch Hannah in the face?" Ginny asks.

"No, that was Miranda, the girl I dumped the week before homecoming."

For years, Ginny would have called Clay and Tristan her best friends. But things are changing. Things *have* changed.

"You know what's so easy about hanging out with you?" Finch says that Monday as they make a loop around a fenced-in green space, where a man with punching mitts lets a woman in boxing gloves rail against him. "I see myself in you. Looking at you is like . . . like staring into a clear pond."

"How do you mean?"

"I mean—it's different from looking into a mirror. I see myself, but I see other things, too. Things beneath the surface of the water. It's like—you help me see parts of myself that I didn't even know were there. Does that make any sense at all?"

"It does." Ginny averts her smile. "And I feel the same way about you."

"It's so stupid, isn't it?" Finch chews on the end of his straw. "That we wasted so many years semi-avoiding each other when things could have been like this all the time."

"It is stupid." They round another bend, headed back in the direction of the Flatiron Building. "But at least we aren't wasting any more time, right?"

"Right."

Ginny knows it's wrong, how much she enjoys being around Finch. It's wrong, the way her heart flutters when she gets her daily lunch text. The way she leaves their interactions feeling energized, pumped full of adrenaline and endorphins, like his very presence is some kind of drug. He has a girlfriend, and she's seeing Adrian. It's wrong.

But it's not like they're *doing* anything, right? They never hug, never kiss, never touch each other at all.

Maybe this is what it's like to find your soulmate, Ginny thinks. The platonic kind. The best friend whose mere presence can lift you from the blackest pit of your mind and leave you vibrating with joy.

So what if, every now and then, they share a glance that lasts a second too long? So what if he calls her beautiful, always in the context of something benign, such as him telling her that she's *so beautiful that of course Adrian wants to be with her*? So what? It means nothing.

They're friends. Just friends, nothing more.

Dinner is always Ginny's biggest meal. Even though she's eating more throughout the day than she has in the last five years, at least half of it comes back up, and by the time she reaches nine o'clock, she's fucking ravenous.

After dinner, Finch usually hangs around the living room, which presents a problem for Ginny. Going into the bathroom every time would be too obvious, so she develops a sneaky method for purging undetected: turn on the faucet, spit-up into her mouth, tilt her head to the side, and pretend to drink from the spigot. Then, with her head blocking anyone else's view, let the mushy food trickle out the corner of her mouth and down the drain.

For Ginny, the best part about throwing up is how easy it has become.

Anorexia was hard; it took superhuman restraint, the total repression of normal human instincts. At first, bulimia was hard, too, but now? She doesn't even have to try. She just stands in front of the toilet, pushes upward with her neck muscles, and the food reemerges, chunky and almost whole. Or she stands before the kitchen sink and spits into the drain while she washes dishes. Or she leaves the dinner table to go for a walk and dribbles into the bushes like a sprinkler. She's inventive with her purging.

She doesn't feel nauseous. She doesn't taste copper or take deep breaths to quell the storm within her. Her body simply readies itself to vomit. The food presses up against her esophagus, ready to climb, a practiced habit. She knows the drill: everything that goes down must come back up.

She's not full-on bulimic. Really, she's not. Yes, she vomits at least once a day, usually twice, but she doesn't *force* herself to do it; it just comes up, easy as turning on the kitchen faucet.

And she's not bingeing, not even close. According to the definition in the *Diagnostic and Statistical Manual of Mental Disorders*— which she looked up shortly after the puking began—bingeing is one-half of bulimia: first you binge, then you purge. So, if anything, Ginny is only *half* bulimic. Bulimia lite.

Late one Saturday morning, Ginny's phone buzzes with a Face-Time. She pulls it out. *Heather*.

For the first time in several weeks, she answers.

"*There* you are." Wavy blond hair. Bronze cheekbones. Face painted like a French portrait. Heather's face, angelic in its beauty, cannot be dulled even by an iPhone. "I've called you, like, forty-seven times since you moved in."

Ginny sits up in bed, shaking out her hair and tucking in her double chin. "Forty-eighth time's the charm."

"You're such a hermit. Where do you even go?"

"Into my hole. No service down there."

Separation. That was all it took for Ginny and Heather to stop fighting. Heather left Michigan for fashion school, and suddenly she was calling her little sister every week to gossip about the girls in her classes, the boys she kissed at parties. Ginny couldn't believe it. For the first few months, whenever Heather called, Ginny would put the phone on speaker, place it flat in her palm, and just stare. Observe. Wait with breath held, as if her sister's voice were a bomb that might combust at any moment.

To this day, Ginny doesn't know what made her sister change

her mind. Maybe it was homesickness. Maybe nostalgia. Maybe, with three thousand miles between them, Heather no longer had to be embarrassed by Ginny's obvious lack of femininity.

Whatever the case, Heather now FaceTimes her little sister every Saturday, just before her daily run, while drinking coffee in bed with her husband. In Minnesota, Ginny always answered. But, since moving to New York—she doesn't know. Something has changed.

"How are you liking the new apartment?" Heather asks.

"Love it." Ginny turns her screen around to show Heather the pint-sized closet, the framed prints that hang over her desk. "My bedroom is tiny, but I wouldn't expect anything less in New York."

"And the job?"

"I still have no idea what the hell I'm doing." Ginny blows a strand of hair off her forehead. "But the free coffee is nice."

Heather snorts. Sheets rustle in the background, and Ginny knows that her sister is getting out of bed to pick out her outfit for the day. "Things are insane over here." The camera bobs as Heather pads down the hallway of her Venice condo. "Our collab with that YouTube influencer flew off the shelves. We sold out of everything in, like, five minutes."

"That's amazing."

Heather sets the phone down on her vanity. "How's your eating?"

Ginny sighs. This question is phrased in the way Heather always asks—as if the act of eating were a creature that belongs to Ginny, a living being that could be well or unwell.

"It's fine," she says. And it is fine. She is eating.

She's just throwing up afterward.

"Good." Heather runs a brush through her hair. "Want me to send you the samples from our next line?"

Heather is married. Heather runs her own business. Heather eats pizza for dinner and cupcakes for dessert and doesn't gain a single pound. One day, Heather will have a baby, and she'll lose the weight in three days flat.

"Always," says Ginny, who was never meant to be like her sister but has never stopped trying.

The phone interview with Disney goes well. Adrian gets a second round, then a third. The interviews are long, grueling, and sometimes involve supplemental components, like aptitude tests designed to rank cultural fit. He takes them in coffee shops; empty conference rooms; or, even once, a supply closet. His coworkers can't know what he's doing; they'll make his life a living hell.

Ginny is remarkably supportive. She checks in with him often, asking how interviews went or helping supply him with three adjectives to describe himself. He finds himself actually responding to her text messages. It's nice to feel like she's in his corner.

The more time he spends with Ginny, the less he understands her. Normally, she's all bubbles and sunshine, but other times . . . there's a certain distance to her eyes, a place she goes. He catches it right after meals, or mid-conversation, or as they lie in bed after sex. She'll blink, and her eyes will get round and drift away. In those moments, he feels clutched by a dull terror, like she has gone somewhere from which he can never bring her back.

Every time he sleeps with Ginny feels oddly foreign. Like he's trying to learn the words to a brand-new song. She's different in the bedroom. In the rest of life, everything about her feels so *large*—her smile and her family and her laughter and her stories. It shocks him, then, when he runs his hands along her soft skin and remembers how small she is. How breakable. He never knows when to kiss her or how far she'll want to go. He doesn't want to assume that, just because they've slept together, she'll want to do it every time.

This whole relationship—it's bizarre. Ginny pops into his

thoughts all the time now. His mind still races—still leaps from one thought to the next like a faulty CD—but it's as if Ginny has been added to the song of his life. Every few minutes—there she is. Every time, he has to shake her off and return to whatever it was he was doing before.

Two weeks into interviewing, Chad eyes Adrian as he returns from the supply closet. "You take a long dump or something?"

"Just wanted a change of scenery."

"Uh-huh." Chad clicks his pen. "Don't we all."

When Adrian sets down his laptop, Chad cranes his neck to get a view of the screen. Adrian shifts over, blocking him out.

Ginny knows she shouldn't. Really, she does. But she can't help it.

She chases Adrian.

She doesn't know what it is about him. Maybe his gentle touch. Maybe the way he flutters his eyelashes—quick, like a hummingbird—when considering his answer to one of her many questions. Whatever the case, when Adrian kisses her, Ginny doesn't feel empty; she feels, from the tips of her toes to the crown of her head, filled with a kind of buzzing warmth.

On their dates, Adrian checks his phone every fifteen minutes. Waiting for an email that will demand he come into the office, stat. He's tired. Ginny can tell. The bags beneath his eyes are purple cinder blocks; they droop from his face, tug his torso, hunch his shoulders, drag him down like a body underwater. Sometimes, just before their date, Adrian will cancel, saying his associate just asked for a deck or analysis. Anxiety whispers to Ginny that these excuses are fabrications, avoidance, evidence that Adrian doesn't like her after all. She takes those whispers and tucks them away. Texts him again the next weekend.

At times, she feels embarrassed. Girls aren't supposed to chase boys. They're supposed to be coy, play hard to get, twirl their bubble gum and roll their eyes and tell them *some other time*. By all accounts, she must look desperate.

But Ginny has never quite understood how to be a girl. Not the way Heather does, with her bikinis and blond hair and knife-length nails. If she's being honest, until she met Adrian, Ginny didn't *care* to understand. She was content to rub away at her femininity, cut her hair short, and play video games and stand with her boys in a huddle at parties, laughing at the girls who showed up in heels and miniskirts. *They must be from Wellesley*, she would think, snickering.

Now she wonders if her disconnect with womanhood is why Adrian still hesitates to kiss her.

In Ginny's past experience, once she and a boy kiss for the first time—and *especially* after they've slept together—a barrier drops. A threshold passed. After that, they kiss freely.

Not so with Adrian. Some dates, she waits hours for him to kiss her. Some dates, they'll sit on the end of his bed, talking about God only knows what, and all Ginny can do is stare at his lips, begging him internally just to lean down already.

Every time she sleeps with Adrian feels like the first. He is so quiet, so closed off, that whenever she takes his clothes off, she's faced with a brand-new puzzle. *Where should I touch him? What will make him feel good?* His body is all muscle and bone, a web of hard angles that never feels familiar, no matter how many times she sees it.

There is nothing rote or boring about being with Adrian Silvas. When he runs his fingers down her spine, she shivers. When he sighs into her mouth, she wishes she could capture his satisfaction, inhale it, and make it part of her own body. When he touches the most sensitive parts of her, a fire blooms, and she has to stifle her cries for fear they'll startle him away.

She is constantly rediscovering him. Rediscovering all the parts he hides from the rest of the world.

But, despite the fire growing inside her, Ginny stays cool. She stays casual. She might set up their dates, but she never pushes him to acknowledge them as such. She doesn't want to pressure him. She doesn't want to ask for more than he can give.

*   *   *

One night, after her usual post-dinner purge, Ginny opens her phone and scrolls through the Instagram page for her sister's business, looking at the bikini models flouncing the tiny pieces of fabric that Heather creates. She looks at the inward curve of their waists, the hard lines of their jaws. Women paid for their flawless femininity. Heather is in the photos with them, laughing, as if her beauty is the funniest joke she's ever heard.

Ginny knows she will never be in any of these photos.

She tries to relax. After all, what does she have to worry about? Work is going well. She lives with her three best friends. She likes a boy who sometimes seems to like her back.

But none of that matters to Anxiety. The moment she registers that Ginny is sitting around, no distractions, no danger, she starts searching. Seeking. Looking for something wrong.

You see, Anxiety is a tricky little devil. She masquerades as your friend, as a necessary part of your life, allowed to dictate where you go, what you eat, who you befriend, and most importantly what to avoid. Her hold is so strong because she thinks she's protecting you. She thinks it's looking for tigers—but you left the jungle centuries ago.

It's why things got so bad in Minnesota. Alone, with nothing and no one to pull Ginny's focus away from her mind, Anxiety took over. She found tigers everywhere: in too many drinks, too many bites, too little exercise. She controlled every action Ginny made, from when she got up in the morning to how many episodes of Netflix she was allowed to watch at night.

Anxiety is a dictator.

But when Ginny is around Adrian, something strange happens. Her Anxiety quiets. Ginny doesn't feel the need to obsessively plan every minute of her day. She can forget about work. She can eat and, at least until she leaves his presence, she doesn't feel the need to throw up.

She picks up her phone. Pulls up his contact. Her finger wavers over the CALL button. She's never done this before. She doesn't know if he'll find it weird or clingy.

She hits CALL.

It's 11:30 p.m. There's a good chance that Adrian is still at the office. That he won't be able to answer, even if he wanted to.

"Hello?"

Ginny's heart skips into her throat. "Adrian?"

"Yeah, hi."

"Are you at the office?"

"No, I'm home. I got out early."

"Oh. That's nice."

"Yeah."

She glances about her room—which used to be *his* room— searching for something to say. After a lengthy pause, she blurts, "Did the lady next door practice her scales in the middle of the night when you lived here, too?"

Adrian laughs, a surprised sound. "Yeah. She did."

"She's really awful, isn't she?"

"So awful. I used to have to put in headphones."

"Lately, I've resorted to banging my fist on the wall and making loud sex noises until she stops."

"I bet your roommates love that."

"Nothing Finch can't drown out with his guitar."

"God, I *forgot* about that." Adrian groans. "Between him and the neighbor, I'm shocked I got any sleep in that apartment."

"You didn't. You were always at work."

"True." Adrian seems like he wants to say more but doesn't. He falls silent instead.

This is not unusual. All throughout high school, Ginny went for boys like Andy and Finch—talkative, confident, eager to add their two cents. Adrian isn't like that. Adrian rations words like bread during wartime: exactly as many as he needs, not one syllable more.

At first, Ginny felt that she must fill every silence. Must come up with some question, some story, some distraction for the lack of words between them. But the longer she spends with him, the more she understands that this filler is unnecessary. If she waits—if she's patient—eventually he'll say what's on his mind.

"Have you tried Morgenstern's yet?" Adrian asks.

"No," Ginny says. "What's that?"

"My coworkers say it's the best ice cream in New York."

"Guess we'll have to give it a try, then."

"Guess we will."

They fall silent again.

They are part of Adrian, his silences. As much a part of him as his hair or his past or the way his forehead crinkles just before he kisses her. If Ginny chooses him, she chooses his quiet, too.

That weekend, the last in June, they get ice cream from Morgenstern's and sit on a bench in Washington Square Park.

"What's your dream role at a movie studio?" Ginny asks. "Producer? Director?"

"I don't know," says Adrian.

"That's okay." Ginny tilts her cone and licks the drizzle running down the side. She no longer worries about the food that goes into her body. She doesn't have to; she knows that as soon as the meal is over she can regurgitate every last bite. "We're twenty-three. We're not supposed to know what we want to do with our lives."

Adrian bites his lower lip.

"What?" Ginny asks.

He hesitates. "I made it to the final round of interviews at Disney."

"You *what*?" She turns on the bench. "Are you fucking serious? When?"

"I got the email last week."

"Holy shit." Her face spreads into a huge grin. "I'm so proud of you. That's amazing."

"Yeah, well . . . it's a long shot. I don't know how many candidates are still up for the role, but . . ." A smile sneaks up behind his scoop of mint chip. Ginny loves that smile. "If I get it, it would be pretty awesome."

Before she can think too hard about it, Ginny leans over and kisses his cheek. "You're going to get it."

She regrets the move as soon as she does it. She and Adrian never display affection in public. They kiss only in the privacy of his bedroom, and almost always at his initiation.

But if the kiss bothers him, he doesn't show it. He licks his mint chip and asks, "How's the writing coming?"

"Oh . . ." Ginny trails off, watching ice cream drip down her cone. "I haven't really been writing much recently."

"You haven't?"

"Nah. Too busy at work, climbing the ladder and all."

"Oh."

Adrian looks strangely dismayed by this news. Ginny feels a jolt of shame and quickly steers the conversation back to Disney: "When is the interview?"

"Next Wednesday."

"Well, I'm sure you'll nail it." She pauses. "If you get this job, you'll have way more free time than you do now, huh?"

"I suppose I will."

A spark of hope flickers in Ginny's stomach. Right now, he's far too busy for a real relationship. But if he gets this new job . . .

She stops that train of thought before it can go any further.

"What will you do with all that free time?" she asks.

Adrian takes a bite out of his cone. "Sleep."

Ginny laughs. "Besides that, I mean."

He looks out across the park, watching the jets of water shoot up from the fountain at its center. "Read," he says at last. "I would read as many books as I can."

"Really?" She shifts on the hard wood of the bench. "Like what? Novels?"

"Definitely. Or short stories. Those are what I usually go for, anyway."

"Oh. Well." Ginny looks down at the melted cookies 'n' cream now pooling inside her waffle cone. *Do it*, she tells herself. *Just tell him.* She takes a deep breath, then looks back up. "You could read mine. If you want, I mean."

Adrian turns to her, eyes wide. Loose waffle cone clings to one corner of his mouth. The effect is that of a startled child. "I could?"

"Of course." Embarrassed, she turns away and speaks to the park, to the hot dog carts and the old men sitting at stone chess-boards, challenging tourists to a game. "I mean—only if you want to. I don't mean to assume that—"

"Yes."

Ginny's eyes dart back to Adrian. "Yes?"

A rare smile tugs at his lips. "Yes." He reaches up with his free hand and grazes two fingers along her temple, sending quiet shivers along every inch of her skin. "I would love nothing more than to take a look inside that brilliant mind of yours."

On her walk home, Ginny's ice cream comes up in little burps, like a child. She pushes with her throat, and the watery, half-digested ice cream floods into her mouth. She holds it there until she reaches a block free from pedestrians, then leans over the curb and spits it out onto the street.

She repeats this act as often as necessary, leaving black-and-white splatters throughout the city, in bushes and street corners, in puddles, behind parked semis. The splatters mark her path home, bread crumbs that anyone could follow, if they knew where to look.

Voluntary purging is nothing like getting sick. Nothing like throwing up because of a bug, because you ate expired sushi, or because you drank too much alcohol. In those instances, something genuinely wrong, genuinely dangerous, swims within you. Your body does whatever it must to be rid of it. Sprints its insides up your esophagus and ejects themselves of its own volition. Your body is fighting to save itself.

When you start to voluntarily purge, your body is confused. Why are we acting like we are sick? Why are we acting like there's poison inside us? There isn't. There is just food. Just sugars and fats and proteins. Nothing wrong. Nothing dangerous.

Yet you have convinced yourself that food *is* wrong. That it *is* dangerous. That it carries some inherent threat against your well-being. Food is a disease. In order to get better, you need to get it out of your body. You need to be empty.

So, you do. You stick your fingers down your throat, or push upward on your esophagus, or whatever other method you have to evacuate the disease from your system.

At first, it's difficult. You are trying to reverse a fundamental process, one developed by millions of years of adaptation and evolution. Food is meant to go down, not come up. Your insides do not sprint willingly up your esophagus. They dig in their heels. They claw with their fingers. They are dragged, against their will, back up and out into the world.

But you don't give up. You tell your body that it is sick. You tell it over and over again.

And, eventually, your body starts to believe you.

t's strange for Adrian to climb the stairs to his old apartment. It's even stranger to be climbing them before eight o'clock at night. He can count on one hand the number of times he made it home while the sun was still out.

Home.

Yet this apartment isn't his home anymore. It's Ginny's.

He doesn't know how he feels about that.

Where is his home? His studio apartment? Harvard? Indiana? Maybe. He likes Indy enough now, but in the beginning, he was miserable. Learning English was a nightmare. Its slippery consonants and inconsistent vowels felt nothing like Hungarian. For a full month, Adrian's classmates jabbered excitedly at him in this ugly new language, and all he could do was smile. America was where Adrian started learning how to fake human emotions. How to play at happiness, or anger or joy, when really all he felt was nothing.

And then, of course, there was his stepfather.

Adrian never had to force smiles in Budapest. His *nagyanya* was stern but tender, his *nagyapa* enthusiastic, a hammer or wrench always in hand. They took Adrian exactly as he came— good moods, bad moods, and anywhere in between.

His sister had a far easier transition than he did. Unlike Adrian, Beatrix actually participated in the English lessons that their mother sent them to before they moved. By the time they arrived in Indianapolis, she could name every object in their new backyard. On Saturday mornings, when she and Adrian watched cartoons on their living room floor, she would translate the dialogue for him, so he could laugh just a second after she did.

No. If he's being honest, when his airplane touches down at Ferenc Liszt International—*that's* when he feels the strongest sense of coming home.

It's Budapest. It's always been Budapest.

Yet, to his Hungarian friends, like Jozsef Borza, Adrian is the boy who left. Who grew up in America. Who went to Harvard. He does not belong there anymore. He does not belong anywhere.

As he knocks on his old door, a bottle of red dangling at his side, Adrian wonders if every twentysomething feels the way he does. Untethered. Searching for a home.

Ginny opens the door in a flurry of flour and oven mitts. White powder dusts her cheeks and the bridge of her nose as if she's been snorting cocaine instead of cooking. Her hair is twisted up into a chaotic bun. She pulls him into a hug, then turns and waves him inside with one mitt.

"Come in, come in." She tightens the straps of her apron as they walk down the hallway. "You're just in time for appetizers."

"Appetizers?"

"Oh, yes. We have a whole feast ahead."

His stomach growls in approval. He hasn't eaten since the salad he had at noon.

"*Dude!*" A mess of red hair leaps into his view first. Clay. As usual, he wraps Adrian in a hug tight enough to squeeze out his insides. Next is Tristan, slapping him once on the back. And then—Finch. He's seated in his usual armchair, guitar propped up on his legs. He doesn't stand. Just keeps strumming and nods once. "What's up, man?"

"Nice to see you."

It isn't, actually.

At first, the apartment looks exactly as Adrian remembers. Only upon closer inspection does he notice the small touches of Ginny that have appeared: a fake plant on the windowsill; Johnny Cash and Bob Dylan record sleeves on the shelves; a full chef's set of knives next to the microwave.

And then, of course, the smell.

The air brims with it—oregano, parsley, sautéed meat, stewing tomatoes. All at once, Adrian is six years old, sitting at the table in his *nagyanya*'s kitchen, where something was always simmering on the stove. His grip tightens on the neck of the wine. He's afraid, suddenly, that he might drop it.

As if reading his mind, Ginny turns away from the stove and eyes the bottle. "You brought wine?"

"I did. I know you're a beer girl, but I figured it might be nice to switch it up."

She grins. "I love wine. Let me see." He hands her the bottle, and she eyes the label. A nice $6 vintage from Trader Joe's. "This will be perfect with the spaghetti. Thank you so much, Adrian."

They smile awkwardly at each other. Adrian wonders if she's having the same realization that he is: this is their first time hanging out with their friends since everything started.

"Spaghetti?" Adrian leans over to eye the food steaming in the kitchenette behind her.

"Yes." Her face shades over with nerves. "I hope that's okay?"

"That's great," he says quickly. "I didn't know you cooked."

"You didn't?" asks Clay from the couch through a mouthful of blueberry goat cheese. "Dude. That's, like, her whole personality."

"I'd like to think there's a *little* more to me than that," Ginny says, but Adrian can hear her pride.

"Seriously. She even went to culinary school."

"What?" Adrian asks. "You did?"

"Oh, yeah," Clay answers. "The summer after freshman year."

Tristan scoops a grainy cracker into a melting wheel of brie. "After she came back, Gin would cook us these dope dinners every Wednesday. Fancy French food, you know? The good stuff."

Adrian can imagine it: the four of them clustered around a scuffed-up coffee table bought from Harvard's welcome-back yard sale, far too dirty to be holding the gorgeous feast sitting atop it. He imagines sweatpants, plastic cups filled with cheap wine, Ginny serving generous portions with a spatula she stole from the dining hall. The way she could take a drab, standard-issue dorm room and fill it with warmth, with butter and sugar, the smell of home.

The boys revolve around her, Adrian thinks. *Ginny is the sun.*

"She said it was the best way to hone her training," Finch adds, "but I'm pretty sure she just likes to show off."

Ginny turns her head over her shoulder, grins, and sticks out her tongue. Finch produces that same impish smile that always needled Adrian when they lived together. When Ginny turns back to the stove, the smile drops from Finch's face, but he doesn't look away. Just watches her work. And as he does, his eyes shift. Soften. Turn almost wistful.

Before Adrian can think too hard about the implications of that expression, Ginny turns around and sets the open bottle of red on the table. "Drink up, boys," she says. "I want you suitably lubricated when the food comes out."

So, Gin." Clay drops his fork onto the empty plate and leans back into the sofa. "How do you like living with boys?"

Ginny snorts. "I lived with you assholes all of college."

"You did?" Adrian asks.

"Oh, yeah." Ginny shifts closer to him on the couch. They went through the bottle of wine before dinner had even been served. Now a rainbow assortment of hefeweizens and IPAs scatter across the coffee table, all chosen from Ginny's personal collection. The alcohol did what it always does—quiets the anxiety, loosens the tongue, brightens the mood . . . and makes her want to sit as close to Adrian as possible. "Not freshman year, but we blocked together and lived in a quad in Lowell for the other three years."

"No kidding. You didn't like any of the girls you met?"

Ginny sips her beer. "Girls have never really been my thing."

"No?"

"Nah. I grew up with three brothers, remember? I spent most of my time playing video games or smearing mud on my face." She shrugs. "I guess it just stuck."

"Yeah." Finch leans forward, grinning. "Gin is just *such* a guy's girl."

Ginny throws a wet noodle at his face.

He dodges, laughing. "What? You are. You know how to hang with the boys." He props his chin on both hands and flutters his eyelashes. "Tell us, oh wise one—what's it like to be a true guy's girl?"

"Oh, that's easy." Ginny straightens, laying both hands on her knees. "If you want to be a guy's girl, all you have to do is become an excellent liar. As a first step, I recommend standing in front of the mirror and reciting these words." She clears her throat: "None of them want to fuck me."

Clay bursts into laughter.

"Repeat this lie until you believe it at least forty percent of the time," Ginny continues. "None of them want to fuck me, none of them want to fuck me, none of them—"

"Stop." Clay waves a hand. "I can't hear about men wanting to fuck you without needing to beat them up." He pauses, then winks at Adrian. "Present company excluded, of course."

Ginny hits Clay with a wooden spoon.

"Hey," Tristan says. "Save some of the Adrian-and-Ginny innuendo for me."

Ginny hits Tristan even harder.

She doesn't look at Adrian. She's too scared of what his face will show. "To change the subject as fast as humanly possible," she says. "Now that we're a year out of college, how does everyone feel about postgraduate life?"

"What in particular?" Finch asks.

"I just feel like . . . I don't know. When I moved to Minnesota, I was constantly plagued by the feeling that I wasn't doing something I was supposed to."

"You mean like . . . homework?" Clay asks. "Come on, Gin. Tell me you don't miss homework."

"No, not that. Well, maybe. I don't know. All I know is . . . for my whole life, my path was prescribed: grade school, high school, college. Then what? We're all thrust out into the world, free to do essentially whatever we want, so long as we can pay our bills."

Tristan tsks. "Not *whatever* we want."

Ginny rolls her eyes. "Well, for everyone who isn't Tristan and didn't come out of the womb modeling leveraged buyouts—"

"I love it when you talk dirty to me," says Tristan.

"You can do essentially anything. You can get a corporate job, or you can go to med school, or you can work for the government, or you can live in a fucking tent on the beach and get all your meals by spearfishing. You can do *anything*. And don't you think . . . don't you think that's chaotic? Doesn't it feel like too much? In Minnesota, I would come home from work and sit on my couch and just think—*What the hell now?*" She sighs. "That's why I started writing. Just to fill the hours."

"I know what you mean, Gin," says Finch. She meets his eyes over the table. "That's how I feel about music sometimes. Like, if I'm not studying or in lecture, I need to be doing something at least semiproductive. I can't just be sitting on my ass."

"*Yes.*" Ginny smacks the table. "That's exactly it. I cannot allow myself downtime."

"Well, I have no idea what that's like," says Clay. "All I ever want is downtime."

"I would kill for a Saturday off," says Tristan.

"No, you wouldn't," says Clay. "You'd kill for more hours to wipe your MD's ass."

But Ginny doesn't listen to their back-and-forth. She's too busy staring at Finch.

She loves this side of him. The one that listens. The one that gets it. Freshman year, she would lie with her head in Finch's lap for hours as they peeled apart their childhoods, their sadness and insecurities, trying to make sense of why they were the way they were. They never ran out of things to talk about.

Her eyes flit to the side, to Adrian, then back to Finch.

No. Stop. This train of thought cannot go anywhere good.

"I just . . ." She pulls herself out of her own thoughts. "Maybe it's because my family was so close growing up, and then, in college, you don't think twice about where you're 'supposed' to be;

but in Minnesota it felt like . . . I don't know. Like I didn't have a home anymore." She shakes her head. "Does that even make any sense?"

"Yes," Adrian says, his first words in several minutes. "Yes, it does."

Ginny looks over in surprise. Adrian has been fairly quiet over the course of the dinner. Several times, she caught herself worrying that he wasn't having fun. They hold each other's gaze for a long moment, and something passes behind his eyes that she can't read.

"Well, Ginny—that won't be an issue anymore." Tristan gestures around the apartment, ignorant of their staring contest. "You're in the big city now. No time to think, let alone have an existential crisis."

"Thank God," Ginny says, pulling her eyes away. "I would pay literally every cent in my bank account if it meant I didn't have to think anymore."

Tristan tuts. "There are far more profitable investments if you're looking for a place to put your money."

"Shut up, Tristan," say Ginny and Clay together.

"Why do you say that?" Adrian asks. "That you wish you didn't have to think anymore."

"I'm . . ." Ginny taps her glass and searches for the right words. "Fairly anxious."

Adrian's eyebrows rise. "You are?"

Ginny is downplaying. Her anxiety is all-consuming, an imaginary checklist her brain goes through every day, hundreds of times a day. If she's satisfied every item on the checklist, her anxiety will temporarily quiet, let her focus on other things. If she hasn't, then she'll spend the next three hours mentally reviewing every piece of food she's put into her body that she shouldn't have.

She can't remember one thought she's ever had that wasn't *over*-thought. For nine-tenths of the day, for no reason whatsoever, she feels like she's going to die.

One of the trickiest parts about anxiety-based fear is that so often the thing you fear does not actually exist. Like rejection. Or loneliness. For that reason, you cannot cure Anxiety simply by going into the world and actively seeking whatever it is that is stressing you out, though if you can—by all means, do it.

"I've always been that way," Ginny says. "I operate at a baseline anxious frequency of about twelve times the natural human standard of stress. It has, as a rule of thumb, ruined nearly every aspect of my life."

All the boys laugh except Adrian. He rubs his thumb over the rim of his beer. "I would never have guessed."

Ginny shrugs. "I don't exactly advertise it."

"No. You don't."

He's looking at her funny. She blushes, looking away, and wonders if she overshared.

There was very little that the Murphys kept secret. They were a wide-open Midwestern family, with too much food at dinnertime and too little discretion about their bowel movements. "Was it a five-wiper or a six-wiper?" Willie would ask Crash when he returned to the table after a twenty-minute trip to the shitter.

"Seven." Crash would drop into his chair and unfold his napkin.

The kids all oohed, clapping. Heather sighed, shaking her head.

"Boys," their mother said. "No bodily functions at the table."

No one except Heather ever bothered to say Ginny wasn't a boy.

Ginny has a suspicion that Adrian's family wasn't like that. In fact, if she had to put money on it, she would guess there was zero talk of bodily functions at their dinner table.

"That's our Gin." Tristan reaches out and wraps an arm around her head, blocking her face. "Anxious little butterfly."

"Eat a dick and die," she says into his elbow.

"I would tell you to do the same," says Tristan, not releasing her from the headlock, "but, with Adrian here, I don't think I have to."

The next Friday, like clockwork, Ginny's text arrives.

GINNY: Hey. Day drinking with the boys tomorrow. Want to come?

He doesn't need to ask to which boys she is referring.

ADRIAN: Yes

On 3rd Street in Williamsburg, between a warehouse and a coffee shop, there's a bar called the Freehold. It's not a fancy bar, but it isn't a dive, either. It's bi-level, half inside, half patio. There are orange painted murals and floors sticky with spilled beer. There are watery $16 margaritas and girls in platform sandals and boys doing lines of cocaine in the bathroom at 2 p.m. There are, above all, hordes of interns, postgrads, and the occasional creepy forty-year-old.

This type of venue is not Adrian's favorite, but it isn't his least favorite, either. It falls in the middle, somewhere between waiting for the subway and watching men put on two-act plays in Washington Square Park. It might ultimately leave him filled with a deep sense of despair, but at least the people watching is good.

"Adrian!"

He finds his friends over by the bar. Clay is paying for their first round of drinks. Finch is scanning the room as if he thinks he's going to see someone he knows. Tristan is looking at the sticky floors with his lip curled in distaste.

And Ginny. She's waving Adrian over, smile wide, margarita spilling over the side of a plastic glass as she bobs up and down.

"What's up, man?" says Clay, putting down the pen.

"Can you believe we're at the Freehold, of all places?" Tristan sighs. "You know, the William Vale hotel has this gorgeous rooftop bar—"

"Shut up, Tristan," says everyone in the circle.

Ginny bounces over to Adrian's side and nudges him with her hips. "Hi."

"Hi."

"Want to dance?"

He nods to the bar. "I need one or two of those before I'll make it out onto that floor."

"Oh. Got it." Ginny frowns for a second, then turns to Clay. "Dance?"

"Duh." Clay takes her hand and pulls her out into the crowd.

"Wait for me!" calls Tristan, apparently forgetting that he would rather be anywhere but here.

"So," says Finch as Adrian watches the group disappear. "You and Gin, huh?"

Adrian picks up his margarita and takes a sip. "Sort of."

"Sort of?" Finch snorts. "You two are together all the time."

Adrian shrugs. "She's cool."

"Yeah. She is cool." Adrian thinks this will be the end of the conversation, but after a pause, Finch adds, "Just . . . be careful, okay?"

Adrian looks over. "What do you mean?"

"I just mean . . . Ginny has this really big heart, you know? Too big. She might not be thinking about this relationship as casually as you are."

"Oh." Adrian scans the crowd for Ginny, Clay, and Tristan. They're right at the center, swing dancing to Lil Nas X. "You think?"

"I don't know. I just know that after everything that went down freshman year—"

"Freshman year?"

"She didn't tell you?" Finch brushes away a droplet from his plastic glass. "We were together. Sort of."

"No. She definitely didn't tell me that."

Finch waves a hand. "Whatever, man. She probably just didn't want to weird you out."

"What happened?"

He runs a hand through his hair. "I liked her. A lot. But ultimately I couldn't give her what she wanted." He sighs. "It almost fucked up our whole friendship. Thankfully, we got past things, but . . . I don't know. I should've been honest with her from the start."

"I see." Adrian's heart is starting to beat unnaturally fast in his chest.

Finch claps a hand on his shoulder. "Don't let my shit get to you, though, man. You seem to know what you're doing."

Adrian watches as Clay and Tristan dip Ginny's head back, her mouth spilling open with laughter.

No, he thinks. *No, I don't.*

Not at all.

Back at his apartment, Ginny and Adrian lie tangled together in the queen-size bed, limbs draped loosely in soft cotton sheets.

It's only five, but Adrian is exhausted. Day drinking always has that effect on him—an early boost, then a steady drain as both alcohol and energy seep out of his system. Under his arm, he thinks Ginny has already drifted off. He strokes her hair absently. A warm feeling seeps through him, the same tendrils he felt growing within him the first time they had sex. He shuts his eyes.

Just before unconsciousness pulls him under, Ginny whispers, "I like you, Adrian."

His eyes flutter open. By now, twilight spills into the studio. Rays of dying sunlight illuminate the kitchenette, the sofa, the unopened whiskey bottles, the barren fridge. Adrian spends almost no time in this apartment. A place built for one, usually empty, now holding two.

Finch's words echo in his head: *I should've been honest with her from the start.*

He likes Ginny. He *really* likes her, actually. She's funny. She's unpredictable. She fills him with a low-level buzz, even when he's sober. But he doesn't yet know whether they have a real future together. He needs time to figure that out.

Unfortunately, time is the first thing he lost when he took a job in banking.

Plus, he's tired. So, so tired.

"Ginny." He rolls over to look right into her eyes. He will say this only once, and he hopes she hears. "I like you. I do." A pause. "But my life is still hell right now. To be honest, I can't even believe my eyes are still open. I can't . . . I don't have the mental capacity for a real relationship."

It's like watching a flower fold back in on itself.

"But that doesn't mean—" Adrian searches for the words. He has only ever ended relationships—never given them a chance to become something more. He doesn't know how. "I do like you. I don't want to stop seeing you."

For a moment, Ginny becomes completely vacant. Her jaw slackens. Her eyes drift away. Her chest ceases to move, going as still as a doll left to gather dust in the attic.

Adrian panics. He thinks she might cry. She's naked in his bed, and she might cry. He starts to reach for her hand, then stops.

Looks around. He didn't want this; he just wanted her to understand. To know what to expect. She can't go into this relationship thinking he'll give her more than he can.

Before he can panic any further, Ginny blinks twice and snaps back to life. "Sorry about that. I just . . ." She clears her throat. Smiles. Nudges his arm. "Got any more of that cherry wine?"

After just one glass of wine, which they drink naked under the sheets, Ginny says that she should leave.

"Really?" Adrian sits up, the sheets slipping down to pool around his waist.

"Yes. I have to . . . I'm working on a new section for next week's newsletter," she lies.

He blinks. "Okay."

Ginny pulls on her skirt, underwear, crop top, and white platform shoes. She works quickly, knowing that the longer she stays, the greater the risk she starts crying. She kept it together as long as she could, but she can feel herself starting to come apart. At first, Adrian just watches, confused. Then he gets out of bed and starts to dress, too. He only makes it into his underwear by the time Ginny slings her purse over her shoulder and is ready to go.

"Thanks for the wine," she says.

Adrian stands with one foot in the kitchenette, his long, bare torso swaying. He doesn't seem to know what to do with his hands. "You're welcome."

Ginny walks forward and wraps him in a hug, quick and tight. "See you."

"Okay. See you."

Then she's out the door and running down the stairs.

Street after street, awning after awning, she runs. She barely takes in the people she passes, all of whom are headed to dinners and drinks, dressed in outfits they tried on six times, just beginning an evening full of promise. Ginny forgot to zip up the back of her skirt; it's now slipping down her hips.

Four years, no romantic feelings toward any man whatsoever, and now she feels like life is leaking out of her body. She cannot believe how much it hurts.

She should have known this was coming. Between his cancellations, how long it takes him to text her back, how *she* has been the one putting all the effort into trying to date him—of course he isn't interested in having a real relationship. All that nonsense about not having the time? What a convenient excuse. He isn't the first man to use "I don't want a girlfriend right now" in place of "I don't want *you* as my girlfriend."

A part of her isn't even surprised. This entire experience only confirms what Ginny already knew: that she is broken. That something about her—something fundamental, sewn right into the fibers of her muscles, the marrow of her bones—prevents Ginny from deserving love.

Love.

That cannot possibly be what she feels toward Adrian, can it? Two months. It's only been two months. If love is a fire, he was barely a candle.

But a candle is enough to start an inferno.

Ginny rounds the last corner onto Sullivan Street. The familiar signs flip past: Brigadeiro, Pepe Rosso's, the Dutch. She didn't know it was possible to feel this empty.

All her life, she sought emptiness by withholding food; she didn't know that all she needed to do was give her heart to someone who didn't want it.

Back in Chelsea, Adrian sits on the couch and turns on a movie. Tries to focus. Tries to take his mind off Ginny.

It doesn't work. He can't stop thinking about her. The flash of hurt. The sudden vacancy in her eyes. How fast she dressed to leave, as if she could no longer stand to be around him. He'd only meant to clarify where he stood *right now*, not end things for good.

A terrifying ache blossoms in his breast. He clutches a hand to his shirt, bundling the fabric in his fist. *What is this? What the hell is happening to me? Am I . . . ?*

No. He won't even think the word. He can't. He knows what happens when love enters the equation. He knows how fleeting it is. How slippery. Nothing is promised. Nothing assured.

He knows that better than anyone. His stepdad taught him years ago.

He just lost sight of the truth.

Adrian thought she married for love. That's how it works, right? You fall in love, you get married. That was the equation that existed in nine-year-old Adrian's brain. For that reason, when his mother announced that they were moving to America so she could marry a man named Scott, he assumed she was in love.

He was happy for her. All his life, Adrian's *anya* had done nothing but work. Work and attend church. Even at the age of nine, he understood her behavior to be a way of coping with his father's untimely death. His *nagyanya* often said as much. And while he loathed the idea of leaving behind his beloved Hungary for a strange new country, he hoped that finding true love would finally make his *anya* happy. Perhaps a mother in love would stay home every now and then. Perhaps she would smile.

Back then, he believed in true love. How could he not? He spent so much time with his *nagyanya* and *nagyapa*, who had been married for fifty years and still held hands everywhere they went. Not to mention that they spoke near constantly of their late son's love for Adrian's mother. How pure it was. How perfect. How devastating when it was ripped apart. "Their love would have lasted a lifetime," *Nagyanya* used to say.

The wedding in Indiana wasn't what Adrian expected. He thought there would be flowers, a tender exchange of vows, a crowd of joyous guests throwing rice. Not an empty cathedral. Not a grey Monday afternoon. Not a priest whose voice echoed off the hollow church walls, reciting the ceremony as if reading from a textbook. There were no flowers. No rice. Only a quick service and an awkward lunch afterward at a place with sticky wooden booths and plastic-coated menus.

Still, Adrian held out hope. His mother might not hold Scott's hand or stare lovingly into his eyes, but, when she finally opened the door to his red-brick house on Meridian Street—when she set down her suitcase and looked around the entryway at the carpeted staircase and hanging still-life of three pears—Adrian thought he almost saw her smile.

A week passed. Two. Adrian settled into his bedroom and re-read his favorite books. Beatrix left the house every morning and didn't return until dinner. She was already making friends. Adjusting. Sometimes, he saw his sister through his bedroom window, pedaling down Meridian Street in a sea of children on bicycles. Her silver helmet and brown ponytail fit right in with the rest of them.

Too afraid to join, Adrian spent his days at home with Scott and his mother. Their marriage was a strange one. His stepfather spoke no Hungarian, and his mother knew only basic English. Their conversations consisted mostly of nods, hand gestures, and silence. On occasion, his mother would smile at something Scott said. Once, Adrian even saw her squeeze his hand.

At the end of August, school began.

Adrian and Beatrix slid out of the back seat of Scott's car—driven by their mother, as their stepfather was too busy "working" at a vaguely described job that Adrian didn't fully understand—with brand-new JanSports on their backs. Beatrix took his hand and led him across the street, toward the stone wall and wrought-iron fence that marked the entrance to Park Tudor. As they approached their new school's front entrance, Beatrix with one hand wrapped around his, the other waving to all her new friends, Adrian thought that this place looked less like a schoolhouse and more like a place where a king would send his children.

Class was a disaster. His teacher made Adrian introduce himself, which consisted of stuttering out a few sentences that he had memorized in the bathroom earlier that morning—*My name is Adrian Silvas, I am nine years old, I am from Budapest*—before quickly taking his seat at the very center of the room. His classmates stared openly. Throughout the morning, he tried to take notes, but all he could do was stare at the teacher's lips as she fired off sentence after sentence in rapid English. His pen hovered uselessly over a blank notebook.

At lunch, Adrian anticipated sequestering himself in a remote corner of the cafeteria. He would pull out one of his Hungarian novels and pretend to study. Instead, the moment he walked through the cafeteria doors, he was swarmed.

Girls. Dozens of them, all Indiana born and bred. They chattered at him. Grazed his shoulders and arms. When he picked up his tray and went to the lunch line, they followed. When he carried that tray to an empty table, they followed. They filled the benches. Girls and girls and girls, all staring at him with wide, curious eyes. They whispered to each other. He caught a few English words, like *so cute* and *that accent*. They fought for his attention. Batted their eyelashes. Played with their hair. He hadn't a clue what to do with it all. Mostly, he smiled and nodded. When the bell rang, a pretty girl with short blond hair took his hand, and he thought he might have unwittingly acquired his first girlfriend.

He went to recess in good spirits. If the girls had accepted him so quickly, surely the boys would, too.

No such luck.

Out on the playground, the boys picked up a game of "soccer," the American version of football. Adrian liked football. Back in Hungary, he often played one-on-one with his best friend, Jozsef. He strolled out onto the field, a smile on his face, ready to join.

When he asked in Hungarian if he could play, the boys didn't answer. They kept their backs to him while dividing into teams. Shoved him out of the way when he tried to join, then ran off to their respective sides of the field. The only boy who acknowledged him was a gangly fourth-grader with green braces. He clenched his metal-covered teeth, hissed a word that sounded like a punch to the gut, and spat on Adrian's shoes.

At home, Adrian struggled through his homework. Eventually, he gave up and switched on the television. He pressed the channel changer until a cartoon appeared. Then he settled in to watch, willing the program to magically project English into his brain.

A month passed. Two. At school, the girls continued to fawn over him like an object in a museum. The blond girl stopped holding his hand but was quickly replaced by a redhead with sparkling amber eyes. The boys continued to ignore him.

Slowly, painfully, he learned English. His notebook went from completely blank to half-filled with half-understood sentences. Some phrases he picked up more quickly than others, in particular the ones he heard over and over, like, *Don't worry, he can't understand you,* or, *Give that one to the foreigner.*

Every day after school, he completed his homework, watched a few hours of television, and ate dinner with Beatrix and his *anya.* Scott was gone all the time. At work. Adrian knew he must do something important, given the size of their house, but he could never figure out what. When he asked his *anya,* she never gave him a straight answer.

When Scott was home, however, Adrian carefully observed his interactions with his mother. Watched them circle each other, sleep in separate rooms, occasionally offer a quiet smile. He watched them, and he wondered: *Is this love?*

It had to be. That's what he told himself. Why else would she uproot his and Beatrix's lives in Budapest, where he'd been happy? Why else would she subject him to classes in a language he didn't understand, to children who laughed at his broken English and threw notes at him with words scrawled on them in shaky pencil? Words that he now understood, like *slow* and *retard* and *Nazi.* Surely she wouldn't put him through this for anything less than true love. Surely it would all be worth it.

That was Adrian's belief. And because of that belief, when he arrived home from school two years later—after he had finally adjusted to life in the United States, after the bullies had forgotten about him and he'd started making friends—to find his mother out on the curb, her stuff in boxes, her eyes puffy and bloodshot, he didn't understand. He didn't understand as she collapsed on Beatrix's shoulder. Didn't understand as she said, "I made the last payment today." Didn't understand as she said, "He's done with us, now. He's kicking us out."

* * *

His mother didn't get out of bed for a month.

After Scott forced them out of the house on Meridian Street, they moved into a tiny two-bedroom duplex in Westside, the only neighborhood they could afford. Adrian pleaded with his mother to take them back to Budapest. "Why stay?" he asked in Hungarian while unpacking boxes. His mother was in bed already. No sheets, no covers. Just a barren mattress. "If your marriage is over, what's keeping us here?"

"Nothing," she said in Hungarian.

"So?"

"That was it, Adrian. My savings. All of them. I used them all to pay him for our marriage." Her voice cracked. "I can't afford to take us back." Then she rolled over onto her side and shut her eyes.

By then, Adrian was eleven. Two years wiser. He took it upon himself to tend to his mother. Beatrix—now fifteen, leaving the house too late and returning home even later, smelling faintly of sour alcohol—certainly wasn't going to help.

Westside wasn't a safe neighborhood. Beat-up houses. Crumbling bricks. Litter in front yards. Shotguns inside closets. "Everyone has one," said a boy he met on their block. "You can buy them at Walmart. My older brother bought ours."

At night, he sat with his mother and read to her in Hungarian. Adult books, even though he was too young for them. His *anya* drifted in and out of sleep throughout the day. When lucid, she rarely reacted to the stories, but he hoped she was listening all the same.

This is what happens when you put your trust in another person, he thought as he watched her twitch in her sleep, fists balled around the sheets as if caught in a nightmare. *This is what love gets you.* He'd thought he would be able to do it, to push past the guilt he felt for his father's death by seeing his mother find new love, to finally flourish in the way he always hoped she would.

Instead, now his guilt was even worse.

He tucked a strand of hair behind his mother's ear. She let out a low whimper.

I don't want it, he decided. *I don't want it, and I never will.*

Ginny shuffles down the hallway and into the living room. She isn't expecting anyone to be awake, so it's a surprise when she finds Finch seated on the couch, feet up on the coffee table.

"Hey, how was the d—?" When he spies her puffy cheeks, Finch pulls up short. "Gin? Shit—are you okay?"

"Fine." The last person she wants to talk to right now is Finch. Or maybe he's the *first* person she wants to talk to, which is even worse. She turns away and heads for her bedroom, but Finch is quickly in front of her, blocking the entrance.

"What happened?" he asks.

"Nothing."

"You're lying."

She tries to sidestep him. He moves, too.

"Was it Adrian?" His voice is angry now. "What did he do to you?"

Her head snaps to look up at him. "What do you care?" she spits out. "You never gave a shit about me in college. When did I suddenly become your problem?"

He steps back. "What are you talking about? We're best fr—"

"Don't you dare say that." Maybe it's all the drinking. She can feel the wine and the margaritas swirling around the inside of her head, pushing out words that she wouldn't say sober. "Don't you dare call us best friends. Yes, we're part of the same friend group. Yes, we *act* like you didn't toss me aside for your ex-girlfriend—*twice*." She swallows. "But we both know that's not true."

And there it is. That night senior year. The one that neither of them has acknowledged, when she drank too much at a Sig Chi party and ended up in Finch's room, on Finch's bed, sobbing, gasping for air, confessing to three years of repressed emotion. The night he told her that he didn't return her feelings. That she was alone. As always.

"Ginny—" he starts.

"No." She moves away. "Don't, Alex. I have enough to deal with right now."

His mouth opens. One hand comes up and around his head to rub at his eyebrow—his quintessential nervous tic. "Just—" His hand comes back down. "I know you do. And I worry about you."

"Oh, do you? Do I keep you up at night?"

"More than you know."

She tries to step around him again, but Finch reaches out and takes her elbow. Her breath catches. She knows she should push him away, but— "What?"

"Just—" He glances about the living room. "Here. Sit down." He heads for the bar cart and pours two glasses of whiskey. Hands one to her. "Tell me what happened."

She thinks of telling him no. Of telling him to fuck off and go find Hannah. That's what he's always done, right? But that would get her nothing. Instead, she sinks onto the couch and takes a sip of whiskey. It's a sultry burn, different from vodka or tequila. "He doesn't want to be with me."

Finch's eyes bunch together with pity. This is how he is— theatrical in his displays of emotion. "I'm sorry, Gin."

"It hurts."

"I know it does."

"I just—" She tilts back the tumbler, downing all the whiskey in one go. "I'm sick of it, you know? Sick of being the one that no one ever chooses."

Finch looks down. Silence roils between them, but Ginny doesn't care. Let him feel bad. Let him know how badly he hurt her.

"I lied to you," he says softly. "That night senior year. I lied."

"You—" She pauses. "What?"

"When you said you liked me. I lied. I . . . I did feel the same way." He sets his glass on his knee. "God, of course I felt the same way, Gin."

"Then why—?"

"That morning, Hannah and I had just talked on the phone and agreed to give it another go." He swallows. "I couldn't—I couldn't tell you without betraying her."

She shakes her head. "That doesn't— I don't—"

"I know." His eyes—they're so familiar, like little circles of driftwood. "I regretted it the minute you walked out the door."

Her chest is heaving now, air spilling in and out of her lungs like a broken dam. "How long?" she demands. "How long have you felt this way?"

A sad smile curls up the sides of his mouth. "Forever." When he releases her elbow, warm summer air drifts in to take his place. "It's weird." He looks away, foot tapping the rug. "Before freshman year, I thought I had it all figured out. I thought Hannah and I would get married, and I'd work, and play music on the side, and we'd have a bunch of kids, and live happily ever after." He looks back at Ginny. "Then you walked into my life."

She takes the bottle of whiskey and pours another glass.

"You ruined all my plans," he says.

"I'm sorry."

"I'm not." He smiles. Then he stands up and heads for his bedroom. He opens the door, then pauses. "I'm happy with Hannah. I am. But sometimes . . ." He looks over his shoulder, eyes meeting hers for just a second too long. "Sometimes I wonder if I made the right choice."

After Finch shuts his door, Ginny sits alone for a full five minutes. She stares at Finch's door, hearing his final sentence on one continuous loop.

Sometimes I wonder if I made the right choice.

Was that a hint? Is he going to break up with Hannah? She's met his girlfriend once or twice when she came to visit Harvard. She was nice. Ginny doesn't want to wish ill upon her, but . . .

Hope, small but intoxicating, flutters at the center of her chest.

Ginny knows she shouldn't do this. Shouldn't place her heart into the hands of someone who isn't hers to want. But when she considers the alternative—when she pictures that sea of darkness into which she felt herself sinking during her walk home—every muscle in her body seizes up at once. She cannot stomach the sadness that seeps inside when she thinks about Adrian. She cannot let herself drown.

So, why not allow herself a new crush? Why not grab hold of the life ring floating so clearly before her, especially when the man in question is already taken, when their relationship cannot actually go anywhere?

She inhales. Exhales.

That's it, then. She won't chase Adrian anymore. She'll stop texting him, stop responding to his Instagram stories. If he genuinely likes her, he'll reach out. And if he doesn't?

She'll have her answer.

Back in her bedroom, Ginny takes out her notebook for the first time in weeks. She stares at its empty insides. Page after page, blank after blank. Nothing since the day she arrived in New York.

She does not have a story to write. She does not have a character or a plot or a setting. She has only one sentence. Twelve words bouncing around and around the inside of her head. She scribbles them out. As soon as they have been excised from her body, she flips the journal shut again, spent.

We only tell each other the truth when it's already too late.

Two weeks later.

No matter how hard Adrian focuses on work, his mind keeps wandering back to his phone. To Ginny.

It's been like this for days. The constant loop of questions: *Why did she run out so quickly the last time he saw her? Why hasn't she texted him since? Was it truly because of what he said?* And look: it's not that he's suddenly decided he wants a relationship—given his miserable schedule, that's still out of the cards—but he'd become accustomed to her presence, her smile, the heat of her tiny body curled up beside his. Its absence is a shock. Like an old friend who leaves without warning.

His phone buzzes. He lifts it up, checking the email that just landed in his personal inbox. It's from the head of international strategy at Disney, the woman with whom he interviewed the day before.

Hi Adrian,

I really enjoyed talking with you yesterday. I've spoken to the team, and we all agree that you would be a great fit.

I'm pleased to extend to you an official job offer as a global analyst for our Eastern European division, working out of our New York City headquarters. Should you choose to accept . . .

Adrian's heart starts pounding. He fumbles with his pocket, pulling out his phone to text Ginny the good news. *He's free. He's* finally *going to be free.* He scrolls down, looking for her contact.

Then he remembers.

PART III

One Year Later

Adrian should be more nervous. That's what he's thinking as his driver—an ancient man in a 1974 Suburban with torn leather seats—whisks him from Ferenc Liszt International to Tristan's house in Hegyvidék, Budapest's swanky twelfth district.

It's strange to not be driving straight to his grandparents' home in Szentendre. The neighborhood through which they now drive is nothing like the artist district. It's gated driveways and European sports cars. Security guards and private mountain compounds. He can practically smell the wealth drifting from the hillside, even through the Suburban's closed windows.

"You got a house here?" his driver asks in Hungarian.

"*Nem*," Adrian says. "My friend does."

Adrian was surprised when he received the invitation to join his old roommates for a week's vacation in Europe. Since things ended with Ginny, he's barely spent any time with them. It's nothing personal; after starting his new job, Adrian was absorbed into the Disney social culture, his calendar packed with happy hours and conferences and corporate retreats. All at once, he no longer had time for his college friends. He would have thought that his absence would put his old roommates off inviting him on a group trip. Apparently not.

Or maybe they simply felt guilty not inviting their Hungarian friend to Hungary.

For him, the trip couldn't have come at a better time. He just wrapped up his first big project at Disney—a ten-month-long slog outlining strategy for the company's new streaming service overseas. His focus area: Eastern Europe, including Hungary.

Working for Disney sounds sexy. It isn't. Though in front of the curtain, Disney's content is nothing short of magical, the machine behind the scenes is purely a multibillion-dollar conglomerate. And like every other multibillion-dollar conglomerate, it runs on bureaucracy, bonuses, and bullshit.

Adrian loves every second of it.

He might not be the one creating the content, but he's the one who ensures it gets into the hands of kids like himself. The ones who watch cartoons from the floor of their grandparents' homes in Hungary, Bulgaria, or Romania.

The streaming service was announced globally two weeks ago, marking the close of almost a year's work and the perfect opportunity for Adrian to head out on vacation. He took off three weeks: one to spend with his friends, two with his grandparents.

The house toward which they are now driving had been rented out by Tristan's father for a company retreat that month. According to Tristan, they hosted them every year in different locales: Costa Rica, London, Singapore, Budapest . . . His father is a terrifyingly successful figure: the head of one of New York's largest hedge funds, once cited by the *Wall Street Journal* for his habit of lying down on the floor of conference rooms and pretending to sleep when he wants a meeting to end. It's no secret that Tristan has spent his entire life chasing his father's success. Get him drunk enough and he'll tell you all about it.

But Tristan isn't the one Adrian is nervous to see. Not even close.

Because Ginny is at that house, drinking with the rest of them, waiting for him to arrive.

After the night they slept together and Adrian told her he wasn't looking for a serious relationship, Ginny never texted him again. Though he should have felt like he dodged a bullet—clearly, she wasn't on the same page—after he stopped hearing from her, he felt oddly like he lost something he didn't even know he had.

Now they're going to spend a week together, and he has no idea how she'll act toward him. Will she be friendly? Cold? Will he feel that same strange comfort from before, the warm blanket that wrapped him whenever she was around, or will things be horribly awkward? A few weeks back, he heard that Finch and Ginny were together, but then separately he heard that Finch was still with his high school girlfriend. He doesn't know which story is true.

He has a feeling he's about to find out.

Ginny is addicted to Finch. As she pours two glasses of wine at the outdoor bar, she can't stop glancing over to where he sits on one of the lounge chairs by the pool. Every time she does, he's looking back at her.

Ginny looks away before Clay and Tristan notice. Not that it would surprise them. Everyone knows what's happening between Ginny and Finch, even if no one will admit it.

Behind one of Hegyvidék's many hilltops, the sun is starting to set, casting Budapest in a burnt orange glow. Tristan's house nestles high into the ridge of a mountain. From the pool deck, they have an immaculate view of the valley below. It ebbs and undulates, peppered with pine trees and multicolored rooftops.

Down the stone steps from the outdoor bar is the pool, connected to a three-tiered waterfall with a hot tub at the very top. Across from the pool is the garden, which is shaded by apple and cherry trees. It is, by far, the nicest property on which Ginny has ever stayed.

The Murphy family mostly vacationed in their motor home, a tricked-out 1995 fifth wheel with three sets of bunk beds, into which they packed all five children, plus a dog, and saw every corner of the United States. If they stayed in a hotel or bed and breakfast, it was the three-star kind, where dinner was the Applebee's down the street and midnight snacks came out of a vending machine.

This house—this entire *life* Ginny now leads—was an unforeseen side effect of getting into Harvard. Ginny had been so focused on doing *exactly* the right thing—following *exactly* the right path, getting *exactly* the right grades, doing *exactly* the right after-school sports, all to guarantee her spot at *exactly* the right school—that she never considered how drastically her life would change based solely on the people she met.

She pulls out her phone to type a quick message to her mother, letting her know that they made it safely to the house and that she's still planning to fly back to New York the following Saturday. If Ginny is surprised by the route her life has taken, her mother is nothing but overjoyed; her daughter gets to explore the world in a way she never could.

Tucking her phone into her pocket and pinching the wine-glasses by their stems, Ginny bumps the outdoor fridge shut with her hip and heads from the bar—a granite island flanked by a grill and wood-burning pizza oven—over to the boys. She settles onto the end of Finch's chair, folding her legs beneath her, and passes him the second glass. He winks.

This vacation came at exactly the right moment. After a year of Ginny working her ass off to impress Kam, her boss finally sat her down for *the* conversation. The one she'd been waiting for—*promotion*. A jump from manager to senior manager. Everything is going exactly according to plan.

Except when it isn't.

Ginny knows it's wrong, how close she and Finch have become. Not because men and women cannot be friends; she herself has proven that myth wrong time and time again. No—it's wrong because he and Hannah are still together. And although she and Finch are friends in name, in truth, they are far more.

There's something seductive about their friendship. Maybe it's the way they look at each other—always for a beat too long, always with something lingering just behind the eyes. Or maybe it's the push and pull, the way Ginny will decide one day that this thing between them needs to end, but by the next, be sitting on the end of his bed, laughing harder than she has all week.

Finch is the first person she calls when something goes wrong, the first person she texts when something goes right. That role used to belong to Clay and Tristan, but she's drifted further and further from her two closest friends. It's sad, but that's what happens, right? That's adulthood. Friendships shift. Draw closer or slowly unravel. She and Finch—they have something special.

In the apartment, she always sits next to him on the couch. He learned how to play her favorite country songs on the guitar, and they sing them together, her voice practically gravel next to his. They spend so much time together that they might as well be in a relationship. They are, emotionally speaking.

At night, when she touches herself, she pictures Finch, lying awake just ten feet away. She pictures getting out of bed in nothing but her bra and crossing those ten feet. Crawling into bed with him. Pulling off his boxers. Sliding him into her. She cannot picture anyone else. She does not want anyone else. She knows he pictures her, too.

"Ginny," Clay said one night as they waited for shots at Dream Baby. Ginny had spent the last half hour letting Finch swing her in circles around their table. "He has a girlfriend."

"I know that." She accepted two lime wedges from the bartender. "We're just friends."

"Are you, though?"

"Of course. Have you seen us kiss?"

"No." Clay hunched over the bill from the bartender and added a tip. "But I just—I worry about you, you know?"

"Come on. This is Finch we're talking about. He's one of your best friends."

"He is. But so are you. And the way Finch is with girls—"

Ginny held out Clay's tequila. "You worry too much."

He doesn't, of course. He's spot-on. But she knew that if she tried to explain the energy, the connection that tied her and Finch together, he wouldn't understand. *She* barely understood it herself. All she knew was that when she was around Finch, time didn't exist. Hours could be minutes.

There were hard moments, too. Finch is moody. As quickly as he can smile, laugh, tell stories at a pace nearly too fast to follow, so, too, can he become sarcastic, jaded. Almost cruel. Ginny hated when that side of Finch came out. She missed her best friend.

"Adrian is almost here," says Clay, setting his phone back on the stone table beside his lounge chair.

"Finally," says Tristan. "I can't believe he stayed an extra day just to work. He's not even in finance anymore."

Adrian.

Adrian is coming. Ginny feels a pinch of nerves at the base of her stomach. It's subtle—not the anxious clamp from months before. But then, nothing has been the same since Finch.

Her relationship with Finch is nothing like her relationship was with Adrian. There are no long silences. No sitting around, wondering what the other person is thinking. They tell each other everything. They tell each other too much. Adrian is like a faraway dream. She can't believe she ever cried over him. How could she have thought that what they had was passion? How could she have thought it was love?

Still. That doesn't mean she isn't nervous to see him.

"Should I get the grill going?" Clay asks. At twenty-four, Ginny and her friends love playing at adulthood—drinking wine, cooking their own dinners. Living in a house that belongs to one of their fathers.

"Sure." Tristan stands, placing his red wine down on the table. "Let's pick out the meats."

Clay and Tristan head for the French doors that lead into the main house. After they're out of view, Finch twists to face Ginny. "So," he says. "Adrian."

She brushes an invisible hair from her arm. "What about him?"

"Think you guys will hook up this week?"

She lowers her hand and looks out at the sunset. "Maybe."

"I see."

This is it. The game they play—each pretending to care less what the other person does. *How well can I feign nonchalance? How far can I push you away before we come crashing back together?*

It's toxic. It's destructive.

Ginny is completely addicted.

Pebbles crunch under the Suburban's tires as they pull into the driveway. Adrian peers out the windshield. Towering well above them is what he can only describe as a villa that should be occupied by the Godfather: stucco walls; bay windows; a grand entryway with double doors; and a snug, east-facing breakfast patio.

Adrian cannot believe this house is where he's going to spend the next week.

The driver puts the Suburban in park. Adrian pushes open the side door, letting twilight filter inside. As he steps out into the pebbled driveway, a clatter sounds from over by the house, and he looks over to find the double doors swinging wide.

"Dude!" Clay jogs out first, red hair flopping about. "You made it."

Adrian grins as Clay pulls him into a hug. "Just barely."

"Walt working you hard?"

"You know he's been dead for, like, fifty years, right?"

Clay heads for the trunk to grab Adrian's suitcase. "Doesn't mean he isn't sending directives down to the C-suite from the great beyond."

"Nah." Adrian shoulders his backpack. "It'll be Gates who figures that one out."

"The latest release: Microsoft Afterlife."

"Outlook Beyond."

"Are you two idiots starting a business without me?" calls a voice from the doorway. They look over to find Tristan leaning against the marble doorframe, glass of red wine in hand.

"We would never dream of it," says Adrian.

"Good." Tristan pushes off the frame and walks over to his friends. "Because you would be hopelessly lost without my financial wisdom."

"I'm sure we would be."

They hug, then Tristan leads them inside and gestures to the different parts of the house with his wineglass. When he remarks offhandedly about how much the Mr. Brainwash on the second-floor landing is worth, Clay threatens to sew Tristan's mouth shut with dental floss. Adrian watches it all unfold with fondness, reminded of countless nights around the coffee table in Sullivan Street.

"And this is the kitchen."

Tristan's voice draws Adrian's attention to the cavernous room into which they've just stepped. Marble floors and high wood ceilings frame a massive grey-and-white-peppered island, around which are dozens of cabinets, double frosted glass refrigerators, and a Bertazzoni stovetop so shiny it looks fresh off the boat from a professional kitchen in Emilia-Romagna. Knowing Tristan, it probably is.

"Well," says Adrian, taking in the adjoining living room, with a couch so big it could comfortably seat twenty-five. "It's not terrible."

As he does one last spin, his gaze catches on the pair of figures seated close together on a lounge chair beside the pool. Ginny and Finch.

Adrian's left fist twitches.

Clay follows Adrian's gaze outside. "Ah," he says. "Yes. The happy couple."

"So, they're . . ."

"No. Finch is still with Hannah." Clay shakes his head. "But none of us know why. He's clearly smitten with Ginny."

"Clearly," says Adrian.

Clay glances sideways at Adrian, as if he wants to say more, but doesn't. And Adrian is grateful, because Ginny chooses that moment to look over from her place beside Finch and spot Adrian through the French doors. Her eyes pop wide. She untangles herself from Finch's legs, hops to her feet, and runs over to the French doors. When she pushes them open, her shoulder-length hair is floppy and wild, her face all rosy cheeks and sparkling teeth. Adrian thinks that no one has ever looked so genuinely happy to see him.

But then—

But then his eyes lower, and he sees her body, and ice-cold water fills his insides.

Ginny has lost weight since the last time he saw her. Her cheeks are freshly dug mounds, their bones the pointed spades left behind. Her collarbone presses so tautly to her skin that it looks like it's trying to escape her body entirely.

He doesn't know where the weight went; she had none to lose in the first place.

It happens in an instant. The minute her eyes land on Adrian, every belief, every certainty she held just moments before—*I'm over him, I feel nothing, how could I ever have thought I felt anything in the first place*—washes away.

In its place . . .

Free fall.

Adrian looks good. Forget that—he looks fantastic, like an entirely different human being. His chest and arms have filled out. His hair is longer, mussed from the airplane. Gone are the bags under his eyes, the sickly pallor tainting his otherwise perfect skin, leaving his face pearly and soft, like freshly poured sand. It must be the new job. The transition away from banking. It's as if a long-flickering light bulb within him was finally replaced.

It takes all her effort not to stumble or pull up short when she sees him. She plows forward, a rickety smile pasted to her face as if she isn't suddenly overwhelmed with panic.

He's here. Adrian is here.

And he's far more beautiful than she remembered.

"Adrian!" she exclaims, voice too high. "Hi!" She throws her arms up and over his shoulders, even though he's at least a foot taller than she is. When she pulls back, she holds on to his arms, scared she might teeter over from light-headedness. "I can't believe it's been almost a year since I last saw you."

"I know," he says.

She releases his arms. "Crazy that it takes leaving the country to hang out with someone who lives right down the street. But that's Manhattan, I guess."

He isn't quite smiling. His eyes keep flicking down to her body as if looking for something. She knew she ate too much on the flight over, but she threw most of it up in the tiny airplane bathroom. Did it not work? Did she gain even more weight than she thought?

"I guess," he says.

She fights the urge to fold her arms over her chest. "Anyway," she says, bustling over to the kitchen island, where a cutting board is set out with avocado, onion, garlic, and cilantro. "I was about to make some appetizers. You hungry?"

She can still feel his eyes on her. "Starving."

Something about the way he says that word makes her blood race through her body. His gaze is a heat lamp, warming every part of her bare flesh. *Relax*, she tells herself. *You will be fine. Continue as if nothing is amiss, as if you still feel nothing for him and this strange sensation will fade of its own accord.*

"Go wash up." She slides a knife into the soft flesh of an avocado. "By the time you're done, this will be ready, and we can get the night started."

Avocado is green. Cilantro is even greener. Onions are clear white, almost see-through, almost nothing at all. Ginny would love to be see-through. Ginny would love to be nothing at all.

Through the open doors, burgers sizzle and the boys laugh. Finch's laugh—short and clunky, like tap shoes—shakes her insides.

Or maybe it's just the shock of seeing Adrian.

With the blade of her knife Ginny scoops up the pile of minced onions and dumps them into the bowl. *Focus. Don't think about Adrian. You're in enough of a romantic mess as it is. Focus on plucking the cilantro, on bunching the leaves into a bundle thick enough to slice.*

As she wipes off her knife, she glances out the window at the boys. Finch is already looking at her. Her stomach flip-flops.

Ginny has become a master at suppressing her desire to be with Finch. To *truly* be with him. She has to, if she doesn't want to lose him. She keeps her desire at a simmer, low-level bubbles at the very base of her stomach. Well below her heart.

But every couple of weeks, the water boils over. Her Anxiety gets bad, and Finch holds her hand and looks at her with those big driftwood eyes and tells her everything is going to be okay, and her feelings for him bubble forth so violently that she's quite certain she'll drown in them.

None of that, unfortunately, changes the fact that he's still with Hannah.

It all came to a head the week before this trip. They met for lunch in Madison Square Park as usual. Finch was talking, something about radial fractures. Ginny was staring at Madison Avenue, having a minor panic attack and not listening to anything Finch was saying.

Midway through a sentence about plaster casts and bone realignment, Ginny turned to Finch and said, "I love you."

Finch stopped. Stared. "What?"

"I love you." Ginny sipped her cold brew without ice. "I don't want you to say it back because I know you can't, but I just needed to tell you. That's all."

Then she stood up and walked the four blocks back to her office.

Ginny knew exactly what she was doing. She knows that Finch loves her back. She knows that he needs the right nudge to get him over the finish line, to give him the strength to break things off with Hannah. She knows that, when all is said and done, he'll choose her.

And she has a strong suspicion that it will happen on this very trip.

Like a proper adult, Ginny sets the outdoor table for dinner. She lays out both wine- and water glasses. Cloth napkins and gleaming china instead of plastic utensils and floppy paper plates. She slices tomatoes and spreads them out in a juicy fan on a patterned serving platter. The others offer to help, but she waves them away, tells them to work on the steaks and drink some more.

As she sets down the last knife, Adrian emerges from the house. His hair is damp and glistening. He scratches the hard line of his jaw, the one she used to trace when they would lie together after sex. She pretends not to notice.

"Whoa." Adrian walks over and lays a hand on the back of one of the chairs. "What's all this for?"

"Our welcome dinner." She smooths out a crease in one of the napkins. "First time in Budapest. Well." She smiles up at him. "For Clay, Finch, and me, anyway."

Adrian runs his fingers along the gilded lip of a plate. "This definitely isn't the Budapest I'm used to."

Ginny looks out over the sprawling estate. "This isn't the *anything* I'm used to."

"No." He follows her gaze. "I suppose not."

They both fall silent, watching the sun sink lower over the valley below.

"Are you going to see your grandparents while you're here?" Ginny asks.

"Of course. I'm spending two weeks with them after you all leave."

"Are they still in that artist village—Zen-something?"

"Szentendre." Adrian smiles, surprised. "You remember."

"Well." She shrugs, feeling her cheeks warm.

"Steaks are done!" Clay calls from over by the grill. Ginny picks up the serving platter and hurries over, grateful for the interruption.

Once the steaks are served, everyone settles into a place at the table and starts passing around the rest of the food. Ginny digs eagerly into the mashed potatoes, whipped with two whole sticks of butter, knowing she can rid herself of them later.

"So," Clay says, cutting into his steak. "What's on the schedule for this week?"

"Well." Tristan stabs an asparagus spear and pops it into his mouth. "Seeing as tomorrow is our first full day in Budapest, I figured I'd start us off easy: a tour of Buda Castle, a walk on the Chain Bridge, lunch on Váci Street, bikes by the Danube, dinner at Mazel Tov, and a ruin pub crawl to end the night."

"Think we could squeeze in a six-mile hike and helicopter ride, too?" Finch asks.

Tristan considers this. "Well, if we leave for Buda Castle early enough—"

"I'm shitting you, dude."

Their host looks suitably put out.

"That sounds like a great day," Adrian says quickly.

"Agreed," says Clay through a mouthful of potato. "Anything that includes the words *pub* and *crawl*—count me in."

"Hold up." Ginny points at Adrian. "Shouldn't the guy who grew up here be the one showing us around?"

"Oh." Adrian shakes his head. "No. It's fine. I—"

"No, Gin has a point," says Clay. "Adrian, don't let the foreigner make all the plans."

"Hey," says Tristan. "My family came to this same house when I was fifteen. I know my way around."

Finch sighs. "Are you really as ignorant as you sound?"

"Honestly, he's made a good list of tourist spots," says Adrian.

"But what about the *non*-tourist spots?" Ginny asks. "I, for one, would love to see where you grew up."

"Seconded," says Clay.

Adrian peeks over at Ginny. As his head turns, his eyes flutter, an action she's seen dozens of times—the sign he's considering something very closely. He holds her gaze with those familiar eyes, so brown they're almost black. The sight makes Ginny's stomach clench in a way she would rather ignore.

"I think we could make that happen," he says, not looking away.

Ginny clears her throat. "What about your Hungarian friends? Would they want to meet up with us?"

He smiles. "I'm sure they would."

At the end of the meal, as conversation winds down and steaks are polished off, Finch sets down his fork and dabs at his mouth with a napkin. "So," he says. "I have some news."

Ginny's neck jolts up.

Holy shit, she thinks. *This is it*. The moment he tells them. The moment he says he's breaking up with Hannah. The moment they finally go public with their relationship. Her hands reach under the table and close around her knees, nails digging into the skin.

Finch dips one arm into his pocket and rummages around. When it reemerges, a small velvet box balances on his palm.

Wait.

The box clicks open. Nestled inside a satin cushion is a white gold band with one big, fat rock at its center.

Wait.

What?

Finch looks around the table, a grin on his face.

"Dude," says Clay.

For one buzzing moment, Ginny's brain short-circuits. She

cannot process the ring hovering over the table. She cannot process the half-eaten scraps of food on everyone's plates. She cannot process the boys' expressions, the red wine staining their teeth, their hair flapping in the breeze. Her brain simply—

Stops.

"I'm proposing to Hannah." Finch's grin widens. "Next week, when I'm home."

And then it shuts off entirely.

As soon as the words come out of Finch's mouth, Adrian looks over at Ginny. Her face has gone completely blank. Jaw slack, lips slightly parted, eyes on the ring. She doesn't look upset; she looks like all the life has drained out of her and pooled on the floor. Adrian has the impulse to check under the table.

All around him, the boys jump up to clap Finch's back. To laugh about finally making him an honest man. Only Ginny and Adrian remain seated. Her eyes drift down to the table. Her shoulders tremble. Adrian starts to lift one hand—to do what, he's not sure, maybe touch one of those trembling shoulders—but, quite suddenly, Ginny stands, too. Her face snaps up, chair rocketing back so abruptly it tumbles to the floor.

The boys fall silent. Turn to look at her.

Ginny's chest heaves in and out. She smiles, a jagged thing that seems to splinter open her entire head, revealing the skeleton beneath. "Congratulations, Finch." She bends, scoops up her plate, and hurries through the French doors into the kitchen.

When Adrian turns to look back at the table, Tristan is rubbing the back of his neck. Clay looks physically pained. And Finch—he stares after Ginny, mouth turned down, like a father whose child is misbehaving again.

After dinner, they open a bottle of champagne and climb the outdoor steps up to the second-floor wraparound patio. Everyone except Ginny, who claims she can't stand to leave a kitchen dirty.

Adrian hangs back. "I'll help," he says.

Ginny waves him off. "Go celebrate," she says. "I want to do this alone."

"Okay."

Adrian exits the French doors and starts toward the terra cotta staircase. Just before ascending, he turns back to look through the windows at Ginny. Her head is down, arms scrubbing thoroughly, violently. As he watches, she leans to the side and spits into the left-hand sink. Though it's hard to make out through the glass, the spit doesn't appear thin and white; it's a chunky green-brown, like dog food. Adrian hesitates. Blinks. Did he see that correctly? He watches a beat longer, but Ginny simply scrubs and scrubs, as if nothing happened.

Adrian shakes his head and climbs the stairs.

Y ou can say it."

Ginny and Clay are the last two awake. Adrian begged off to bed early, and Tristan and Finch tapped out after drinking too much champagne and getting into a fight over Bitcoin versus Ethereum. Now Ginny and Clay sit at the outdoor table where they ate dinner, looking out over the lights sprinkling the valley.

"Say what?" Clay pours another thimble of whiskey into his tumbler.

"'I told you so.'"

Clay sighs. "I'm not going to do that, Gin."

"Well, you should."

"Well, I'm not going to, okay? You're my best friend. I'm never going to gloat over something that's hurting you."

"Nothing is hurting me. I did this to myself." She keeps her eyes away, pinned to the lights in the valley. "I lied to myself. I got in too deep. I let myself fall, even when I knew I shouldn't. It's freshman year all over again."

"Come on. Finch is as much a party to all that as you were. He knew exactly what he was doing." Clay taps the side of his glass. It pings twice. "I mean, God—I love the kid to death, but I rarely understand his decisions."

Ginny is silent. Then, quietly: "I love him, too."

"Oh, Gin." Clay reaches across the table and takes one of her hands. "And he loves you."

"No." Her eyelashes flutter as she blinks at the valley. "No, he doesn't."

"He does. He's confused."

"He wouldn't have bought that ring if he was confused."

"He wouldn't have bought that ring if he *wasn't* confused."

They both fall silent after that. Clay squeezes Ginny's hand. Tears start to gather at the corner of her eyes. She fights them. The other boys could come back downstairs anytime; the last thing she needs is for Finch to find her glassy-eyed.

"What about Adrian?"

Ginny finally looks back at Clay. She blinks, and two tears run down her cheeks. She wipes them away with her sweatshirt sleeve. "What about him?"

"He cares about you."

Her heart flexes when she pictures Adrian—the tender way he used to touch her, the soft sighs during their nights together. But then she thinks of the strange, almost disgusted look on his face when he first saw her today. She huffs out a laugh. "Right."

"He does." Light from the patio lamp cuts across their table and over Clay's face, making a stripe across his freckles. "And he's a good guy."

"Unlike Finch?"

Clay holds up both hands. "I never speak ill of my friends."

"Except Tristan."

He grins. "Except Tristan."

She sighs, rubbing her forehead. "How did we do it, do you think?"

"Do what?"

"Stay friends." She lowers her hand and plops her chin into her palm. "And I mean *just* friends. No repressed sexual tension, no nothing."

Clay shrugs. "You're too important to me."

"So are you. And I *tried* to tell Finch freshman year. I tried to tell him this would happen. I was so afraid of losing you guys." She bites her lip. "I still am."

"You're not losing anyone, Ginny." When Clay smiles, little crow's-feet wrinkle by his eyes. "You're stuck with us, whether you like it or not."

She waits until they're all asleep. Until Clay goes upstairs, and the lights click off in Tristan's room, and she hears snoring coming from Finch's. When the house is still, she slips into the kitchen. On the counter is a bag of assorted candy from the airport. Tristan's, no doubt—the man has an alarmingly aggressive sweet tooth.

She hesitates, staring at the bag. At its crinkly plastic wrapping, the sea of Reese's and Snickers and Milky Ways and Twixes inside. She walks over. How long has it been since she ate a piece of candy? How many years? How much restriction, how many pastries chewed up and spit out?

And, you know what? Today has been shit. She deserves something sweet.

Before thinking too hard about it, she reaches into the bag, plucks out a single Snickers Mini, and carries it into her first-floor bedroom. Shutting the door behind her, she sits down on her bed, folds her legs, and unwraps the candy. The chocolate lump rolls out onto her palm. She flattens her hand. There it is: chocolate, caramel, peanuts, and nougat. Fifty calories of pure sugar. Delicious, addictive. Completely forbidden.

Ginny pops it into her mouth.

The sugar hits her all at once, spreads atop her tongue like a river. Pleasure centers light up her brain, heightening her senses, narrowing them, until every part of her being focuses only on her mouth. She swallows.

"Whoa," she says aloud.

More.

On instinct, she shakes her head. One is already too many.

But another voice whispers: *Don't worry. You don't have to keep it down.*

That voice is right, she realizes. She can do it. She can have the best of both worlds. She can taste something she has long denied herself, and then it can come right back up.

She slips out of her room, scoops out a handful of candy, and returns to her bed. She unwraps a Reese's this time. Pops it into her mouth. Chews and swallows. It's just as good as the Snickers. She unwraps another candy. Then another. And another. Before she even knows what's happening, five pieces of candy are gone.

It isn't enough. She needs more. She gets another handful. Eats it without blinking.

The fourth time she goes out to the kitchen, she gives in and grabs the entire bag. When she returns to her bedroom, she locks the door.

Ten, eleven, twelve pieces of candy. Thirteen, fourteen, fifteen. A small mountain of shiny wrappers starts to build beside Ginny's left knee. She doesn't stop. She can't. *What the hell is happening?* She feels . . . strangely out of control. Like her hands and mouth are operating without her permission. She keeps telling herself to stop, that fifteen is enough, that it's *too many*, but then she reaches for another. And another. Whatever mechanism within you that tells you to cease eating, that you've had enough—it seems to have broken. She has broken.

I am bingeing.

The words come to her from far away, a flicker in a long, dark tunnel.

I am bingeing.

Only when the entire bag is empty does she finally cease chewing. Her hands hover over the chocolate-flecked comforter, quaking. Even after thirty-two pieces of candy, even as her body twitches with the overload of sugar, it isn't enough. She wants more.

More.

More.

She stands up and slips out into the living room. Opens the refrigerator. Every cabinet in the kitchenette. She's looking for something sweet, anything. A pastry. Ice cream. Honey-coated peanuts. She finds nothing.

She glances over the staircase. Tristan is asleep, and she would bet every cent in her bank account that he keeps a couple of king-sized Snickers bars squirreled away in his bedside table. Her fingers twitch. Does she risk going inside?

Ginny stands, rooted to the spot with indecision. Her breath comes in shallow little gulps.

While she ate, Ginny felt strangely numb. She could almost detach from herself, could watch the girl in that beautiful bedroom eat those beautiful candies. All that kept her inside her body was the press of each sugared bite onto her tongue, the feel of it sliding down her throat. It was easy, in the middle of her frenzy, to detach from the reality of what she was doing. What she was putting into herself. What it would do to her.

That numbness ends as soon as she stops eating.

Imagine this: you go from five years of wholehearted restriction, of believing that to eat too much or to eat the wrong thing will ruin your entire life, straight to stuffing your face with as much candy as you can find.

Ginny is fucking terrified.

The fear rolls over her in long waves. *What did I just do? What did I just do? What did I just do?* Each wave sucks her in, pulls her under, clogs her nose and mouth until she can no longer breathe.

She runs into the bathroom, shuts the door, turns on the shower, and waits.

Normally, this would be the point at which the food comes up. Ginny would push with her throat, and her dinner would be right there, waiting. Eager to leap back into the world. But when she pushes, nothing happens. The candy doesn't come up. Neither does the alcohol, nor anything else.

"Come on," Ginny grits out, hands on either side of the toilet bowl. "Where are you?"

Nothing comes; it's as if her throat has closed itself off for the night.

So Ginny does the one thing she never wanted to do. The line she thought she had drawn.

She sticks her fingers down her throat.

There is nothing calm or discreet about this style of purging. It isn't quietly spitting up into the bushes or pushing mush into a coffee cup. It is sudden. It is violent. Your middle and index fingers hit the back of your throat over and over. If you haven't clipped your nails recently, they scratch at the tender flesh, leaving behind marks you'll never see. But you don't stop. You push those fingers farther, deeper, seeking the trigger that will open the gateway between your stomach and your mouth. You push those fingers in over and over, even though your body is crying out for you to stop, please, stop. But you don't. You keep going. You violate yourself. It is punishment. It is rape.

Eating disorders are abusive relationships. They coax you in with kisses and promises of love. They tell you they will treat you right. They tell you that only they know how to love you properly. They make you promise after promise. And, for a while, they keep that promise. They keep you skinny. They make you like what you see in the mirror. They make you feel good about yourself.

But it's never enough. You will fail. You will eat. You *have* to if you want to stay alive. And when you do, your eating disorder will punish you. She will yell. She will hit. She will tell you that you are nothing without her. That, on your own, you are ugly, fat, unworthy of love. And you will believe her. And you will return to her. Over and over. Over and over.

The next morning, the boys gather in the kitchen, coffee bubbling in the high-tech Black + Decker in the corner. It took Adrian three tries to figure out how to start it. Tristan, who, for reasons Adrian cannot fathom, doesn't drink coffee, was of little help.

The group trickled in slowly that morning—Clay first, then Adrian, then Tristan, then Finch. According to Clay, Ginny was up the earliest but left right away to go on a hike. Adrian wonders why she didn't wait for any of them to accompany her; going alone feels distinctly un-Ginny.

Now the boys sprawl out on the boa constrictor of an L-shaped sofa in the living room. Adrian sits at the angle of the couch, taking long drags from his mug. Finch reads the news on his phone. Clay calls the patisserie down the road. Tristan lies with his head on a pillow, hands behind his head, yelling pastry orders at Clay.

The front door bangs open. Seconds later, a red-faced Ginny emerges into the room, ponytail matted to her sweating neck. Her breath is deep and heavy, the way Adrian's sounds when he finishes a run over the Brooklyn Bridge.

"Did you just"—Tristan pauses—"go for a *run*?"

Ginny bends double, hands atop knees. She nods.

Tristan looks aghast. "But . . . it's a fucking *mountain*, Gin. Sheer uphill and downhill."

She nods again, eyes never leaving the floor.

"Dude." Clay sits up, swinging his feet around to set them on the coffee table.

"You're a psycho," adds Tristan.

Finch, noticeably, keeps his face buried in his phone.

"Shower," Ginny coughs out. She stands and limps toward the stairs, leaving the boys to finish the coffee without her.

Tristan's father's car is a red five-seat Audi convertible. When he pulls it out of the garage, Ginny feels no surprise or excitement. She feels nothing really, having just eaten four of the pastries he ordered and thrown them all up afterward.

No one was in the kitchen when she found the box. The boys were all off showering, shaving, or otherwise getting ready for the day. She intended to eat only one. Only half of one, actually. But, similar to what happened the night before, the second that chocolate croissant hit her tongue, she couldn't stop.

She polished off the croissant. Then she moved on to a muffin. Then she cleared away a coffee cake. Only when the final pastry, a sort of cream-filled roll, was gone and the box was empty could she cease chewing. She shut the box, shoved it into the garbage, and ran straight up to her bathroom.

Now all she feels is the cool, even buzz that follows a good purge.

They pile into the car, Clay in shotgun, Ginny squished between Adrian and Finch.

Great.

As the car crunches down the driveway and out the front gate, Ginny shifts closer to Adrian, careful to ensure her thigh doesn't touch one slice of Finch's bare skin. She might imagine it, but she thinks that Adrian scoots closer to her, too. Up front, Clay plugs in his phone and puts on something called Friday Beers Tasty Licks playlist. The convertible rolls down a road called Béla király út, passing one gated mansion after another until they round a bend and the houses disappear altogether. They're left with an open view of Budapest, all the way from one side of the Danube to the other.

Clay whistles.

"The view is even better when you fly in on a helicopter," Tristan says.

"Shut up, Tristan," says the rest of the car.

During the forty-five-minute drive to town, Finch tries to engage Ginny no less than twelve different times. Ginny deflects each attempt, offering one-word answers, singing along with the music, talking over him, or just ignoring him altogether. She has decided to deal with this situation the mature way: by pretending he doesn't exist.

As it turns out, the Tasty Licks playlist is quite good. Ginny dances in the back seat—arms above her head, pelvis twisting, air rushing through her fingers. A few times, she even grabs Adrian's hand and pulls him into the dance. She doesn't care if Adrian finds it weird. She has nothing to be embarrassed about anymore. She has already endured the greatest humiliation of all.

The drive is gorgeous. Hegyvidék is all curving gravel roads and leafy green trees. The pavement winds through the valley like a snake at the center of the earth.

Soon enough, they reach Buda Castle. Tristan parks the car in the all-day lot, saying they'll pick it up later, after the pub crawl.

"You mean . . . when we're fucking hammered?" Clay asks.

Tristan waves a hand. "If we have to leave it overnight, so be it."

Ginny and Clay exchange glances, wondering what it must be like to be comfortable leaving such a ridiculously expensive piece of machinery lying around.

Buda Castle is named after the side of the river upon which it sits. As Adrian explains on their way inside, Budapest is divided into two areas: Buda to the west of the river and Pest to the east.

To Ginny, it looks less like a castle and more like an enormous library, or perhaps an ornate prison, all grey stone with a long army of windows and greenish neobaroque roofing.

"Do we want to do a tour?" Clay asks as they head to the ticket window.

"Absolutely not." Ginny links an arm through Adrian's elbow. "This man will know far more than any tour guide could tell us."

"That's not—" Adrian starts, but Ginny is already dragging him inside.

Adrian has never introduced his city to foreigners before. In the past, when he visited, he hung out only with his grandparents or childhood friends, and none of them was particularly interested in sightseeing.

He did visit Buda Castle on a school trip once. He remembers filing inside, his classmates in their navy uniforms, his best friend, Jozsef, at the front of the pack, tugging Adrian along with him. He remembers their teacher explaining the castle's long history, the many times it has been destroyed and rebuilt.

Adrian leads them straight to his favorite part of the castle: the view over the Danube. You can see everything: the Chain Bridge; the massive, red-domed Parliament Building; Gresham Palace; Fisherman's Bastion; and Eötvös Loránd University, way down south. His gaze lingers on the university buildings. On instinct, he scans for the spire of the math and science department.

"I can't tell you much about the castle itself," Adrian says, clearing his throat and turning back to his friends, who are staring out at the view in awe. "But I do remember that it was first built as a fortress in the thirteen hundreds, and when Sigismund became the Holy Roman Emperor in the fourteen hundreds, Buda was named Europe's political capital. I remember this quote our teacher told us. They said that Europe had three crown jewels: Venice on the waters, Florence on the plains, and Buda on the hills."

"Damn." Clay cups a hand over his eyes. "You know more than you think you do."

Adrian shrugs. "I guess I do."

He points out the landmarks to them, talking at length about parliament and the current corruption that is Hungarian politics. He's warming up now, recalling facts that his friends and grandparents mentioned in passing. Stories of kings and queens, invasions and affairs, scandalous court intrigue.

As the boys take selfies with the view, Ginny leans in to Adrian's shoulder and says, in a low voice, "Eötvös Loránd University— is that where your father taught?"

Adrian pauses. His eyes flick down to Ginny, then over to the school. "It is."

She nods. They stand together in silence, staring at the ridges and clock towers of the university.

Eventually, Adrian turns back to the group and says, "I have something to show you."

He leads them into the castle, through a series of hallways, then down a staircase marked THE LABYRINTH.

"What is this?" asks Clay, running a hand along the rough stone wall. The lower they descend, the cooler the air becomes.

"There's a huge network of tunnels beneath this part of the city," Adrian says. When they reach the bottom of the staircase, they enter a long arched stone hallway lit by eerie orange lights on the floor. "Criminals used to hide here when the authorities were after them." His voice echoes off the tunnel. "When I was a kid, my grandpa told me that vampires lived down here, too. He said Dracula himself moved from Transylvania to Budapest because he liked the climate better."

Ginny laughs at this story, a burst of unexpected noise, and the sound bounces off the tunnel walls. Adrian glances at her. Her choppy, layered hair glows a burnt orange. She's acting happy. She danced in the car, chattered about nothing, and skipped ahead as they walked up to the castle. But it isn't a happiness that Adrian believes. Not after last night. It's a hostile sort of happiness, a saw-tooth smile, sugar-sweet words with barbs at the center. In the dim light, her laughing mouth is like a black-filled breach in the earth.

As they walk the labyrinth, Adrian tells a story about Jozsef, who, during their field trip to Buda Castle, hid behind one of the stone statues and, in the middle of their tour guide's lecture on vampires and mythology, jumped out and scared the guide so badly that he wet himself. The prank earned him a round of applause from the students and a week's detention.

In Jozsef's words: *érdemes. Worth it.*

Even as Adrian speaks, he keeps one eye on Ginny, on the distance to her normally watchful gaze, on the tremble of her fingers as she reaches out to brush the stone gargoyle at the entrance to Dracula's Chamber. If the rumors about her and Finch were true, he wonders how she can stand to be near him right now. How she can plaster a smile onto her face—however barbed, however filled with wounded hate.

They will eat lunch on Váci Street, just as Tristan planned. Váci is, unsurprisingly, a complete tourist trap, but the outdoor terraces are great for people watching. Plus, Adrian knows a café that serves excellent *paprikás csirke.*

On their way to the café, they pass the towering statue dedicated to Mihály Vörösmarty, a famous Hungarian poet and playwright. The boys walk right past it, but Ginny stops and stares. Vörösmarty is seated high above her on a platform surrounded by Hungarian men and women—workers, couples, families, all carved from stone. Representatives of the population that Vörösmarty's words touched so deeply.

After a long moment, Ginny says, "They built this . . . just for a poet?"

"He wasn't just a poet." Adrian glances over his shoulder. The boys, seemingly unaware, have continued out of the square. He looks back at Ginny. "He was a beloved patriot. Like the Hungarian version of Shakespeare."

"And they made a statue for him," Ginny says.

"They did."

Ginny continues to stare up at the figure. For the first time all morning, she seems focused, entirely drawn into the present. Slowly, she climbs up onto the platform and runs her hand along the inscription below Vörösmarty's likeness.

"'Be steadfastly faithful to your homeland,'" Adrian translates. "The opening lines of one of his poems. It's like a second national anthem here."

"A second national anthem," Ginny repeats. She says nothing else. Just stays up on the platform, one hand hovering over the words, the other dangling at her side, fingers rubbing together, as if aching to grip something between them.

At lunch, they talk about trauma.

"There's just far too much emphasis placed on it," Tristan says, pinching a cracker from the bowl at the center of their table. "I'm sorry, but not everyone has experienced real trauma."

Clay says, "You're wrong, man. Trauma comes in many forms."

They're seated on the terrace of a small café just off Váci Street. No real food has arrived yet, but the group has already gone through an entire bottle of white wine.

"It's true." Clay signals for the waiter to bring another bottle. "People think that PTSD only happens to war vets. Men who watch their friends get blown up and come home and can't sleep at night because they keep seeing it happen over and over. And, yes—lots of vets have PTSD. But death isn't God's only trauma. He's got plenty more in store for us."

Adrian thinks of his father, then. Of a death that happened when Adrian was still inside his mother's belly. Could he call his father's death a trauma? Could he lay claim to grief or sadness when he and his father had never even existed in the same world?

Of course not.

Not when he knows that the blame for his father's death is his own.

He snaps out of his thoughts in time to hear Tristan ask Finch, "So, where do you think you'll do it?"

Beside Tristan, Ginny stiffens.

Adrian blinks. He wants to kick Tristan, who, as usual, is the only one at the table blissfully unaware of the tension between Ginny and Finch, rippling like a dangerous undertow.

Finch runs one hand over his jacket pocket as if he's still keeping the ring inside. As if he brings it everywhere he goes. "Well, we met my sophomore year of high school, when we both auditioned for *West Side Story*. I thought I might do it there. At the theater."

"Onstage?"

"Yeah."

Ginny snorts into her wineglass.

Finch raises his eyebrows. "Something to say, Gin?"

"Nope."

"Adrian," Clay says loudly, playing with the corner of his plastic menu. "I've been really impressed with the way Disney pivoted its Marvel content so seamlessly to streaming."

Adrian grabs hold of the change in subject. "Me, too, man. I wish I could take more credit, but that's a completely different division."

"Can we go back to trauma?" Tristan is talking even more loudly than normal, no doubt a result of his empty third glass of wine. "I mean, what—we're supposed to just nod along when a therapist says that getting a wedgie in the middle of the hallway was *traumatic*? How is that anywhere near as bad as fighting in the military?"

"Trauma has nothing to do with how 'bad' something is," says Ginny. This is the first full sentence that she's contributed since they sat down. Until now, she has just been drinking. Steadily.

Everyone turns to listen.

"Trauma happens when you aren't processing or acknowledging feelings as they happen to you." She swallows another mouthful of white. "When you experience hurt but push down the pain, or when you experience fear but push down the terror."

"How do you know that?" Tristan asks.

Ginny shrugs. "Novels aren't *all* that I read."

"But if men with PTSD—"

"Men *and* women," Ginny corrects. "In fact, today, right now, far more women experience PTSD than men." She drains her glass in two more sips and pours herself another. Her cheeks are turning the light pink Adrian remembers from their dates. "Think about it. Think about the people you know. How many men do you know who have actually gone into battle and seen their best friends blown up? Any? And how many women do you know who've been raped or sexually assaulted?"

No one responds.

"Almost all of them, probably. And do you think that they just move on without playing back the events in their heads? And not just when they're trying to fall asleep. No. PTSD is far less predictable. Far more insidious. It happens when they're just going about their day, just sitting at their desk or folding laundry or arranging a fucking vase of flowers."

"Ginny," says Finch.

"No." She looks straight at Finch for the first time all day. "No, *you* don't speak. You shut the fuck up, okay?"

He does.

They all do.

Adrian thinks, then, that Ginny is like a top spinning faster and faster, losing control, and he wants to catch her before she spins right off the table.

He clears his throat. "Ginny?"

Everyone looks over at him in surprise.

"Want to . . . go for a walk?"

Ginny does not look like she wants to go for a walk. She looks like she wants to murder someone—preferably Finch, but if not him, she'll settle for whoever is closest. Her eyes flare, seeming to burn at the edges. For a moment, his question hangs awkwardly between them.

Finally, she exhales. "Yeah. Fine." She stands and storms down the side street, heading toward the river. Adrian nods to the boys before leaving. Finch doesn't notice; he's staring after Ginny, a strange expression on his face.

The Danube looks dirty in downtown Budapest. Ginny walks along the riverside, eyes glaring at the clouds of dust that puff up around her white sneakers. Adrian falls into step beside her, saying nothing. She walks fast, arms swinging, but her short legs barely match Adrian's leisurely stroll.

"So." Adrian clears his throat. "Are we going to talk about it?"

"No."

"Okay, then. Should we talk about Tristan's massive imposter syndrome instead?"

"What?" Ginny pulls up short. His question took Ginny entirely by surprise.

"I mean, come on." Adrian grins. *Bring her back*, he thinks. *You can do this.* "Don't tell me you haven't noticed him trying to be a European for the past two days."

She pauses, scrunching her forehead. "Now that I think about it . . . he *is* wearing a completely different wardrobe than he does in New York."

"I've never seen so much linen in one place," he says. "Not even Positano."

Ginny lets out a laugh. The sound makes Adrian want to pick her tiny body up and spin her around.

"And the pastries this morning," he continues. "He wouldn't shut up about how famous the bakery is. Then, when they showed up, he made me sit and listen while he walked me through what each pastry was."

"Because *he's* the Hungarian expert here."

"Exactly." Adrian sighs. "I didn't have the heart to tell him that no one in Hegyvidék would use an iPhone app to order breakfast pastries."

Ginny laughs again, loud and unfettered, the way she used to. Just as it did a year ago, her laughter fills him in places he didn't realize were empty.

"Feeling better?" he asks.

"Yeah." She smiles up at him. "Should we keep walking?"

"Sure."

They continue along the river, watching sunlight dance off the waves.

"I just . . ." Ginny starts, then gathers herself. "It's just . . . I'm just fucking sick of it."

"Sick of what?"

She kicks a small pebble. "Do you know what it's like," she asks, "being the only girl in a group of boys?"

"Can't say that I do."

This gets another laugh out of her. Short, throaty. "Right. Well. Sometimes, it's great. Sometimes, I feel like I have access to this secret club, one I've worked my entire life to join. I mean—I grew up with three brothers and a sister who hated me and a mother who would sooner put on a pair of waders and spend the whole day fishing with my father than put on a stitch of makeup. Femininity never interested me. *Girls* never interested me."

Ahead, the road slopes upward. They begin to climb.

"When I got to college, the first people I met were the boys. Practically overnight, we were best friends. It felt . . . it felt like proof. Like God was telling me I was always meant to live among men."

Adrian's breath deepens as they climb.

"But the thing about being a woman in a group of all men—" Ginny pauses to exhale. "The thing about being a woman in a group of all men is that no matter how close you are, no matter how many secrets they share with you, no matter how comfortable they get around you, no matter if they can fart and burp and cuss and talk shit and not think twice about your presence— you're still a girl. And you will always *be* a girl; and for that one simple, stupid, arbitrary fact, you will never be fully a part of them."

Her words make Adrian's chest ache. He wants to reach for her hand, to reassure her—about what, he isn't entirely sure. He keeps his palm flat to his side.

"Sometimes," Ginny says, "the loneliest place isn't standing by yourself. It's standing just a few inches away from what you want."

They reach the top of the hill. "Ginny—" Adrian starts.

"I'm just . . ." She shakes her head. "I'm just sick of it."

"Of being the only girl?"

"No." She shades her eyes with one hand, looks right up at Adrian. "Of never being the one that they choose."

Her face looks so open, so alone. Adrian wants to lay his palm on her cheek. He wants to run his fingertips down her bare shoulder, the way he would when they lay naked in his bed after their dates.

I would choose you.

The words pop into Adrian's head unbidden. He tries to wipe them away, to gum up the cracks in the wall he keeps bricked so tightly together, because he knows they aren't true. He can't choose her. He can't choose anyone.

But it's already too late.

"What happened?" Adrian asks quietly as if to cover the thought. "With you and Finch?"

A car whizzes past. Ginny's hair flutters around her chin. She doesn't look away. "The same thing that always happens," she says. "I fell in love with someone who could never love me back."

They skip the ruin pub crawl. "We'll come back later this week," Tristan promises. "I think we're all pretty jet-lagged today."

We're all pretty jet-lagged, Ginny thinks. Code for: *Gin is too drunk and pissed off.*

"We should drive to Lake Balaton tomorrow," Adrian says as they climb back into the Audi. "It was one of my favorite day trips as a kid. It'll be a gorgeous drive in this car, and we can swim and relax and rest up for a proper pub crawl the next day."

"Done," says Tristan.

On the drive back, as Ginny sobers up, she begins to suspect that she shared too much with Adrian during their walk by the river. And yet, she thinks as she glances at his profile, as he stares quietly out the side window, she talked about her doubts, her insecurities, and he barely even blinked.

He's like that, Ginny is starting to realize. Unruffled. Unruffleable. Kind to a fault. Like a stone in a great river, taking anything that comes at it without shock or complaint. She could probably tell Adrian that she once murdered a man, and he would simply wrinkle his brow and ask how she hid the body.

Lake Balaton is exactly as beautiful as Adrian remembers. Nearly fifty miles long and as crystalline turquoise as a thermal bath, Balaton is the country's largest freshwater lake. Lush green hills circle the water, peppered with red-roofed towns and sprawling vineyards. The occasional harbor nestles into the lakeside, filled with teetering sailboats and inflatable rafts.

They used to take trips here as a family—Adrian, Beatrix, his mother, and his grandparents. Besides Christmas and Easter, these day trips were one of the few things Adrian remembers doing with his entire family. As a child, he assumed this separation was due to how busy his mother was. Now he can't help but wonder if it was purposeful—if his grandparents were a painful reminder of the husband she lost.

They park near Siófok, Balaton's infamous party town. As they head down from the parking lot to the beach, Adrian guides them toward a stand filled with colorful water toys: kayaks, paddleboards, giant inflatable flamingos.

"Three paddleboards and two kayaks, please," Tristan asks the rental attendant in English.

"Two paddleboards, not three," Ginny says over her shoulder. She's staring out at the waves. "I'm sharing with Adrian."

Tristan glances at Adrian, who shrugs. *Sure.*

The attendant tilts his head, not understanding. Adrian steps in to translate, handing over a wad of blue and red forint as he does.

Once Ginny sees that he has their board in hand, she runs ahead toward the lake. She doesn't pause or squeal when her feet touch the waves; she plows through and dives in headfirst. When she bobs back up, her hair is slicked back. Water runs down her arms and chest.

Adrian drops the board into the waves. Ginny climbs on word-lessly and sits up front, legs crossed. Adrian stands in the back. He paddles them steadily out past the pier, where the water is smoother.

For a few minutes, they drift in silence. Then, Ginny says, "We do this back in the Soo."

"Do what?"

"Paddleboarding. On Lake Huron. There are all these little in-lets and bays where the water is calm. Flat, like this. My brothers and I bring kayaks and boards and floaties and just spend the day adrift, drinking beer on the water." She glances over her shoulder. Then, seeming to make a decision, she spins all the way around and pats the space in front of her. "Sit."

"Okay." Adrian sits, letting his long legs splash into the clear water.

"Ask me anything," she says.

"What?"

"I'm serious. Whatever you want—ask away. I'm an open book."

Adrian pauses. He knows that she isn't lying, that she *is* an open book. It's one of the things he likes most about her.

"With which of your brothers are you closest?"

Ginny's eyes light up. "Tom. The eldest. Growing up, he made sure I was included in everything the boys did, whether that was video games or catch with a football or stopping Crash from blowing up our neighbor's cat."

"Are you still close?"

"Definitely. We have a sibling group chat, and Tom calls me every week."

"That's nice." Adrian should call Beatrix more often. "Okay. Your turn."

"Really?" Her eyes widen. She looks like a child receiving a present with a big red bow.

"Of course."

"Okay." She tilts her head, squinting at him. "What was your father's name?"

Well. That was the last thing he expected.

He hesitates, then says, "Adrian. Adri, for short."

"How did he and your mom meet?"

"That's two questions."

"You asked two."

He rolls his eyes. "They were high school sweethearts."

"Really?"

"Really. Back then, the communists were still in power, and the schools had basically no money. Students had to share textbooks, pencils, things like that. My mom and dad sat next to each other in class, so they made a habit of sharing—first books, then homework, then quality time, and, eventually, an entire life."

"That"—Ginny blinks—"is the sweetest story I've ever heard."

"A sweet story with a tragic ending."

She nods. "It is."

Adrian kicks his foot in and out of the waves, watching water run down his shin.

"Your turn," she says.

As Adrian thinks, Finch paddles through his line of sight, hunched over in a bright red kayak. He's gunning full tilt for the back of Tristan's paddleboard. Tristan spins around, but it's too late—the kayak makes contact, sending Tristan whirling as he howls, "*Dick!*" and falls into the water with a great splash.

I'm sick of it. Of never being the one they choose.

I would choose you.

"Tell me something you've never told anyone else," he says.

Ginny looks down into the water. It's clear enough that he knows she can see all the way to the bottom, to the sand and muck and rocks and reeds. She watches them for a long time.

Then, as if making a decision, she looks up and says, "I used to be anorexic."

"You—what?"

"Yeah." She chews her bottom lip. "All throughout college. And the year I lived in Minnesota. It's not that I . . . It's not that I wouldn't eat at all. I would. But I ate small portions and cut certain foods out entirely, like bread and other starches. That's how I got away with it. You have to eat *something*, or people start asking questions."

Adrian stays quiet, sensing that she has more to say.

"I knew I needed help, but I couldn't tell anyone. It's such a . . . a *girl* thing, anorexia. I know men suffer from it, too, but . . . I just didn't think the boys would understand. Or my brothers. I thought it would separate me further from them. I *still* do."

Adrian leans forward, trying to catch her eye. "You know that isn't true, right?"

Ginny traces small circles on the board's rubber surface. Then, she asks, "Do you ever feel unlovable?"

"I . . . what?" He blinks. "Is that how *you* feel?"

Her eyes flick back to his. "I asked you first."

"Ginny, you're—"

"Don't." She shakes her wet hair. "Don't tell me I'm lovable. I won't believe it." She swallows. "Especially not from you."

You're not just lovable; you're fucking sunshine. That's what he was going to say.

He could ask why he, in particular, isn't allowed to say she's lovable, but he already knows the answer. The answer is in long sighs tangled up in his sheets, in warm bodies pressed together

long afterward. The answer is in the wilting of Ginny's eyes when
he said he couldn't give her what she wanted.

"Just forget I asked anything." She starts to shut down, to turn
away. Her hands press to either side of the board and lift her pelvis
to spin around.

"Wait," Adrian says.

Ginny pauses.

"I do." He rubs a hand on one of his knees. "Know what it's like
to feel unlovable, I mean."

"Okay."

"I don't . . . I've never been in love. I don't think I'm even *capable* of falling in love. And if I can't . . . if I can't give that to
someone else, I don't think I deserve to receive it." Adrian has
never spoken these words out loud. They've pinballed around the
inside of his head for years, but he's never let them out. He's never
wanted to.

Not until now.

With anyone else, he'd worry about the effect of his words.
He'd expect the hearer to recoil, to call him a heartless robot. Not
Ginny. She just settles back onto the board and tilts her head.
"Why do you think that?"

"What? That I'm incapable of falling in love?"

She nods.

"Because it's true."

"No, it's not." She doesn't say it argumentatively. She states it
like plain fact. "You're not incapable of love, Adrian. No one is."

He watches her a moment. Then he asks, "How do you think
people see you? If you had to guess."

"Hmm." She unfolds her legs, leaning forward and wrapping a
hand around each side of the board. "I think . . . the boys see me
as kind of ridiculous. Emotional. Zany. The girl who cooks for
everyone and gets too drunk at parties. Who can never hold down

a stable relationship." She exhales through her lips. "My brothers and sister see me as the smart one, but a little scatterbrained. Always losing things. Never looking both ways at a crosswalk. That sort of thing."

He bites the inside of his cheek. *She took all her positive traits and spun them into negative ones.* "That's . . . not how I would describe you."

"No? Well, then—how *would* you describe me?"

Carefree. Thoughtful.

Beautiful.

"Is that your official question?" he asks.

"No." Ginny chews at her bottom lip. "Okay. I've got one: At what age do you think we come of age?"

"What," Adrian asks, "does that mean?"

She shrugs. "Well, it used to be, like, sixteen, right? I'd be a girl living on a farm, and at sixteen, my parents would sell me off in marriage for a load of cows or pigs. Now all sixteen-year-olds do is learn how to parallel park. And drink Busch Light. Hopefully not at the same time." She smiles. "So, when do you think we grow up? Like, *really* grow up?"

Adrian considers the question. From his perspective, his life can be divided into four parts: Budapest, Indiana, Harvard, and New York. He had to grow up when he moved to America. He had to grow up when he went to college. And he certainly had to grow up when he left college to live on his own.

"It depends what you mean by grow up," he says. "For some people, it's financial independence, which can happen at eighteen or twenty-two or, in the case of Tristan, never."

Ginny laughs.

"For others, it's settling down into a serious relationship. But our generation is so fucking stunted when it comes to love that I don't know if that's the best metric to use, either."

"Are we using *our generation* in the royal sense here, Adrian?"

At that, he laughs. "I think my answer is that it's different for every person. We all undergo change or trauma at different parts of our lives that forces us to grow up. It could be at nine or it could be at sixteen or it could be at forty-three. I don't know."

"That's one stunted forty-three-year-old." Ginny pauses. "You left Hungary when you were nine."

"That was just the first number that came to mind."

"Right." She eyes him closely, then says, "Your turn."

Adrian is ready. "What do you think you would be like in jail?"

"*What?*" She chokes out a surprised laugh.

"Well, you know how there are roles in prisons? Gang leaders, information gatherers, cigarette dealers." He's getting warmed up now. "Don't you ever think about where you would stand in that ranking?"

"Absolutely not."

"Well, take a guess."

"Um . . ." She scans the shore. "Cigarette dealer?"

"No way." He shakes his head. "Uh-uh. Stop being modest. Obviously, you would befriend every single inmate in there, whether they liked it or not, and eventually become their benevolent dictator."

She shakes her wet hair slowly back and forth. "Who are you and what have you done with Adrian Silvas?"

He winks. "Your turn."

"Fine." She leans backward, relaxing onto her palms. "Last question: What was the hardest part about learning English?"

"Ooh." He folds his knees up on the board. "Good one. Hmm." He taps his chin. "There's a lot. English is a weird fucking language."

"That it is, my friend."

"Okay." He claps once. "This doesn't really answer your question, but for a long time I used to get the words *hostel* and *brothel* mixed up."

For a long beat, Ginny stares at him in silence. Then, without warning, she bursts into laughter. "What in God's name," she asks through gasps, "was a nine-year-old doing thinking about *brothels*?"

He shrugs. "Little boys are horny."

She splashes him, and he laughs, batting the water away.

He says, "I can't believe you remember the age I moved to the United States."

She shrugs. Dips one hand into the water and spoons out a handful. "I remember everything about you."

And the funny thing is—he believes her.

As he paddles them back to shore, board bouncing in the waves, spraying them with cold water, Adrian watches Ginny's face. She laughs every time they hit a wave. Her eyes close, but her lips spread wide, teeth flashing, as if she wants to catch the water on her tongue. He realizes, as obvious as one sentence following the next, that he would do anything to keep that smile on her face.

When they reach the sand, Ginny helps him tug the board ashore. She straightens, then turns to look at him.

"What?" he asks.

"I forgot," she says.

"Forgot what?"

"How easy it is to talk to you."

"Oh." He pulls at his swim trunks. "I feel the same way about you."

She smiles just a little.

"Clay said something funny to me," she says.

"What's that?"

"He said you care about me."

"I do care about you, Ginny."

"That's weird," she says.

"Why?"

"Because you said . . . in your apartment, after we . . ." She seems to process several things at once. She closes her eyes and shakes her head. "You know what? Whatever. Fuck it. I like being around you."

Adrian tries to follow her train of thought, but she's like a minnow, darting from one subject to the next. All he can do is swallow and say: "I do, too."

She nods as if they are discussing the weather. "Good," she says. "Friends, then."

Friends. Good. That's what he wants, right? That's the safest option. To keep Ginny in his life, not committing to anything serious, ensuring that they don't explode and lose each other forever.

He says, "Friends."

Adrian's best friend does, in fact, join them for the ruin pub crawl. Not only that—he chooses the route. "'I'll take you to the good spots,'" he writes in a text that Adrian translates aloud to the group. "'Not the crap tourist ones.'"

Jozsef Borza is half the size of the rest of the boys with twice the personality. Ginny's first impression of him is a head of unkempt blond hair flapping in the breeze as he bounces down the street toward their group. "*Haver!*" he yells, one arm waving frantically over his head. "*Haver!*"

Adrian leans over to the group, a smile tugging at his lips. "That means *dude.*"

When Jozsef reaches them, he bounds into his best friend's arms, tackling him in an over-the-shoulder hug. Adrian is so much taller than Jozsef that he ends up lifting his friend off the pavement and swinging him in a circle.

"Welcome to Budapest!" Jozsef says to the group after Adrian sets him down. "Sophisticated, cosmopolitan, and filled to the brim with politicians so corrupt they'd make your US senators blush." He winks. "But at least the nightlife is great, eh?"

"I like him already," says Clay.

They start at Szimpla Kert, the most famous ruin pub in the city. As Adrian and Jozsef explain, ruin pubs first popped up in District VII, a section of the city left to decay after World War II. Over time, an underground bar scene developed, with colorful pubs opening inside the ruins of abandoned stores, warehouses, and homes. From the street, the buildings are unmarked and unassuming; only flickering lights and the faint thump of music hint at revelry. But within—

Szimpla Kert is a circus. Tucked inside an old factory, among crumbling brick walls and rusted handrails, a bar has been cobbled together out of worn wooden high tops and rickety stools. The space is decorated with lush plants, neon lights, old advertisements pinned to the walls, and even chairs suspended from the ceiling with cables. Ginny wanders the crowded maze, mouth agape. Each room is different: some hold foosball tables or bathtubs filled with padding and converted into benches. Every wall has been scrawled over in spray paint and permanent marker, a cloud of names and messages.

For a brief moment, Ginny forgets all about Finch. She forgets all about Adrian. She forgets about purging, about anorexia, about all the pain that exists outside these walls. She sees only color and light.

Jozsef leads them out to the open-air patio. Hanging lamps illuminate the space. At the very center, an old car has been painted, stickered, sliced open, and transformed into a booth, inside of which a group of friends laughs loudly. Jozsef cuts around the car and points to a picnic table.

"I'll get the first round," he yells, then elbows his way toward the bar.

The group sits—Ginny, Clay, and Finch on one side, Adrian and Tristan on the other. Out of the corner of her eye, Ginny sees Finch lean into Clay's ear, speaking with fervor. Every few moments, his eyes dart over to her. She pointedly ignores him.

After a few minutes, Jozsef returns with a cluster of glass mugs. He sets them at the center of the table and slides in between Adrian and Tristan, launching immediately into a story about the couple that was standing next to him as he ordered the drinks.

Ginny likes his Hungarian accent. It's crisp and precise, each syllable distinct from the other. Unlike Americans, Jozsef does not mumble or swallow any of his consonants; he pronounces everything as carefully as a computer.

Yet his personality could not be less mechanical. He tells stories like an excited puppy, jumping from subject to subject too quickly for Ginny to follow. She laughs every time he circles back, trying to remember how he got there in the first place.

"Tell me a word that's unique to Hungarian," she says when Jozsef reaches a lull in one of his stories.

"What do you mean?"

"Like . . . people always say that German has these unique words for highly specific emotions or actions. Things we don't have in English." Overhead, the soundtrack switches abruptly from thumping pop to an oldies remix. "Does Hungarian have anything similar?"

"Let's see . . ." Jozsef lays his chin on his palm, tapping his jaw with one finger. "*Haver*, you could answer this question, too."

"Not as well as you," says Adrian.

Jozsef's eyes light up. "I have one! Have you heard the word *elvágyódás*?"

"Ahhh." Adrian smiles.

"Can't say that I have," says Ginny.

"It describes a very specific feeling." Jozsef leans forward. "The intense desire to get away from where you currently are."

Ginny's mouth spreads into a slow smile. "*Elvágyódás.* That's an incredible word."

"It is. A very useful one, too." Jozsef taps the table twice with his middle finger. "I have another. We have a word, *rosszarcú.* It can be a noun or an adjective, and it describes someone with an 'evil air.'"

Ginny cocks her head. "Like . . . an evil person?"

"No." Jozsef shakes his blond hair. "Not necessarily. They just have an evil *air* about them."

Without meaning to, Ginny glances over at Finch. Adrian sees her do it. He bursts out laughing. Ginny's cheeks burn, but then she starts to giggle.

"What's so funny?" Clay asks.

"Nothing," Ginny and Adrian say together. They glance at each other.

A slow smile spreads across Clay's face. "Is that so?"

"It is." Adrian turns to Ginny. "I have one."

"What is it?"

"*Szöszmötöl.* It's a verb that describes when you're doing something and get so involved in it that the entire rest of the world falls away."

"Oh," she says.

Neither of them speaks after that. Adrian's brown eyes watch her so intently that her stomach starts to warm, low and steady, right at the base of her pelvis. She feels as if she has crawled into his eyes, as if they are a warm, dark cavern that cocoons her, protecting her from the outside world. She tries to stay still, to keep from moving her pelvis or heaving her chest, but it's nearly impossible; a strange, tight fire seems to have lit inside her.

She exhales. "That's . . . a beautiful word."

"It is."

"I have another," Jozsef announces, cracking open the cave in which Ginny was huddled. She turns to him, blinking rapidly, as if his blond mop of hair were a sudden burst of sunshine. "*Nincs.* Or *sincs.*"

"Wh—" Ginny clears her throat. "What is that?"

"It's a word that quite literally refers to the absence of something. A lacking. A thing that isn't there but should be."

"Oh."

And as Adrian stands from their table, brushing off his jeans and heading over to the bar to collect more beer, Ginny thinks she knows exactly what he means. That she has always known. That *nincs* describes what she has long felt about herself—an absence, a lacking, a thing that isn't there but should be.

The next bar isn't a bar at all. It's an outdoor food hall inside the alleyway beside Szimpla Kert. Pebbles crunch under Ginny's shoes as she crosses under a wooden archway with a neon sign that reads: KARAVÁN. Food stalls line each side of the alley, and a crowd of people mills about the inside, queueing for orders or eating at one of the wooden high tops.

As they elbow their way through the throng, Ginny spies every type of food imaginable: gyros, some sort of deep-fried pancake, burritos, sweet potato fries, marshmallow cones, burgers with patties made entirely of cheese. The farther they walk, the faster her heart races. What should she eat? How can she possibly choose? Her mind darts from one option to the next, considering each, trying to imagine their flavor, to taste them without tasting them. The boys start to peel off, headed for one stall or another. Ginny remains frozen. She spins in a tight circle. Her neck jerks from left to right. People jostle her on both sides. She scans the crowd for a glimpse of the boys to see what they've chosen. She sees no one.

Going into every meal since the night she arrived, Ginny's brain has been on high alert. She's certain that she'll slip up, that one bite will turn to two and two to a thousand. And sometimes, it does. Sometimes, she gives in to the panic, to the rabbit scanning the room in search of more, more, *more*.

She doesn't want that to happen tonight. The last hour at Szimpla Kert was the closest she has felt to calm in a long time; she doesn't want to ruin that with yet another binge. Yet another descent into the total absence of control. She will have to pick her dinner carefully. To ensure she doesn't choose something addictive, likely to trigger—

"Having trouble deciding?"

Ginny spins around. Behind her stands Finch, a cheese-and-chicken taco in one hand.

She narrows both eyes. "No." She starts to turn away, to march toward the nearest stall, but Finch grabs her wrist.

"Ginny, wait."

"*What?*" She spins around. "What, Finch? What could you possibly have to say to me?"

Maybe it's the alcohol. Maybe it's the light-headedness. Maybe it's the crush of people, the thumping music, the overwhelming shimmer of food at every corner of her vision. Whatever it is, something tells Ginny that she needs to have this confrontation here, *now*.

Now that he has her attention, Finch seems to have forgotten how to speak. He looks down. Shifts from foot to foot. The *taco* shifts on its plate, too, sliding from one edge to the other. When he looks back up, his eyes are so warm and sad it almost breaks Ginny's heart.

"I miss you," he says.

Ginny laughs once. The sound is harsh, biting. "Nice try. Fool me once."

"I do." His words plead with her. "You have no idea how difficult this decision was for me."

"For you?" Ginny steps closer, voice rising. "For *you*? No, fuck that, Finch. *Fuck* that. You spent the last year leading me on. I should have known it was all bullshit." She shakes her head. "It's the same fucked-up shit that happened freshman year. It's just a rerun."

"It's not a rerun." This time, Finch is the one who steps closer. He takes Ginny's hand and pulls her in until she is just an inch from his chest. "I did want to be with you. I *do*. But I have to consider my future. To break up with Hannah—it would destroy her. And it might destroy me, too. I don't know. But that doesn't— I can't—" He looks down at the pebbled ground. After a long pause, his eyes inch back up to find hers. "I love you, too, Ginny. I always have, and I always will."

Ginny inhales. She feels the urge to press both hands to his cheeks, to pull his mouth down to hers. But she fights it and takes a step back, instead. "That's not—" Her voice wavers. "That's not fair."

"But it's true. It's true, and I—" He runs his hand along her cheek. "God, I—"

Then he leans down, and he crushes his lips to hers.

Ginny gasps against his mouth. On instinct, her hands come up and knot themselves in his hair, pulling him tighter to her. The kiss—it's everything she's wanted. Everything she's waited for.

Everything she cannot have.

She pulls away, gasping. Her hands fall from Finch's face and clutch at her stomach.

"Ginny?"

The music has become too loud, the scent of food so thick she could suffocate in it. "I can't— I don't—" There is too much she wants to say. Too many speeches she has written in her head over the last few days. None of it comes out. She feels empty, depleted. She wants, suddenly, to fill that emptiness in any way possible.

She spins on her heel and pushes into the crowd.

"Ginny—"

She runs until his voice is swallowed by the music. Until she reaches the very end of Karaván, string lights and potted plants dangling from the metal pagoda above. Only then does she find the rest of the boys—Clay, Tristan, Jozsef, Adrian. All clustered around a high top, a sea of paper plates spread between them.

Clay spies Ginny, waving her over. "There you are. We were just wondering—" He stops when he sees her face. "What happened?"

"Nothing." Ginny elbows her way into a gap around the table. "I'm starving." She picks up a sweet potato fry and pops it into her mouth.

The boys exchange glances. "Where's Finch?"

"Who cares?" says Ginny. She picks up three more fries. Eats them all at once.

The boys fall back into uneasy conversation. They pick at the food on the paper plates. They appear to be sharing everything, so Ginny does the same.

At first, she tells herself that she'll just pick, too. That she just needs a few bites, just enough to fill the emptiness, the *nincs* at her very center. Quickly, however, she finds that a few bites do not satisfy her.

Ginny doesn't make a conscious decision to overeat. She simply tells herself that she needs another handful of fries, then another, then another, then another, and suddenly the tureen is empty. She simply tells herself that she wants another bite of the delicious deep-fried pancake on the table, the one she heard Adrian call *lángos*. Then another. Then another, then another, and suddenly the plate holds nothing but crumbs. She makes her way around the table, mopping up the boys' leftovers. Food has become everything. She stuffs herself with it. She becomes the most deplorable species of glutton.

They're watching me. They see me bingeing.

It consumes her, bulimia, the same way anorexia did. The same way anorexia told her to starve until all she could eat was her own body—taking whole bites of herself, the way one eats an apple, bite and bite and bite until only the core is left—bulimia tells her to eat until her body is so achingly full she misses the comfort of starving.

She can feel it, when the gluttonous part of her brain turns on. It's a switch. It's what she imagines a werewolf would feel when the beast within the man tears its way to the surface. It comes alive, this deep hunger, all instinct and animal, and it demolishes Ginny's every impulse toward self-restraint.

We all have a beast. They might desire different things—some crave sex, some power, some chemically induced happiness. And Ginny? Well. After five years of feeding herself just enough to get by, just enough for the pain to be chronic but livable, and one more year of throwing up almost everything that went into her body—

Well.

Her beast wants to eat.

Adrian is the first to notice that Ginny is missing. Fifteen minutes earlier, she excused herself to use the restroom, and she still hasn't returned. He's starting to get nervous. He didn't like the feverish look in her eyes when she showed up to their table. Didn't like how she barely spoke a word, only ate and ate until there was nothing left.

At first, as he watched her dig into the food, Adrian was thrilled. He was glad she opened up to him about her anorexia, but, if he's being honest, he didn't fully believe that her illness is as far in the past as she claims. She's so *thin*. But as he watched her take down a whole carton of sweet potato fries, he thought: *She's eating. She's finally eating.* It filled him with a strange sense of elation. One that only grew the more she ate.

When she finished, Adrian watched out of the corner of his eye as she dabbed at her mouth with a paper napkin. He waited for her to settle into herself. To become wrapped in the comfort that accompanies a full meal.

Only it never came. Ginny did not smile. She did not pat her belly or settle back onto her heels. Her shoulders tightened. Her hands drew into fists. Her eyes stared straight forward, wide and unfocused in the way that indicates someone is far, far away, sunk into the unreachable depths of the mind.

Adrian wanted to touch her shoulder. To say her name. Something, anything, to bring her out of what he could only imagine was a place of fear and overwhelming panic.

Just as he was about to reach for her, however, Ginny came to.

Her eyes snapped into focus, her neck straightening like a whip. "Bathroom," she announced. Then she turned and vanished.

That was fifteen minutes ago. So, under the pretense of needing the bathroom as well, Adrian leaves to search for her.

It doesn't take long. He finds her just outside Karaván, wandering back and forth on the sidewalk, a paper cup in one hand. Every couple of seconds, she lifts the cup up to her mouth and takes a sip. Her wrist trembles slightly.

"Ginny?"

She flinches so violently you would think Adrian yelled her name, not speaking it as gently as he could. Her wrist jolts, sending the liquid inside the paper cup splashing over the edge. To his surprise, it isn't water; it's an oddly thick, yellow-orange substance that spatters the pavement like paint.

For a tense moment, she just stares at the spill, mouth ajar.

"What is—" He steps forward, squinting at the ground. "What are you drinking?"

"Nothing." She steps sideways, blocking it.

"Ginny—"

"It's *nothing*, Adrian. Okay? Just some weird Hungarian drink I didn't even want." She paces over to the garbage and tosses the cup inside. "See?"

"That didn't look like any—"

"God, Adrian, *stop*. Just stop." She covers her eyes with one hand. "Go back to not speaking. Go back to not caring about me. Okay? I don't want your help. I don't even want to be in this stupid country, with its stupid tourist bars and disgusting drinks. Just mind your own fucking business and leave me alone."

Adrian watches Ginny, whose tiny face is still buried in her palm. He opens his mouth, then shuts it again.

"*Haver!*" Jozsef's voice cuts through the tense silence. Ginny's palm falls away from her face. She straightens, pastes a tight smile on her face. Jozsef sidles up behind Adrian and throws an arm over his shoulder. "You ready to head to the next bar?"

Adrian stares at Ginny, who won't meet his gaze. She looks at the ground, the garbage, the entrance to Karaván. Anywhere but at him.

"Yeah," Adrian says. "Yeah. Let's get out of here."

The third stop is a nightclub. It's called Instant-Fogas, and it consists of not one club but seven, all stacked together inside a single warehouse. Jozsef drags them to one of the smaller clubs, a dark, boxy room called Robot, featuring live rock 'n' roll groups. He orders tequila shots for the group.

"Not tequila." Tristan puts his hand on his stomach. "I'll hurl."

Ginny laughs in a way Adrian can't decipher.

"*Tequila for all!*" Clay passes the shots around. Each one has a sliver of lime balanced on top. Clay raises his glass. "To our intrepid host, Jozsef."

"I have no idea what *intrepid* means"—Jozsef knocks his glass against Clay's—"but I'm going to assume it has to do with how unspeakably handsome I am. Let's get fucked up, brother."

All six glasses come together over the bar, stinging liquid sloshing over the rims. They toss them back. Adrian swallows, thinking it tastes like stomach acid. He mashes the lime against his teeth.

Ginny grabs Clay and Tristan. "Let's dance, boys." She tugs them out into the crowd. After a brief hesitation, Finch slips in after them.

"So." Jozsef sets his glass on the bar and signals for two more. He looks directly at Adrian and switches into Hungarian, saying, "You and Ginny."

"What about us?"

"You're together, right?"

Two more shots appear before them. "No. Not even close."

"Ah." Jozsef pinches his glass and lifts it from the bar. "But you like each other, right?"

Adrian shakes his head. "I don't think so."

Jozsef snorts. "*Haver.* Are you dense? Do you see the way she looks at you?"

"She doesn't look at me like anything."

"She looks at you like *everything*, my friend. Listen." Jozsef leans in. "I've known you since we were in diapers. I know you aren't one to chase girls. I mean, *szar*, you could have any girl you wanted in this club. But that's not your style."

Adrian looks down at his shot. The liquid inside is a light yellow, almost gold.

"But that girl? Ginny? She's special."

He meets Jozsef's gaze. "You barely know her."

"Ah, but I know *you*. And I haven't just seen the way she looks at you, *haver*." In one clean motion, Jozsef downs his shot. He sets the empty glass back on the bar. "I've seen the way you look at her, too."

Ten minutes later, Ginny and the boys spill out of the crowd. Jozsef has spent most of the time leaning over the bar, deep in conversation with the bartender; Adrian gets the feeling that whatever he ordered is going to be extravagant.

He isn't disappointed. As his friends catch their breath, the drinks arrive. The bartender sets them down on the mottled wood: six tiny tubular spirals made of fluffy cake, toasted until golden brown.

"What the hell are these?" Tristan asks.

"Hungarian chimney shots!" Jozsef looks twice as ecstatic as normal, a true feat. "They're a classic Hungarian dessert: tube-shaped cake, toasted over an open fire and filled with ice cream. I asked the bartender to fill them with alcohol instead."

Tristan leans over the bar. "But these are empty."

"Not for long," says their bartender. In his right hand is a handle of vodka, which he pours down the line of Hungarian chimneys, filling each to the brim. "Better take them now before they melt."

"Onward!" Jozsef scoops up his shot and jams it into his mouth, cake and all.

Adrian glances over at Ginny. Her hand hovers just above, as if she cannot decide whether to take it or not. Her eyes dart back and forth. She seems to be looking for somewhere else to put it, but then Jozsef elbows her in the side and says, "Bottoms up."

Resolution snaps into place in her eyes. She stuffs the shot into her mouth. As she does, her body tips backward, her shoulder accidentally bumping into Adrian's chest.

"Well?" Jozsef hops back and forth. "Do you like it?"

With effort, Ginny swallows. Her tongue moves about, licking her bottom lip. "Wow."

"I knew it!" Jozsef claps. In Hungarian, he shouts, "Two more, good bartender."

Adrian watches as Ginny and Jozsef do two more chimney shots together. With each mouthful, Ginny grows looser, more bubbly. Her cheeks redden. Jozsef throws an arm over her shoulder and laughs, turning to Adrian. "This one can drink."

"Let's do another," Ginny says.

Adrian puts a hand on Jozsef's arm. "That's probably enough."

"Oh, is it?" Ginny narrows her eyes. Her words don't slur, not yet, but they seem to slope downward at the ends, like lazy penmanship. "I wasn't aware that you were entitled to an opinion over what goes into my body, Adrian."

"I'm not. I'm just watching out for you."

"Well, don't." Ginny turns to the bartender and says, "Two more chimney shots, please. And an extra chimney. Just for fun." When the shots arrive, Ginny drains the liquid first, then eats both cakes in quick succession. She eats them with aggressive enjoyment as if making a point.

"Looks like we've found a new chimney cake fan," Jozsef says.

"Sure have," Ginny says. But as Jozsef turns away from her to chat with the other boys, she doesn't look happy. She looks . . . lost. Her eyes are withdrawing again, sinking into themselves the way they did when she finished eating back at Karaván. As Adrian watches this change take place, the same sense of panic rises within him, as if she's traveling to a place from which he can never bring her back.

"Bathroom." She mumbles the word almost inaudibly, like she doesn't think anyone cares. Then she's gone.

For a full minute, Adrian doesn't move. He stares into the crowd at the gap into which her head just disappeared, debating. Does he go after her? Does she *want* him to go after her? Should he just leave her alone, the way she asked?

"Dude," says Finch, peering around Adrian's head. "Are you good?"

Adrian doesn't answer. He pushes past Finch and into the crowd.

The bathrooms are all the way at the other end of the room. When Adrian finally elbows his way over, he finds a long, black hallway lined with single-stall doors. Two are occupied. Two are not. He begins to wonder why he came over here. What is he going to do, bang on the door of a stranger's stall and hope it's Ginny? And to what end? She doesn't need a babysitter.

He sighs. While he's here, he might as well pee. He walks over to one of the doors and pushes it open.

Which is how he finds Ginny on her knees, bent over the toilet, fingers down her throat.

Adrian freezes. His hand slips on the knob. He sputters, "Wh—what the hell are you doing?"

Ginny looks up. Her eyes are glassy and bloodshot. Vomit trickles out one corner of her mouth, lumpy and cream colored—the remnants of a chimney cake.

For a long moment, they stare at each other. Several emotions cross Ginny's face at once: surprise, terror, confusion. Adrian expects her to yell, to tell him to get the fuck out.

Instead, she crumples up into a ball and starts to cry.

Adrian steps forward. The door swings shut and he pauses to lock it. Then he falls to his knees and scoops Ginny up into his arms. She's so tiny. Her body folds up onto his lap like a rag doll.

Her sobs come in heaves. Her face falls into his shoulder, her chest onto his. Great shudders accompany each gasp. They grow louder and louder as she gives into the sadness and lets it take over her entire body. She quivers in his arms, a bundle of skin and bones, far too breakable. He doesn't move. He doesn't speak. He's afraid that, if he does, she will coil back into herself and disappear forever.

Adrian doesn't know how long they stay like this. It could be five minutes. It could be twenty. After a time, Ginny's sobs subside enough for her to lean back and look him in the eye. Her face is puffy and red.

"*Elvágyódás*," she whispers.

"What?" Adrian leans in, thinking he's misheard.

"*Elvágyódás. Elvágyódás.*" Her voice cracks. "Please. I can't go back in there. I can't be around him anymore."

Adrian doesn't need her to clarify to whom she is referring. He reaches over to the toilet paper roll and pulls off a few sheets. He crumples them up, using the wad to dab the vomit off Ginny's chin. Then he stands, keeping her bundled up in his arms, tosses the wad into the toilet, and unlocks the bathroom door.

Surely the crowd is difficult to push through. Surely Adrian and Ginny receive confused stares and annoyed elbows. But Adrian notices none of it. He moves with a singular purpose, a ship plowing through the ocean, focused only on holding tight to the woman in his arms.

When he reaches the bar, the boys look up, ready to shout a greeting. Then they see Ginny. Confusion crosses their faces, then alarm.

"Ginny?" Finch's voice rises. "What the hell? Is she okay?"

"She's fine." Adrian looks past him, straight to Clay and Tristan. "I'm taking her to my grandparents' place for a few nights. She needs a break from . . ." He glances over at Finch. "The house. I'll call you tomorrow to fill you in, okay?"

Clay and Tristan glance at each other. Both seem unwilling to look at Finch. Finally, they nod.

Jozsef asks no questions. "I'll help you get a cab." He pushes away from the bar, skirts around Adrian, and starts to clear a path to the door.

Outside, Budapest is chilly and bustling. Neon-clothed ravers jostle Adrian as he carries Ginny to the curb. They barely glance at the pair, doubtless assuming she's just another partier too drunk to walk. Jozsef hurries out into the street and flags down the first empty taxi that drives past. He opens the back door and holds on to its handle as Adrian steps inside, careful to protect Ginny's head from hitting the top.

"Text me when you make it home," says Jozsef. He seems completely sober now.

Adrian nods. Then Jozsef shuts the door and the cab rumbles forward, Ginny still huddled up on Adrian's lap, her body trembling like a child faced with daylight for the very first time.

PART IV

How did I get here?

Ginny wakes to find herself in a warm, yellow-painted bedroom. The sheets are clean. A handwoven quilt drapes over the end. In one corner of the room is a fluffy white rocking chair. In another, a light blue armoire with a mirror hanging above. She sits up. In the mirror, she sees a scared girl with choppy blond hair. It takes her a moment to register that girl as herself.

Out the window, she sees a line of houses: one yellow, one blue, one red, all so bright they seemed to be yelling. Paper lamps hang across the street. Everyone outside looks happy.

It's then that she realizes she is at Adrian's grandparents' house.

Her theory is confirmed after she slips out of bed and pads over to the armoire, where she finds a framed photograph of Adrian with two women—one young, one old—whom she can only assume to be his immediate family.

This room must be Beatrix's, she thinks. She's never met Adrian's sister, but there are too many feminine touches for the room to belong to Adrian—the quilt, the flowers, the drawer filled with bronzer and moisturizer.

In that same drawer: a notebook with an embroidered butterfly on the cover. She picks it up, turns it over. The notebook seems to hum, to call to Ginny. She carries it over to the bed and tosses it onto the quilt. Beatrix won't mind, she thinks; the notebook is dusty and old, the spine uncracked. Probably her grandparents gave it to her ages ago.

She finds a pen in the bedside table, flips open the notebook, and begins to write.

*I'm trying to piece together last night. I remember flashes. I
remember Adrian finding me in the bathroom. I remember
crying. I remember being in his arms. I think . . . God, I think
he carried me here. That feels entirely impossible, like a super-
hero rescuing someone dangling from a rooftop by their fingertips. But it's the only explanation I have.*

*I'm scared to leave this room. It's safe in here. Some sort of
twilight zone, an eight-by-eight box cut off from the dangers
of the outside world. The happy houses across the street, the
happy people carrying groceries back to their happy families.
If I leave, all that will disappear. I will have to face the truth
of what happened last night. And I'm not ready for that. I'm
just not.*

Eventually, she leaves.

She has to. She knows that she is inside someone else's home,
and that to hide in the bedroom all day would be disrespectful.
So, reluctantly, she cracks open the door and tries to slip sound-
lessly into the hallway. But when she steps out of the room, she
finds herself not in a hallway at all, but in a sun-drenched kitchen
with painted brick walls and a high wooden ceiling. Spices and
preserves line the windowsill. Dish towels hang from the oven
and the kitchen sink. The dishwasher is painted a faded sky blue.

Standing around the cozy kitchen island—Adrian and his
grandparents.

They all turn to face her at once.

"Hi," Adrian says.

"Hi," she says back. She doesn't know what else to say, so she
waves to his grandparents and adds, "I'm Ginny."

"They know," he says, not unkindly. "This is Eszter and Imre.
We're going to stay with them until you all fly home on Saturday."

She opens her mouth, maybe to argue, maybe to protest, she doesn't know. Then she glances at Eszter, Adrian's grandmother. She wants to find comfort there, the sense that her presence is not an annoyance or a burden. She doesn't find it. Eszter isn't even looking at her. She is staring out the kitchen window, face unreadable. Ginny tugs nervously at her pajama pants, suddenly conscious of the fact that Adrian must have undressed and redressed her the night before.

"We were about to sit down to breakfast," Adrian says, completely unaware of the chill radiating from his grandmother. "Would you like to join?"

"Oh, I don't—"

"I insist." Adrian points over at the dripping coffee machine. "Coffee?"

"Yes, please."

Not wanting to be useless, she walks over to the wooden shelf that holds a line of white ceramic coffee mugs painted with blueberries. She reaches up to take a mug, but before she can grab one, a delicate, wrinkled hand closes around her wrist.

She jumps and looks down. To her right stands Eszter, a full six inches shorter, looking as hawkish and terrifying as anything Ginny has ever seen. Eszter doesn't speak. Just shakes her head and produces a clear mason jar with a handle instead. She pushes it into Ginny's hands.

Stunned, Ginny carries the mason jar over to the coffee machine. As Adrian pours from the carafe, he leans in close and whispers. "They don't really speak English. But don't worry—I'll do all the translating."

They sit down around the breakfast nook, a little wooden table beside bay windows. Eszter and Imre lay out the food: a bowl of scrambled eggs, a plate of toast, a tureen of butter, little homemade jellies and jams. Ginny waits, uncertain how to proceed. Apparently, she waits just a smidge too long; with a sigh of annoyance, Eszter picks up a spoon and starts ladling eggs onto her plate.

As they eat, Adrian chats with his grandparents in Hungarian. Every so often, he translates for Ginny—statements about the weather, his job, his aunts and uncles who live nearby. He seems more at ease than Ginny has ever seen him. Several times, he laughs loudly at something his grandparents say. Ginny waits for his translation so that she can force out a laugh, too.

No one asks her any questions, for which she is extremely grateful.

It's the first time Ginny has eaten breakfast in several days, and the first time she's kept it down in over a year. She has no choice. When they finish eating, she tries to excuse herself to use the bathroom. Without a word, Eszter places a surprisingly firm hand on Ginny's shoulder and pushes her back into her chair. She says something Ginny can't understand, something in Hungarian. Adrian translates it as, "We like to enjoy a bit of after-meal conversation in this house."

After breakfast, she isn't allowed to help with dishes. She isn't allowed near the sink at all.

She's not sure what Adrian told his grandparents when he showed up on their doorstep last night, but it must be the truth.

"Do you want to shower?" Adrian asks. She says yes. He looks at Eszter, who picks up the newspaper from the kitchen counter and leads Ginny up the stairs and into what appears to be a master bedroom. She crosses the room and steps into the adjacent bathroom, where she hands Ginny a towel. Once they're both inside, Eszter shuts the bathroom door behind them. Then she closes the lid of the toilet, sits down, and opens the newspaper.

Ginny hesitates, waiting for Eszter to leave. She doesn't. Ginny understands, then, what is happening. She doesn't have the energy to argue. She strips down to nothing and steps into the shower. When she turns on the water, it's freezing. It takes a full minute to warm up.

Eszter never looks at her. Never speaks, never pries. Eventually, Ginny grows accustomed to her presence. She knows why she's there. It's a warning. A reminder that, if Ginny does something she shouldn't, Eszter will know.

Her bedroom doesn't have its own bathroom. If she wants to pee, she has to use the powder room in the front hall. Eszter keeps it locked. Ginny has to ask for the key if she wants to use it, and then Eszter stands outside and waits until Ginny is done. The door is thin; if Ginny throws up, Eszter will hear it.

Ginny is alone in Beatrix's room right now, writing about breakfast in the little butterfly notebook. Adrian asked if she wanted company, and she did, but she said no anyway.

She doesn't know why she's writing any of this down. She's barely written at all since leaving Minnesota, and it's not like she has any story ideas. But, to be honest, there isn't much else to do in this house. All the books are in Hungarian. The TV barely works, and only shows Hungarian cable television anyway. Adrian seemed displeased about that; he talked about it with his grandparents for a long time. Ginny could tell because he kept pointing over at the old set, and she thinks she heard the word *Disney*. She's sure they'll have a brand-new flat-screen by the time he leaves, whether they want one or not.

But, for now, there's nothing to read, nothing to watch. There's just Ginny and her notebook. And her anxiety, which keeps trying to remind her about the eggs and toast she just put into her body.

She's tired. So, so tired.

She thinks she'll take a nap.

Ginny has to eat lunch, too. She was hoping she'd sleep through it, but when she shuffles out of her room at two o'clock, Eszter has a sandwich waiting. She sets it down in the breakfast nook and pulls out a chair, gesturing for Ginny to sit.

For a while, Ginny just stares at the sandwich. She doesn't particularly want it, but she's equally afraid that, once she starts to eat, she won't be able to stop. She will go for the cabinets. Eat the potato chips and cookies and anything else she can find. Wipe their kitchen clean.

After a few minutes, Adrian walks down the staircase. "You're awake," he says.

"I'm awake."

He sits in the chair opposite hers. He doesn't say anything, just sits with her. She starts to eat. She moves slowly, tearing off the crusts. It takes a while, but she eats the whole thing.

After lunch, they play cards. Adrian teaches Ginny a Hungarian game called Snapszer that uses cards with Roman numerals. She doesn't really understand what's going on, but it occupies her mind as she tries not to think about the food stewing in her stomach. That's all she can really ask for.

When they finish the game, Ginny fetches the notebook from inside her bedroom and returns to the living room. Adrian is in front of the television, fiddling with its antennae. He turns around when he hears her enter.

When he sees the notebook, his eyes light up. "You're writing again?"

"I guess," she says. Then she lies on the floor and starts a new entry.

Adrian doesn't say anything while she writes; but every couple of minutes, she feels his eyes flick over, searing her cheek with just a glance.

> *I think writing is the only form of communication in which I can truly say what I mean. When I speak, I feel like a broken dam—my words are spilling water, with a life and purpose all their own. I have no control over where they will go or what they will destroy along the way. But when I write, I have time to think about exactly what I want to say. To place every letter, every comma, every colon exactly as I intend. I control my words; I control myself.*
>
> *I'm scared to eat dinner tonight.*
>
> *Eszter has been cooking for practically the entire day, and whatever she's making smells incredible. Which is exactly what I'm afraid of.*
>
> *Anyone with an eating disorder knows that nights are worse than days. Especially if you tend to restrict. By the time the sun sets, you're like a bear coming out of hibernation. Your body needs food, and it needs food now.*
>
> *If I'm being honest, I haven't eaten much today. A few bites of breakfast, a sandwich with no crusts. To my anorexia brain, that feels like a lot, but I'm cognizant of the fact that it isn't, really. I'm hungry. And the better the house smells, the hungrier I get.*

Dinner goes surprisingly well.

Ginny is careful. She eats only half of what she is served, and then she sits on her hands. She can feel the beast trying to edge his way through to the surface. Can feel her brain starting to dart back and forth, taking in all the serving platters, all the options on the table. She feels it happen, and she wrestles it back under control.

Maybe this will be easier than she thought.

I just binged. I didn't mean to, but I did.

At around eleven o'clock, I got hungry again, probably because I didn't eat my full dinner plate. So I went out to the kitchen to look for a snack. I found a jar of peanut butter. I like peanut butter. I opened the jar and ate three spoonfuls. Then I shut the jar, put it back in the cabinet, and got into bed. I'll just eat that, I decided.

For thirty seconds, I lay in bed, thinking about the taste of that peanut butter on my tongue. How smooth it was. How creamy. The taste played like a loop in my head, a siren's call, beckoning me back out into the kitchen.

Fine, I decided. I'll have just one more spoonful.

I didn't have just one more spoonful. One turned to two, which turned to four. It tasted so good, and it went down so easy, and the excuses started piling up in my head—but I'm hungry, but I didn't eat much today, but I was anorexic for so long, but I deserve this peanut butter, I deserve to eat half a jar, maybe more, just a quarter jar more, that's not so bad, is it, and maybe just another spoonful, it's so good isn't it, and, shoot, is that the bottom of the jar, how did I get here, holy shit, I just ate an entire jar of peanut butter, that's, like, three thousand calories, I just put three thousand calories into my body without even blinking, holy shit, holy shit, oh fuck, what did I just do to myself, oh my god, oh my god . . .

The panic descended like a familiar pair of arms, a hug that starts tender but grips tighter and tighter, constricting my chest and cutting off my windpipe.

Fuck.

Fuck.

I took a deep breath. Then I cleaned everything up, all of it. I wiped peanut butter smears off the counter. Put the spoon in the dishwasher. Screwed back on the lid. I didn't even put the empty jar into the garbage—that would be too much evidence. I took it into my bedroom and hid it under the bed, making sure the skirt draped down far enough to obscure it from view.

I'm on my bedroom floor now. I'm curled into a ball, one hand gripping my ankle so hard I'm sure it will bruise, the other scrawling manically in this butterfly notebook. Dread spreads thick and sludgy along my insides, like fresh jam atop stale bread.

I'm so hungry. I'm too full. I'm so hungry. I'm too full.

I want to vomit so badly. I want to expel everything, all the food and the sadness and the fear and the danger I just put into myself. But I can't. If I do, I'm afraid that Eszter will kick me out, and I'm not ready to leave the sanctuary of this home quite yet.

I am leaking peanut butter out of my esophagus.

I am so sick of having an eating disorder.

I don't know what to do with all of this body. I think I'll just break it instead.

The next day is miserable. Ginny feels like she's exploding. Like her organs are going to burst out of her skin.

She almost threw up last night. She came dangerously close. When she finished writing in her journal, it was well past midnight. She slipped out of her bedroom, thinking she could throw up in the sink and then wash it down the drain. But on her way across the kitchen, a stair creaked behind her. She whipped around. On the landing stood Adrian, one hand on the light switch.

"Ginny?" he asked. "What are you doing?"

"Nothing," she said. Then she ran across the kitchen and into her bedroom, locking the door behind her.

Ginny thinks that she used to be vibrant. In college, and throughout most of her life, she was the bubbly one. The thin little pixie. Crop tops. Rollerblades. Quick with a joke, even quicker to laugh at someone else's. She used to love meeting new people. She loved that strangers are blank canvases, friendly facades containing lies and secrets and years of mystery to pick apart. Each their own past. Each their own story.

Now she thinks of nothing but food.

She's sick of it. Sick of food taking up every last inch of her mental space. But she also knows that, in order to sweep it all away, she has to eat, and keep it down; and when she does, her body will start to expand, and she cannot survive living in a larger body. She can't.

She saw an eating disorder specialist for a month back in Minnesota. For anorexia. The sessions took place at one of those dual inpatient-outpatient clinics. Once, on her way out of the therapist's office, she saw the girls who were living there full-time. They were seated in what looked like a conference room, crafts spread out between them. There were feathers and glitter, paints and markers, hearts and googly eyes. They pasted things together, sometimes onto each other. They smiled and laughed. They looked happy.

The sight depressed her so much that she never showed up again.

As I picked at my bagel and cream cheese at breakfast today, I thought about anxiety.

One of the trickiest parts about anxiety-based fear is that, so often, the thing you fear does not actually exist.

When anxiety comes up, when you start down that road of no return, you cannot "think" or reason your way out of it. That's the mental equivalent of chasing down cars that have no regard for whether you want them on the road or not. In this case, of course, the road is your mind.

That being said—don't try to reason your way out of anxiety. She will not listen to logic or reason. She has no use for them. Anxiety will always look for reasons to keep herself alive.

So it is with my anxiety around food. I keep trying to reason myself into eating normally, but it's fucking impossible. Anxiety has already identified every possible trap: too little, too much, too many, not enough. At every meal, my brain darts between these possibilities, backing me ever further into the corner I already know too well.

Take now, for example. Adrian is gone, picking up my bags from Tristan's rented house in his grandfather's truck. I'm lying on the couch in the living room, notebook open, recording every stupid, useless detail of the twenty-four hours I've spent in this house. To Adrian's grandfather Imre, who is sitting on the armchair across the room, it looks like that's all I'm doing. Lying on the couch and writing. I probably look calm to him. Relaxed, even.

Yet, if you could see the inside of my head, you wouldn't think that that was the case. You would think I'm seriously cracked out or something because my thoughts are moving so quickly it feels like I'm stuck on one of those whirly teacup rides at an amusement park.

• You ate too much.

- *You need to throw up.*
- *You can't throw up.*
- *You haven't exercised in two days.*
- *You need to stand up and walk around.*
- *You're going to get fat.*
- *You're going to feel awful about yourself.*
- *Return to first bullet point. Repeat.*

You know, if there's one positive to this whole situation, it's that, with all my time and energy devoted to feeling like I could fucking die at any moment, there's very little space left for thinking about Finch.

As I think about him right now, I don't feel sad; I feel angry. I think I might genuinely hate him. I do. All the sadness I felt about his engagement—it's gone, leaving in its place a burning hot anger unlike anything I have felt toward any human being, ever.

And to think—not a week ago, I thought I was in love with him!

How is that even possible? Can we trick ourselves into thinking we're in love? And, if so, how am I ever supposed to know when it's the real thing? Maybe I can't. Maybe that's the point. Maybe, when it happens, I'll just have to throw myself in blindly and pray my emotions aren't trying to deceive me.

Every meal is a fucking mountain. Ginny both cannot wait to eat and dreads eating so intensely that she wishes she could brutally murder the human need for sustenance. She's never felt such contrasting emotions about one simple event before.

At mealtimes, she picks at her plate, tentative, embarrassed. She knows they're all watching. That they're wondering if, after they go to bed, she'll throw up out her bedroom window. They probably think she's weak, that she's disgusting. She can't stand the sight of her empty plate. She can't stand the feeling of existing inside her own skin.

But throughout it all, there's one constant—Adrian. He never says so, but she can tell he's watching. He sits close enough for her to know he's there, to ask for help if she needs it, but far enough that she doesn't feel him breathing down her neck.

Tonight, she finishes her whole plate, then is overcome with the urge to grab his grandparents' plates out of their hands and dump them down her throat, too. Both urges scream at her at once: *Don't eat. Eat everything. Don't eat. Eat everything.*

As if he can read her mind, Adrian nudges his plate toward her. "Want it?"

She shakes her head.

"Are you sure? Because it's okay if you do."

Whatever she takes from his plate, she cannot give back. Whatever she puts in her body, she must keep down. She eats his potatoes. She eats Imre's potatoes. Then she sits in her chair and wants to cry.

Tentatively, Adrian lowers his hand and places it over her fist, clenched so tight atop her napkin. Her eyes dart up, but he doesn't look down at her. Doesn't make a big deal of this small gesture of comfort.

He keeps his hand there until her fingers loosen, eventually coming apart altogether.

After dinner, they move into the living room. Adrian plays Snapszer with his grandparents. Ginny lies on the couch. She thinks that Imre and Eszter must believe there is something seriously wrong with her; all she ever does is lie around and scribble in her notebook.

Well, joke's on them, she thinks. *There is something wrong with me. Many, many things.*

Adrian glances at her several times. By the fourth or fifth glance, she raises her eyes and meets his gaze. Instead of acting embarrassed, he smiles. "It's good to see you writing," he says in English.

She looks down, cheeks burning.

She wonders what he would think if he knew she isn't doing this for fun. That she's writing because it feels like the only thing keeping her tethered to the face of the planet. That, if she doesn't write, she will binge, or purge, or simply erupt in a cloud of smoke and float away, never to be seen again.

The next morning is different. After breakfast, Adrian asks if Ginny wants to go for a walk.

For the last two days, she hasn't wanted to do much of anything. She's been too exhausted. But this morning, she's surprised to find a touch of energy buzzing through her body. She says yes.

There is just one issue: by now, the initial shock of her current situation has passed, and she's started to feel the embarrassment she believes she should have felt since the very first day. She's in a foreign country, intruding in the home of the grandparents of a boy with whom she used to have sex. Her common sense has finally caught up with her, and she's humiliated.

All of that to say—she doesn't want Adrian to feel like he has to babysit her.

"You don't have to accompany me if you're busy," she says.

"That's okay. I'd like to stretch my legs." He pauses in tying his shoes. "Plus . . . Well. I don't really want to leave you alone right now."

Oh. Right. Because she could easily find a bush to throw up into on the side of the road.

She's such a fucking liability.

* * *

On their walk, Adrian leads her down the hill through winding cobblestoned walkways flanked by alternately colorful or crumbling houses. He points out landmarks as they go: art galleries, famous homes, small statues done by famous artists. She tries to pay attention, but she can't stop perseverating over her own guilt. Adrian's words, chipper as they are, seem, in that moment, to be coated in a thick layer of pity.

It only gets worse when Adrian says, "I think it's time we talk about treatment."

She freezes on the cobblestones. "What?"

Adrian stops, too. "Getting you into recovery. *Real* recovery, I mean, not just the low-grade version we've thrown together here."

The thought of going into a treatment center, with its white walls and sterile bedsheets . . . "I don't—"

"I know it's scary, Gin." He steps forward and takes her hands. "I know you don't want to disrupt your life. But I've been reading about eating disorder recovery, and the thing is—treatment centers are the gold standard. They really are. If you're serious about making a change . . ." He eyes her meaningfully.

"I am," she says hastily. Because she is. *Right?*

"Good." He nods. "Then it's settled. As soon as you're back in New York and ready to tell your parents, we can call them together. Unless you want to do it alone, of course. Just as long as we get the process going." He lets go of her hands and keeps walking. Ginny follows, numbness seeping into her with every step.

After ten minutes, they reach the main shopping road, Bogdányi. They turn left and walk downhill. Adrian gestures to a marzipan candy shop on one side of the road. It seems as if he's gearing up for an enthusiastic explanation of marzipan's importance in Hungarian culture. But before he can get much headway, Ginny stops walking.

For a few steps, Adrian continues on as if nothing is amiss. When he realizes she is no longer with him, he turns around, confused.

"Ginny?" he asks. "Do you want to go inside?"

She inhales once, twice, three times. Then, she blurts, "I'm sorry."

"What?" He steps closer. "Sorry for what?"

"For—" She gestures vaguely to herself. "For all this. For having a meltdown. For ruining your trip with your friends. For forcing you to bring me to your grandparents' house and being such a fucking imposition on them."

"Ginny." Adrian closes the distance between them. "You didn't force me to do anything. I chose to bring you here."

"But it's my fault. If I wasn't such a complete and utter mess, you would never have had to make that choice. I'm so—" Her voice breaks a little. "I'm so fucking selfish. I'm sorry, Adrian. I'm so sorry."

"Ginny." He puts his hands on her shoulders.

"I don't—" She swallows. She can feel them coming. The tears. She doesn't want to cry in front of him again. "I don't want to be a burden on your family."

"Shhh." He pulls her into a hug. "It's okay, Ginny."

"I don't—I don't ever want to be a burden. To anyone. I hate it. I hate it so much."

"Shhh. You aren't a burden."

"Yes, I am." She hiccups. "You don't have to lie to me, Adrian."

"I'm not lying."

"I'm standing here, in the middle of your hometown, sobbing my eyes out, and you're seriously saying I'm not a burden?"

For a moment, Adrian doesn't speak. She thinks she has trapped him, that he is finally going to push her away, revealing the annoyance underneath. Instead, after a few seconds, his shoulders start to shake.

"Are you—" She pulls back, thinking he's crying. But when she looks up, it isn't tears she sees; it's laughter.

Through her own tears, she lets out a surprised laugh. "What?" she asks. "What is it?"

"If someone had told me in college," Adrian says, shoulders still shaking as he cups a hand over his mouth, "that I would one day be holding Ginny Murphy as she cried her eyes out on the most public street in downtown Szentendre"—he wipes a fake tear from his eye—"I would have called them mental."

She cracks a small smile. "Rightfully so."

Adrian shakes his head. Then he takes her by both arms, leaning down to look her directly in the face. "If you can't burden your friends with your troubles," he says, "then who can you share them with?"

She thinks about it for a moment. Biting her lip, she whispers, "No one."

"That's bullshit."

Her eyebrows must jump up to her forehead. She can't remember Adrian ever cursing before.

"I'm serious. It's bullshit. I mean, I get it. I'm the king of being emotionally unavailable. You know that better than anyone else."

At that, she can't help but laugh. "True."

He smiles. "But Clay was right, Ginny."

"What do you mean?"

"I do care about you. As does Clay. And Tristan, and even Finch, in his own fucked-up way. Not that we're talking about him." Adrian raises one of his hands and tucks a loose strand of hair behind her ear. She inhales in surprise. "We're talking about you, and the fact that—that—"

"That what, Adrian?" It's barely a whisper.

His eyes search hers. After a pause, he says, "That I care about you. That I care about you getting healthy. I care about you living, for fuck's sake." He looks away, over at the marzipan sweets glistening in the window. "I know what the endgame is when it comes to eating disorders. I know where they lead. And I won't—" His voice cracks. "I refuse to let that happen to you." He looks back down at her. "Okay?"

Her voice is barely audible. "Okay."

"Good." He releases his hold on her arms, puts one arm over her shoulders, and tucks her into his side. Then, together, they start back down Bogdányi.

"Adrian?" She squeezes his side. "I'm sorry."

"What did I just—"

"No." She shakes her head. "Not about that. I'm sorry that you're going to have to give me that tour all over again because I really want to learn about your hometown, but I wasn't listening to literally anything you said."

Adrian laughs, a sound so warm and genuine it gives her a brief rush of elation. As they continue down Bogdányi, she wishes she could bottle that sound up, slip it into her back pocket, and keep it forever.

Walks become their daily ritual. One in the morning, one in the afternoon.

On their first afternoon walk, Ginny makes Adrian reeducate her on all the history she missed that morning. When he points to a building and says there is an art exhibit beneath it, she tells him she wants to go inside.

"This building is called the Lajos Vajda Studio," Adrian says as they descend the staircase. "Named after Lajos Vajda, a famous Hungarian artist who lived during the early twentieth century. He was a weird dude. Did a lot of abstract paintings and charcoals and collages."

They reach the bottom of the staircase, which opens up into what she can only describe as a brightly lit dungeon. The walls and floor are all made of dusty, deteriorating brick. High archways line the space. The whole thing reminds her of the crypt in *Game of Thrones*.

Except for the art.

The art is everywhere: affixed to the walls, wrapped around the arches, standing upright at the center of the room. Paintings, pastels, collages, photographs, sculptures, installations. Each one stranger than the last.

"This studio opened in the seventies." Adrian leads her over to the closest painting. It's an abstract piece painted in bright primary colors that reminds her of the houses that line the street in Szentendre. She can make out no distinct shape but a small eye down in the left corner. "It's a cult collective dedicated to supporting the underground art scene in Hungary. You get some weird stuff down here."

"No kidding," she says, eyeing a sculpture that appears to be coated in a thin layer of human hair.

They continue their loop of the room. "Do you like art, then?" Adrian asks.

"I don't know," she says honestly. "I've never studied it in any depth."

"Well, you don't need to study art to appreciate it."

"Don't you, though? Unless it comes naturally to you, like some kind of gift? I look at stuff like this and I think—I have no idea what the artist is trying to say. I get a general feeling from the work, but I don't know how to analyze it, to make any meaning out of it. Not the way I do with a written text. I look at paintings and feel kind of stupid, to be honest."

Adrian shakes his head. "You're not stupid. Art analysis is a muscle, just like literary analysis. Were you able to identify metaphors and alliteration and mood and tone before you started studying them in earnest?"

She thinks about it for a moment. "Actually, on some level, I think the answer to that question is yes. Writing has always come naturally to me. It's one of the only things that does. Everything else—math, science, sports, music, whatever—I had to work hard to achieve even a modicum of success." She stops before a charcoal portrait. The woman holds a hand to either side of her face, barely touching her cheeks. Her chin is tilted back, mouth slightly ajar. It is a posture of surprise, though her eyes look utterly in control. "I'm not saying I came out of the womb knowing what a metaphor was. Obviously I didn't. But I've always . . . I don't know. I've always known how to make a piece of writing dark, or light, or gruesome, or funny. I've always known that characters need backstories and motivations. I didn't think of things in those terms, of course. I just thought . . . I was just writing about people. I was just writing a story."

Adrian is quiet, then, watching her.

She thinks back over her words. "That sounded really arrogant, didn't it?"

"No." He shakes his head. "It didn't."

"Oh." She looks down at the dusty stone floor. "Well, enough about me. This whole damn week has been about me. I'm sure you're sick of it. Tell me about Disney. I haven't even asked you about it once."

When she looks back up at Adrian, he opens his mouth as if to say one thing, then shuts it again. He nods, then, and says, "It's good." He smiles. "It's great, actually. I just finished my first big project."

"Oh? Go on."

Adrian fishes his phone out of his pocket and types something into Google. When the page loads, he turns the screen to face her. It's open to a *USA Today* article titled, "Disney+ to Expand Streaming Service in Fourteen Countries." She takes the phone out of his hand and scrolls through the text. Much of it is standard corporate jargon—the kind of thing she would write about Sofra-Moreno in her job—but in the fifth paragraph, there is a list of the countries in which the service would be launching: Bulgaria, Croatia, Hungary . . .

"Hold up." She raises her hand, palm flat. "Are you telling me that you helped launch a streaming service that will bring movies and TV to children growing up in Hungary?"

Adrian just grins.

Ginny whacks his shoulder. "Are you fucking kidding me, Adrian? This is amazing. How did I not know about this before?"

He shrugs. "It wasn't announced publicly until last week. Plus, you know." He raises one hand and scratches the back of his neck. "We haven't really talked much since . . ."

They let the sentence trail off.

He clears his throat. "Anyway. Have you seen enough?"

"Down here? Absolutely." She points to his phone. "About your project? Not even close. You better tell me everything." She nudges his shoulder again. "I'm so proud of you, Adrian."

When he smiles, it reaches the very tops of his ears.

Here's what babies and bulimics have in common: we both love to spit up.

Unlike bulimics, babies are not trying to shrink. They are trying to grow, but they do not know how. They cannot feed themselves. So they eat, and they eat, and they eat; and they do not know when to stop, so they eat far too much and then burp half of it up.

Sometimes, I feel like a baby.

Sometimes, I soar up and out of my body; and when I do, I see myself for what I am: a human being who is not fully formed, who is trying to grow into an adult, but does not know how. Who cannot feed herself. Who needs someone to tell her when, how much, and how little, but who cannot actually ask for what she needs because she cannot speak. She can only cry and cry and cry and hope, eventually, someone will listen.

Ginny doesn't want to go home yet. She still has two days in Hungary before she has to board a plane and head back to New York, but she's already dreading it. She doesn't want to go back to that apartment, where Finch lives a mere six feet away. She doesn't want to go back to her job, no matter how good it feels when Kam nods in approval at how quickly she turns in her tasks. She wants . . .

She doesn't know yet what she wants.

But she knows she can't stay here any longer. Adrian might claim that she's no burden, but that's because he doesn't notice the way Eszter glares at her, the noise of displeasure she makes when she strips the sheets from her bed and carries them to the laundry. Ginny tries to interrupt, to say she can do it herself, but Eszter shoos her away.

Four days have passed since she last purged. It's crazy how quickly her body is expanding. An outsider would probably tell her that she's being ridiculous, that there's no way she could have gained weight already, but Ginny can tell. It's like her body was desperate for it, for an extra pound, an extra ounce of fat. Her skin rumples in so many places now. Around the waist, the thighs, the back of the arms, beneath her chin. It almost mocks her with how easily it folds.

She feels like she's drowning in her own insecurity. Given the choice, she would curl up into a little ball and sleep through the rest of her life.

Later that day, Ginny lies on the couch, journaling as always, while Imre reads quietly in his armchair. Just as she finishes her entry, Imre stands up and walks over to the bookshelf. She assumes he's going to pick out another book, but after searching around for a minute, he pulls out a tome so large it could only be an encyclopedia. He turns around and starts to carry it toward Ginny. She thinks that maybe it's a Hungarian-to-English dictionary, that he has something to tell her. It isn't until he settles on the couch beside her and opens the book that she realizes it isn't a book at all.

It's a photo album.

Imre opens the first page and points at a picture. Ginny's face splits into a huge grin, because captured in that photograph is a dark-haired, chubby-cheeked, unbearably adorable baby that could only be one person.

"Adrian?" she asks.

Imre nods, smiling. He points to another photo, this one of two toddlers waddling along the Danube—Adrian and Beatrix. They sit in silence for a few minutes as Imre turns the pages for Ginny. Whenever they come to an especially cute one of Adrian, they pause to grin at each other. About four turns in, Imre reaches up to flip to the next page, but she stops him. There, in the top corner of the page, is a faded photograph she wants to ask about.

She holds up a finger, then pulls out her phone and googles the translation she needs. When she finds it, she points at the photograph and asks, *"Apa?" Father?*

The photograph in question shows a pale, lanky man standing beside a yellow car, a stack of books under one elbow. He wears a grey overcoat and glasses perched on the end of his nose. But it's the slight smile that gives it away. That smile belongs to Adrian.

Imre lays two fingers atop the lanky man's face. His son's face. His eyes crinkle at the edges as he says, *"Igen."*

That word Ginny knows. *Yes.*

She types something else into the translator. When the Hungarian result appears, she shows the screen to him: *Van több képed róla? Do you have more pictures of him?*

Imre nods, smiling. He sets the album aside, then stands up from the couch and walks across the room. Instead of stopping at the bookshelf, he walks further to a wooden chest in the corner. He cracks open its lid. Ginny had assumed the chest was decorative, filled, perhaps, with more quilts and throws.

Instead, when she peers over Imre's shoulder, she spots a mess of books, papers, cassette tapes, even a pair of glasses. Ginny wonders if they're the same glasses in the photograph she just saw. But before she can get a closer look, Imre shuts the chest and returns to the couch, this time bearing a smaller photo album.

This album only holds photos from before Adrian was born. First comes a young version of his *apa*, high school age or so. He has a girl on his arm, slight, with dark hair and red lipstick. Adrian's mother. Ginny recognizes her from the photograph on Beatrix's dresser. Imre flips through the photographs until he finds the one he's looking for—Adrian's mother and father standing outside a church.

Ginny takes out her phone to ask another question, but a voice surprises her from behind.

"What's going on?"

Ginny and Imre jump. Behind them is Adrian, who had approached so silently that neither of them heard. Her face warms. She wants to reach down, to shut the album and pretend she saw nothing. With Adrian standing there, face unreadable, she feels as if she's done something deeply wrong.

Adrian's eyes flit over the album spread out on Imre's lap. His gaze lingers on the photograph of his parents getting married. In it, his mother and father stand outside a grey cathedral, his mother's bouquet waving in the air. Adrian holds out a hand and says something to Imre in Hungarian. Imre passes him the album.

Adrian leafs through the album with a blank expression. He flips so quickly that he doesn't seem to take in the photographs at all. He asks his grandfather another question. Imre responds. Adrian nods. Then he passes back the album, turns around, and walks away.

Imre and Ginny look at each other. She's sure he can tell from her expression that she feels guilty, and he just shakes his head. She opens her phone and googles a translation:

What did he ask you?

Imre holds out his hand. She passes him the phone. He types in a few words, then shows Ginny the English translation: **He wanted to know why I had never shown him those photographs before.**

Ginny tilts her head, hoping he will understand her question: **And why didn't you?**

Imre types in another sentence, then turns the phone around to face her again:

Because he never asked.

One morning, during their walk, Adrian asks Ginny a question.

"Did you mean it?" he asks as they round Bogdányi and head for the Danube. "What you said at lunch our first day?"

"Which lunch? The one on Váci Street?"

He nods. "You said that trauma is something that happens when you experience something but push down any emotion around it."

She isn't sure what she expected him to say, but it wasn't that.

She thinks about it for a little, then says, "It's something I read about in an article a few years ago. A piece in *Psychology Today* about processing emotions." She looks out at the milky waves of the Danube. "Say you endure something sad, like the death of a loved one, but instead of letting yourself feel sadness, your body just shuts down. You feel nothing. Or maybe you actively run from the grief. You use booze or drugs or sex, or you get really into working out, or whatever—I don't know. Whatever it takes to turn it off.

"In the moment, you aren't processing your emotions. You're avoiding them. But that doesn't mean they go away. They're always there, just below the surface. Watching. Waiting." While she talks, she fiddles absentmindedly with the strap of her tank top. When she thinks about it, it's strange that she can wear tank tops in front of him at all, terrified as she is about the expansion of her body. "They find you in moments of silence or stillness, flashes of memory or tears you can't explain. And the process repeats itself, over and over, until you finally let yourself feel." She lets her hand fall to her thigh. "That's trauma."

"And that's why trauma can come from anywhere," Adrian says. "Not just extreme circumstances, like war."

"Right."

"Has that ever . . . I mean, have you ever . . . ?"

Her eyes travel up and over Adrian's shoulder, to the ridge of buildings beyond. "Having anxiety is chronic trauma. That's what the article said, anyway. Everything is bigger and more terrifying than it should be. Sometimes, it seems fucking impossible to live your life feeling all that, all the time, so . . ."

"So you repress," Adrian says.

Several moments pass, then she continues: "Anorexia is a coping mechanism. I know that. Starving yourself—it keeps you from feeling anything. And I did that to myself for five years. *Five years*. But I don't—" Her bottom lip wavers, then. "I don't know what I was hiding from."

Adrian says nothing.

"What about you?" she asks.

"What *about* me?"

"Are you hiding from anything?"

He doesn't respond. He turns to the Danube, his shoulders rising and falling with the lilt of the waves.

It's my second to last night in Hungary, and something bizarre just happened. I was sitting on the sofa next to Adrian. Eszter was on his other side, Imre in the armchair. Adrian had somehow fixed the old TV set, and we were watching a movie on VHS. Seriously. VHS. I couldn't tell you the last time I even saw one of those, but his grandparents have a whole collection.

Eszter chose the movie. She rattled on about the collection, pulling options and showing them to the room, to which Adrian and Imre would either yell, "Igen!" or "Nem!" They couldn't agree on anything. Finally, Eszter waved them both away and picked out a movie herself.

"What are we watching?" I asked Adrian.

"Pirates of the Caribbean," he said.

I almost spit out the water I had just sipped. "That's the movie your grandmother chose?"

"Don't let her hardened exterior fool you, Ginny. She's a romantic at heart."

Thankfully, the movie was subtitled in Hungarian, not dubbed. It had been years since I watched Pirates. *I forgot how fun the movie was. I laughed. I gripped the sofa. I almost grabbed Adrian's hand at several points but managed to stop myself.*

None of that was unusual. I always get too invested in fictional characters. I always feel exactly what the writers and directors want me to feel. What was unusual was this: at the end of the movie, when Elizabeth and Will Turner finally kissed, I started to cry.

And I don't just mean a few tears. I don't mean glassy eyes and a trickling nose. I mean sobs. I mean a full, gushing, torrential waterfall. Hiccupping inhales and a shaking chest. As the credits rolled, Adrian turned to me, alarmed. "Are you all right?"

"Yes," I said through a gasp. "Yes, I'm fine. I just, um. I need—" I stood up. "I'll be in my room." Then I ran away before I could see the look on his grandparents' faces.

I closed my door and buried my face in my pillow. Only then did I let the full extent of my emotion come out: heaving sobs, gasping inhales, cries that, were they not blocked by a pillow, would have sounded like a strange mix between screaming and laughing uncontrollably.

I'm still crying. I can't make it stop. Even as I write this, tears are falling onto the page, blotting the paper, creating little wrinkles. Several times, I've had to stop writing altogether because my eyes were too filled with water to see.

I'm scared Adrian is going to walk in. I'm scared he's going to see the truth of what I am: a wreck, a disaster, a being filled with unexplainable darkness.

I don't understand what's happening to me. Pirates of the Caribbean *isn't even a sad movie. It's the opposite. It's a happy movie with a happy ending. Where the fuck did all these tears come from?*

My only guess is this: at the very moment when Will kissed Elizabeth, when it became clear that they would get their happy ending, I thought to myself: I will never have that.

The thought played over and over in my head, a song I did not want to hear; but the moment it began I knew I believed it to be true. I hate men. Yet I crave love so badly it feels like a gap is sawing its way open in my chest, starting as nothing more than a pinprick and working its way out, hollowing me, making real the emptiness I feel.

I will never have that.

I will never have that.

I will never be loved.

I don't even deserve it.

As I write those words, I cry harder, but the sadness does not diminish. It expands. It fills every limb of my body. I don't think I'm even upset about the movie anymore. I'm just upset. And I can't make it go away. I can only conclude that I do not like myself one bit. That the sadness I feel is a sadness without cause, a despair capable of sitting at bay for long periods of time or of washing over me all at once, without warning and often at the most inopportune moments.

That's it. That's my secret. Nothing more, nothing less. This is the beast, the one I've feared for so long. I see now that everything I do, all day long—the obsessive exercise, the heady starvation, the hunger that cannot be satisfied until it is stuffed to the point of physical pain and then released in a bundle of stomach acid and salt—is done to keep that hurt at bay.

The creature within me—it is made up of every insecurity, every ounce of low self-esteem, every wrongdoing, every mistake, every man I slept with who never loved me. Every reason to hate the very skin I walk in. It craves validation and fears failure. It dictates my every decision, from what time I wake up in the morning to how many slices of bread I might eat in a given day.

I don't think I was even capable of experiencing true sadness before now. That's what anorexia and bulimia do—they numb you out, erase your emotions, make it so that all you think about is food, food, food. But now that I'm eating—and keeping it down—everything else is coming back up. All of it. Every emotion I spent the last seven years suppressing.

I wish my heart would fall out of my chest and pull my misery with it.

A few minutes after Ginny finishes writing in her journal, she hears a soft knock on the door. She knows who it is without even asking. She doesn't want him to see her like this, with tearstained cheeks and puffy eyelids, but she says, "Come in," anyway. Her back is to the door.

Adrian turns the knob gently, the same way he does everything. "Are you okay?"

She pauses, then says, "No."

Footsteps on the wooden floor. "Can I . . ."

"Yes," she says. "Lie with me. Please."

Adrian hesitates. Then the mattress dips as he kneels onto it. She feels his body stretch out behind her. His head settles on her pillow, arms wrapping around her chest. She scoots her pelvis back until it lays flat against his.

"Is this okay?" she asks.

"Yes," he whispers. "I can't stay all night, though."

"I understand." She reaches up and squeezes one of his hands. "Thank you, Adrian."

And they lie like that, body to body, until at last they drift off to sleep.

* * *

On Ginny's last day in Hungary, she turns her phone on for the first time in almost a week. She let it run out of battery the night of the ruin pub crawl and hasn't plugged it in since.

But she has to now. And she's terrified.

The minute it turns on, texts start to roll in. She shoves the phone under her pillow, but it barely muffles the chorus of buzzes and pings. Each one makes her pulse tick faster. What are the boys going to say? How is she supposed to explain herself to them? She's hidden from reality for five days now—but reality is always there, waiting.

When the phone finally stops making noises, she creeps over to the pillow and pulls the phone out from underneath:

137 text messages.

16 missed calls.

3 voice mails.

"Jesus Christ," she says aloud.

Fifty messages from Finch alone. She ignores those, clicking first on the conversation with Clay.

CLAY: Gin, are you ok?? What happened?

CLAY: The message didn't go through. I think your phone is off.

CLAY: I'll try you again tomorrow

CLAY: Helllooooo

CLAY: Still not going through. Ok. I'm calling Adrian.

CLAY: Ok. Just talked to Adrian. He filled me in on the situation. Please don't be mad at him for telling me, Gin. He just wants you to get healthy.

CLAY: I haven't told the others yet. I just said that you were having a health issue and were recovering at Adrian's. I won't say anything else until you tell me otherwise.

She rereads the messages several times. To be honest, it hadn't even occurred to her to be angry with Adrian for telling Clay. She feels grateful, actually. A big part of the reason she dreaded turning on her phone is that, once she reconnected to the outside world, she would have to start telling people what was happening. And the idea of doing that, of sitting down with her parents or brothers or sister or best friends and telling them that she's bulimic—it makes her want to fucking throw up. Both literally and metaphorically.

She sets down her phone without reading any of the other messages.

"Don't go home."

This comes from Adrian, who sneaks up behind Ginny when she's packing the last of her bag. She turns around to find him leaning against the doorframe, arms crossed.

"What?"

"Don't go home. You're not ready."

Ginny sighs. "I have to. My ticket is for tomorrow."

"Extend it."

"But my job—"

"Do you not have vacation built up?" Adrian pushes himself off the frame. "Tell them you need more time. Tell them you're having a health emergency. Because you are, Ginny. You can't just go back to normal life and pretend everything will be all right."

She bites her lip because she knows he's right. But she also knows she can't stay here. She can't continue to intrude upon his grandparents' hospitality.

"I'll figure it out," she says, tucking shirts into the corners of her suitcase. "I'll get Clay to keep me accountable. I'll call my mom and start the process of finding a treatment center. I promise. But I can't—"

Just then, Eszter appears in the doorway, cutting her off. As usual, she doesn't speak. Her eyes travel the room. Take in the sight of Ginny's half-filled suitcase, the shirt dangling from her hand. Eszter clucks once. Marches forward and brushes Ginny aside. Ginny steps back, watching as Eszter pulls things out of her suitcase and puts them back into Beatrix's dresser.

When Eszter is finished, she turns and stares at Ginny. She's such a tiny woman that Ginny has to look down to meet her gaze. She points up at Ginny and says, in English, "You not go."

Then she turns around and marches back out of the room.

So, she's staying. She's staying not one but two extra weeks. "Just take the same flight home that I'm taking," Adrian says. So she does. LX 2251, BUD to JFK, connecting in Zurich, departing at 9:40 a.m. She has no idea if it's a good or bad decision. She also doesn't know how she's going to explain this to her mother.

She'll think of something.

A few days later, Eszter proposes they take a trip to a farm owned by friends of theirs, where they collect eggs and fresh honey and wild berries to make into jams.

"They don't even have to be home when we get there," Adrian translates on Eszter's behalf on the drive over. "We're allowed to just waltz onto the farm and pick things as we like."

"Did she seriously just say waltz in Hungarian?"

Adrian smiles. "No. That was some artistic liberty."

"Look at you." Ginny nudges him with her shoulder. "Who's the wordsmith now?"

Laszlo Farms is owned by distant cousins of the Silvas family, a childless couple who devoted their lives to raising crops and tending bees and goats. The farmhouse sits on a remarkably green stretch of land, far different from the cornfield farms of the

Midwest. If anything, the area reminds Ginny of the greenest parts of the Upper Peninsula—the few fields left untouched by corporate farming.

They stop by the farmhouse—a grey stone building with a red roof—to say hello to the Silvas's cousins, a man and woman, probably in their forties, named Áron and Klara. They welcome their visitors with cups of tea and coffee. Klara holds out a jar filled with opaque white liquid and asks Ginny a question in Hungarian. Ginny looks to Adrian for translation.

"Goat's milk," he says. "For your coffee."

"Oh." Ginny smiles and shakes her head. "*Nem, köszönöm.*" *No, thank you.*

Klara doesn't give up. She shakes the bottle, talking excitedly.

"She knows that Americans find it weird to put goat's milk in their coffee," Adrian says. "But says it's delicious. She really wants you to try."

What Ginny can't say is that she didn't refuse the milk because it came from a goat. She refused it because she never takes milk with her tea or coffee. Too many additional calories.

But she doesn't want to be rude, so she holds out her cup and waits while Klara pours in a splash. Then she raises the cup to her lips and takes a sip. "Mmm," she says.

Klara nods with satisfaction, then turns to speak to Eszter and Imre.

The farm itself is magical. Klara leads them out the back door, onto a wide-open field lined with fruit trees and vegetable plants. She points out each species to Ginny, which Adrian translates in her ear: "Sweet corn over there," he whispers. "Apples over there. Green peas and sour cherry in the field opposite." The whisper tickles the back of her neck and makes her shiver.

"Sour cherry!" Ginny perks up. "That's the wine your grandmother makes."

Ginny can't read Adrian's expression. "That's right."

"Can we go over there?"

"Of course."

Adrian tells the others where they're headed, then leads her over to the opposite field.

The sour cherry tree is the most beautiful tree Ginny has ever seen.

The cherries are at peak ripeness. Unlike regular cherries, which are so dark they could be called purple, sour cherries are a vivid red, bright as apples or lipstick or the color you use to draw hearts all over your paper when you're in love. From a distance, they don't even look like fruit; they look, impossibly, like roses that have defied the laws of nature and grown from a tree instead of a bush.

Ginny walks through the field slowly. Every now and then, she reaches out to touch a cherry, rubbing her thumb gently along its smooth skin.

"Want to try one?" Adrian asks.

"Yes, please."

He searches the closest tree until he finds the two brightest, so red they look ready to burst. He places one in her palm and keeps the other for himself.

She stares down at the berry. She doesn't bring it up to her mouth.

"Nervous?" he asks.

She nods.

"Why? Because it's sour?"

"No." She bites her lip. She'd never told him about the fear that clutches her before each meal. The anxiety over what might happen.

"What is it, then?"

"It's just . . ." She inhales and looks up at Adrian, sour cherry still wobbling in her open palm. "The thing about bulimia is . . . it's not just throwing up. You probably already know this, of course. Most people do. But, um . . . it's also about overeating. Bingeing, I mean. Bingeing and purging."

Adrian watches her. His hand closes around the cherry and lowers to his side. "I did know that."

"Yeah?"

"Yeah. I, um . . ." He uses his free hand to scratch the back of his neck. "I've sort of been researching bulimia since the day after the pub crawl."

"You have?"

"Yeah." He laughs nervously. "I don't know if that's weird or anything. But. Yeah. I've learned a lot. Especially about the binge-purge cycle and how one feeds into the other."

"What do you mean?"

"Well, obviously, when you binge, it makes you want to throw up. That's the obvious part of the cycle. The part that people don't often think about is that purging is actually a catalyst for binge-ing, too." As Adrian speaks, he picks up speed, as if he needs to spit all this information out while he still has the nerve. "You throw up all your food before your body gets the chance to absorb the nutrients it needs, so, even though you feel like you just put way too much food into your body, you actually didn't get enough. You're starving. Your body is starving. It thinks you're living through some sort of famine. That food is scarce. So, once you finally go to eat again, even if you have no intention of bingeing, your body will want to. Your body will think, *Oh, you're finally feeding me? Great, then let's stuff as much food as possible into ourselves; Lord only knows when we'll get another chance to eat.*"

Adrian pauses to catch his breath. "Does that make sense?"

Ginny stares down at the bright-red cherry in her palm. "Actually, yeah," she says quietly. "It makes perfect sense."

"But you don't have to stay stuck in the loop forever, Ginny. All the research says that once you start to eat regular intermittent meals and snacks, your body will recalibrate. It won't feel the need to stuff itself every time it eats."

"Well, that's a relief." She casts her eyes down the long line of sour cherry trees. "You know, it's funny, the way you're describing bulimia. How you make it sound like my body is separate from me. That it has instincts of its own that are capable of overriding conscious decisions I think I'm making."

"Does that feel untrue?"

"Quite the opposite. It actually feels like it explains something that has been bothering me since the moment I started bingeing."

"What's that?"

"Whenever I overeat, it doesn't feel like I'm the one deciding to do it. It feels like my body has been taken over by another being—the beast inside me, that's how I think of it—and that being now has total control over my decisions, my actions, the movement of my hands and mouth. I know it's ridiculous, of course. No creature is inhabiting my body. It's just me. I'm weak. I'm a glutton." She sucks air in through her teeth. "But if . . . if you're right . . ."

"You're not weak, Ginny. You're not a glutton." He reaches out and takes the hand dangling at her side. "Your body is just trying to save itself. It's trying to survive."

She nods. Then she nods some more. Then, just as she is about to suggest they leave, Adrian says, "Here," and holds up the sour cherry in his hand.

"What?" she asks.

"I'm going to feed you," he says. "That way, you know you're safe. The beast can't come out if you aren't the one feeding yourself."

She swallows. She nods and opens her mouth. With his right hand holding hers, Adrian uses his left to feed her the sour cherry.

He doesn't let go of her hand. Not as she bites into the cherry and the first rush of tart juice fills her mouth. Not as she yells, "Oh my—" and spits the cherry out. Not even as he doubles over with laughter.

"What the hell was that?" she demands.

"It does have the word *sour* in its name, Gin," Adrian says through laughs.

"Does anyone actually *eat* those?"

"Yes." Adrian uses his free hand to cover his mouth. "But, in all fairness, you normally boil them first to make them sweeter."

She whacks his shoulder as hard as she can, which only makes him laugh more.

"Come on," he says, tugging her back toward the house. "Let's go get you some more goat's milk."

Ginny used to care about calories. She used to count them, each one as precious as gold. She doesn't, anymore. She can't. Not after the bingeing. Not after putting away thousands upon thousands of calories in just one sitting, letting them slide into her body as easily as slipping into a dreamless sleep.

She's been here for a week now. A week of eating her food and keeping it down. There have been a few more binges, too. She doesn't write about them in her journal because she's too embarrassed, even just to tell it to a notebook that no one else is going to read. She manages to keep the food down after she binges, but only by lying in her bed and sobbing her eyes out.

It's a strange feeling, watching your body grow back without your permission.

Her body grows less childlike every day. Her boobs inflate to twin pillows of fat that bounce with every step. Her body—while perhaps only now, at twenty-four years old, filling out into the size

and shape it should have occupied for the previous five years—
feels as if it is growing with a mind of its own. Try as she might to
flatten it back out, to push her curves back where they came from,
her body says no. Her body says, *Let me grow, let me blossom, let
me sag and dimple in the places I desire.*

She hates it.

She hates herself.

She hates this new body in which she lives.

But she refuses to run from it any longer.

Ginny is lying in bed, as usual, staring at the ceiling, when she
starts thinking about *sajtos*.

Sajtos are heavenly little cheese pastries that Eszter makes with
dinner sometimes. Tonight, Ginny ate about three of them—an
eagerness that, if she wasn't mistaken, actually made Eszter smile.
Or, if not smile, at least look minutely less disgruntled than normal. After dinner, she tried not to think any more about the pastries.

Thus began the typical nighttime war in her head: to eat or not
to eat.

The thing is—if Ginny eats one *sajto*, she'll probably eat four or
five. And then she'll want to throw up. She always wants to throw
up. And at night, when everyone else is asleep, the temptation is
even more potent.

She can't help but think of Adrian. Of his words in the cherry
tree field, about the body having instincts of its own. She can't
help but wonder if the war taking place inside her at that very moment is really a war of the body versus mind. The need for food
versus the learned desire for thinness. She thinks it might be.

I should start doing my own research on bulimia, she thinks. *It
might be good for me.*

She used to be in denial about her disease. That's the first stage, right? Denial. Except, she's fairly certain that denial is the first stage of grief, and she doesn't know what she's grieving.

That night, Ginny can't sleep. She paces around her room, trying not to go out into the kitchen to get more *sajtos*. Then, when that doesn't work, she leaves her bedroom and just stands beside the kitchen island, telling herself she won't open the refrigerator. But the desire to open the refrigerator is so overwhelming that she has to do something else, anything else.

So, she does the first thing she thinks of: she turns around and walks up the staircase.

Creeps is more like it. She assumes Eszter sleeps with one eye and one ear open.

When she reaches the top-floor landing, she glances between the doors. She has never been to Adrian's room before, but she goes inside his grandparents' for her daily shower. The door furthest to the left, then.

She turns the handle and cracks it open, not bothering to knock. If Adrian is already asleep, she doesn't want to wake him. And if he's changing—well, it's nothing she hasn't seen before.

His lights are off. Asleep, then. She starts to shut the door, but Adrian rolls over, squinting through the moonlight. "Ginny?"

"Yeah. Sorry. It's me." She backs away from the door. "I didn't mean to wake you. I'll go."

"No, it's fine." He sits up in bed. "What's up?"

"Oh. Just." She steps inside and closes the door behind her. "Can I maybe . . . lie down with you?"

"Of course." He scoots over in bed, pulling down the comforter to let her crawl inside. It's warm but not hot beside him, as if his body barely gives off any heat at all. She lays her head on the pillow, facing the white-painted ceiling, where plastic glow-in-the-dark stars shine dimly.

"Imre put them up when I was a kid," Adrian whispers. "Back then, I wanted to be an astronaut." He pauses. "Or a movie star. Either way."

"You could easily be a movie star."

"But not an astronaut? You wound me, Ginny."

She laughs. "I just mean that you're handsome enough for it."

"Hmm."

They lie there quietly for a few minutes.

"Adrian," she says finally. "Do you think I'm fat now?"

"What?" His head turns on the pillow. "What are you talking about?"

"The weight. I've been gaining weight, obviously. I mean, I wasn't keeping my food down before, but I am now, so . . ."

"So, you're gaining weight. You're *supposed* to gain weight. But from what I've seen, you've barely gained any at all."

"That's not true." She starts to get frustrated. "Really. I'm not crazy. I can prove it to you." She reaches down and takes his hand. "You and I, we've been together before. You've seen my breasts. You've felt them, too." She places his hand atop her right breast, over her T-shirt. "See? It's bigger. *Much* bigger."

Adrian doesn't move his hand. He doesn't seem certain of what he's supposed to do. "I don't—"

"Look." She moves his hand down and slips it underneath her T-shirt, sliding his fingers up her stomach until his palm rests flat atop her bare breast. "There. Can you feel it now?"

Adrian doesn't answer. He seems to have stopped breathing.

"Do you believe me now?" she asks, impatient.

Instead of answering, his palm draws back, just a touch. Just enough to allow his fingers to run light circles around her nipple.

She exhales in surprise.

"Do you like that?" he whispers.

She whimpers quietly in response.

Soft lips press to her collarbone, just above the neck of her T-shirt. "I like it, too," he says against her skin. "I want to feel more of you."

She says, "I'm afraid."

All at once, he pulls back. His eyes, black circles illuminated by the moonlight, are wide with alarm. "Should I stop?"

"No! No. God, no."

Adrian's mouth crooks into a small smile at how fervent her reply is.

"I just mean—I, um. I mean. The last time we were together, I was . . . you know . . ."

"Bulimic."

She nods.

"And you're afraid that I won't like the way that you look now."

She nods again.

"Ginny." Adrian lowers onto one elbow, using the other to lay his palm against her face. "Bulimia is a disease. You were sick. You still are, but you're recovering, and you're doing an amazing job. And if I ever, ever make you feel like you have to go back to your illness to feel attractive," he says, moving his hand down her cheek and cupping her chin with his palm, "I want you to get my grandpa's hunting rifle out of the basement, take me out back, and shoot me." He pauses, eyes searching. "Okay?"

She laughs. Or maybe it's a quiet sob, she doesn't know.

"You don't ever have to be afraid with me."

"Okay," she says.

And then Adrian presses his lips to hers, and whatever she was thinking before sort of melts away because his hands are running down her sides now, slipping under the soft cotton waistband of her shorts.

"The last time we had sex," he asks, "did you come?"

She hesitates. Considers lying. That's what she's always done, right? Lie to preserve the man's feelings, lie so that it can be over when it's gone on too long and it's starting to hurt. But with Adrian . . . she doesn't feel the need to lie. To pretend or put on any kind of a show.

"No," she says.

Adrian leans back. He tilts his head, and for a moment, she thinks he's going to be angry. To demand to know why she lied. Instead, he says, "All right, then. Teach me how."

"To be honest?" she says. "I've never come from regular sex. The kind you see in porn, where the girl is just bobbing up and down on top of the man? It's never worked for me. But I know how to do it to myself. I can teach you that."

He nods. She takes his right hand, the one cradling her ass, and moves it around to lie on top of her pelvis. He presses down lightly, entering her with just the tip of his middle finger, and she lets out a little whimper.

"You're wet," he says.

She nods. Then she lays her hand atop his, matching their fingers to one another. "Okay. Start like this." She presses his fingers, then starts moving them in little circles. His fingers are long and lithe, just like the rest of his body. They pick up her rhythm quickly. She lifts her pelvis upward, already wanting to feel him inside her.

"It's okay," he whispers. "Just relax. What's next?"

She pulls his fingers up, laying them atop the sensitive little bump at the top. She pushes his fingers from side to side, the pressure harder than before, the movement faster. A little groan escapes her mouth.

"Now," she says, breath coming faster, "play with me."

And he does. Or, rather—they do, together, her hand atop his. His touch is light, barely there at all, but it presses against all the right places, sending little shudders up through her stomach. Her breath deepens. She whispers his name, and he makes a noise at the back of his throat. She can't tell who is controlling the movement at this point—whether it's him, or her, or both of them, no distinction at all.

"Adrian," she whispers. "I want to feel you inside me."

"Not yet." He slips one finger down, sliding it over her opening but not quite going inside.

"Fuck." She pulls her hand out of the covers and grips his biceps. "Adrian, please."

"Not yet. I want to get you close."

He keeps working, alternating between rubbing the sensitive spot at the top of her pelvis and playing with the rest, sliding his fingers along its wet surface. She tries to keep her breathing steady, to stifle the moans coming unbidden from her lips, but it's impossible. She has to turn her head, to press her mouth to the fabric of Adrian's shirt. It feels nothing like the sex she had in the past. She isn't putting on a show for Adrian's benefit. In fact, she's trying to control herself, but she can't. Each touch of his fingers sends little sparks through her, and the sparks multiply, and they gather together at her very center, pulsing, tightening, until she knows they've reached their limit.

"Now," she whispers. "Now, Adrian, please."

"Condom." He slips his hand away from her pelvis. She keeps hers there, not wanting to lose all the heat he just created, and within seconds he's back, ripping the wrapper off the condom.

"Let me." She sits up, and he hands her the rubber. She takes him in her hands. Before pressing the rubber atop the head, she pauses to rub her thumb along its top. He shivers. Then she slides the rubber all the way down and lies back against the pillow.

He positions himself above her. She feels the tip of the rubber. He shifts his hips back and forth, teasing himself against the outside. "Like this?"

She groans. "Fuck's sake, Adrian."

He laughs silently. "As you wish." Then he pushes inside her.

It doesn't take long after that; she was so close already. When she comes, she wraps her arms and legs around his torso, pulling him as deeply into herself as she can.

When they're both finished, Adrian rolls off her but keeps one arm around her shoulders. She huddles into his body, laying her head atop his chest.

After a minute, he asks, "Did you come then?"

In response, she just laughs into his chest. He wraps an arm around her back, pulling her in tighter. And even though she can't see his face, she knows he's smiling.

On their walk the next day, Adrian holds Ginny's hand. They take their usual route down the hill, but before they reach the river, he pulls Ginny into a coffee shop. In Hungarian, he asks for two iced Americanos and a chocolate *fánk*—a donut. They wait beside the front window for the barista to call out their order. Adrian holds her hand the whole time. Once, he leans down and kisses her forehead, and it is such a natural gesture that Ginny thinks she might die.

They take their coffees down to the river. They walk and walk, going much farther than usual, as if they never want the walk to end. They walk so far, in fact, that when they finally turn around, Adrian says it will take them an hour to get back. He pulls Ginny into a bike rental shop and tells the owner they will return them first thing tomorrow morning. Then they bike back along the Danube. Ginny's hair whips against her face and the air smells brackish. It's the happiest she can remember being since arriving in Hungary.

When they return home, Ginny FaceTimes her mother from her bedroom. She shows her the bed, the armoire, the colorful houses across the street. Her mom wants to see the rest of the house, too, so she walks her through the kitchen and the living room, then sits down on the couch.

"I thought you were coming home last weekend," her mom says. "Did you extend your trip?"

"Yeah," Ginny says. "It's a long story. I'll explain when I'm home again."

Ginny hasn't told her she's bulimic. She knows that telling your secrets can be therapeutic, can make them feel like less of a burden, but she isn't ready for her secrets to extend beyond the safety of Szentendre just yet.

After a long goodbye, in which her mom asks Ginny twice whether she is eating—to which Ginny can, for the first time in years, honestly reply *yes*—they finally hang up.

Ginny sits on the sofa for a long time, staring out the window at the blue plaster of the house next door. She is thinking about the strangeness of her situation, wondering how she got here. She snaps out of it only when she hears a noise behind her.

She turns to find Imre ambling into the living room. She smiles at him, and he smiles back. She expects him to head straight for his usual armchair. Instead, he walks over to the couch and settles down beside her.

With a little wink, he pulls out his Samsung phone and points at its screen. He opens a translation app and types something in. When he turns the phone around to face Ginny, he looks rather proud of himself. She grins at him, giving him the thumbs-up. Then she squints at the screen.

He has never brought a girl home before.

Her eyes widen. She takes out her own phone and types hastily: *Oh, I'm not his girlfriend.*

When Imre looks at the screen, he clucks. He types into his Samsung: *Titles are meaningless. Love is what matters.*

Then, without giving her a chance to argue, he tucks his phone back into his pocket, pats her shoulder once, stands up, and walks away.

Ginny makes it seventeen days without vomiting. Not long ago, that was unthinkable. Not long ago, she was shoveling candy into her mouth with all the joy and satisfaction of a starving zombie, then running up to her bedroom and puking it all back up.

Recovery is not fun. It is not relaxing. It is to feel consistently like you are three breaths away from losing your mind.

But she's trying.

The first time she thinks it is on their walk.

They go up that day instead of down. Adrian wants to take her to Kada csúcs, a lookout that's a short hike up the hill. They load sandwiches and potato chips into a backpack that Adrian carries, and Ginny takes pictures of the wildlife they pass along the way: purple flowers, yellow rosebuds, a stream carrying just a trickle of water.

Kada csúcs itself isn't much to see: a small clearing with one bench, barely large enough to hold both Adrian and Ginny. They have to balance their sandwiches on their legs, prop the potato chips up against the bench.

But none of that matters because the view from Kada csúcs is the second most spectacular Ginny had seen in Hungary, surpassed only by Buda Castle. It feels as if she can see the entire countryside: undulating waves of red rooftops, long green stretches of farmland, the spires of church towers, the winding Danube.

Ginny is picky about food. Almost everyone with an eating disorder is. They have preferences, rituals, safe foods, unsafe foods. The rules and regulations are part of what keeps them in their disorder. For example, Ginny never eats the crusts on her sandwiches. She doesn't like them. Today, she peels them off before even starting to eat. On the one hand, it's fine, because she doesn't like how they taste. But in the back of her mind, she also knows that it's an excuse. A way to cut out calories in a manner that doesn't look suspicious.

Adrian doesn't fall for it. When he looks down at the foil on her lap and sees a pile of jagged crusts, he says nothing, just reaches over and picks them up, dropping them onto his lap. Then he rips off a crust-less slice of his own sandwich and places it before her. No questions. No reprimands. A simple act ensuring she eats a full meal, no cheating.

God help me, she thinks as she looks at that slice of sandwich. *I think I'm falling for him.*

She keeps her face very still, as blank as she can, nodding at all the right parts in his story. When he finishes talking, he smiles expectantly. She opens her mouth and laughs, even though she doesn't know if he just told a joke. She needs to do something, anything, to smother the words echoing inside her head.

She knows, then, that it's true. She *is* falling for him. No—if she's honest, she fell for him long before that. She fell for him a year and a half ago, on the night he held her in his bed for the first time. All the bullshit with Finch—the crying, the drama, the addictive back-and-forth—that was all a distraction. A lid to cover up the truth.

But how can I know? she wonders. *Two weeks ago, I believed I was in love with Finch. How can I possibly trust that what I feel for Adrian is real?*

The answer is that she can't. No one can. You can only follow what *feels* like the truth of your emotions, trusting that, eventually, the rest will become clear.

* * *

Two nights later, she accidentally falls asleep in Adrian's room. By the time they wake up, it's already 8 a.m. the next day, well past the time his grandparents normally wake up. When they register the sun streaming through the blinds, they look at each other with wide, panicked eyes.

"Shit." Ginny scrambles out of bed, pulling on her pajama shorts. "Shit, shit, shit." She turns around and points at Adrian, who hasn't moved. "Okay. I go out first. God willing, they're out for a walk or something. If not, if they're already in the kitchen, I'll take down a towel and say I was in the shower."

"But your hair is dry."

She waves an impatient hand. "I'll figure it out."

When she cracks open the door and shimmies outside, she finds no one on the landing. She sighs in relief and shuts Adrian's door.

Then, just as she turns around, the door to Adrian's grandparents' room opens.

Out walks Imre.

They both freeze. For a moment, they just stare at each other, his hand on one doorknob, hers on another. He takes in her messy hair, her wrinkled pajamas. Her back seizes up. She waits for his reprimand. For him to call her a trollop and tell her to get out of their house this instant.

Instead, without a word, his face stretches into a grin. He winks and walks down the stairs.

I've been researching my disease. Did you know that throwing up isn't the only way to purge? Some abuse laxatives instead, draining themselves of food before it can be absorbed into the body. Still others have the "nonpurging" subtype of bulimia,

*where they fast or overexercise to rid themselves of excess
calories.*

I found this on WebMD:

> "In bulimia, also called bulimia nervosa, you usually
> binge and purge in secret. You feel disgusted and
> ashamed when you binge and relieved once you purge."

*I must have reread that paragraph five or six times. It felt
so true, my eyes welled up.*

*I think I will never be cured. I think I will always feel dis-
gusted and ashamed about myself, regardless of whether I'm
bingeing or purging or just sitting on the couch, existing.*

Ginny loses track of how many days she's spent at Eszter and
Imre's house.

Today, they're going to Jozsef's house. "He has a pool," Adrian
says.

"That sounds nice," Ginny says.

She's lying. With every day that passes, she is utterly convinced
that Adrian will wake up, take one look at her, and decide that
this is it. This is the day that she's gained too much. That her arms
have grown too thick, her face too wide. How could he possibly be
attracted to her when she's no longer the pin-thin girl he wanted
to fuck in the first place?

It hasn't happened. Not yet.

But the idea of him seeing her in a bikini is so terrifying she
can hardly breathe.

Jozsef is a delight. He mixes Ginny and Adrian drinks and puts
out snacks like they're a normal bunch of adults without any eating disorders between them. Ginny hasn't drunk anything since

that night, so she sips hesitantly at the gin cocktail he hands her, which comes in a green plastic glass with a pineapple spear.

Adrian sits on the side of the pool. He wears dark blue trunks with little white palm trees. The shorts are a normal length, but on his long vine of a body, they look too small. His hair is damp and curly from the water. Stubble peppers his chin. It is in that moment, as Ginny paddles slowly through the pool, that she first thinks the words in their entirety:

I love you.

As soon as the thought occurs to her, she wants to take it back. She wants to wipe it from the fabric of her mind. But something is building inside her. A tight, strangling feeling, like a belt wrapped around her chest. She watches Adrian laugh with Jozsef, concentrating on the soft pink skin of his lips. It hurts to look at him, but it would hurt more if he wasn't there at all.

Is this what love feels like? Is it just pain and confusion? Ginny cannot fathom why people actively seek this feeling out.

Does he love her, too? She can't tell. Really, she can't. She sometimes thinks that Adrian has entire conversations with her that take place only inside his head. At times, he'll reference a subject about which they have never spoken. Mention it in passing, as if it's a well-established idea between the two of them when in reality, she has no idea what he's talking about.

It's almost as if he believes she is capable of reading his mind.

Here's how love works: first, you think it. You are staring at someone, and the words pop into your head unbidden. I love you. You cover them up. You try not to think about them again.

But you do, of course. You think of them the next time you see that person. And the next. And the next. The I love you's stack one atop the other, building until they take up all the available space inside your head. Soon enough, you have no choice. Soon, I love you *will come spilling out, whether you like it or not.*

Tonight is Ginny's last night in Budapest. She has to tell him, she decides. It's now or never.

She doesn't want to do it when they're in bed together; it's too much of a cliché. Plus, it didn't work out well the last time she tried to have a serious conversation with him in bed. So, she decides to do it after dinner, when his grandparents go for their evening walk.

She's fucking scared. But she thinks he feels the same way that she does.

She thinks everything is going to be okay.

~~Well. That was~~
~~I don't~~

Here's how it happened:

She's sitting on the couch. Eszter and Imre are out for their walk. Adrian has his head stuck behind the flat-screen TV that was just delivered to the house, something fancy that would allow his grandparents to access Disney+. He's been at it for a half hour, while Ginny pretends to read the only English book in the house: an early edition Hardy Boys mystery. In reality, she's just running her eyes over the lines, planning a speech in her head, taking in absolutely nothing.

"Adrian," she finally blurts out. Then she squeezes her eyes shut.

"Yes?" he says, head still behind the TV.

"Can I—talk to you for a second?"

"Of course." He stoops over, extricating himself from a tangle of wires. "What's up?" He walks over and sits next to her on the couch. "Is everything okay?"

"Yes. Everything is—yes. I'm good. I'm great, actually."

He tilts his head, eyebrows furrowed. "Okay."

"I wanted to say . . ." She looks down at her hands, which are twisted into a knot atop the Hardy Boys book. "I will never be able to thank you for what you did these last few weeks. I can't—I don't even know what to say."

"Ginny." He shakes his head. "You don't have to say anything. You're my friend. I know you would have done the same for me."

You're my friend. Is that what she is? Is that what she wants to be?

She already knows the answer to the second question.

"I just—" She inhales and exhales. Fiddles with the book's spine. "God, I'm nervous."

"Nervous?" Adrian leans forward, concerned. "About going back to New York?"

She almost laughs. "No, Adrian. Not that."

"What, then?"

"I'm nervous because—" Inhale. Exhale. "I don't know. I don't really know how to describe what's happened between us the last two weeks."

"Ah. That."

"Yes. That."

"Well." Adrian shifts on the couch, turning to face her. "You want to talk about it, then?"

"I do. The thing is—" She clears her throat. "My time here should have been hell. And in some ways, it has been. I've been miserable. I've hated myself. I've cried more than I can remember crying in my entire life."

Adrian's face kind of crumples then, but Ginny keeps talking because she doesn't want to see any pity in his eyes. She just needs to say what she needs to say.

"But in other ways, my time here has been fucking magical. You and Eszter and Imre—you've taken such good care of me. You made me feel like I wasn't a burden, like I genuinely belonged here. And I feel like I *know* Szentendre now. Like it's some kind of second home." She takes a breath then. Because this part—this is the part she's afraid to say. "You took me in. You shared your home with me. You fed me. You—you saved me. I was—" Her voice cracks a little there. "I was killing myself, Adrian. Even if I didn't know it. I was dying. And I couldn't—I couldn't save myself."

"Ginny—"

"No. I'm not done." She shakes her head. "I couldn't save myself. But you did, Adrian. You picked me up and you put me back together." She swallows. "And I will always, always, always be in your debt."

Adrian is the one shaking his head now. "You don't owe me a damn thing. Don't you see that? I did this because I wanted to. Because I care about you." He reaches down and takes her hand. "You're so afraid of being a burden. I have no doubt that that's one of the reasons this disease has kept its hold over you for so long. Because you're too afraid to ask for help. But the people who care about you—me, Clay, Tristan, your brothers, your sister, your parents, all of us—we want to help you. It's no burden to us. And if it is, then we don't deserve you."

He looks away. She thinks, for one crazy moment, that he's going to start crying. Instead, he blinks once, then looks back.

"You're one of the best people I know, Ginny. You're like—you're like sunshine. I'm just grateful that I know you at all."

She's breathing deeply then, her chest heaving up and down. They stare right at each other, his dark eyes wide open and unguarded in a way she's never seen. She thinks, *He looks fucking beautiful.*

She wants to say that. She wants to tell him that *he* is the one who is sunshine. That he seeped warmth into her at a time when she couldn't feel anything at all.

She tries to say that. She does. But the words in her head—the ones that had been growing all week, stacking one atop the other, filling every corner of her mind—they choose that moment to reach their tipping point. They choose that moment to come spilling out.

She can't breathe. She can't think.

This feels nothing like the confession she made to Finch on a park bench. There's no ulterior motive behind it, no last-ditch desperation, no attempt to bend the will of another man, to force him to choose her over someone else. She just needs to tell him. She needs to tell him now, or she never will.

"I love you," she says.

"You—" His eyes widen. "What?"

"I love you," she says, her voice rising in volume. "I fucking love you, Adrian, goddammit. And I'm tired of hiding it."

Silence.

The longest silence of her life.

His eyes rove her face. They seem to be looking for something. Or maybe they're just taking in as much information as possible because his thoughts seem to move rapidly, as rapidly as the darting of his pupils—from her nose to her chin to her forehead to the shape of her lips. He's weighing all the options. She can see it plain as day: he's not thinking with his heart; he's thinking with his head.

She knows what his answer will be before he says it.

His face crumples.

And that's when she starts to cry.

~~Sorry. I don't know how to~~
~~I'm finding it hard to~~
Let me just record what I can.

After Adrian didn't tell me he loved me, I sort of blacked out. I don't remember everything about the conversation afterward. I know I was sobbing—and not the cute kind of crying. The gross kind, where snot dribbles down your face and your eyes hurt afterward.

When I black back in, I remember him saying:

"Not you. Nothing to do with you. It's all me. I'm the one who's fucked up."

I didn't reply. I just sobbed into my open palm.

"I'm the one who has never held down a serious relationship. You're the closest I've ever come. This here, it's the closest I've ever come."

"You don't love me back."

"Ginny, I—"

"It's the weight, isn't it? All the weight I've gained? Fuck. I knew it."

"No, Ginny, it's not that at all. It's just—this was just—I don't know what this was."

"You don't know what this was," I repeated.

"That's not what I meant. When I meant was—I don't know. I don't know what I want. I care for you so much—more than you could ever know—but I don't . . . I don't know if this will last forever. If our relationship would last forever. If I knew that it would, I would be all in, but we're so young still, and . . ."

"Together forever?" I shook my head. "Together forever? That's a fantasy, Adrian. You can't know that anything will last forever. Not the job you take, or the person you date, or even the lives of the people you love. Don't you see that?"

"I don't—"

"That's life, Adrian. Everything is a calculated risk. Everything is partly chance. You can never have all the information. That's life."

He fell silent, eyes on his lap.

"Just say it."

He looked up. "Say what?"

"Say you don't like me. Say we'll never be together."

"I don't— God, I don't know about never. *I just know that, right now, I don't know how to be in a relationship. I know it's fucked up. I know that I'm* fucked up. *But I've always been like this, Gin. For as long as I can remember. And I wish . . . God, I wish . . ."*

I covered my mouth with my hand again. "I feel like there's a hole in my chest."

"I'm so sorry, Ginny."

"I don't want you to be sorry. I want you to love me back." *I sobbed, the sound rippling up my chest. I leaned into his chest, soaking his shirt. He let me. He put his arm over my shoulder, pulling me in close.*

"I'm so, so sorry," he whispered again.

I cried for a long time. I can't even say how long. When I finished, when the tears subsided just enough, I looked up and met his eyes. I needed to hear it. I needed to know for sure. "No part of you—none at all—wants to try? To even try *a relationship?"*

He was silent for a long time, eyes at the foot of the couch.

"Ginny . . ." he said finally.

I didn't think the hole in my chest could split open any wider.

He says he tried. She says he didn't even begin.

She says her heart holds so much more. He says that's all he can give.

He can't fix himself. She can't take her love away.

They both wish they could.

Ginny wants to throw up so badly. She wants to stuff herself with every last bag of potato chips in that kitchen, feel fucking awful about herself afterward, then throw it all up. What's the harm in doing that, anyway? It's not like anyone cares about her or finds her attractive.

She knew Adrian was going to stop liking her. Did she not guess it? Did she not know from the start?

Look at her now.

Pathetic.

She's going to do it. She's going to binge. She waits until she hears Adrian climb the stairs to his room, then grabs every snack she can find in the kitchen, intending to carry them back to her bedroom. Who cares if they figure it out tomorrow? By then, she'll be gone.

But when she turns around, she finds herself face-to-face with Eszter.

Eszter stares at Ginny. Takes in her puffy eyes. Her red cheeks. The mountain of food in her arms, colorful and egregious. She doesn't say anything. Doesn't even frown. And for some reason, that blankness, that total lack of judgment—it does Ginny in. Her face crumples. Her arms give out. The food falls to the floor and rolls out in all different directions. She starts to bend over, to pick everything back up, but Eszter stops her with her small, strong hands.

"Imre," she calls over her shoulder, never taking her eyes off Ginny.

"*Igen?*" he calls back.

She yells instructions to him in Hungarian. Then she uses both hands to lift Ginny's shoulders back to vertical and guide her over to her bedroom. She follows Ginny inside, closing the door behind them. She sits on the bed, pulls Ginny into her side, and, for the next thirty minutes, lets her cry as hard as she needs. As hard as she can. She wails against Eszter. Every so often, Eszter rubs Ginny's back and murmurs soothing words she can't understand.

When Ginny is done crying, Eszter pulls back the sheets and helps her into bed. Ginny lies down, helpless to protest, body limp like a caterpillar. Eszter tucks the quilt around her. Sleep closes in as soon as she shuts the door.

I'm on the plane now. Adrian and I had the most awkward ride to the airport in all of history. I didn't know whether to cry or avoid looking at him or thank him for everything he's done for me. I ended up kind of doing all three.

Imre and Eszter took my tears in stride. When we reached the airport, I hugged them both, starting with Imre, and said, "Thank you so much. Köszönöm. Köszönöm. I can never repay you." Imre pulled me in under his arm and said "Brave girl" over and over again, which only made me cry harder.

Then I hugged Eszter. She didn't smile at me, didn't acknowledge any of the tenderness that had passed between us the night before. But when my head was bent down next to hers, she pressed her lips to my ear and whispered two sentences, both in English:

"Do not give up on him," she said. "He did not give up on you."

PART V

When Adrian gets back to his studio in New York, he drops his bags onto the floor and stares out the window at the street below. There are no colorful houses. There are no cobble-stoned streets. There is no girl in the bedroom below, waiting to go for their daily walk.

What do you do when the person you love cannot love you back?

The first thing Ginny does is cry. A lot. On the plane. On the cab ride home, after keeping fifty feet from Adrian at the baggage carousel. All the way back to Manhattan. All the way up the stairs to her apartment.

If nothing else, the journey home gave Ginny time to think. To reflect. When she first woke up in Szentendre, she was afraid to recover. She feared that she would gain mountains of weight, would explode, would become something that no man could ever desire. Not Finch, not Adrian. No one.

But she did it anyway. She did it because Adrian and Eszter and Imre wanted her to. She did it because they wouldn't allow her to do anything else.

But it doesn't have to be that way. Ginny sees that now. She spent so long being afraid that men wouldn't be interested in her because of the shape of her body; she didn't realize, back then, that the size of her body would make no difference. Adrian did not want her at her skinniest, and he does not want her in whatever shape she is now.

So, why should he get to decide?

Why should she let someone else's opinion of her decide whether or not she is allowed to recover? Why should she let anything external decide? Why not recover for her *own* sake? Why not recover because she is a human being, and all human beings deserve food?

Why not?

As she climbs the four flights of stairs up to their apartment, she makes a promise to herself: she would do it. She would feed herself. Not because Adrian or Eszter or anyone else wants her to, but because she deserves it. Because she deserves to be fed, to be nourished, to be cared for and watched after, all by virtue of being a human being.

All by virtue of being alive.

Clay and Tristan come home from work to find her sitting on the couch, arms wrapped around her legs, tears streaking her face. They hurry over and gather her into their arms.

"It's okay," Clay whispers, smoothing back her hair. "It's okay. He's not here."

Finch. They think she's upset about Finch.

Oh, how much three weeks can change.

She realizes, then, how little she has actually shared with her best friends. How fully she shut them out, all for the sake of maintaining a disease that was killing her and a relationship that was no better. That ends now, she decides. She will tell them everything.

So she does.

The following Monday, Adrian returns to the Disney office. He greets his coworkers, waving to their familiar faces seated behind their familiar open-concept desks. He chats with the members of his team about his time in Hungary.

"Was it amazing?" everyone asks. "Being home again?"

"It was," he says. "It really was."

The Disney office is one of his favorite places in the city. It's here that he dragged himself out of the darkness that overtook him when he worked at Goldman. It's here that he helped build a product that would bring TV and movies to his grandparents and friends for years to come. It's here that, before his vacation, he always felt the most like himself.

Why, then, as he sits at his desk, does he feel like he's missing something essential, like a piece of his body has been sawed clean away?

Ginny isn't expecting her. When the knock comes, she looks at the boys, wondering if they invited someone over. "Guys?" she asks.

No one answers. No one even looks at her.

"Guys," she says again. "Why are you—"

"Virginia Murphy," comes a high-pitched female voice from out in the hallway. "Open this damn door before I kick it in myself."

Ginny's eyes narrow as she looks at the boys. "You didn't."

"It was Clay's idea," Tristan says.

"Traitor," mutters Clay.

"*Virginia Murphy*," the voice calls again.

Ginny sighs, easing herself out of the chair. She walks along the short hallway and places a hand on the doorknob. Glances once over her shoulder. Then she twists the knob and opens the door.

"Who the fuck," Heather says before she even makes it through the door, "gave you the right to exclude me from helping my little sister recover from fucking *bulimia*?"

She pushes past Ginny, dragging her suitcases down the hall-way. Even in the dim light Ginny can tell that Heather brought at least two—unsurprising, as her sister never travels with just one suitcase. "One for shoes," she always says, "and one for everything else."

"I knew it," Heather says as she stomps into the apartment. "I knew something was up. You were ignoring all my calls, and being cagey when I asked how your eating was going, and God only *knows* how many articles I've panic read about how anorexia can easily turn into its sister disease, and . . ."

When she reaches the living room, she stops, her suitcases rolling to a halt at either side. She takes in the scene before her: Tristan in the armchair, Clay on the couch, and boxes of takeout scattered on the coffee table. She's just deplaned after a five-hour flight from Los Angeles, but she looks perfect. Her skin is bronzed, her hair long and brushed, curly extensions clipped into place. She wears leggings and a cropped jacket that says GUCCI across the front.

Ginny's hair is in a bun. She wears an oversize Mackinac Island sweatshirt and thick, fuzzy socks. It's the same look she's worn for the past twenty-four hours, one that requires zero effort and hides all the growing parts of her body, the parts that make her wish she owned a vacuum for her insides. Around the boys, she never once felt insecure about how sloppy she looked.

But now?

It's not just the clothing. It's her face, too. The sweatshirt might hide her swelling arms and stomach and thighs, but it does nothing to obscure the ever-rounding edges of her face, her mushy chin, which doubles so easily now it almost seems to be laughing at her.

Heather spins around and zeroes in on her little sister. Her eyes travel the length of Ginny's body.

As she stares, her face screws up into an expression Ginny has never seen before. At the peak of her anorexia and bulimia, Ginny was the same size as Heather. Maybe even smaller. But there's no doubt in Ginny's mind—her sister can see how much weight she's gained. She can see how large she is now. How weak. How ugly. Heather is judging Ginny. Thinking, *Thank God I don't look like that.* It's obvious. It's written all over her face.

Heather lets go of her bags. She takes a step toward Ginny.

Another. "Oh, little sister," she says, face twisting even further. "You look—"

Ginny inhales, pinching the soft skin of her thigh, waiting for her sister to say it.

"God," Heather says, shaking her head. "You look *healthy.*"

Then she bends over and scoops Ginny up into a hug so tight it squeezes her very insides.

"Right." After forcing the boys to clear out of the apartment and "look at overpriced sneakers or whatever you do for fun, I don't care," Heather settles onto the sofa. "Tell me everything."

Cautiously, Ginny sits beside her. "Everything about what?"

"Everything about everything." Just as soon as she sat, she's up, heading to the coffee machine to put a pot on. "You've been ignoring my calls for months, Gin. Now I know why; you were puking your guts up and knew I'd sniff it out, even from across the country." She opens the cabinets one by one, in search of filters and grounds. "I always do."

"Right," Ginny says.

Heather opens the last cabinet to the left, where she finds both a bag of Peet's and a stack of filters. She takes out both. "But none of that explains how you got *here,* stuffed into a tiny apartment with two dudes doing their best to simulate outpatient therapy."

"Yeah. Um." Ginny looks down at her fingers, which are folded up into the creases of a blanket, the soft fabric spilling up through her knuckles. "It's just temporary. I'm taking a week to pack my stuff, tie up loose ends at work, and find a good in-patient program in Michigan. Mom and Dad want me to be close by while I recover."

"Damn straight." Heather pours a steady stream of grounds into the coffeepot. "Mom said you didn't want her and Dad here while you packed up. Just your roommates. Which is killing her, by the way. You owe her a FaceTime." She slams the lid on the coffeepot shut and turns to face Ginny, arms crossed. She glares down at her little sister. Behind, the coffeepot starts to bubble. She glares for so long that Ginny has to look down at her hands.

"I didn't . . ." Ginny stops, then exhales. "I didn't want . . ."

Heather's voice softens. "Gin," she says. "Look at me."

She does.

Quietly, Heather asks, "Why didn't you tell me?"

"I—" Ginny squeezes a bundle of blanket in one fist. "It's hard to explain."

Heather walks over to the couch and sits. "Just try."

"It's just—" Ginny cobbles the words together, searching for the right way to say it. "It's a weird thing, having a sister. Genetically speaking, they're the closest thing that exists to another version of yourself. So, if you're vastly different from your older sister—if she's effortlessly beautiful and thin and feminine and confident and successful, and none of those things come easily to you . . ."

Heather lays a hand on Ginny's knee.

"Hold on. I'm not done." Ginny inhales. "I'm not trying to blame my eating disorder on you. Obviously, it has far more to do with my own psychology than anything else. I just—I don't know. When your older sister is already the perfect version of what you could have been, how can you explain to her that you've spent seven years killing yourself to attain that same perfection? It's completely insane."

"Ginny." Heather moves her hand to take Ginny's. "It *is* insane. You think I'm perfect? Jesus Christ, do you not remember all the fits I threw as a child? Do you not remember the times I ran away, the screaming fights between me and Mom, or me and Dad, or me and anyone, for that matter?" She leans in, squeezing Ginny's hand. "*You* were the perfect one. You were the one who followed all the rules, and did all the homework, and got into fucking *Harvard*, for Christ's sake."

"Yes, but—"

"Did you ever stop to think," Heather interrupts, tilting her head, "that *I* might be the one who's envious of *you*?"

Ginny opens her mouth. She looks down at their intertwined hands, both pale and slim, though she could have sworn that her fingers were thickening by the day. "No."

"Then you're even crazier than I thought, Sis." Heather lifts their hands and shakes them in the air. "Do you have any idea how perfect your life looks from the outside? The Harvard degree, the fancy job—"

"Which I haven't been to in three weeks."

"The unhealthily intelligent brain, the perfect skin, the face that could make men cry?"

"Now you're just being obnoxious."

"I'm serious. And your relationship with our brothers? How close you four have always been? Didn't you ever think that I might be envious of that?"

Ginny's mouth opens and closes. She stares at her sister. Her impervious big sister, who has never felt insecure or confused about anything in her life.

Or so Ginny thought.

Heather tilts her head. "That's it, then? That's the only reason you didn't tell me about your bulimia?"

"Well, that," says Ginny, "and the fact that I was terrified you would fly straight to New York, duct tape me to the bed, and force-feed me cupcakes."

Heather nods. "Now *there's* that Ivy League intellect at work."

It doesn't take long for Heather to go full business owner on the entire situation.

"First things first," she says, bustling around the living room and tidying up all the snack wrappers the boys left strewn about the floor. "We need to get you into a proper outpatient program while you pack up your life here. I know you leave in less than a week, but there's no sense dawdling. We need your recovery to start *now*." She tosses the wrappers into the trash can. "It can even just be a Zoom thing. I did some reading on the plane, and it sounds like the best practice is to set up weekly meetings with a therapist and a nutritionist, plus maybe group sessions if we can find one in your area. Which, duh, it's New York, there are probably eating disorder support groups on every block."

Ginny follows Heather around the living room, not touching anything or helping in any meaningful way. "But how will I know the right therapist to sign up with?"

"You research and get referrals. Duh. How does one do anything in life?" Heather shakes her head, plucking a pillow off the floor and placing it on the couch. "I swear to God—you Harvard types. All book smarts, absolutely no common sense. Right." She pulls out her phone and opens the Notes application. "Second order of business—your job. You took a leave from Sofra-Moreno, right?"

Ginny nods.

"Good. I know you love your job, but if for whatever reason the corporate tyrants won't give you enough time to adequately recover in treatment, you can always quit. You'll have no problem finding a new one when you get out of treatment. In the interim, I'll update your résumé, just in case."

"You don't have to do that," Ginny says quickly.

"Nonsense." Heather waves a hand. "I need you to focus on recovery and recovery alone. And, of course, when you get out of treatment, we'll need to find you a new place to live—"

"No."

Heather looks up from her phone and raises her eyebrows.

"I don't want to leave New York permanently. I want to move back in with Clay and Tristan when I return."

Heather exhales through her bright red lips. "Fine. But we need to figure something out about this Finch boy. He is bad news, and I don't want you living with a trigger like that."

Finch isn't home. He hasn't been back since Budapest. He has a full month off from med school, so he flew home to propose to Hannah, who said yes, and he's stayed in Cleveland under the guise of getting wedding preparations underway. But she knows better.

"You're right," Ginny says. "I know you're right. But I have a feeling that the problem will resolve itself on its own."

"How so?"

"I heard Clay talking with him on the phone the other night. Finch is moving in with his fiancée. Apparently, she wants to make a go at Broadway—"

Heather snorts. "All my best to her."

"So, when our lease is up, he's going to look for a place in Greenwich Village."

"I see." Heather taps her chin. "Right, then. That's sorted. Hopefully, you won't even have to see him before you leave."

Ginny nudges the bottom of the sofa with her toe. "I don't want to hide from him forever."

"And you won't have to, Ginny." Heather puts one finger under Ginny's chin and lifts her face to look at her. Ginny tries not to think about the soft skin of her neck that Heather must feel right now, the dangling fat. "But you're in a delicate state right now. We need to do everything we can to remove stressors and triggers from your life while you recover, and I'm fairly certain that Finch might be both."

Ginny pulls her sister's hand away from her chin and smiles. "Wow. One plane ride and you're an eating disorder expert."

Heather winks. "How do you think I built my company in less than a year? Now." She spins around and marches toward Ginny's bedroom. "Final order of business."

Ginny follows. "What's that?"

"I'm taking you shopping." Ginny finds Heather's head stuck in her closet, rummaging through the hangers. She pops back out. "Because, honey"—her eyes fall to Ginny's chest—"there is no way those fabulous new tits of yours are going to fit into these anorexic-ass tank tops."

Wednesday, after work, Adrian can't take it any longer. He calls Clay for an update on Ginny's progress. He needs to know if she's okay. He needs to know if she's keeping her food down.

Clay picks up after the second ring. "Hey, man."

"Hey. How is she?"

Clay pauses. "She's doing okay. Her sister flew out here and is basically running all our lives now, which is . . ." He laughs. "An experience. Oh, and Ginny quit her job, too."

"She . . . what?"

"Yeah. I actually think it was the right move." Something *dings* on the other end of the line, as if Clay is heating food up in a microwave. "She has a bit of money saved up, and that job was making her fucking miserable, man. She hasn't been herself in a long time."

"Oh." Adrian had no idea. "That's good, then."

"Yeah."

"Is she eating?"

"She is, actually. And we're helping her research recovery programs. There's one close to where she grew up that's ranked pretty highly. We're thinking she might head there."

The thought of Ginny leaving Manhattan makes Adrian's heart squeeze, though he knows he has no right to feel that way. "Good." He hesitates, then: "I'm guessing she told you what happened with us."

"Yeah," says Clay. "Sounds like things were pretty intense over there."

"They were."

"I get it. And listen, man—I know it's none of my business, but . . ." He hesitates, and Adrian hears the microwave door slam shut. "I don't know. I've seen the two of you together, and"—the sound of plastic ripping in the background—"all I'm trying to say is that if anything is up on your end . . . if there's anything going on in your life that makes you feel like you have to, I don't know . . . push people away? I'm here for you." A clank of ceramic on wood. "That is, if you even need it."

Adrian shifts the phone into his other hand. He looks out the window again, half wishing he'd find his *nagyapa* out in the garden, pulling weeds.

"Thanks, man," he says finally. "I appreciate it. But I'm all good."

He hangs up. Waits to feel something—anxiety, sadness, confusion. Nothing comes.

It's a familiar feeling. Yet another instance in a long line of relationships where he attaches himself to someone, lets *them* attach to him, and then feels nothing when he leaves. It happened with every girl in college. It happened with Ginny. Where does his sadness go? It's like he can't process goodbyes.

Where has that gotten him? Sure, he might have made a girl fall in love with him, but he's good at that, isn't he? And the more unrequited love he collects, the more alone he feels.

He thinks, then, of his conversation with Ginny about trauma. About how trauma occurs when something bad happens to you, but you feel no emotion around it.

Maybe that's where my trauma comes from, he thinks. *That's my story. A long line of unacknowledged goodbyes.*

Every night, after dinner, Ginny, Heather, and the boys watch an episode of *Grey's Anatomy*. They want to keep her busy, to keep her from purging. She knows it. At first, they suggested games, but Ginny found that, after enduring yet another day of being alive, she was too exhausted to pay attention to the cards. So. *Grey's Anatomy* it was.

They made Ginny choose what to watch. She picked *Grey's* at random, hoping the rainy Seattle weather and the simplicity of early 2000's television would put her at ease. Part of her was embarrassed; she couldn't have picked a girlier show, and she assumed the boys would roll their eyes. And they did, at first. But by episode four, the boys were the ones yelling at the TV, Clay throwing popcorn kernels at the screen and saying things like, "How the fuck could Meredith do that to George?"

In her free time, she writes. She doesn't know exactly what she's working toward—a book of essays, or a novel, maybe? It doesn't much matter. She writes not with a project in mind but purely because she has to, because when it's 9 a.m. and she crawls out of bed, looks in the mirror, and loathes every inch of her body, or when it's 3 p.m. and she feels, for no specific reason whatsoever, that she is going to die, writing is her first instinct. It's the only thing she *can* do.

By the time she goes to bed each night, she doesn't even have the energy to hate herself.

I want Adrian so badly it hurts. I crave him the same way I once craved the donuts I was never allowed to eat.

Whenever I remember that he doesn't love me, I press to-gether all five of the fingertips from my right hand, making a cone, and then I grab that cone with my left hand and squeeze as hard as I possibly can.

Everyone says—wait until. Wait until you're secure with yourself, and have yourself figured out, before getting into a serious relationship. But what if this is it? What if I'm always going to be this anxious, this unhappy, for the rest of my fuck-ing life?

He is never going to like you, he is never going to like you, he is never going to like you, he is never going to like you, you are living a fantasy, you are living a fantasy, you are living a fantasy, you are living a fantasy, stop crying.

Ginny opens up Google. Types: **how to stop loving someone**. Stares at the search bar for too long. Deletes the words without searching.

The package arrives on his doorstep five days after he gets home. The return address is Szentendre. He turns it over in his hands, curious. It's heavy. Multiple objects rattle about inside. Did he leave something in Hungary?

He fetches a knife from the kitchen and slices open the packaging. Inside, the first thing he sees is a two-liter Coca-Cola bottle filled with a dark red liquor. He smiles, knowing exactly what it is. He picks it up and sets it on the counter.

Underneath, he finds a thick, leather-bound book with a blank cover. He blinks, trying to place it. He knows he's seen it before.

And then he remembers.

He's back in his grandparents' house, staring from the bottom step of the staircase at Ginny and his *nagyapa*, seated on the couch. There's something on Ginny's lap, something he cannot see. She and his *nagyapa* are smiling at each other like they've been best friends for ages.

That's when he feels it. When his heart does that weird squeezing thing, and he has the abrupt thought that, if anything were to happen to either of the people on that sofa, he would descend into a darkness so black that he would never be able to find his way back out.

He hates the feeling as soon as it hits him. He wants to erase it. He wants to crawl out of his skin and replace it with someone else's body.

Then he walks over and sees what they're looking at. He sees his father. Dozens of versions of him—maybe even hundreds. Photographs he's never seen, never even knew existed. And all thoughts of the previous sensation are quickly wiped from his mind.

Now Adrian reaches down and picks up the photo album from inside the box. He lifts it gingerly as if afraid it might break. When he does, he sees one last item sitting on the cardboard: an envelope with his name on it.

The envelope is green, the same color as his bedroom in Szentendre. His name is written in his *nagyanya*'s familiar scrawl. Adrian stares at the envelope for a long time, the photo album dangling at his side. He stares so long that his eyes start to dry. Then he lays the album back inside the box, over the envelope, opens his closet, and tucks the whole thing into the back, behind his dress shoes.

I don't see how anyone could possibly love me when I look like this. I don't see how anyone could love me, period, riddled as I am with anxiety, obsession, sadness, and these long, rolling hills of fat.

Where do people get self-confidence? Are you born with it? Or is it earned, fought for, won, all part of some fucked-up battle with your own mind?

I am so fat, and everyone else is so thin.

Okay. I'm not actually fat. But there's this selfie I took of Heather and me where my arm and my shoulder and my tits and my face look just . . . round. That's the only way I can say it. I used to be lean and hard. Now I am round and soft. It makes me want to die.

Anxiety is both delicate and all-consuming. It buzzes within Ginny, a tightening of the heart, a breeze in her veins. She didn't hate her body before. That was the whole point of her eating disorder: to keep enough weight off that she didn't have to think about her body one way or another. But she does now. God, does she ever. She cannot believe that this is what she looks like. She cannot believe that this is the way she will look for the rest of her life. It makes her want to restrict, restrict, restrict.

As she recovers from the trauma that is bulimia, she feels her sister return. She sees her beckon with open arms and a blade-thin smile. Anorexia. Beautiful, perfect Anorexia.

How does everyone sit down all day and make it look so easy?

How do they live inside their skin and make it look so easy? Why does Ginny hate herself? Why does she look in the mirror and see only fat, fat, fat, fat?

Two weeks she spent out of control, eating things she didn't want to eat. Four weeks she has watched her body grow, thicken, stretch, and pucker. She doesn't know how to stop it. She repeats over and over that it will be okay, that she will be okay, that there is far more to a person than a size. She pictures her best friends approaching her, telling her they hate their bodies, that they're fat, disgusting, will never be loved. All the things she repeats to herself hour after hour, day after day. She knows what she would say to them. She would tell them not to be ridiculous, that they're beautiful no matter what, that their heart, above all, is why she loves them. And to them? She would mean it. But to herself?

Not a chance.

Every twentysomething has asked herself this question at one point or another: Is this it? Is this all there is to adulthood? Day after day, breakfast after breakfast, job after job. Will I be single forever? Because, goodness—marriage sounds awful, but dying alone sounds worse.

The boys are out drinking. Ginny lies in bed, listening to the water run in the next room.

Her sister takes baths when she's stressed. When she told Ginny that she planned to take one here, Ginny called her "institutionalizably mental," to which Heather responded, "Pot, kettle, darling."

"But this is an *apartment in Manhattan*," Ginny said. "You have no idea what's gone on in that bathtub before."

"I'll spray it down with Lysol."

* * *

After ten minutes, the water shuts off. Ginny glances at her phone: ten o'clock. She's tired. She needs to brush her teeth, but doesn't want to go into the bathroom while Heather is in there. Which will be ages, knowing her sister.

Eventually, she gives in. She walks into the hallway and squeezes through the bathroom doorway. Heather sits up. Ginny keeps her eyes averted. She walks to the sink and turns on the faucet. She's wearing only a tank top and shorts, so she knows Heather is watching her shoulder blades undulate beneath thickening layers of flesh as she moves.

"Want to get in?" Heather asks.

Ginny turns in surprise. Heather is propped up on her elbows in a foot of water, completely naked, completely unashamed. Normally, Ginny would laugh and tell her not to be a freak. Despite being six years her senior, Heather dresses like a carefree teenager, in crop tops, teeny dresses, and, of course, bikinis.

Ginny stares at her sister for a long time. Then she wordlessly grabs either side of her tank top and pulls it over her head. Goose bumps rise on her skin.

The water burns as she slides down the side of the tub. She lowers her head onto the porcelain next to Heather's feet. Their figures, which began in—and were shaped by—the same body of water, form an inverted reflection. Heather's body all bone, Ginny's all flesh. The burning heat turns slowly to warmth. Ginny huddles as much of her body underwater as possible. As the goose bumps slowly dissolve, she realizes that she hasn't been properly warm in almost seven years.

Since the day Heather arrived, Ginny has been thinking about their relationship. About their past, their differences. In their family, along with Male and Female, the five children were further divided into Problems and Not-Problems. Heather and Ginny sat on opposite sides of that line. Ginny, the anxious ten-year-old desperate to please everyone within a hundred-foot radius. Heather, the angry sixteen-year-old who could sweep into the room and not only take it over but become the room itself.

"Heather knows what Heather wants," said every member of the family, raising their eyes in condescension. "And she's not afraid to scream."

Ultimately Ginny sided with the boys, and Heather sided with herself, a move that at the time made her look selfish and petty. It's only now that Ginny sees her choice for what it was: an act of bravery. The courage to be a woman in a family of men.

Friday morning, Adrian's boss, Lawrence, puts time on Adrian's calendar. **ADRIAN/LAWRENCE 1:1**, the meeting subject reads. **10 a.m.–10:30 a.m.**

At 10 a.m., Adrian pokes his head through the doorway of the conference room indicated in the meeting invitation. Lawrence looks up from his laptop, where he's drafting an email. He pulls out an empty rolling chair and gestures for Adrian to sit.

"Adrian," he says, shutting his laptop halfway and crossing his arms. "You've been with us for just over a year now."

"Yes, sir."

"I don't know how many times I'll have to tell you to call me Lawrence before it finally sticks." He taps the table twice. "That aside—in just a year, you've established yourself on your team and played a central role in the launch of a product key to our overseas strategy."

"That's true, sir."

"It's impressive stuff, Silvas. Unusual for someone of your level." He pauses. "Which is why you're no longer going to work on that level."

Adrian leans forward, hands flat on his knees. "Sir?"

"I'm promoting you. Effective immediately. If you're to lead content strategy for Disney+ in Eastern Europe, I want your title to reflect your responsibility."

"I don't—" Adrian sits back in the rolling chair. He blinks up at the monitor on the wall. "Lead strategy? As in—with my own team?"

"That's right. You'll have two direct reports, whom I will help you choose from within the organization. Or from outside, if we can't find the right talent internally."

"I don't know what to say."

"Say yes." Lawrence thumbs the edge of his laptop screen. "It's obvious to everyone on the team how passionate you are about your job. I want to foster that passion. I want you to have a long, fruitful career at Disney." He smiles. "We're lucky to have you."

"I'm—" Adrian shakes his head. "Thank you, sir."

"Good man." Lawrence reopens his laptop. "Now get out—I have a Serbian streaming crisis to manage."

Adrian grins. "Yes, sir." He stands and walks out of the conference room.

On the way back to his desk, several of his colleagues stop to congratulate him, slapping him on the shoulder and saying it's well deserved. Apparently, everyone knew he was getting promoted except Adrian.

He reaches his desk and sits, stretching his legs out until they almost pop out the other side. He opens his laptop. The welcome screen glows warm and bright.

This is it. This is what he waited for, why he worked his ass off for a year straight. *Lead dissemination strategy.* He would have a real say in what content was brought to countries like Hungary. What kids like himself would watch from the floor of their grandparents' living rooms.

He should be thrilled. He should be high on his own success.

He isn't.

He's plagued by that same feeling that has haunted him since the moment he returned from Budapest—the sensation that he is missing something he cannot put his finger on. A part of him wonders if this is a common feeling. If inexplicable emptiness is just a side effect of being alive.

Another part of him wonders if it has to do with Ginny.

That would be the logical explanation, right? Girl disappears, hole opens in chest. But Adrian has never been like that. He made sure long ago that his own happiness would never rely upon the absence or presence of another human being. He is independent, a fully self-sustaining ecosystem.

And, besides—he knows he made the right decision by breaking things off with Ginny before they ever really got off the ground. She deserves someone who is fully committed to the idea of a relationship. Someone who is unafraid.

By now, Adrian has sat before his laptop for so long that the screen went dark. He shakes the mouse. He enters his password, six letters long, and the welcome screen disappears, revealing a desktop cluttered with work programs: Excel, Outlook, Word, Microsoft Teams. He ignores all these windows, instead opening a browser and, with a quick glance over his shoulder, typing *www.instagram.com*.

When the home page loads, the first thing he sees are all the circles at the top of the screen. Each one is attached to a specific user. Beneath the very first circle is the username @ginmurph. Adrian moves the mouse to hover over the circle. After a few seconds, he clicks it.

A photograph pops up on screen. A screenshot, actually. An airplane ticket with service from JFK to Detroit International Airport. Atop the ticket, Ginny has written with white text: **See ya later NYC**.

Adrian stares at the screenshot for a long time. He holds down with his mouse on the picture to keep it from disappearing. His eyes linger over the time and date: 9 p.m., Friday.

Tonight.

His breathing becomes shallow. The screen blurs slightly before him. He knew this was coming. He didn't know *when*, but still. The idea of Ginny leaving New York should not send him into a panic.

But it does.

Somewhat erratically, Adrian closes the browser and clicks into Excel. He scrolls through the data he's already begun to compile about Disney+ usage in Romania. His eyes skim over the percentages. When he reaches the bottom, his mouse drifts down to hover over the icon for Microsoft Word.

He thinks about Ginny, unemployed and in recovery. He wonders if she's still writing. He wonders if she'll copy any of it over to her computer. If she'll send it out for others to see.

He hopes she will.

Tonight, Ginny flies home. To her Michigan home, anyway.

Her day is busy. There are bags to pack, therapy sessions to attend, Heather and Tristan to keep from tearing each other's heads off. Her day is so busy, in fact, that it isn't until 4 p.m. that she's finally able to open her notebook and complete the writing prompt assigned by her therapist.

Today's prompt: write down a few things you love about your life. The purpose of this one is obvious, she thinks as she clicks open her pen—to remind herself of the happiness that exists outside her eating disorder.

She begins to write.

I love my family. I love my friends. I love this little home, where I live with my friends. I love my little room, big enough only for a bed and a desk and a tiny window. I love our little kitchen and the boxes of cereal pushed up against the wall, and the bathroom whose fan is too loud, and the couch that takes up the entire living room. I am sad. I am always sad. But, sometimes, it's possible to be sad and still be glad you're alive.

An hour later, Ginny walks out of the bathroom holding her toothbrush and a plastic baggie. She starts to call out to Heather. "What time did you say we need to catch the ca—" she starts, but cuts off when she sees her sister standing over her desk, holding her notebook.

"Whoa, whoa, whoa." She walks over and tries to snatch the

notebook out of her sister's hands. "Keep your nose out of my stuff."

It's only then that she sees the expression on Heather's face: shock, verging on horror. Ginny glances down at the page to which the journal is open. It's dated several weeks prior, when she was still in the thick of things back in Szentendre. Ginny stiffens. She can only imagine what her sister was just reading.

"Ginny," she whispers.

Ginny turns around, snapping the journal shut.

"You never said things were that bad."

"Yeah, well." She walks over to her backpack and stuffs the journal inside. "It's not really something you go around advertising, is it?"

Heather doesn't respond, and Ginny busies herself with rearranging books that don't need rearranging. After a moment, Heather walks over and lays a hand over Ginny's, stilling it.

"Gin," she says. "What happened with Adrian?"

Ginny blinks rapidly several times.

"Gin?"

"I—" Her voice is barely a whisper. "He saved my life."

"What?"

"He saved my life." She looks over at her sister. Tears start to well at the corners of her eyes. "I love him. And . . . and he doesn't love me back."

"Oh, Ginny." Heather wraps her arms around Ginny and pulls her into a hug. Her arms are slim and delicate. Her hair smells familiar, the same perfume she's worn since she was sixteen. Ginny doesn't hug her back, just leans into the embrace, letting her face fall onto her sister's shoulder. "He's a fool."

"You're required to say that," Ginny says into her collarbone.

"Maybe. But that doesn't make it untrue."

Ginny hiccups.

"But, hey—you know the good news?"

"What's that?"

"I've figured out your next career."

"What?" Ginny lifts her head and squints. "What do you mean?"

Heather reaches into Ginny's backpack and pulls out the notebook. She shakes it back and forth. "You're going to be a writer."

"That's ridiculous." Ginny reaches for the journal, but Heather moves it behind her back. "Those are just ramblings."

"They're ramblings with a *voice*. I'm serious. I could hear you talking through those pages."

"Having a voice doesn't qualify you to write."

"I disagree."

"Well, you can disagree with whatever you want. It doesn't make you correct."

"Ginny." Heather lays her fists on her hips, the notebook dangling from one side. "Do you remember the journal that you carried with you everywhere when we were growing up? The ugly purple thing with the fuzzy cover?"

"It was *turquoise*." Ginny snatches the journal out of her sister's fist. "And there wasn't just one. There were, like, twenty."

"That's what I mean. Every memory I have of you from that age, your nose is in some kind of notebook. And every time I tried to ask what you were writing, you told me that it was none of my business."

Ginny crosses her arms. "It *was* none of your business."

Heather starts to laugh. "Nothing changes, does it?"

Ginny sticks out her tongue.

"You're talented, Gin. I'm serious. I'm not just saying it because I'm your older sister. I'm saying it because it's true." Heather tilts her head and arches an eyebrow. "In fact, have you *ever* known me to compliment someone when I don't mean it?"

"No." Ginny laughs, wiping her eyes. "You're more of the *so blunt you make them cry* type. It's what makes you a good businesswoman."

Heather grins. "Those fabric vendors had it coming."

"I don't know, Heath." Ginny sighs, sitting on the end of her bed. "I don't have any formal training as a writer. I don't have a giant Instagram following, the way you do. I don't know how to go about getting an agent or an editor. I'm a nobody."

"Everybody starts out as a nobody, Gin. You know how many bikinis I sold in my first month in business?" Heather pauses. "Three. Three bikinis." She looks at Ginny gravely. "And they were all purchased by our mother."

Ginny laughs.

"All I'm saying is that we all start from nothing. And you— you're a Harvard graduate! And you already have half of a memoir written in that thing." She gestures to the journal. "That's hardly nothing."

"I guess."

Heather lays a hand on Ginny's knee. "Just think about it. That's all I'm asking."

"I will. I promise."

Heather smiles, then her eyes flick back to the notebook. She studies it for a long moment, her lips turning steadily downward.

"What is it?" Ginny asks.

Heather's eyes flick up to Ginny's face, then back down to the notebook. Then, without warning, she wraps her arms around Ginny again and pulls her in close.

"You don't have to make yourself suffer anymore, little sister," Heather whispers into her ear. "You're safe, now. You're safe."

After Heather leaves, but before Ginny finishes packing, she re-opens her journal. She flips backward several pages until she finds the entry she's looking for. It's short, only a paragraph or so. She rereads the entry:

> I read today that, when given proper treatment and medication, only 70 percent of women recover fully from bulimia. 70 percent. That might sound like a high number, but that means 30 percent of women who go through treatment—who take all the steps and try to do everything right—never make it to full recovery. That, ten years out, their disease still has a hold over them. The vise grip of temptation, of the release that they know will come from the purge.
>
> Today, I made a vow. I will not be part of that 30 percent. I will not let my disease win. I will take back my own life. I will piece it back together as best I can, tape over the cracks, give it legs and wings. I will learn how to live with the hurt. To carry it within me, to not fear it, to make it my friend.
>
> And I will write. Because on the day I can no longer put pen to paper, I will know the creature has won.

After work, Adrian walks home. It's forty blocks, but he needs the air.

Disney has a casual dress code. Unlike at Goldman, it's perfectly acceptable for Adrian to show up to work in Nikes and a nice T-shirt. He finds himself especially grateful for this policy as he picks up speed, his black joggers far looser and more forgiving than a pair of slacks would be.

He starts on 10th Avenue, flanked by the towering all-glass buildings of Hudson Square. The skyscrapers are so clean and reflective that they seem to blend in with the sky.

All morning and throughout the afternoon, thoughts of Ginny plagued Adrian. He tried to focus on work, on the excitement of his new position. He poured himself a cup of coffee, stuck on his headphones, and did a full sweep of his hard drive, reviewing the many files he'd created over the past year. He was looking for the most important data points, the ones that would help drive his strategy in the year to come.

Normally, that kind of work sucks him right in. Adrian has lost entire days to playing with numbers in Excel. He'll look up from a pivot table and find that, somehow, it went from one o'clock to five o'clock in three minutes flat.

Not today. Today, Adrian's mind couldn't stay on his work. It kept picturing that screenshot, the plane ticket that would take Ginny away from New York for God only knows how long. Four or five times, Adrian returned to Instagram to stare at the screenshot as if checking and rechecking could somehow change the eventual outcome.

As he veers right, headed for the West Side Highway, Adrian wonders why he even cares if Ginny leaves. They live in a city of eight million; the absence of one should not affect him. Plus, it's not like he was going to see her. If Adrian had to guess, he would bet that, of all eight million people in New York, he's the last one that Ginny wants to see.

Up here, the Hudson River Greenway is a study in opposites: highway on one side, lush green parks on the other. Bikes and rollerbladers skirt around him. The rollerbladers remind him of Ginny, who showed up to their first date with a pair dangling from her right arm. Every goddamn thing reminds him of Ginny. Adrian wishes he could turn his head sideways and shake it until all the memories poured out.

But he can't. He can only see her choppy blond hair under her stickered helmet, her bright smile as she walked up to Dante in nothing but a pair of socks. She seemed completely different back then. Like she had never known sadness or suffering. Like her entire life was air.

He couldn't have been more wrong.

It's then that he starts to run.

He wasn't planning on running home. In fact, he's already been for his usual Monday morning run that day, six miles down to Battery Park and back up again. This extra jog will wear on his muscles; he'll be sore tomorrow. But walking is not enough right now. His limbs ache to stretch, to push against the pavement in long, satisfying strides.

He doesn't put in AirPods. He listens to the sounds of the city: the rumble of cars, the whiz of bikes spinning past, the laughter of groups gathered on the greens, the gentle crash of waves on the pier.

At Pier 45, there's a long break in the trees, affording an unobscured view of the Hudson. Under the partly cloudy afternoon sky, the waves are a chalky blue grey, reminding Adrian of the Danube. Reminding him of long walks in the morning, of Americanos and chocolate-filled *fánks*.

He redirects his thoughts. Ginny isn't the only memory he has of the Danube, right? He grew up next to that river. He and Jozsef used to kick footballs against the rocky ledge that guards the walkway from the river, seeing who could get it closest to the top of the ledge without going over. They must have lost dozens of balls that way, each one swept away in the tide, bobbing up and down as it drifted toward the Parliament Building. His *nagyanya* would have scolded him if she knew how wasteful he was being, but he never had to tell her; Jozsef's family seemed to have an endless supply of footballs.

He would always have mixed feelings about that river. He spent some of his happiest moments there—from football with Jozsef to riding his rusty little bike along its pathway to sitting with his skinny legs crossed upon the ledge and throwing bits of bread to the seagulls.

But the Danube would also always be the river that swallowed his father.

For many years after he learned how his father died, he couldn't go near the Danube. He would take winding routes that obscured the view of the water, only drawing near when he absolutely had to. When he looked at the bridges that connect one side to the other, all he could see was a car skidding on black ice, crashing through the railing, soaring through the air, diving nose first into the water. All he could feel was metal and rubber sinking to the bottom. A door that wouldn't open. A tight space filling until there was no room left to breathe.

Stop.

Why is Adrian thinking about this right now? He doesn't like to think about his father in that way. He likes to think of him as he was when he was alive: intelligent, charismatic, beloved by his students. Adrian's thoughts seem to have grown steadily darker as the day wears on. He needs it to stop.

He's almost home now. Only a few blocks to go. His breath is labored. Sweat trickles down his back, pooling at his waistband, dampening the soft fabric of his T-shirt. His legs ache. He pushes his pace. He wants to outrun these thoughts, the eerie feeling that has dogged him all day. When he turns onto his block, he does not see the restaurants and bodegas that line the street; he sees his father's face, a yellow car, a stack of books.

Adrian takes the stairs two at a time. He fumbles with the key. When the door opens, he spills into the room and falls to the floor, panting.

One photograph. The only image he has of his father. A photograph he does not even possess, that he held for only a few weeks before returning it to his mother's hiding place. He doesn't even know if the image in his mind matches his father's true likeness. It could be completely false, warped by the passage of years. He might not even know what his father looks like.

This realization makes Adrian want to curl up into a ball and cry.

But he can't, of course. Adrian doesn't cry. Adrian doesn't feel, period.

His eyes drift about the room, passing over the kitchenette, his desk, his sofa, and landing finally on his open closet. On the dress shoes lining the top shelf.

It's then that he remembers the package.

Adrian is off the floor and up on his toes before he can think too hard about it, feeling about the shelf for the cardboard box. He finds it and pulls it out so hastily that he knocks one of his shoes to the floor. He doesn't stop to put it back on the shelf. He carries the box over to the sofa and sits down. The box balances on his lap, the top half-open. A partial invitation.

Adrian opens the flaps one by one, smoothing each crease until each lies flat. Inside is the black leather album. He lifts it from its box and wipes off the cover. Exhales lengthily. Then he flips open the cover.

The first photo is of a young version of his mother and father. They're dressed up, perhaps for some school function. They can't be older than sixteen. Was there prom in communist Hungary? He doesn't know. Yet another thing he's never asked his grandparents.

He flips to the next page. In this photo, his father is a touch older and dressed in a sports uniform, a football under his arm. The uniform reads KÖLCSEY FERENC.

Adrian stares at this photo for a long time. His father played football. *Football*.

In the photo to the right, his parents are again together, only this time Eszter is there, too. They're on a picnic blanket spread out on the shore of Lake Balaton. His father wears dark blue swim trunks, his mother and *nagyanya* long bathing costumes. Adrian recognizes *lángos* and *dobostorta*, glasses filled with dark red wine. Their smiles are bunched, eyes squinting in the sunshine. His father's mouth is open as if he's in the middle of saying something. Adrian fills with a strange ache. A desire to know what, exactly, his *apa* said.

He flips the page again. Again. There are several more pictures: his parents at university, his parents at a sporting event, his parents on holiday in what looks like Sofia, his parents at graduation.

And then, on the next page—his mother in a white dress, his father in a pale grey suit. They stand with their arms around each other. Behind them, the doors to a cathedral are open wide. Flower petals drift through the picture, which appear to have been thrown by people standing off frame. His father is smiling. His mother is smiling. He has never seen his mother smile that wide. Not once.

It's here that Adrian's eyes first start to water. He blinks rapidly, pushing down the tears, and flips quickly to the next page.

He sees his parents buy their house. He sees them throw dinner parties and tend the garden in his grandparents' backyard. He sees them on a hike in the hills around Szentendre. He sees them riding bikes along the Danube, just as he used to do. And then, all at once, he sees a bump in his mother's stomach, and he knows that Beatrix is on her way. He sees the bump grow over the course of the next few photos, and then he flips the page, and there they are, his mother in a hospital bed, baby Beatrix in her arms. His father stands beside his mother, one hand on her shoulder. Their eyes are tired, but their smiles are genuine, filled with shock and wonder.

The more Adrian flips, the harder his eyes sting. Water wells up in his eyes, blurring his vision until he's forced to blink, to allow the tears to run down his cheeks. He can't remember the last time he cried. He didn't even think his body was capable of producing tears.

He turns the page again. He sees his parents with baby Beatrix, out for a picnic in one of the city's parks. He sees Beatrix in his father's arms. He sees Beatrix in a stroller as Eszter and her mother visit Eötvös Loránd. He sees them out to eat at a restaurant in Pest. He sees playdates and first steps and a little family snuggled up on an unfamiliar sofa in a house that Adrian never lived inside. He sees an entire life unfold. He sees a childhood he never had, a family that was happy, that was unhurt and unbroken. The tears come faster and faster now.

When he flips the page and is faced with a photograph of his again-pregnant mother, his father crouched at her side, one hand on her belly, he freezes. There he is. Adrian, in utero. They look elated, ready to bring yet another member into their little family.

But they don't know the truth: that Adrian's conception is the beginning of the end.

He can barely look through the rest of the photographs. Beatrix, a toddler now, their pregnant mother, and their excited father. He can't look at the cups of coffee, at the walks along the river, at the birthday parties and saint's holidays at their grandparents' house. He doesn't want to see it. He knows what comes next.

His mother is massively pregnant. His sister is grinning with only six teeth. His father has his arms around them both.

Then Adrian flips the page, and there's nothing. No photo. Just an empty plastic sleeve.

He flips to the next page. The next. He's in denial. He's certain that if he just looks a little harder, he will find something. The photos will not end here. They cannot end here. *They cannot end here.*

He flips the very last page. He has reached the end of the album. There is nothing left. He shoves the book off his lap. It lands on the floor facedown, pages bent and smushed at an angle. Adrian bends over and wraps his arms around his legs. He tips over onto his side. He is sobbing now. The gasps come in deep and heavy, shaking his body. He cannot breathe. He cannot think.

He fumbles in his pocket for his phone. He pulls it out with unsteady hands. The screen is a blur. He presses the screen several times, finally finding the call icon. He scrolls until he finds a contact that says **MOM**. He hits call.

She picks up after just two rings. "Adrian!" she says, but before she can say anything more, Adrian interrupts:

"It's my fault." He sobs, speaking in Hungarian. "It's my fault."

"Sweetheart, calm down." His mother's voice is alarmed. "What is it? What are you talking about?"

"It's my fault, Mom. He would never have died if it wasn't for me."

"Who—"

"He died on the way to the hospital. On the way to meet me. It's my fault." He can hardly breathe, can hardly get the words out. "He died for me. I'm so sorry, Mom. I'm so, so sorry."

His mother says nothing.

Adrian makes a noise somewhere between a gasp and a wail. "I didn't mean to take him away from you."

No one speaks. The only noise comes from Adrian sobbing into the telephone. Some part of his brain recognizes that he should feel ashamed for acting so irrationally, but another part of him—an overwhelming majority—wishes that he could cry even harder. That he could push out every ounce of water in his body. Maybe if he did, it would expel the pain that built up in him while he flipped through that photo album. Maybe it would drain away the grief now filling every crevice of his body.

After a minute or two, his sobs subside. As they do, he begins to hear his mother's breathing on the other end. He tries to focus on that, on the sound of her breath. To let it pull him in and out of himself, too.

"Adrian," she says finally. Her voice is soft. "Your father's death is not your fault. You know that, right?"

He says nothing.

"It was an accident. One of the worst accidents that has ever happened, but an accident nonetheless. Yes, he was taken—but it wasn't by you. It was by a patch of ice." She pauses. "You understand that, yes?"

He sniffles.

"God may work in mysterious ways, but he does not take a life for a life," she says. "That is not his way."

"But his way meant that Dad had to die before I could be born."

"That may be, Adrian. But that does not make it your fault."

He inhales raggedly. "I can't take it, Mom." His voice cracks. "It's too heavy."

"What is, honey?"

He exhales. "Everything."

Though he cannot see his mother, he thinks that he can feel her nodding through the phone. He can imagine the expression on her face: grave but understanding, lips pursed, two thin lines in her forehead. It's an expression he's seen hundreds of times—the same she wears in church when the priest says that we are all sinners and we must repent for our sins.

"I know, honey," she says soothingly. "I know."

"How do I make it go away?"

Quietly, she says, "You don't. You just learn to live with it."

After that, they fall silent. They listen to each other's breathing through the phone. Adrian has never cried to his mother before. Has never gone to her to have his hair stroked, to be held. He imagines that it must feel something like this. The silent comfort of knowing that someone else is there.

"Do you want to come home?" his mother asks.

Adrian considers it. Maybe going home is what he needs. Maybe he needs the sunlight slanting through their living room, the soft green hills, the golden fields of corn. There was something very healing about going home to Budapest; maybe it would be to go to Indiana, too.

That's why Ginny is going home, after all. To heal.

Adrian sits up on the couch. He looks down at the box, at the bottom of which still sits a green envelope with his name on it.

"Mom?" He bends over and picks the envelope up. "Can I call you back?"

"Of course, honey. I love you."

"I—me, too." Adrian winces as he presses end on the call. Even to his mother, he struggles to say the words in their entirety.

He turns the envelope over. Like all his grandparents' letters, it's sealed with a blue mark bearing a tulip. The envelopes themselves are also licked and sealed the regular way; the mark is purely decorative. He runs his fingers over the seal. Then he peels it away and slips his fingers under the flap of the envelope.

From inside slides a single piece of cardstock, on which are scribbled just a few lines in Hungarian:

Adrian,

These belong to you. Keep them safe; keep his memory safer.
All our love to Ginny.

P.S.—Have you told her that you love her, yet, too?

The bags are packed. Heather's air mattress rolled up. The toiletries swept off the counter, the garbage sealed up and ready to be hauled away. Ginny is finally leaving Sullivan Street.

"Dude," says Tristan across the living room. Ginny is tying her shoes and cannot see to whom he's speaking. "Who are you texting? You've been staring at your phone for, like, ten minutes."

"No one," says Clay.

"Is no one a girl with whom you're currently sleeping?"

"No," says Clay. "It's no one."

Ginny stands up. She squints at her best friend. "You're being sketchy."

"No, I'm not." He pockets his phone and turns to Heather. "We'll miss you, Heath."

"I know." Heather pretends to pout. "Who am I supposed to bully now, with no Tristan in my life?"

"Well," says Tristan, "there's always text."

Ginny is about to start laughing when she hears the sound of a key turning in the front door. She turns around just as the door creaks open. In steps Finch.

The room goes very still.

Finch walks forward, suitcase wheels bouncing on the cracks in the floorboards. He passes out of the shadow and into the light of the living room. The first thing she sees are his warm, familiar eyes, the curve of his lips. Her stomach drops to her feet.

"I thought you weren't coming back until Monday," she says.

"Hey to you, too."

"Hey, Tristan," says Clay loudly. "There's something really cool I wanted to show you in my bedroom."

"Nice. I like cool things." Tristan hurries after him and shuts the door.

"Is this—" Heather steps up beside Ginny and grips her elbow. "Is this Finch?"

"Nice to meet you," says Finch.

"Ginny." Heather squeezes her elbow. "Say the word and I'll rip his testicles off."

"Um." Finch glances at his crotch.

"No," Ginny says. "No, it's fine. I've got this."

"Are you sure?"

"Positive. Go hang out with the boys. I'm sure they've got their ears pressed to the door, anyway."

"No, we don't!" yell Tristan and Clay, voices muffled.

Heather squeezes Ginny's elbow one last time, then turns around and heads into Clay's room. Ginny and Finch stand four feet away from each other, as far apart as the Manhattan living room will allow.

"So." She doesn't cross her arms. She doesn't want to look like she's hiding. "You're engaged."

"I'm engaged."

"Congratulations."

"I don't—" He clears his throat. "I came home early because I wanted to catch you before you left. I wanted to—apologize."

"You've already apologized, Alex. Several times."

"And you don't—you won't ever forgive me?"

"I'm not saying that. I'm just saying that, for now, what I need from you is space. Not an apology. I need to recover, and you need to make things right with your fiancée." Ginny takes a step toward him. "Have you even told her about what happened between us?"

"I—" Finch fiddles with the handle of his suitcase. "Not yet."

"How convenient."

"But I will," he hurries on. "I swear I will."

"I can't say I believe you. But thankfully it's no longer my issue."

"You're saying . . . you're no longer in love with me?"

Ginny laughs, a throaty sound of disbelief. "No, Finch. I'm no longer in love with you. And, you know what? I don't think I ever was."

"But what about—"

"No. Stop." She places a hand over both ears. "I don't want to hear this. I don't want to get pulled back into your games." Her hands lower, but her voice raises. "What you felt for me, Finch? Whatever fucked-up, ego-stroking shit you got out of our relationship? It wasn't love. And what I felt for you? That wasn't love, either." She draws in a ragged breath. "It was fear."

"Fear?" He shakes his head. "Fear of what?"

"Fear of being ugly. Fear of being alone. Fear of being unlovable. You were my safety net. And I bet you could smell my fear. I bet you could smell it from the moment I walked in the apartment door. It's what drew you to me in the first place; I was just an easy target."

"That's not—"

"I can't have this conversation with you, Finch. I'm sorry. I can't trust anything you say. I don't know what's truth and what's fiction. And the worst part is—I don't think you know, either."

Finch's jaw snaps shut.

"Now, if you'll excuse me." Ginny pushes past him and over to the bathroom door. She twists the handle and steps inside. Finch doesn't call after her.

The door bangs shut. She presses her back against it, palms flat on the wood. It's a tiny bathroom, so tiny that her strangled exhales ruffle the plastic shower curtain less than a foot away. Tears flow freely down her face now. She wants to collapse to the floor. She wants to curl herself up into the tiniest version of herself, one free from wide thighs and rolls of fat and breasts that block her arms from crossing over her chest. She wants to fall asleep and make it all disappear.

But she can't. Instead of sliding down the door, she steps away from it. Instead of folding over herself, she straightens up. Rolls her shoulders back. And instead of turning away from the mirror, the way she so often does when washing her hands, she pivots to face the mirror head-on.

She looks at herself. At her newly rounded face. At her generous breasts. At her collarbone, now slightly buried beneath skin. At the soft line of her shoulders.

And that's the first time she thinks it:

This is what I look like when I'm healthy.

The tears run faster, turning her cheeks a glowing pink. Her lips part. Her nose starts to run. She gasps for air: *please, more, fill my body.* She doesn't look beautiful; she looks peeled back, raw. All soft angles and wide eyes. As if every protective layer has been shed from her body. As if the only thing left is her.

This is what I look like when I'm healthy, she thinks.

This is what I look like.

Adrian stares at the note for a long time. He follows the loops and curves of his *nagyanya*'s handwriting. Studies the blank spaces, each one in turn, as if they might obscure some hidden message. As if the card were really a cipher.

Abruptly, he drops the card and picks up his phone. With shaking hands, he unlocks the screen and selects Messages. He scrolls until he finds Clay's contact.

ADRIAN: Has she left yet?

He sets the phone and waits. He shakes out his shoulders, as if the action can release the tension in his body. Clay's answer arrives within seconds.

CLAY: No. Just finished packing.

CLAY: She's leaving soon, tho

CLAY: So if you have something you want to say . . .

Adrian doesn't bother to reply. He jumps up, grabs his keys off the bedside table, and hurries out the door.

Down on the street, he hails the first taxi he finds. Normally, he would order an Uber, but he can't waste time waiting for it to arrive. "One sixteen Sullivan Street," he tells the driver, and they're off.

They turn onto Seventh Avenue and immediately hit traffic. Adrian's foot taps rapidly, his thigh drumming against the seat. He takes out his phone and opens Safari. He stares intently at the screen, typing things here and there. He loads a new page, a longer one, and fills in more boxes. When he reaches the end of the page, he presses a button. A set of terms and agreements appears, which he ignores, pressing yet another button. When he reaches the final page, he clicks off his phone and shoves it into his pocket.

The car inches forward a few feet, then a few feet more. In his pocket, Adrian's phone vibrates once, then twice, then three times. He doesn't check it. He doesn't want to know if he's already too late. He wants to make it all the way there, regardless of the outcome.

Five minutes pass. Adrian feels like he's going to explode out of his skin. His foot is tapping so fast and so loudly that it's a wonder the cabdriver hasn't told him to stop. He rolls the window down and sticks his head out. The traffic seems to go on for ages, maybe even all the way down to the Freedom Tower.

"Fuck this," he mutters. He thrusts a few dollars into the compartment in the driver's protective glass. The driver unlocks the door, then Adrian is out, and he's running.

He weaves through the sedans and semis backed up on Seventh Avenue. He weaves around rearview mirrors and jumps over steaming grates. When he spots a gap in the biker's lane, he veers left and bounds up onto the sidewalk. He doesn't slow. He keeps running. He passes West 4th Street, then Bleecker. He elbows through a crowd of drunk underage kids gathered outside Caliente Cab Co. His phone is buzzing in his pocket; he thinks it's a call this time. He doesn't stop to pull it out. He skirts around a woman with a baby stroller, narrowly avoiding falling into an open cellar door outside a coffee shop. He's breathing hard now. Three runs in one day, his legs are screaming at him. Finally, finally, he spots the intersection of Seventh and Houston in the distance. He pushes even harder, reaching Houston just as the walk light disappears. He curses and runs across anyway, causing half a dozen drivers to lay on their horns. He reaches the other side unharmed and hangs a left. He passes Sixth Avenue, reaching the blessedly short blocks of SoHo. Just MacDougal to pass, and then—

And then—

There it is. Sullivan. Adrian leans forward, pumps his arms. He can hardly breathe now, but he's so close. Ginny could be waiting just around that corner. Or it could be too late, she could be gone, and all this will have been for—

Ginny.

There she is, standing by the curb, surrounded by Clay, Tristan, and someone Adrian can only assume is her sister. A smile spreads wide across his face. But then she turns to the side and looks right at him, and the smile disappears, because he's here now, and God help him, he doesn't know what he's going to say.

Adrian and Ginny stand three feet apart, halfway down Sullivan Street. Ginny is frozen, one hand resting on her suitcase, the other covering her mouth. Adrian is bent double, breathing so heavily he cannot speak.

"Oh, God." Ginny steps away from her suitcase. She looks for somewhere to hide—behind Clay, behind a lamppost, anywhere. She doesn't want him to see her like this. She doesn't want him to see how much weight she's gained, to witness the new body in which she is living. Even if she's started to accept it for herself, that doesn't mean she's ready to show it off to the world. "You can't— I don't—"

"Wait," Adrian gasps out, putting a hand on Ginny's shoulder. She jumps visibly at the touch, turning back with wide eyes. "Wait."

Everyone waits. Everyone watches as Adrian straightens, heaving deep breaths. His cheeks are pink, his hair tousled, a faint beading of sweat on his forehead.

"Gin," Heather says slowly, "is that who I think it is?"

"Yes," Ginny says. She's shaking now. She wishes she could fold herself up into her suitcase and zip the whole thing closed. "Yes, it is."

They watch as Adrian draws himself up to his full height. He rolls his shoulders back but doesn't puff his chest out. Instead, he stands neutrally, almost limply. He looks down, then back up, eyelashes fluttering the way they always do. Ginny feels all the breath leave her body.

She says, "Adrian—"

"I love you."

He says the words so quickly they blend together.

"You—" Ginny's voice sticks in her throat. "You what?"

"I love you, Ginny." His arms dangle at his sides. "I'm sorry it took me this long to figure it out. And I'm not—I'm not really one for giving speeches—"

From behind, Tristan snorts. Clay stomps on his foot.

"But I just—I had to tell you. I'm sorry, Ginny. I'm sorry I hurt you. I'm sorry I was afraid. Fuck, I'm *still* afraid. I've never been in a real relationship before, and this, all this"—he gestures between them—"it terrifies me. I'm fucking terrified. I don't let myself get close to people. Not close enough that it would hurt if they left. But with you—with you, it's already too late. And I'm terrified that, if we get together, things will blow up, because I have no fucking clue what I'll do without you."

Ginny can hardly breathe. Adrian never once looks at the people surrounding them. He speaks only to her.

"Back in Hungary, you told me that it was absurd to think that I needed to know before it began that our relationship wouldn't end. That no human has ever made any decision about which they have absolutely zero doubts. And you know what? You were right. I had doubts about Harvard. I had doubts about Disney. I even had doubts about what I should eat for breakfast this morning. They were tiny doubts, almost insignificant, but they were there. They're always there. Because it's human to worry, right? To ask, *what if*? To question every decision you make." He takes a breath. "So. Yes. It's absurd to think that you need to be able to tell the future of a relationship before you jump in. But, Ginny." He steps forward once again. He reaches down and takes one of her hands. "None of that matters because, right now, I *can* see the future. I'm so in love with you, Ginny Murphy. And I know with a hundred percent certainty that if I have to spend another minute away from you, I'm going to lose my fucking mind."

She opens her mouth. Closes it again. Shakes her head, eyes darting about the street. "But I don't—I don't understand." She shakes her head again. "How can you love me *now*? After I've gained all this weight? After my arms have grown and my thighs have grown and my face has grown and . . ." Her breath comes fast now, little gasps for air. "How can you love me when I've gotten so—so *ugly*?"

For a moment, silence falls between them. Ginny's chest rises and falls. Her cheeks are pink, her hair knotted back in a low bun. Adrian looks at her, at the sad tilt of her eyes, the hunched shape of her back.

"Ginny." He moves his hands up to hold her arms. "Whatever you are feeling about yourself right now, I can promise you—it isn't real. It isn't what the rest of the world sees. Because, to me— Jesus Christ. Right now, you're so beautiful it's hard for me to even look at you."

Ginny laughs, a choking sound that rattles her stomach. She wants to hug him, to press her body to his and feel the familiar ridges of his torso.

Instead, she looks down at her suitcase and lays a hand atop it. "Adrian." She squeezes the handle. "I'm—I'm leaving. I'm going home. Not forever, but—"

"I know. I know." He nods, pulling his phone out of his pocket. "I'm coming with you."

"You're—" She blinks. "What?"

"I bought a plane ticket. On the cab ride over." He raises the phone and shows her the screen, which displays a ticket from JFK to Detroit. "I already asked my boss, and he gave me the okay to work remotely for a few weeks. I want to be there for you during your recovery. I want to be there for *everything*—the good stuff, the bad. Unless"—his eyes withdraw—"unless you don't want me to."

Ginny stares at the plane ticket, mouth ajar. No one—not the boys, not her sister—says a word. The pause stretches long and thick between them, between all the bodies crowded together on the sidewalk. Out on Sullivan Street, a food supply truck rumbles past, exhaling a cloud of exhaust over the block.

And then, without warning, Ginny starts to laugh.

Adrian's eyebrows bunch. He lowers his phone. "Is that—is that a no?"

"No, you idiot." Tears start to gather at the corners of Ginny's eyes. She's still laughing. "It's a yes. Of course it's a yes. I want you to come home with me. I want you to come everywhere with me."

A small smile tugs at his mouth. "Yeah?"

She smiles back. "Yeah."

"Well?" Heather calls from behind Ginny. "Kiss him, then."

Ginny takes the last step toward Adrian, throwing her arms over his shoulders and jumping up into his arms. He catches her under her legs. She leans down and presses her lips to his. Just a few feet away, the boys cheer. Heather puts two fingers into her mouth and lets out a wolf whistle. Drivers lay on their horns. Strangers across Sullivan Street start to clap. Half the block has no idea what's going on, but everyone seems happy about it anyway.

And just beside the curb, Ginny and Adrian hold each other close. Ginny knots her fingers in his hair. Adrian smiles against her teeth. He spins her around just once, then lowers her carefully back to the pavement.

They pull apart but don't let go of each other. Ginny ducks her head into his chest and squeezes her arms around him.

"I love you," she whispers.

"I will always love you," he says, loud enough for everyone to hear.

ACKNOWLEDGMENTS

I entered treatment for anorexia and bulimia in September 2020. I was twenty-five years old and had suffered silently for over seven years.

It was far easier to admit to being anorexic than it was to being bulimic. In society, "eating healthy" and exercising regularly—the two excuses that cover up anorexia—are seen as positives, while there is nothing good about throwing up. Throwing up is dirty, private, something to be hidden away. The shame that I felt around bulimia haunted me for years, making it almost impossible to share the truth even with those closest to me.

I wrote this book because I didn't want to be ashamed anymore.

To start, I want to thank every doctor, nutritionist, and therapist who guided me through the recovery process, in particular Kelley, Kristi, and Kathy. I could not have written this book without you. Thank you for saving my life.

To my agent, Kimberly Whalen—my dream-maker extraordinaire. Thank you for taking a chance on me and this book. Thank you for championing my work, for believing in me no matter what wild tale I dream up. I could not be prouder to have you in my corner.

To my editor, Kristine Swartz—thank you for seeing the promise inside this book and turning it into something better than I ever could have dreamed. Thank you to the entire team at Berkley who worked so hard on this book: Mary Baker, Chelsea Pascoe, Yazmine Hassan, Jessica Mangicaro, Christine Legon, Jennifer Lynes, Martha Schwartz, Colleen Reinhart, and Jacob Jordan—this book could not have landed at a better home. I also must give a special thank-you to Clio Cornish and my UK team at Michael Joseph, who welcomed me so warmly to their London office.

I owe endless gratitude to my parents, Nick and Susan, who gave me shelter and love as I went through the recovery process. Mom, our *Grey's Anatomy* marathons got me through my first month without purging. I also must thank my motley band of older siblings who taught me how to laugh, tell stories, and never take myself too seriously. A special shout-out to Gramsie, Susie, Ian, Edie, Charlie, Jo, Lucy, Willie, and every other family member who has been with me along the way.

To every single friend who supported me through the long and nerve-racking publication process: Lauren, Zizi, Kendall, Jamie, Cece, Caroline, Lou, Chris, Dylan, Tristan, Cathy, Danielle, Hunter, Hermosa Dan, Jack, Gabe, Maxx, Gray, Matt, Scottie, Sam, Jess, Lydia, Alisha, Vanessa, Katie, Makayla, Merit, and many, many more that I'm sure I'm forgetting.

To my Swedish meatball, Pontus. I had no idea when I walked into that coffee shop that I was meeting my soulmate, but here we are. You are my biggest champion and my best friend. I love you like crazy.

From the bottom of my heart, I must thank every reader, reviewer, BookTokker, Bookstagrammer, and anyone else who took a chance on this book. You are the people who keep the beautiful art of reading alive. I love you all.

And, last but never least, to anyone who has struggled or continues to struggle with any type of eating disorder: I see you. I was you. You are not alone—and you are so much more than what you put on your dinner plate.

GUY'S
GIRL

EMMA NOYES

READERS GUIDE

DISCUSSION QUESTIONS

1. What did you know about anorexia and bulimia before reading this novel? How has your perception of these diseases changed?

2. How would you describe the dynamic between Ginny and Finch? How does it compare to her friendships with Clay and Tristan? Do any of the friendships remind you of yours?

3. What is one thing you learned about Hungarian culture by reading this book?

4. Were you rooting for Ginny and Adrian as a couple? Why or why not?

5. The two main characters reflect quite a bit on what it's like to be a young professional. What are the biggest hurdles they face? Would you describe your own experience similarly?

6. What does Ginny and Adrian's story tell us about modern dating?

7. Do you relate more to Ginny's perspective or Adrian's perspective in the story? Why?

8. Ginny and Adrian have a difficult discussion around commitment and whether one can be absolutely certain before

jumping into a relationship. Do you think this applies to other aspects of life?

9. Many people experience difficulties around food without ever actually being diagnosed with an eating disorder. How do you think the culture around eating could be changed to better facilitate conversations about these issues?

Keep reading for a preview of
the next novel by Emma Noyes,

HOW TO HIDE IN PLAIN SIGHT

from Berkley!

PROLOGUE

Here's what you need to understand about my family: all of our money came from drugs.

Nothing illegal, of course. Not crack, or quaaludes, or even marijuana. All government-sanctioned. The good stuff, you know? Prozac. Insulin. Cialis. (That's a PDE-5 inhibitor, the drug that helps men get it up—the alternative to Viagra. I know. The assholes at Pfizer ruined any chance we had at brand recognition. There's only so much brain space Americans are willing to commit to boner medication.)

Another thing you need to understand about my family: it's big. I couldn't tell you the number of times I've said those words. At parties, on the job. *Tell me about yourself*, says someone I've just met. *Well, I grew up in a big family.* It's a great opening line. People trust me right away, which makes no sense. As if being born into a big family says something about your character. As if there's a reproductive threshold above which none of your children become psychopaths or serial killers. As if Ted Bundy would have turned out okay if only he'd had a brother or two.

I was a happy kid. How could I not be? I was raised the way all parents dream of raising their children: in a big house in the suburbs of Chicago, right on the shore of Lake Michigan. Our town was just large enough for me to run free on the weekend, but just small enough to come home with nothing worse than a skinned knee. Our school district liberal enough to preach universal love, but so white that I didn't discover racism until we reached the chapter on slavery in our fifth-grade history textbook.

I was given everything—including, but not limited to, that

most elusive of gifts: the Happy Family. Undivorced parents. Siblings who can actually stand each other. Who vacation together and eat family dinner around a worn wooden table and only try to kill each other on special occasions. Who even—when the climate is right—*like* each other.

There were unhappy moments, too, of course. And chaos. Plenty of chaos. In a family of eight, if you want to be heard, you yell: at dinner, during card games, on long road trips, when the back two rows of the Suburban become louder and more political than the floor of Congress. Everyone talks over each other. Facts are not as important as volume.

As the youngest—and therefore least authoritative—member of the family, I was never going to be the loudest. So, instead, I watched. Listened. Took in the laughter and the chaos and the secrets and the broken parts. Because yes, the Beck Family is a Happy Family. But behind the curtain, we fight. We hurt each other. We even hate each other, for a time. But we forgive. We always forgive.

We have to.

We're family.

1

Now

In the thirteen hours it took me to drive from New York City to Port Windfall, Ontario, I drank three cups of coffee, started four podcasts, engaged in countless lively debates with drivers who couldn't hear me, and listened to every single one of my Spotify playlists. Twice.

When I ran out of background noise, I took reality and shaped it into copywriting templates. I do that sometimes.

HEADLINE: Disgraced Daughter Returns to Family's Private Island for Four-Day "Wedding of the Century"

OFFER: Ready to face your demons, relish in lavish excess, and suffer through nightly political diatribes, all while wearing a smile that says you're having the time of your life?

CTA: Click for Free Trial!

When I tell people I'm a copywriter, most often they picture *Mad Men*: long rows of women in smart wool skirts pounding at typewriters, dodging the advances of male executives, locked out of the meetings where *real* decisions are made. You don't need talent to be a copywriter. You just need to be able to type.

Let me tell you a secret: copy is far more than words on an advertisement. It's everything. It's everywhere. We copywriters are the engine that moves society forward. Without us, progress grinds to a halt. Instruction manuals are blank. Street signs don't exist. Travel becomes impossible. No sentence comes from nothing, after all: from the saccharine Christmas message on the side of your soda to the *screw u bro* written on a bathroom stall; from the seat-back sign telling you "Life Vest Under Seat" to the greeting that welcomes you to a website. Even the highway sign telling you that you're now leaving Ohio, bidding you farewell and asking that you come back soon. Do you ever think about who wrote those words? Of course not; those words are not words to us, with authors and backstories and spellcheck. They're background. They're grass and trees, part of the landscape. EMERGENCY EXIT signs say EMERGENCY EXIT because that's how it is. Car mirrors tell us that OBJECTS IN THE MIRROR ARE CLOSER THAN THEY APPEAR because they do. Because they always have. These words, these pillars of society—they weren't *written*. They sprang into existence at the exact moment society needed them. Perhaps they were even created by God: *And on the third day, God created the sun and the moon and the instruction manual for how to set up your Google Edge TPU™ Application-Specific Integrated Circuit.*

Anyway.

My destination was Cradle Island: a mile-around private paradise purchased by my father during the coked-up height of his second marriage. He found it in a newspaper advertisement. ISLAND FOR SALE! I imagine the ad said. EXCELLENT VALUE! 100% SURROUNDED BY WATER!

The way Dad tells it, he almost flipped right past. But then he saw the birds-eye shot of Cradle Island at the bottom of the advertisement. And the island looked like a cradle. An abstract cradle. A cradle on drugs. My father was also on drugs. He found this coincidence so funny that he laughed until he cried.

Then he bought it.

That was a different lifetime. By the time I got into the car borrowed from one of my coworkers to travel from Brooklyn to Ontario, Dad was almost thirty years sober.

As was I. Recovered from my addictions, I mean. Not to drugs or alcohol—to other things. Thoughts, food, people, places. Oh, yes—you can be addicted to a place. It happened to me as a kid. Every year, in the middle of February—deep in the bowels of the Chicago winter—I started to crave Cradle Island. The sound of sparrows in the afternoon. Its curving beaches, peppered with cattails. In the first light of morning, when the lake turns to glass. It was the strangest feeling. More potent than desire for food. Because when you want ice cream or crispy, hot buttered bread, the feeling pools right atop your tongue, but when you want a place, it calls to you with *every* sense, sight and smell and touch and sound and, yes, even taste.

When I moved to New York, I cut all cravings out of my life. All of them. I had to. *"No seas tonta,"* Manuel would have said, waving a bottle of beer in my face. "Just have one."

I gripped the steering wheel. Squeezed my eyes closed and open. Blinked his face from my memory. *No. That was before.* Before I took control of my life. Before I worked my schedule down to an exacting science, to a well-oiled machine that left no room for darker thoughts. Before I learned to ignore the siren's call of my memories, their taunts, daring me to jump down, down, down, into that all-too-familiar place—a hole into which at times I fall accidentally and at others I climb willingly, allowing the rest of the soil to tumble in after me, shutting off all oxygen and blotting out the sun.

The nerves didn't set in until just before I arrived at the marina, but they probably should have set in long before. Frankly, they should have set in the minute I pulled the glossy RSVP card from its envelope and laid it against the plug-in coffeepot in my studio and left it there, untouched, its cheerful calligraphy mocking me every time I walked in or out the apartment's front door. Even then, in my hesitation, I wasn't nervous. I wasn't anything, really.

But I should have been.

See, the issue was this: on the day I arrived at the marina for Taz's wedding, I hadn't seen my family in three years.

It wasn't that I'd been *avoiding* them. Not at first, anyway. I was still there, still included in all the group chats and email threads and family conference calls during which Dad explained for the fourth or fifth time *exactly* how capital gains or fixed-interest mortgages work. But I rarely contributed to these conversations. Instead, I sat silently in my apartment in New York, a spectator to the continuing life of my family in the Midwest.

I listened to what my parents told me growing up: make your own way. Live as if you will inherit nothing. Do not rely on anyone else to save you—including us. So I did. After high school, I skipped the pointless charade of college. Moved to Brooklyn. Lived on a couch. Worked my ass off to find a job. Paid my own rent and taxes. Never touched a dime of The Trust Fund, that grown-up allowance that leaked tens of thousands of dollars into my bank account each year. Doubtless they would prefer that I had a college degree, but such things are neither here nor there. I did it. I achieved financial independence. And at twenty-one years old, I did it well before anyone else did.

I imagined my solo arrival to this wedding as a moment of triumph. *Here she comes*, they would say. *Eliot Beck, Corporate Woman in the Big City!*

But when I crossed the bridge into Port Windfall, the port town where we store our boats in the winter, I started to actually picture the scene that would be waiting for me. They'd be there, all of them, loading their bags into the *Silver Heron*, a 54-foot Bertram yacht purchased by my father in 1975. Mom would be whirring around in one of her usual states. Dad would be up on the flybridge. Karma would be giving directions. Clarence and Caleb would be standing off to the side, arguing about God knows what—probably who would get the bigger bed in Tangled Blue that year. I never understood my half brothers' relationship; they hate each other, yet they insist on staying in the same cabin every year. Both claimed it was their favorite and neither was the type to relent.

Every family reunion begins with a round of hugs. A round of hugs and the promise you've missed one another. For me, that promise is always true. But that summer, after three years away, it was truer than ever.

And yet. And *yet*. I avoided everyone for a reason. For multiple reasons, actually, and it was only at the last minute, when I turned the steering wheel to pull into Kilwin Marina and heard the familiar crunch of gravel beneath the tires, smelled the algae and hull wax and molding rope—that I realized the full depth of what I was doing. Where I was going. I was driving toward not just a wedding but also a week spent trapped on a tiny island with no control over my diet. My routine. My exercise. No East River to run beside in the morning. No cabinet full of gluten-free, dairy-free, paleo-keto Whole 30 nutrition bars stolen from the pantry at work. Just me and my family. And suddenly, I felt nothing short of naked.

I parked the car. Unclipped my seat belt. Rolled down the car window.

The wind blew warm and lazy off Lake Huron, heavy with the smell of gasoline and fried fish. In the slip where the *Silver Heron* normally waited—tall, beastlike, built for function; the floating equivalent of a sensible boot—sat nothing. Just water.

I stared at the empty slip, dumbfounded.

They left without me.

Here's a riddle for you: how do you form meaningful relationships with a family you didn't grow up with?

Sometimes, I think my entire life has been one long attempt to answer that question. When you grow up with a gap between you and your siblings as wide as the one between me and mine (eight years at its smallest, twenty-eight years at its widest), you don't grow up with them, you grow up behind them. The rest of the family shares a wealth of memories to which you'll never have access. Those memories—the earliest, most formative moments— become the backbone of your family history. They're the stories you tell at dinners, at reunions, over beers at a bar your older siblings used to sneak into together, and, six years later, you snuck into alone. Those memories become your origin story. An origin story you didn't get to write.

For a few minutes I sat in the driver's seat, unwilling to believe my eyes. How the hell was I supposed to get to Cradle now? Swim?

But then I spotted the *Periwinkle*, a twin-engine whaler used mostly for grocery runs. Next to the boat was a tall figure with dark hair—one of my brothers, probably. Left behind to pick up the spare.

I unloaded my luggage—one backpack and one gas station bag full of empty cans of sugar-free cancer—and walked down the dock, craning my neck to see which of my brothers it was.

But then the figure turned around and smiled. "Hey, Beck."

I froze.

No.

Only one person called me by my last name, and there was no way that person could be there, at that very moment, standing on the dock in front of me. I blinked hard. Tried to make his face go away, just as I had in the car. *Blink. Blink.* But he was still there.

No.

This cannot be happening.

He looked different. He'd let his hair grow long and wild, the way my mom and I always told him he should. That was all I noticed, at first. His hair. How unfamiliar it was. And why shouldn't it be? Three years at college will do that. Will transform the lanky teenager you once knew into something resembling a man.

An old feeling, long forgotten—or, more accurately, long bound, gagged, and stuffed away in a corner of my mind from which I bade it to never return—yawned and stretched its wings inside my stomach.

No, no, no.

He took a step forward. I took a step back. "Surprise," he said.

Saliva edged up the back of my tongue. *He's here. He's really here.* What was he doing here? The first few days of the wedding were *family only*—it said so in clear, shimmering letters on Taz and Helene's invitation. So, why was my ex–best friend standing two feet in front of me, soft chestnut eyes watching me warily beneath wild curls?

He reached out one hand. For one terrifying moment, I thought he might hit me.

Instead, he grabbed my shoulder and pulled me into his chest.

Despite being skinny as a willow branch, Manuel Garcia Valdecasas gives hugs that feel like drowning. He sucks you into the void of his arms, drags you to the very deepest point of comfort.

"You're here," he said into my hair. That was it. Nothing else.

I thought I didn't miss him. Really, I did. For three years, I pushed him from my mind. Focused on my life in New York. That's what you do, that's what *everyone* does; you grow up, you fly the coop, you leave the other birds behind.

I knew I shouldn't let myself take comfort in his embrace. I'd been a bad friend. An awful friend, really. But I did. I let myself sink, just for a moment. And it felt good. God, it felt *so* good. It felt just the way they say it does—that clear, heady euphoria of death by drowning.

©Magdalena Iskra

Emma Noyes told her mother she wanted to be an author when she was six. She grew up in a suburb outside Chicago and attended Harvard University, where she studied history and literature. She started her career at a beer company, but left because she wanted to write about mermaids and witches—eventually publishing her first YA fantasy series, *The Sunken City*. She now lives in Chicago with her Swedish fiancé and miniature Pomeranian. *Guy's Girl* is her adult debut.

VISIT EMMA NOYES ONLINE

EmmaVRNoyes.com
EmmaNoyesMaybe
EmmaNoyesMaybe

Ready to find
your next great read?

Let us help.

Visit prh.com/nextread